A   P   L   A   C   E

A PLACE APART

— a novel by —

MAUREEN LENNON

THE DUNDURN GROUP
TORONTO

Excerpt from "Revelation" and "The Road Not Taken" from THE POETRY OF ROBERT FROST edited by Edward Connery Lathem. Copyright 1962 by Robert Frost, copyright 1923, 1934, 1969 by Henry Holt and Company. Reprinted by permission of Henry Holt and Company, LLC.

Editor: Barry Jowett
Copy-Editor: Jennifer Bergeron
Design: Andrew Roberts
Printer: Transcontinental

Library and Archives Canada Cataloguing in Publication

Lennon, Maureen
  A place apart / Maureen Lennon.

ISBN-10: 1-55002-544-9
ISBN-13: 978-1-55002-544-6

  I. Title.

PS8623.E56P52 2005   C813'.6   C2005-900171-2

1   2   3   4   5   09 08   07   06   05

Conseil des Arts du Canada   Canada Council for the Arts   Canadä   ONTARIO ARTS COUNCIL
CONSEIL DES ARTS DE L'ONTARIO

We acknowledge the support of the **Canada Council for the Arts** and the **Ontario Arts Council** for our publishing program. We also acknowledge the financial support of the **Government of Canada** through the **Book Publishing Industry Development Program** and **The Association for the Export of Canadian Books**, and the **Government of Ontario** through the **Ontario Book Publishers Tax Credit program**, and the **Ontario Media Development Corporation's Ontario Book Initiative**.

Care has been taken to trace the ownership of copyright material used in this book. The author and the publisher welcome any information enabling them to rectify any references or credit in subsequent editions.

J. Kirk Howard, President

Printed and bound in Canada.
Printed on recycled paper.

www.dundurn.com

Dundurn Press
8 Market Street, Suite 200
Toronto, Ontario, Canada
M5E 1M6

Gazelle Book Services Limited
White Cross Mills
Hightown, Lancaster, England
LA1 4X5

Dundurn Press
2250 Military Road
Tonawanda N
U.S.A. 1

To David, with love,
and in fond memory of Barney, with gratitude for
all the life lessons so gloriously taught.

CHAPTER 1

We make ourselves a place apart
Behind light words that tease and flout,
But oh, the agitated heart
Till someone really find us out.

It could happen any time. Late on a Thursday night, after the eleven o'clock news, with the garbage pails toppled at the foot of the driveway, forgotten, abandoned to the rain and the dark; in the middle of a dead silent Sunday afternoon, the clocks ticking and the rich aroma of roasting meat and browning vegetables seeping under closed doors; at five o'clock on a weekday afternoon, just as foil-covered meatloaf leftovers were about to be lifted from the oven. Out of the blue, a voice would shrill, or glass would shatter against a hard surface. Sometimes the cutlery drawer crashed shut. More often, though, a door just suddenly, violently slammed, shaking the whole house to its foundation. If it was Sunday, and a lemon meringue pie sat cooling on the kitchen counter, you might see a shiver pass through it.

For fifteen-year-old Cathy Mugan, waiting up in her room for the night or the weekend to end, the vibrating walls and floors always meant the same thing. But there was never anything that she could do to save herself. Her room was upstairs at the end of the hall, the last door on the left. Running was out of the question. She'd never get past her mother on the stairs. And even if she could, it wouldn't matter. Outside, the neighbours' blinds were drawn. Inside, there were no locks left on any of the doors.

If it was still early, and she was seated at her desk doing homework, she would have to put her pen or pencil down because her trembling hand made writing impossible. If it was late, and she had already gone to bed, she would back closer to the wall, pull her knees up, and mound the covers around herself. Then she began to count, *one-Angela, two-Angela, three-Angela*, waiting for the door to her room to blast open.

And blast open it had, right on the count of thirty, hundreds of times. As a little girl hearing what was coming, she had taken refuge in corners, wedging herself between a piece of furniture and a wall, squatting close to the floor, her thin arms covering her bowed head, her splayed hands protecting her exposed skin. But now, at fifteen, she knew these actions were futile. She needed to be behind a wall, not crouched against one. So she counted. *Ten-Angela, eleven-Angela, twelve-Angela*. Through the floor, she could hear the other telltale sounds: feet pounding along the downstairs hall, the closet door in the room beneath hers sliding on its rails, slamming into the wall, the tinny jangle of unoccupied hangers, the zipping sound of a belt being pulled briskly free from a pair of trousers, feet pounding again, this time up the stairs. *Twenty-eight-Angela, twenty-nine-Angela*. She had absolutely no memory of a time when things were different. Even her earliest, most shadowy recollections all twitched with alarm.

★ ★ ★

Cathy Mugan's teachers judged her to be a passive, dreamy sort of kid, not outstanding in any way, not someone likely to distinguish herself. Watching how she conducted herself, always choosing a

8

seat in the middle of the class so that she could bury herself behind the other students, always keeping her eyes down, never volunteering to answer questions, always having to ask for the question to be repeated if she was called upon, seemingly satisfied with mediocre, passing grades, it was easy to draw the conclusion that she was uninterested, lazy, dreamy, perhaps even incapable.

The nuns at St. Joseph's Convent School often summarized her in those terms, writing on her report cards that she lacked initiative, she seemed uninterested in her school work, she spent too much time lost in her own little world.

"She's doesn't show much interest in her work," they told her mother at parent-teacher meetings. "Nothing seems to interest her. She just does enough to get by."

"Preoccupied," was the sternly delivered verdict of Sister Lumina. "She seems totally preoccupied with something outside of her school work."

The English and home economics teacher, Sister Anne Rochelle, was more forgiving.

"I think she just needs lots of encouragement. I sense something going on inside that head of hers, but she is more comfortable keeping it to herself right now. She needs time to find herself."

"Find herself, my ass," was the seething response Adele Mugan spat out, pounding across the school parking lot on her shiny beige high heels.

Twice a year Adele patted clouds of talcum powder under her plump arms, shellacked her bright red fuzzy hair firmly into place with hairspray, greased her mouth with tangerine lipstick, and dressed in her Sunday-best beige to attend the mid-term parent-teacher evening sessions. Twice a year she returned home, stormed up to her daughter's room, bent her face to within an inch of Cathy's, and told her that she had had a long talk with each of her teachers.

"And they have my full permission to watch your every move, young lady, do you hear me? I will not have any nonsense going on behind my back. You are there to learn and nothing else."

Cathy, who was nearly always seated at her desk during these encounters, kept her head bent respectfully, taking care not to move her eyes too much lest she be accused of not paying attention and earn a smart slap across the mouth. Living with her mother was like living with a pool of gasoline. But occasionally, with extremely obsequious posturing by Cathy, Adele might grow bored and wander off to watch television. So Cathy kept her head down and her eyes still, suffering Adele's hot breath and spittle landing on the side of her face.

During the school terms, Sister Anne Rochelle tried to cheer Cathy out of her lethargy with praise and overly jolly encouragement. Circling the classroom, talking, she often stopped behind Cathy and laid her hands gently on the shoulders of her shy, nervous pupil.

"Cathy, you can tell me the answer to this one. It's right up your alley. Just take a moment to consider and then tell us what you think."

The smooth, white, damp hands of this nun, weighing down on her shoulders like servings of cold porridge, always repulsed Cathy. There was something presumptuous about them, the way they landed without invitation, claiming her as some sort of pet.

"Hello, hello. Anybody home in there?"

Within seconds of the hands landing, cold, moist thumbs would begin to slowly, rhythmically stroke the bare flesh at the back of Cathy's head, running upwards, disappearing into her hair.

"How's that feel? Hmm? I'm trying to get the blood flowing to your brain."

Cathy wanted to shrug, shake the hands off and scream, "Leave me alone!"

But she didn't dare.

"Just relax and give us your answer, Cathy."

Answering would make the hands go away. So Cathy stuttered out some sort of brief answer and then dropped out from beneath the hands back into the safety of her seat. There she poured all of her energy into burying her emotions before someone asked her what was wrong; what was the matter with her that she couldn't ever look anyone in the eye, that she never seemed to want to talk to anyone? She told herself that everything was fine; no one had noticed anything. Then she opened her eyes as wide as she dared without attracting attention, tilted her head subtly backward, and looked at the ceiling so that tears wouldn't drop down her face.

By contrast, Sister Lumina, the homeroom and mathematics teacher, never touched anyone except by way of her withering remarks. She remained rigidly upright behind her desk at all times, vigilantly surveying her pupils with her mica black eyes, her arms folded and hidden inside the wide black linen sleeves of her habit. Behind her back, the students referred to her as "Lipless Lumeanie" and "Nolips." This was because at the spot on her face where her lips should have been there was nothing to indicate the presence of the instrument of her scorn but a small horizontal slash. Even in profile, a mouth was not even slightly hinted at by either an upper or a lower lip. When the slash in her face parted for her to speak, teeth the colour of maize, as hard and cruel as her remarks, ground their sharp, jumbled edges together in sound.

Occasionally this nun thought she could prod Cathy into working by embarrassing her in front of the whole class with a sneering remark about her laziness.

"In the name of efficiency, I see you have maintained your devotion to the path of least resistance, Catherine."

Cathy did not react outwardly to this treatment any more than she did to Sister Anne Rochelle's touch. She merely kept her head down and waited for the moment to pass. In the silence, her sweaty fingers quietly rolled a pencil back and forth in its groove on her desk. Sometimes, with her head bowed and her voice barely audible, she responded with a brief, mumbled answer to a question, hoping to shift the nun's black-eyed glare away from herself. This reaction, of course, convinced Sister Lumina of the accuracy of her assessment of Cathy.

★ ★ ★

On the last day of school, in the year that Cathy was fifteen, Father McCoy came into the Grade 10 class to hand out final report cards. He took the cards from Sister Lumina and began circling the room, his black linen cassock making delicate little swishing sounds as he passed up and down the aisles. He read aloud selections from the character assessments of each student. Cathy had to wait for twenty minutes before he came to the M's. By then, she was trembling. The instant she heard her name called, she rose swiftly upward, a balloon, a kite, passing right through the ceilings and floors of all five storeys of St. Joseph's, through the roof and up past the tops of trees until the classroom and her desk and herself sitting in it became small specks below her.

"It says here that you appear to have potential that you do not live up to, Cathy, that you are secretive and uncommunicative. Is that true?"

From afar, she saw her body rise to stand beside her desk and look the priest in the chin. She was a slight girl, thin, standing a full head shorter than most of her classmates, with coal black hair, milk white skin, and violet-blue eyes that flagged, unmistakably, her Irish heritage.

"I don't know, Father."

"You don't know? You don't know whether you have secrets or not? That seems to me to be an easy enough question to answer. Just tell us, yes or no? Do you have any secrets?"

"No, Father, I don't have any secrets."

"Why would your teachers say that you have secrets, then?"

"I don't know, Father."

"Ah! You don't know. The famous repeating answer. You sound like a parrot with only one trick, do you know that? I wonder if I can get her to say anything else besides 'I don't know.' Does she ever say anything else to the rest of you?"

With both eyebrows raised in expectation, he looked out over the tops of the students' heads. The girls shifted slightly in their seats, glancing sideways at each other. Father McCoy turned back to Cathy.

"Now then, Miss Mugan, let's see if I can get you to look me in the eye, first of all."

Obediently, Cathy looked up. She could tell by the way he searched her face that he was trying to gain access to her thoughts. Inside her head, her secret voice whispered to her.

Just keep still. Look through him. He'll go away in a minute.

She gazed steadily back at Father McCoy, noting that his grey irises had little green shards of colour in them and that he had small broken blood vessels in the whites of his eyes. As she observed these things, two vessels beat nervously beneath the skin at her own wrists.

After a moment, Father McCoy exhaled.

"If you have secrets, you've got them well hidden in there. I don't see anything except nice blue eyes. You have an older brother, don't you?"

"Yes, Father."

"I forget his name."

"Richard, Father."

"Ah, yes. He's finished at St. Mike's isn't he?"

"Yes, Father."

"What's he doing now?"

"He's working at Robinson's Grocery, Father."

"Ah! Robinson's. What does he do there?"

"He works in the produce department, Father."

"Ah! The produce department. And what does he produce in this produce department?"

"I don't know —"

"Ut-tut-tut!"

"— Father. Vegetables, I think."

"You were doing pretty well there until you snuck in that last 'I don't know.' Vegetables, then. So, your brother Richard is a producer of vegetables over at Robinson's Grocery store and you, his sister, are a producer of secrets here at St. Joseph's, right?"

"No, Father."

"But you just told me he worked at Robinson's."

Here he looked over the top of Cathy's head, raised one eyebrow, and flared his nostrils at the rest of the class. The girls giggled restrainedly. Cathy saw herself drop her gaze to her desktop.

Just be still.

"I meant that I don't have any secrets, Father."

"No secrets at all?"

"No, Father."

"My goodness. Life is no fun without secrets, did you know that? I'll bet everyone in this room has a secret. Even Sister Lumina, there, don't you, Sister?"

Sister Lumina sat up a little straighter; her slash parted to reveal clenched teeth.

"I had a secret when I was your age," Father McCoy continued. "I thought everyone did. Shall I tell you my secret?"

He glanced around the room for permission and then continued.

"Whenever my mother served tomatoes, I used to feed them to the dog under the table when she wasn't looking. Then, when she asked me where they went in such a hurry, I just said they went straight down the hatch, as usual, which was the truth, of course. I didn't lie, you see, I just didn't say whose hatch the tomatoes went down. And when my mother asked me if I wanted some more tomatoes, I always said, no thanks, I'd had enough, which was also true, of course. I'm certain my dog did not agree, but what could he do? So you see, that was my secret. But you, Catherine Mugan, you say you have absolutely no secrets at all then?"

Cathy looked back up.

Hold still.

"No, Father."

"You poor child. What a dull imagination you must have. I suggest you try to acquire at least one secret before you graduate, even if it is only a secret desire to put all of the gifts that God gave you to good use."

He held out the report card for her to take from his hand. Floating so high above the classroom, Cathy barely heard the remarks.

★ ★ ★

The same morning that report cards were being handed out at St. Joseph's Convent School, word went around the neighbourhood that Linda Thompson, the fourteen-year-old who lived across the street from the Mugans, was pregnant. Adele Mugan heard the news at the foot of her own driveway where she was sweeping. Next door, Dot Monroe was preparing to hose down her driveway. She caught Adele's eye and strolled to the corner of her lawn where the two properties met.

At the end of their conversation, after Dot disappeared around the side of her house to turn on the tap, Adele squinted across the street to the living room windows of the Thompson house and then slowly retreated back to the garage to put away the broom. As she did so, the gossip turned slowly on a spit in her mind, growing darker and beginning to sweat; soon it began to sizzle and hiss over the hot coals of her imagination, embellishing itself, slowly ballooning outwards until it had crowded out everything else.

She came in from the garage and began to clean the kitchen.

"Can you imagine?" she began, clattering cutlery and china as she cleared the counters. "Fourteen-year-old little miss hot pants. Just couldn't wait. Must have been sleeping all over town. By Jeezus, no kid of mine had better ever get herself pregnant, that's for darn sure. No siree! I'm not having any little hussy carrying on behind my back, thinking she's pulling the wool over my eyes, the whole town talking behind my back. I wasn't born yesterday."

She piled the dishes noisily into the sink, turned the taps on full blast.

"Little tart," she said, wringing the dishcloth violently. "Little mincing hussy tart!"

She wiped the counters vigorously, rinsed the dishcloth, and wiped the counters again.

"Over my dead body," she said, slamming the butter dish down on the shelf in the fridge. "Over my dead body, let me tell you."

She returned to the sink and carefully piled all of the utensils together beneath the sudsy water. Then her restless hands fell still and her gaze fixed dead ahead through the window on the row of evergreens at the back of the yard.

"There will be no boys in this house until you're out of high school, missy, do you hear me, or by God, you'll have me to answer to. Is that understood? This is not the Thompson household."

★ ★ ★

At one o'clock every afternoon, Adele stopped cleaning, took off her apron, and went into the dining room to sit down with a cup of tea. She began by sitting among the heavy pieces of mahogany furniture, looking out through the French doors at the birds on the back fence. She studied the habits of the birds carefully, hoping to discern some sign, although she didn't know what it would be, that the birds had flown north to Ontario from Washington, D.C. It wasn't impossible, she reasoned, that one of these same birds might have, just the morning before, perhaps, spent time in the President's Rose Garden. It was possible that one of these plain-looking little brown sparrows had sat outside the President's window yesterday, been seen by him, maybe even eaten out of his hand, and then flown straight up here to alight in her garden. It might even have brought a molecule of dirt on its claw from one garden to the other. Something to link the two gardens. Wouldn't it be amazing if, one day, she and the President met and talked about gardens and birds? And he might mention a one-eyed sparrow, or a bird with one yellow leg and one orange one who came to his garden for two or three seasons, and she might suddenly recognize the description of a bird she had watched in her own garden.

The American President's picture sat in a simple brass frame in a froth of doily lace on the buffet. Beside it, brass bookends pressed a volume of the poetry of Robert Frost. After observing the birds and re-imagining all the possibilities concerning their migrations between various gardens, Adele reached back, picked the picture up, and brought it to the table with her. She held it out at arm's length, turning it this way and that, examining the different effects of the light upon the President's expression. The photo was a close-up of him sitting at his desk. She had clipped it out of a magazine the year he was elected. His eyes were uplifted, and he held his chin in his left hand. In her head, Adele heard, with crystal clarity, his peculiarly accented speaking voice.

"How are you today, Adele?"

His office was on the ground floor of the White House, his desk beside French windows that opened out onto the famous Rose Garden. Adele looked through those windows during the afternoons, loving the details — the wicker-backed rocking chair, the blue rug, the naval pictures, him.

She knew the Rose Garden well; it was where she went most often to meet him. It was easy for her to approach from the White House lawns; the security guards knew who she was and left her alone. She was able to slip through the hedge and stroll up one of the paths to sit on a stone bench where she could look in through the double French doors and watch him work. Sometimes the room was crowded with aides, and other times he sat in solitude, sifting through a sheaf of white paper with curled corners. Occasionally he looked out through the small windowpanes; sometimes, if he saw her, he waved. If he was too busy, she went upstairs to have tea with his wife. The First Lady dwelt beneath the snowy white linen tablecloths in a drawer of Adele's dining room buffet. Every afternoon, Adele reverently lifted out the several glossy magazines that contained her and arranged them in a semicircle on the dining room table. As soon as the magazines were opened to the accustomed spots, the exquisitely beautiful young wife of the President rose up from the pages, filling the room with her presence.

Young, glamorous, wealthy, well educated, fluent in several languages, beautiful, a mother, a wife, a former career woman; she set fashion trends with her hair, her simple sleeveless dresses and her little pillbox hats; she was devout, refined, self-possessed. When interviewed, she spoke intelligently about art, music, history, and literature. The press even published a list of her most recently read books.

Adele greedily turned the pages of the magazines, devouring details, willing the First Lady into existence right beside her.

Sometimes, Adele spoke aloud to her; sometimes the two women communicated only through their thoughts.

"Where should we go today? What do you feel like?"

Often, they strolled together, barefoot, on a New England beach, clad alike in pedal-pushers and loose, long-sleeved cotton shirts. Adele's stout limbs grew long and tapered beneath these clothes; her large bust shrank, her plump upper arms became slim. She listened to the surf crashing at their feet and filled her lungs with salted air, thinking that it was good to get away to this type of life once in a while, to experience a bit of it, at least.

Other times, she and the first lady stood poised together at a reception in the White House, elegantly attired in white designer gowns and elbow-length gloves. Adele wandered through the crowd, recognizing faces of presidential aides, television journalists, and Hollywood stars, enjoying her anonymity, her privileged position as the mysterious family friend who had not been explained to anyone. The puzzled whispers about her identity thrilled her; she wandered the room gorged on her own importance.

One magazine photo showed the First Lady poised for an interview in a fireside wingback chair in one of the elegant sitting rooms of the White House. Honey-coloured sunlight poured into the room through tall windows, spilling over antique American furniture and thick, hand-wrought carpets. She told the American people the story of their own heritage, the details of the carpets and the cherrywood tables and the scenes in the paintings adorning the White House walls. On another page, the cameras even roved over the dark wood furniture of Abraham Lincoln's bedroom. Adele hovered behind the cameras and the interviewer's chair, a notebook and pencil in hand, pacing, listening to the interviewer's questions, ready to prompt her friend with details about White House treasures.

Sometimes, the two women met earlier. Adele witnessed the beautiful young debutante floating down the staircase of her parents' mansion for her coming-out party; at her private girls' school the future first lady wore a simple strand of pearls and a pageboy haircut for the yearbook photo. Still another picture took Adele someplace unfamiliar, where she watched the President's future wife, now wearing short-cropped, wind-blown hair, clinging to the rigging of her then senator-fiancé's sailboat; and of course, again and again, Adele attended the wedding.

The bride wore her grandmother's train-length rose point veil, which the wind picked up and tossed into the air behind her, like a mist. The groom wore a morning suit. The two stood on grass, on a sprawling mansion lawn with a simple, split-rail fence in the background. The wind had momentarily pushed the thick hair of the president-to-be down onto his forehead.

Adele was not the maid of honour, she was not a brides-maid, she was not even a member of the wedding party. None of the family members knew her or even seemed to notice her. She slipped through the crowd like a ghost, finding a spot to stand where her friend's eyes could find her. When the photog-rapher called for someone to spread the bride's train out across the grass, a flock of bridesmaids knelt down around the dress and pulled the yards of satin into a wide white fan over the grass. Someone tugged too heartily on the dress, momentarily tipping the bride backwards. The groom reached out and steadied her by the elbow. The bride looked directly, meaningfully at her ghost-friend in the crowd — if *she* had spread the train, it would never have happened.

★ ★ ★

An hour after learning of Linda Thompson's pregnancy, Adele fin-ished the dishes, made a pot of tea, and went into the dining room earlier than usual. She set a place with a teacup and saucer for her-self and then brought the pictures out of the buffet drawers and laid them out in their usual semicircle on the mahogany table. She found that she liked a picture of the First Lady standing in the White House dining room above all others at that moment, and so she drew back her own chair, picked up her teacup, sat back, and slipped herself effortlessly into the room.

"I saw your little girl this morning. She's the sweetest little thing, isn't she? All those angelic blonde curls. You're so lucky. It's such a tragedy, the kind of trouble that young girls can get themselves into these days, isn't it?"

The light from the elegant White House dining room window poured onto Adele's dining room table and carpet, enveloping both women. Adele offered cream for their tea, eagerly telling her news, pausing to listen intently to the quiet, mellifluous voice of her companion.

There she sat, statue-still, all afternoon, gazing into the centre of a magazine picture, her eyes bright with emotion, her cheeks flushed pink with excitement. Every so often she would stir, her head would lean to one side, a smile would cross her face, and she would speak into the empty air before her.

★ ★ ★

At three-thirty that afternoon, the mail slot in the front door clinked sharply; paper hit the hall floor with a soft *whoosh*, and the President's wife, her teacup, and her carpets faded away instantly. Adele blinked to alertness and found that her tea had gone cold.

Rising from her seat, she wandered into the front hall, where she found a small white envelope, like one of those bearing invitations, along with some advertising flyers and the phone bill. The envelope was addressed to Cathy. It bore no return address but had a local postmark. Adele stared at it, trying to recognize the childlike printing. To her knowledge, Cathy hadn't received any mail before, except for the odd birthday card from a school friend. But her birthday was months away.

The contents of the envelope felt stiff between Adele's fingers. Piqued, she inserted her chubby index finger under the sealed flap and worked it along, rupturing the top crease of the envelope. Inside lay a three-and-a-half-by-five-inch index card with a printed message:

Dear Cathy:

A very precious gift I send to you
One very old, very special Indian head nickel
To bring you good luck always,

Your Secret Admirer

Taped to the bottom left-hand corner was an American Indian head nickel. Adele's eyes flickered suspiciously over the message, settling on the words "Your Secret Admirer."

That little Thompson tart had obviously had a secret admirer. And what had Louise De Finca said just yesterday? Bloated with sanctimony, the alto voice of the Italian neighbour from three doors down now rose in Adele's mind.

Now this might not be what you want for your girl, of course…

Just a day ago, at the shopping plaza, Louise had said something like that, in reference to raising teenage daughters. At the time, the remark had seemed vaguely insulting, but Adele had let it pass because she wasn't really sure what it referred to. Now she narrowed her eyes at the memory of it.

Louise De Finca's husband, Angelo, owned a butcher shop on the far side of town. They had four daughters, one of whom was the same age as Cathy. Adele wondered if Louise had known something else the other day, some item of gossip —

about Cathy and a boy — brought home from school by her daughter Sandra.

Maybe Louise had been mocking her, having a little bit of private fun. Enraged, Adele stuffed the index card back into its envelope, dropped it on the front hall table, and churned down the hall to the bathroom on her fat legs. She grabbed the can of cleanser from the edge of the sink, knelt down beside the tub, and began shaking green powder up and down its length, talking in a loud voice.

"As if I don't know what my own daughter is up to. Do you think I don't know what my own daughter is up to, Louise? Are you the only one who knows anything about raising children?"

She hollered the last question into the bathtub. Startled by her outburst, she paused, and then resumed her conversation in a harsh whisper.

"Secret admirer, my ass! There had better not be any nonsense with a boy going on behind my back, my lady, or your behind will be so red you won't sit down for a week."

By now, Adele's fat, red hands were abruptly twisting the water taps on, and the small room filled with the sound of thundering water. She wet a scrubbing cloth and bent her girth over the tub rim, planting her left hand on the tub floor for support, and her right arm began to scrub, churning round and round in clockwise circles, grinding the cloth and the green cleanser over an imagined ring on the tub wall. Her breasts slipped over the tub edge and hung down into the empty space, swaying and jiggling with the motions of her arm. Fine gritty powder rose into the air.

"A very precious gift I send to you indeed. I'll give you a precious gift, my girl, once I find out what's been going on. My father didn't have any nonsense in his house, by God, because he knew how to use a belt, and I don't intend to have any either."

Louise's voice returned.

Neither Angelo nor I are prepared, Adele, to put up with any of today's nonsense.

Adele's arm ground the cloth around the curve of the tub, coming upon the water-spotted chrome faucet and taps. She shrilled aloud at her own bobbing reflection.

"Who do you think you are anyway, Louise?"

Adele felt cleanser grit collecting along her lips. She bent forward and took a mouthful of water from the faucet, swished, and spat.

Angelo and I made a rule, Adele. We decide these things together, as I'm sure you and Gerald do.

Huffing and puffing as she resumed scrubbing, Adele spoke aloud with an ever-rising pitch.

"Angelo, Angelo, Angelo! Big dumb Angelo! Doesn't look as if he could decide his way out of a wet bag; only knows how to tie a bloody apron over that big stomach of his and stand behind a meat counter all day; he's probably told when to go to the bathroom."

Adele leaned close to the faucet to make a point and hollered above the din of the running water.

"We know he makes money, Louise. Everybody eats meat. It didn't take brains to figure that business out."

The heat of humiliation suddenly flashed through her as she remembered what her own husband, Gerald, did for a living. An itinerant pharmacist, a wanderer from the business of one to the business of another, always a fill-in, never an owner, never even acquiring the status of full-time employment with a single employer. The reminder fuelled her rage.

"Lackey! Spineless lackey, Gerald. No ability whatsoever to stand on your own two feet."

The sight of her own teeth flashing in the wet chrome arrested her. She hauled her heavy breasts back over the tub rim and began to scrub in silence. Her thoughts continued to swirl.

In a minute she was speaking again.

"By the gods, Cathy, you'd better be home here right after school, or you won't live to tell about it."

We told our girls, Adele, no dating until they're eighteen and then only with young men we approve of beforehand. Neither one of us is prepared to put up with any of today's nonsense. And if they don't like it they can go board with the nuns. They know that I have all of that information handy in my dressing table drawer. I can have it all arranged in an hour. Now, this might not be at all what you want for your girl, of course.

Adrenaline shot through Adele. Both arms pumped furiously underneath her, up, down, up, down, up, down, as she bellowed into the trough of the tub: "What do you think this is, Louise? Open house? No rules? I let my kids run wild?"

The cloth flew out of her hands and landed on the floor behind her with a loud, wet splat. Defeated, she slumped back on her heels.

★ ★ ★

The school bus departed on its last journey of the year at its usual time that afternoon. By then, the day was darkening rapidly with an approaching thunderstorm. Behind the bus, the sky had already turned a deep steely blue, and dust and paper litter blew up at the sides of the roads, scurrying ahead with the message of impending rain. Cars began to drive with their headlights on, and the greengrocers in the centre of the city were out on the sidewalks in front of their shops in their long white aprons, hurriedly winding their canvas awnings back into retracted positions and dismantling their displays of fruits and vegetables.

The students riding home together from St. Joseph's and St. Michael's were jubilant with the anticipation of two months of summer holidays. The dramatic clouds, rising wind, and dropping temperature heightened their excitement. They shrieked and hollered at one another, tossing a melon-sized green foam rubber ball back and forth across the aisle. The driver followed the proceedings in his mirror, occasionally trying to spike the errant ball back into the seats with his free hand.

Cathy Mugan sat with her head resting against the bus window, watching the telephone wires turn from black to copper green against the dark sky. As a little girl, she had interpreted this strange metamorphosis as a mysterious, private sign from heaven that a storm was coming. Out of the corner of her eye, she watched the other students playing their game. If the ball came near enough to bounce off her head, she swatted it away, smiling, and then went back to her wire-gazing. Beside her, her classmate and best friend, Janet St. Amand, popped up and down in the seat, participating vigorously in the game, calling out loudly for the ball to be passed to her.

When the bus began to slow down for her stop, Cathy looped her school bag over one shoulder and pushed herself out of the seat past Janet. She felt sick to her stomach. The words "secretive and uncommunicative" escaped from the report card at the bottom of her schoolbag and scrawled themselves in a mean-lipped script across the air in front of her in dark, navy blue ink. Instead of letting the canvas bag hang at her side, she scooped it up and folded her arms across it so that it pressed against her queasy stomach.

The two Miller boys who lived next door and Dan O'Neil from across the street had been up in the aisle playing furiously since the bus left the school parking lot. Now, along with Cathy, they descended the stairs of the bus to depart, still in possession of the ball, looking to make one last great serve. At the last moment, Scott Miller lobbed the ball into the centre of a mob of friends and skipped out of the bus.

The three boys called goodbye to Janet, who hollered out over the din that she would phone Cathy later. Cathy waved to her friend but turned her head away from her neighbours without saying a word.

The bus stop was at the foot of the Mugan driveway. Cathy crunched up the gravel shoulder of the road towards the pavement, surreptitiously watching for movement behind the white lace curtains on the laundry room windows. She could see nothing.

The laundry room was empty when she stepped into it, but before she had completely closed the door behind her, she heard footsteps approaching. Her mother snapped on the overhead light and the two of them stood for a moment in the yellow glare, observing one another. Cathy noticed the fired-up, glassy eyes and the fine dusk of perspiration glistening on her mother's upper lip and cheeks. Coming down off the single step leading from the kitchen into the laundry room, her mother advanced towards her, cracking a yardstick in front of her on the plastic runner that protected the carpeting.

"You'd better be here, miss."

The final hiss was pressed out from between her mother's teeth as if from between steel rollers. Carefully, Cathy leaned back on the door, pushing it gently closed.

"It's almost past 4:15. You're to be home here on that bus by 4:15, sharp, miss. No excuses! Do you hear me? And don't think I don't know what goes on, on the way home, my lady."

Cathy dropped her gaze to the carpet. It was a long way from here up to her room.

"I saw you getting off that bus with those kids from next door, little miss hot pants secret admirer."

Startled, Cathy looked up, her head cocked quizzically to one side.

"Thought I wouldn't find out, didn't you? Who is it? That O'Neil kid across the street? Huh? You might as well tell me because I'll find out who it is."

Like a missile, the yardstick suddenly flashed past Cathy's face, landing with a brittle smack against the hot water tank beside her. At the sharp sound of wood cracking against metal, Cathy peed herself. Instantly, she squeezed herself as tightly as possible to stop the flow. Tight, tight, tight.

Please God, not now.

She choked the flow in time. Nothing ran down her legs. Her cotton underwear would blot up what had escaped. Now, though, her stomach really began to churn. She parted her lips slightly, cautiously, to breathe through her mouth. Pores on the surface of her skin dilated. Her mouth flooded with saliva. She was going to vomit.

"So. It's starting already, is it? Every mother's nightmare. A slut of a daughter."

While her mother's voice rose in pitch, Cathy's sense of the present suddenly became distorted; everything began moving at half-speed. Her mother, in slow motion, wagged a white index card in front of her. There was a coin taped to a corner of the card. The words that her mother spat out floated past her.

"I told you no boys in this house until you're finished school. Do you hear me? You go to school for one reason and one reason only, and that's to learn. There'll be no hanging around after school, joining clubs and teams and other nonsense and walking home with boys just to be popular, let me tell you."

Her mother's glazed, frenzied gaze looked right through her.

Cathy let her school bag strap slide off her shoulder and fall to the ground. Her bladder continued to threaten. She was going to have to run.

"I'm watching your every move, young lady."

Had her mother seen her wave to Janet and mistakenly thought it was meant for one of the neighbourhood boys?

"By God, you should have had *my* father for a parent. Then you'd understand discipline, my dear."

Her mother's teeth flashed wet and shiny as she spoke, and little bits of spittle flew about, some landing like cold little pinpoints on Cathy's face. As Cathy raised an arm to wipe her face, her mother slapped it away, buried her fingers in Cathy's hair, and jerked her face up to greet her own.

"I want to know who this secret admirer is, right now. Tell me or I'll tan your hide until the skin blisters off of it."

Cathy heard the wheezing breath squeezed out of her mother's asthmatic throat, a sign that she might have been shouting recently.

"I don't know what you're talking about, Mom."

"Don't remind me that I gave birth to you. The President with that obedient, angelic little girl and what do I get?"

Adele pushed her backward, letting go of her hair. Then, with an abrupt flick of her thick wrist, she presented the white card again, so closely that it almost brushed the tip of Cathy's nose. Pee began to trickle down the inside of Cathy's thighs. She jammed her legs together, tightly crossing one knee over the other.

"Who's this secret admirer of yours sending you things through the mail, then, if you haven't been up to anything?"

"I don't know."

"You don't just get mail from strangers, young lady. Who sent you this?"

"I don't know. What is it?"

"This. Right here. It's addressed to you."

"I didn't ask anyone to send me anything in the mail."

"Well somebody's got your address from somewhere, missy, and I want to know where. This boyfriend thing is going to be nipped in the bud right now. Do you hear me?"

Cathy bit her tongue hard to halt the advance of tears and clenched her thighs together, desperate not to wet herself further.

"Caught you, haven't I, miss? Mrs. De Finca told me about it at the plaza."

29

So that was it. She'd been out to the plaza and run into Mrs. De Finca! It was impossible to know what Mrs. De Finca had said to set her off. It could have been a disagreement between the two about the length of hems this season or which way a daughter should be taught to iron — starting with the sleeves first or leaving the sleeves to the end. Or it could have been something that one of Mrs. De Finca's daughters did that she didn't do. Or the reverse.

It didn't matter, really. In the end, her mother would have stormed across the parking lot of the shopping plaza, thrown her parcels into the back seat, and jetted her car out into the traffic, driving in a rage, grinding the gears of her Volkswagen, talking loudly to herself all the way home.

Cathy slowly hooked a hank of hair behind one ear and bent down to remove her shoes, carefully avoiding putting any extra pressure on her bladder. A foot away from her face the tip of the yardstick twirled on the plastic runner. She watched it from her bent position. It rose and fell with her mother's words, ticking nastily, leaving small pocks in the plastic's surface.

"How is it that Louise De Finca knows you're up to something if she didn't hear it from Sandra? Huh? Answer me that? How do you think I felt, standing there, listening to that woman tell me about your antics? That woman was laughing at the whole family behind our backs because of your behaviour!"

Tick, tick, went the yardstick.

Cathy pushed her shoes carefully to one side with a stockinged foot and straightened slowly, keeping her eyes down. Very soon, she would pee down her legs onto the plastic.

Her mother had advanced as far into the room as she could, and now she manoeuvred herself into a position that left Cathy no option but to cross in front of the twitching yardstick.

"Get your little arse up to your room right now, miss."

Tick, tick. Time was up.

Cathy dashed past the twitching stick. It caught her, landing regular stinging whacks on the backs of her calves as her mother chased her through the main floor of the house to the foot of the stairs. Through the blur of tears, she noticed a buffet drawer hanging open as she passed through the dining room.

★ ★ ★

The sound of the phone ringing in the downstairs hall of the Mugans' suburban household was lost amid the overlapping claps of thunder outside and the loud spraying of wind-driven rain against the windows. The maple trees in the backyard flailed violently as the wind tore at them, ripping away their silver-backed leaves and driving them in helpless wet, green clumps against the downstairs windows, making sudden dull thwacking sounds against the glass. All around the house tree branches repeatedly raked and beat against the roof; the sound travelled through the empty attic like a restless knocking from another world.

When the lights flickered momentarily, died and revived, Adele lost her rhythm and halted in mid-sentence. Her bright red face was wet with perspiration and her heavy bosom heaved up and down rapidly. Only as she paused did she notice, for the first time, the dishevelment that lay around her on Cathy's bedroom floor. Glancing critically at it, she called Cathy a dirty pig and ordered her to clean up the mess. Then she spun out of the room in a dissipating eddy of rage.

Cathy crouched behind her open bedroom door, listening, despite the thunder, making sure that the footsteps really were dying away down the hall. When she was certain that they would not be returning, she quickly pushed the door across the blue shag carpet and pressed it silently into place. She controlled the doorknob carefully, letting the glass ball spin beneath her hand in short, hesitant measures, so that the latch would slip noise-lessly into the socket.

It was the hairbrush that had caught her under the left eye, right on the cheekbone. She should have remembered to hide it. Staring at her reflection in the dresser mirror, she took inventory of her other injuries. Her hair was dishevelled and matted to her face. There was a partial print of the hairbrush on her left cheek, and a long superficial scratch down the side of her neck where a sharp fingernail had passed by. Her tongue investigated tiny craters in the wall of her mouth, tasting salt in the stinging raw flesh where her teeth had gone through the back of her lip again. The nail on one of her fingers must have caught on something and pulled back upon itself because it was no longer attached to the nail bed beneath it. She saw blood on the end of her finger and pink, meatlike flesh under the torn flap of nail. Two toes on her right foot screamed with pain when she moved them; one of her knees wouldn't support weight easily and hurt when she tried to bend it. In an effort to prevent a book from being shoved into her stomach, she had raised her knee swiftly, ploughing it into the wooden footboard of the bed. The exposed skin on her calves above her drooping knee socks, like the skin on her forearms, was dotted with red welts. She knew that beneath her uniform her back looked the same.

Outside, the storm slowly dissipated. It continued to rain steadily, but the wind died down and the thunder retreated. After taking off her wet underwear and hiding them in a corner of the closet and pulling on a pair of pyjamas, Cathy opened the window that stood at a right angle to the foot of her bed and stood quietly, listening to the rain, feeling the cool breeze puffing through the screen and across her burning cheek. After a moment, she turned to her desk, picked up a pencil that lay on top of a geography book, and bent to peer beneath the desk drawer. When she located three parallel pencil marks on the

rough unfinished underside of the drawer, she pressed the pencil against the wood and made a single swift short stroke. Four
years down; three years to go. Then she straightened, replaced
the pencil, and lay down on her bed.

There wasn't much noise downstairs now, only an occasional slam of a kitchen cupboard door and the faint haze of audi-
ence laughter from the television. Soon the early evening news
would be on. But it would blare out into an empty living room.
Cathy knew that shortly her mother would take something from
the fridge, the jar of olives, perhaps, and closet herself somewhere else.

Cathy wasn't sure where her father was at the moment.
Driving home slowly through the rain, or working late somewhere. She'd lost track of his schedule.

Because of her injured cheek, she could only lie flat on her
back. She lay still with her injured finger resting carefully on top
of her other hand. She would not be able to move it all night,
lest she catch the nail and tear it further.

Her head rested directly above the hiding place of her stolen
movie magazines. She lay absolutely still, breathing quietly, wishing that it were safe enough to bring one of Angela Gordon's
pictures out of its hiding place. It didn't matter, though. Angela
would have seen everything. She sensed her sitting beside her on
the bed, looking down at her closed eyes.

"*What happened this time?*"

"I don't know. I just got off the school bus and she was waiting for me. I think she thinks I have a boyfriend."

Angela crinkled her nose in disapproval. Then she settled
herself on the foot of the bed, propped up against the wall, with
one hand resting gently on Cathy's foot.

"*This okay?*"

"Ah-huh."

"*I'll sit here until you fall asleep then.*"

Although it was far too early to go to bed for the night, Cathy began to drift off to sleep. There wouldn't be any supper now anyway, and sleep would help her heal. If she were still red-eyed and swollen-faced in the morning, Adele would accuse her of trying to get attention.

Her breathing slowed. She sank deeper. Secret admirer? Admirer? Who...? Nobody admired her. The faces of classmates drifted past beneath her heavy eyelids. No. None of them. There were a few boys from St. Mike's at the bus stop after school, but they never bothered with her. None of them would have sent her anything like that. No. Something must have gotten mixed up. She stretched her uninjured hand across the bedspread and slipped it into Angela's. The last injury that she noticed before finally falling asleep was the throbbing in the roots of her teeth, just below the swelling.

CHAPTER 2

While Cathy drifted off to sleep, the fridge door opened, glass bottles knocked sharply against one another, the fridge closed. Then footsteps chuffed across the carpet and a moment later a metal door latch clicked sharply.

Occasionally, Adele remained hidden only for the remainder of the day and night, emerging the following morning, stepping back into her routine as if nothing had happened. "Porridge for breakfast, kids," she'd call up the stairs if it were a school morning. But most often she withdrew for days, closeting herself in the master bedroom or the den or the guest room. Her fury, though, potent and palpable as her physical presence, seeped out beneath the door, smothering everything to stillness. Only the diligently ticking clocks dared to defy her.

During these times, her husband, Gerald Mugan, came and went like an automaton, speaking in whispers to Cathy and Richard, staying away at his work for as long as he could, coming home only to undress silently in the dark and crawl beneath a blanket on a couch if his bedroom was barred. Although he was nearly six feet tall, he appeared to be shorter because of his stooping posture. A door had fallen on him during the war, damaging several discs in his back. During damp weather, the old injury grew painful, causing him to stoop and walk with a curious rocking gate, shifting his weight from side to side. Cathy thought she noted lately that the stoop seemed less and less dependent upon the presence of dampness. His hair, which was dark as tar but streaked with a bit of grey, hung, much to his wife's annoyance, straight down the front of his forehead unless it was creamed firmly into place. He had blue eyes, a fair Irish complexion, and round, protruding ears.

"Monkey" was what Adele called him.

"No slip-ups from you," he'd whisper to Cathy as they passed in the hall. "I want this to blow over as quickly as possible."

The silences didn't seem to affect Cathy's brother, Richard. Unlike his father, he behaved completely normally. As tall and lanky as a young, uninjured Gerald, he moved with a confident stride, coming and going as he always had — just as he pleased. His only concessions were that he didn't speak much, beyond one-word greetings, and he didn't play any music in his room. Like his father, he spent most of his time at his job, coming home hours after Robinson's had closed, never mentioning to anyone where he had been.

Only Cathy was left behind — the beast-keeper, as she thought of herself — left to come and go from school by herself, to preserve the tomblike silence and her own safety by taking extraordinary care not to step on squeaking floorboards, by soundlessly opening and closing doors, by depressing the toilet handle only halfway so that the water trickled quietly rather than gushed into the bowl. She didn't dare try to stay away like her brother or bring a friend home to use as a buffer between herself and her mother. In the past Adele had burst out of a room at the sound of a school companion's voice and demanded to know who Minnie the Moocher was and didn't she have her own home to go to after school since this wasn't a damned orphanage.

Even the telephone, suddenly shattering the quiet, ringing repeatedly in the kitchen, could not be answered during the silences. Adele would not come out to talk to anyone, but she would roar out from behind her closed door to snatch away the receiver and smash it down onto the cradle if she heard Cathy talking to anyone. And so, while her father and brother stayed away, Cathy spent hours up in her room, waiting for time to pass, carefully and quietly turning the pages of her magazine collection, one ear cocked to the door for any sign that her mother was emerging.

Sometimes Cathy woke from a deep sleep to hear her mother moving about in the middle of the night. At first, not knowing what had woken her, Cathy would lie in her bed, puzzled. But then she would hear it again: the soft clack of a door closing, a light switch snapping on or off, the fridge door falling shut. Suddenly her room would fill with the aroma of fresh toast. In the morning there would be a crumb-covered plate and a knife, sticky with the residue of strawberry jam, sitting in the kitchen sink. But still no Adele.

In warm weather, Adele slipped out of the French doors in the dining room, taking her rage to the back corner of the yard, where she sat alone on the lawn swing. She stretched her stout legs across to the opposite seat and threw her head back towards the sky. You could see her from the dining room, a bone china teacup and saucer resting in her lap, sometimes an empty jar of olives abandoned on the seat beside her. She sat out there for hours, eyes closed, swinging, not responding to anything around her.

The swing stood beneath an old hawthorn tree, and during May, the small white circular petals of the tree's flowers drifted down like confetti, settling over everything below. Adele would lie there, undisturbed, while hundreds of delicate petals collected in her teacup, in her lap, in the crooks of her folded chubby arms, on her eyelids, and in her bright red hair. Several times Cathy had looked out late in the evening and seen her mother sitting on the swing, her head tilted toward a dark or a moonlit sky, with the petals falling silently over her pyjamas and bathrobe.

"The Abominable Snow Mother," she said quietly to Richard, who peered over her shoulder one evening.

"One too many adjectives, Cath," he said, continuing down the hall.

On the evenings when she was home alone, caught in the grip of the stillness, Cathy took to eating bowls of puffed rice for dinner because the rice slid silently into the bowl and didn't crunch when she chewed. She carried the bowls up to her room, where she sat on the foot of her bed. From there she looked out the window at the falling summer twilight, or the nearly impenetrable winter darkness, watching the road, waiting to spot the slow-blinking yellow turn signal of her father's approaching car.

She always wished that there were some way to warn him, to tell him that tonight wasn't a good night to come home, that it had happened again or that the silence from yesterday or the day before still hadn't gone away. For years, she had imagined signalling to him somehow, warning him away. Hundreds of times, she had imagined exactly how the car would crawl past the end of the driveway without stopping, how the red tail lights would disappear into the dark.

But she never spoke to him about a secret signal. He would never risk being found working in league with her against Adele. Her father never resisted Adele. All her life, Cathy had witnessed her mother repeatedly beating him across the head and shoulders with one of the throw cushions from the living room couch, screeching at the top of her lungs that he was a fool and a failure. With each blow, brown and white chicken feathers

jetted out of burst seams in the cushion, moving in curious contrast to the surrounding violence, gently drifting to resting spots
atop silk lampshades and in the crannies in the ornate frame of
the mirror that hung above the couch. Her father barely ever
even raised a hand to shield himself. Instead, he simply removed
his glasses and sat still, with his eyes lowered to the floor.

Cathy couldn't remember a time when she didn't want to
run and wrap herself around her father's head to spare him the
blows. But as a small child, she had learned the one and only rule
of engagement — you never, ever challenged Adele. And so she
would walk past her father's bowed head, go up to her room, and
close the door against the horror. Afterwards, she would watch
for a moment when she could climb up into his lap and lay her
head on the soft cotton of his shirt and feel the warmth of his
body. And as long as Adele wasn't around, he would let her stay
there as long as she liked. But then, one day, he had suddenly
said, "No," and pushed her away. She looked up in time to see
his eyes flash up to the doorway. Her mother was just stepping
into the room.

"Get outside and ride your bike," she hollered. "You're too
big to be sitting in your father's lap. That's for babies. Get going.
And you! What are you trying to encourage, huh? Keeping that
child a baby until she's thirty years old, sitting around on your
lap like a pet, for God's sake. If you want something to moon
over get yourself a dog."

From that day forward, her father either shooed her away or
made himself inaccessible behind his newspaper. She had
become just one more danger to him, like mud tracked in on
the carpets.

Cathy never stopped trying to win him back, though. On
nights when she could hear her mother snoring loudly from
behind a closed door, she often tiptoed through the house to
meet her father at the back door. It pained her greatly to see

how tentatively he stepped through the laundry room door at nine-thirty in the evening, shoulders drooping, a pitiful uncertainty about him as he tried to gauge whether or not he was welcome in his own home that night. In silence, she helped with his coat, took his damp gloves and set them on the hot water tank, held his grey fedora while he bent over to take off his rubbers. Too often, after removing his shoes, loosening his tie, and finding the bedroom door resolutely closed against him, she would see him return quietly to the kitchen to stand alone in the wedge of yellow light that sliced into the dark room from the open fridge and eat a piece of cheddar cheese and drink a glass of milk. And it was there, as she asked in a whisper if there was anything else that she could get for him, that his beseeching blue eyes found her.

"I can't take too much more of this," he'd say, in a low, unhappy voice. And when he'd stop chewing and turn and look directly at her a knife would slice through her heart. Every time he came home late to find the house shrouded in a dark silence, without any supper set aside for him, she felt as if she'd let him down. No matter what the catalyst had been, she felt as if she should have somehow been able to prevent her mother's rage.

"I can make you a tuna sandwich, Dad, instead of just that piece of cheese? And a nice cup of tea?"

"I can feel tachycardia starting up again," he'd say, turning back to stare into the open fridge.

The first time he had used the word "tachycardia" she'd been eleven years old and hadn't known what it meant. But she had looked it up, painstakingly substituting each vowel with another until she hit upon the correct spelling, and now she knew that it meant an irregular heartbeat. She also knew by the lifelong absence of a paternal grandfather and several uncles that the men in her father's family did not live into old age.

"Your grandfather was dead and buried of a heart attack long before you were even thought about, missy," her mother had told her. "Nobody in that family has ever made it past sixty-five. So get used to it."

She knew the story about her grandfather calling the house the night he died. It was before Richard was born. Her father said he could only hear gasping on the other end of the line. But he recognized the sound from having heard it before. That's how he knew to call the ambulance. When her parents got to her grandfather's house, the ambulance was just pulling out of the driveway, so they followed it to the hospital. Her grandfather died four hours later, at the age of sixty-four.

For years, Cathy had been counting and recounting the number of years that remained between the present day and her father's sixty-fifth birthday. At night, before falling asleep, she added sixty-five to her father's birthdate over and over again, never able to be confident that she had added the numbers correctly. According to her calculations, he would turn sixty-five in 1985. She would be thirty-seven by then. Richard would be forty. But her father could die anytime between now and then. If he lived to his maximum age, he had twenty-two years left. That was a little over two decades, but it was spread across three decades: the rest of the sixties, all of the seventies, and half of the eighties. Medical science might have time to make a breakthrough and be able to save him. Or she might.

For most of her life, Cathy had been preparing herself to outwit death and save her father from his inherited fate. For years she had been watching him, secretly staring intently at the side of his face in church on Sundays, or when she found him asleep in a chair at home, studying him for any slight change.

"Your grandfather's blood was so thick the night he died they could hardly get it up the needle," her mother had said. "Saw it with my own two eyes. Black as tar."

41

Cathy was convinced that thick dark blood would be visible in the skin, and that she had come to know her father's skin so intimately she would notice it darkening even before he did. But her hope of saving her father faded on the evenings when he stood drinking milk by the light of the fridge and she saw how he had aged. Lately she had noticed that, although he was only forty-three, the flesh at the base of his throat was beginning to collapse. The sight frightened her. In bed at night she closed her eyes and tried to feel her own heart beating, but felt nothing. Hearts were just like all the other organs of the body, working away silently, for years, except that they suddenly rose up at the last minute, demanding to be noticed for all their hard work before stopping for good. She imagined her father's heart, pumping erratically, racing, slowing, racing again, all this destructive activity taking place out of sight, without any way to know about it, and, even if she could know, without any way to get in there and calm his heart down in time to save him. She thought about the thick black blood just sitting in his veins, congealing like chocolate pudding, not moving. In her dreams she saw images of white-haired men toppling over, dead, one after another, receding back into her father's history: grandfather, great-grandfather, great-great-grandfather. Each one of them suddenly clapping a hand to his chest and slumping forward, blue at the lips and dead before he hit the ground. She worried that she would find her father cold beneath a blanket one morning, his heart having sped up so fast it finally stood dead still.

But how could she help him? What could she do? She had asked the question her whole life. She asked it now as she roamed through an uneasy sleep. What could she do to stop her mother's terrible anger? To end the horrible silences? Sometimes it seemed to help if she kept her room immaculate, if she was quick at a chore that her mother had given her, if she bent with visible effort over some small spot somewhere and scrubbed with determination. Other times, nothing she did seemed to help. If she could just figure it out, she would do what was required, and then the rages would stop and her father wouldn't come home to this withering silence. What hadn't she thought of? She should try harder at school. She should stand up straighter, shoulders back. Her mother hated slouchers; she hated disorder; she could hate something brand new in the morning, something that Cathy had overlooked. Cathy should be ready. For anything.

The next morning, Cathy got up early and tiptoed cautiously past her parents' bedroom to the bathroom. The door to the den was closed, so she knew her father was in there, trying to sleep on the small red loveseat that was too short for anyone but a child. She'd seen how he did it, lying on his back with his legs hanging off one end of the couch, or lying on one side, facing the room with his legs folded up accordion-style. Neither position could be comfortable enough to accommodate a full night's sleep. If this was going to be a long silence, he'd have to move somewhere else.

Cathy pressed the bathroom door quietly into place behind her, passing her fingers over the useless lock that her mother had destroyed a year ago. After listening at the door for a moment, she turned and stood in front of the wide mirror. The glare from the overhead light highlighted everything.

"*Yikes! You're a mess, kid. Red eyes, swollen lids, puffy cheek. Let's get a cold compress going. Turn on the tap. If she sees you like this, you'll only catch it again.*"

"I know."

Adele could wake up at any moment, blast open the bathroom door, and see the damage for herself.

You played with that during the night to get it to swell up, didn't you? Don't think I don't know your tricks, missy, trying to get attention. You didn't look like that last night.

Cathy decided to concentrate on her swollen eyes. She made a cold compress out of a wet facecloth and held it against one eye. Without the swelling, her eyes wouldn't look too bad. They'd be only slightly bloodshot and inflamed, and their appearance could easily be passed off as irritation from hay fever.

"*That's good,*" Angela said. "*Keep it there for a few minutes. What else needs doing?*"

Cathy had brought along last night's damp underwear, hiding them beneath her pyjamas. Now, with one hand, she held them under the running tap, making certain that not a trace of stain or smell of urine remained. When she had wrung them out, she tucked them back inside her pyjamas.

The lump under her cheek was less swollen than it had been last night, but it was still quite visible. She doubted whether a cold compress would have much effect on it but nevertheless reached into the cupboard for another facecloth. Thankfully, the bulk of the swelling rose up at the outer edge of the cheekbone rather than in the dead centre of her face. She shook her head gently, letting her hair fall experimentally over that part of her face. She twisted and turned, examining herself from every possible angle, finally concluding that the injury could be mostly hidden behind an artfully arranged hank of hair.

While she dampened the cloth, she slowly pulled open a vanity drawer and silently withdrew a roll of adhesive tape and the cuticle scissors. She repaired her uprooted nail, carefully holding the roll of tape and the scissors over the carpet in case she dropped either one. The job completed, she reversed her actions, lowering the tools into the drawer, letting go only after each was resting securely on the drawer bottom. After slowly closing the drawer, she lay down on the blue carpeted floor and covered her injured cheek with the second cold cloth. Beside her, the tub filled slowly, the tap barely running, another cloth placed beneath the waterfall to dampen the splashing sound.

Lying on the floor reminded her of seeing her mother on the floor a couple of years ago. It was in the middle of an afternoon, and she had caught her mother laughing alone in the upstairs hall. The hem of her apron was tucked into her mouth, and tears were spilling down her face. The sheets from Richard's bed were piled in a mound in the middle of the hall. When she spotted Cathy, she pulled the apron out of her mouth, threw her head back and cackled, and then slid down the wall to the floor, her legs splaying out across the carpet.

"Oh my dear that's a funny word," she said, using the apron to wipe the tears from her cheeks. Cathy had been on her way to her room, but now she hesitated, unsure of what to do. It was so rare for her mother to laugh like this.

Another wave of hysterics seized her mother and she began to tilt to one side, gasping for breath, propping herself up with one arm and holding her other across her jiggling abdomen. Hardly able to speak, she struggled to look up at Cathy.

"Do you know what a *penis* is?" she asked.

The word "penis" shot from her mouth like the cork from a champagne bottle, and then she slapped the floor with her hand as more hysterical laughter welled up. Cathy stared at her. Adele wiped the corners of her eyes with the apron.

"Isn't that a funny word, 'penis'? That's what it's called. A penis. A man has a penis."

Then she rolled over onto all fours and climbed to her feet.

"Ah, me. I haven't laughed that hard in years."

And that was the end of it. She picked up the bundle of sheets, stepped past Cathy, and headed downstairs.

Then, a day or two later, in a fit of rage, she had taken the screws out of the lock plate on the bathroom door and dug frantically at the wooden frame, gouging pieces of it out until the plate fell to the floor.

"I don't need you in here behind a lock doing God-knows-what for hours while the rest of us wait to get in," Adele had shrilled at Cathy.

"Hey. Let's not fall asleep down there. Hurry up and get in."

"Right."

Cathy got up, turned off the water, and slipped into the tub. Only when the tepid water washed over her legs did she rediscover her injured knee and toes. Seduced by the comforting warm water, she stretched out, immersing everything but her nose. She lay there, peacefully, her hair dark ribbons drifting around her, her weightless arms floating beside her, the steady rasping of her own breathing magnified in her submerged ears. Breathe in. Breathe out. In. Out. Drifting. Warm. Quiet. The sun on her face. She was in California. On a beach. Where Angela lived.

Then a tremor came up through the water from beneath her. The whole tub was vibrating. A truck passing by on the California highway. No. She heard pounding. Footsteps. The bathroom door abruptly jerked open. Adele marched in and wheeled around to face the tub. She was wearing pink pyjamas and a pink bathrobe and her fuzzy red hair was squashed flat on one side.

Cathy shot forward, splashing water over the rim of the tub, and curled herself over her knees.

"It's no wonder I can't sleep with you whaling about in here. Did you wash your vagina?"

Adele's finger jabbed towards an unseen place beneath the water.

"Use lots of soap and get it clean down there."

Cathy, cowering, trying to fold herself up and disappear, wrapped her arms around her knees and turned her head to the wall.

47

Adele abruptly turned away from the tub to lean against the bathroom sink and began examining her teeth in the mirror. Her eyes scanned her gums and the vertical crevices between her teeth. In the bright overhead light, the inside of her mouth appeared pink and glossy.

After a moment, she suddenly gagged and had to bow over the sink.

"Dirty, filthy thing probably never brushes," she said into the sink.

Cathy quickly ran her tongue over her own front teeth, wondering if her mother's remark was aimed at her.

Rising up to the mirror again, Adele pulled down her lower lip. She gagged a second time and bowed to the sink again. While she hung there, waiting for the waves of nausea to stop, Cathy lunged for a towel on the back of the door. She managed to wrap it around herself while kneeling in the tub, before her mother straightened up.

"My God, some people are pigs," Adele said, finally rising up out of the sink. "Yuck."

This time, she dropped her jaw and looked at the gums at the back of her bottom teeth. Her tongue swept over the tooth surfaces. Next, she shot her tongue straight out, examined it quickly, and frowned when she saw that it was white. Disgusted, she retracted it, and then her eyes lost their focus and roamed over the empty space in the mirror just to the right of her head.

"*There it is again,*" Angela whispered. "*That weirdness of hers. She's seeing something in the mirror.*"

The bathroom fell silent.

Don't stare.

The secret voice always gave good advice.

Cathy looked down at her wet bare feet.

The tanned, handsome face of the President of the United States smiled out of the mirror at Adele.

"How are you this morning, Adele?" he asked in his peculiar New England accent.

Adele noticed the faint pepperminty odour of toothpaste in the air. The President was such a nice clean man, such a gentleman. His parents had raised all nine of his brothers and sisters to be such well-mannered kids. His wife was so lucky to have found such a wonderful man, such a good father for her children.

She reached absently beneath the sink and pulled out a can of green powdered cleanser, thinking about him in the beach pictures, lying on his bad back, holding his small daughter in the air. The pictures revealed that he wore plain ordinary white sports socks with two coloured rings at the top, one red, one blue. Socks like she bought her own son, Richard. His millions didn't mean anything to him. He was just a lovely, ordinary family man.

When she looked up from sprinkling the cleanser onto her toothbrush, she noticed Cathy shivering in the corner of the mirror where the President had just been. Her shoulders were bare and wet, and her folded, goosebump-covered arms held a blue bath towel against her torso. Her dark wet hair, hanging down the left side of her face, partially covered her eye and dripped down onto the towel. Adele narrowed her eyes and stared at the reflection of Cathy's face. Suddenly, she whirled around and flicked Cathy's hair aside.

"Huh! Is that all? Big baby. A little tap and you think it's the end of the world. All that wailing and carrying on over nothing. I tell you, if you think you're hard done by, you should have seen some of the swats *my* father doled out."

She let the hair drop and turned back to the mirror. Cathy kept her gaze down.

"No siree boy," Adele started up again, "nobody is going to call me dirty, that's for sure. You should have seen this woman in front of me in the grocery yesterday morning. I tell you, I've never seen such dirty teeth in all my life."

Adele bent over the sink, plunged her brush deep inside her cheek and began to scrub vigorously, talking despite the obstruction.

"Honestly, some people are just born pigs, too lazy to brush their own teeth. I don't know how people can live like that. Yuck! And when she smiled…"

Here Adele pulled herself up to look directly into the mirror at Cathy.

"You should have seen how all of her gums showed above her teeth. Big wet horsy gums. Ew, I hate that."

She dropped back into the depths of the sink. Cathy kept her eyes down, watching her bare big toe trace a circle in the pile of the royal blue carpet.

"Brushing off all the enamel, my ass. I don't need a dentist to show me how to keep clean. I know what feels clean, by God, and this stuff really cleans. It's people like that woman who need a dentist, not me. Somebody should tie her down and give her a good scrub. God, she was dirty!"

She fell silent, spat, ran her tongue over her teeth and began to brush again. Cathy watched her own toe, listening to the steady, unbroken *whoosh* of running tap water beneath the chugging rhythm of her mother's brushing.

"Somebody else who looks like they need a good overhaul, I tell you, is that new helper priest of Father Lauzon's. What's his name? Father Martin or something? I ran into Father at the shopping plaza yesterday and he had this other priest with him. The man looked neglected, positively unkempt. He said he came back into this neck of the woods to pick up a few things for his new place."

Adele removed the red brush from her mouth and held it in the air as if she were going to use it as a pointer.

"Honest to God, you should have seen this man, a priest … his hair was greasy, his shoulders were covered in big chips of dandruff, and he had these big dirty sores on his face and neck. Whiteheads and boils. Ew! I've never seen such a walking mess in all my life. It was enough to make me sick."

Adele's voice was beginning to rise and whine. She bobbed back down into the sink and resumed brushing.

"Poor things have been struggling over at that new rectory for almost a month without a housekeeper. Old Mrs. Dupuis died on them, you know. Can you imagine, three men trying to take care of themselves? Father was asking if I knew anybody…"

She stopped to spit, stood up abruptly, and watched herself in the mirror.

"I told him you could fill in during the summer, until they found someone permanent."

Cathy's foot froze on the carpet. Her eyes flashed up to the mirror.

"Me? You told them me?"

"Yes you, miss sitting-around-all-summer-with-nothing-to-do. It's time you worked for a living. When I was your age I was already out in the world. It'll do you good to get out and earn a few dollars. Now that school's out, I don't need a big lazy fifteen-year-old lying around all summer getting ideas about boys. What happened across the street is not going to happen in this house. The rectory will be a good place for you. You're to be there the beginning of next week, early, before morning mass is finished."

She dropped abruptly from the mirror into the sink, drank from the tap, swished noisily from cheek to cheek, and spat triumphantly.

"Hmm. Wonder what went on across the street?"

Don't ask, Cathy thought back.

"You just have to get their meals, clean the rectory up a bit, make beds, do a bit of laundry. Nothing that'll kill you."

Cathy's eyes dropped down to rest on Adele's feet puffing up out of their pink feather-trimmed slippers. Adele slurped noisily from the tap a second time, swished, spat, and finally rose. Looking into the mirror, she retracted her lips and brought her bottom teeth forward to rest under the edges of her top teeth.

"See? Look at that. Sparkling clean, white as snow, and all my own, too."

She held a pose in the mirror. Cathy thought she looked like a chimpanzee.

Adele banged her brush loudly several times on the rim of the sink, sending a spray of excess water in several directions, and then abruptly shot the toothbrush into its nearby holder.

"Let's see if you can say that, missy, when you're my age."

Blotting her mouth on a hand towel without removing it from the rack, she pushed past Cathy.

"And don't hog this room all morning."

Cathy dried herself off, put her pyjamas back on, and stepped cautiously out into an empty hall. Her mother had vanished and the house had fallen silent again. Hurrying, she opened the hall closet where the cleaning supplies were kept, gathered up what she needed for her chores, and raced up to her room.

"Great news, huh?"

Cathy dumped all the aerosol cans and spray bottles and dusters into the middle of her unmade bed.

"Oh, Angela, I've got a job."

"So I heard."

"I've got something to do all summer."

"Cool."

"I can't believe it. All of a sudden I feel so grown up."

Cathy plunged into the closet and hung her wet underwear on a nail in the back corner.

"A summer job. I'll have a bit of money and something to do."

She popped back out and tore open a dresser drawer to begin changing into work clothes.

"I can go somewhere every day for two whole months."

"Hot dog!"

"I'm so excited."

"So I see."

"I've always wanted to go away. For years, I've been thinking about it."

"I've seen the pencil marks under your desk."

"But I thought it wouldn't be until I could go to university. But that's still three years away."

"Lucky break, huh?"

"But this is right out of the blue. It's not the same as going away to live somewhere else, like residence, but it's at least a start."

Angela smiled. Cathy plunked herself down on the bed to pull on a pair of socks.

"It's housekeeping … for three priests … at St. Alphonsis rectory … across town."

"I was there, remember?"

"It's supposed to be old, but maybe it's going to be really nice, like those parish churches in the old Christmas movies, you know? All that nice dark old woodwork, some of it halfway up the walls in some of the rooms, like the dining room, you know? I wouldn't mind polishing all that."

"You just might be out of your mind, you know?"

"I get to cook, too."

"That's always fun."

"I know how to make sloppy joes, grilled cheese sandwiches, and tuna casserole."

"Gotta start somewhere."

"And I can barbecue things, steaks and chicken and burgers. I'm sure they'll have a barbecue."

"Well, you hope they'll have a barbecue."

"I've always wanted to try baked Alaska too. You know, it's ice cream that gets baked inside a cake and it doesn't melt?"

The whine of the vacuum cleaner suddenly started up in one of the downstairs rooms. Cathy saw that she was sitting motionless, gazing at herself in the dresser mirror. The side of her face was swollen, her eyes bloodshot, and one finger was bound in white tape.

She got up and opened the two small windows in the room. The droning of several lawn mowers and the smell of fresh-cut grass and newly blooming roses floated in through the screens. Unmistakably, it was summer.

"You've got a summer job," she whispered, "a real live summer job."

She picked up the bottle of glass cleaner and a rag and began cleaning the mirror. Her Saturday morning routine had been set in stone for years: bedroom, bathroom, dining room, front hall, dishes. Always in that order. Within each room, the various chores were also ordered. Remove stale sheets or towels first. Then work from the top of the room down: walls, windows and sills, mirrors, furniture, baseboards, floor. Finally, make the bed with fresh sheets or hang fresh towels. Her arm went round and round across the smooth glass surface, the cloth buffing away imagined smudges. How many mirrors would there be in a rectory?

When I was your age, my dear, I could work rings around anyone. My father taught me the meaning of hard work early, by golly, and it's never hurt me one single bit.

How her mother loved the idea of work. Especially if it was hard physical work where you had to bend over or reach up to lift or pull heavy things; where you had to apply force and scrub hard; anything that made you huff and puff and tired you out and gave you rough red hands at the end of the day. That was work, by golly. The backbone of character.

Cathy sprayed the mirror and began buffing it again. At least it had to be better than working for nuns. Priests were a lot more easygoing than nuns. Father McCoy flaring his nostrils like a horse, raising his eyebrows practically up into his hair to get a laugh. She'd never known a nun to make faces. Sister Anne

Rochelle sometimes laughed at her own feeble little witticisms, but generally nuns didn't clown around. And was there a priest anywhere who could come even close to Sister Lumina in sourness? Father Lauzon was very businesslike, perhaps impatient, but she had never sensed cruelty in him.

The vacuum cleaner stopped and the house fell silent. The skin on the back of Cathy's neck contracted. How long had she been cleaning the mirror? Panicked, she put down her cloth and pulled open a dresser drawer. She would tell her mother that she was taking a moment to go through each drawer, refolding everything neatly.

The vacuum started up again, sucking, whining, thumping into the baseboards. At least while it was moving she knew where her mother was. She picked up another duster and the can of furniture polish. How much furniture would there be in a rectory? What would it be like? White French provincial, like this?

"In a guy's room? What are you thinking?"

"Well, there are rooms other than bedrooms."

"Yeah, at Marie Antoinette's house."

"She retired to a hat box, didn't she?"

"Oh! Excellent."

Cathy smiled as she sprayed a lemon-scented mist of polish over the surface of her dresser.

"I'm sure if the place is old, it will be all dark. That'd be better. See this? I can hardly tell where I've been. It's better when the wood's dark and you can just cut a path through the polish like plowing through snow."

"As you wish."

Working through her morning tasks, digging into crevices, rubbing vigorously, pulling things taut, her mother's endless opinions flowed through her mind. Only dirty filthy pigs slept for more than one week in the same sheets; this wasn't a museum, with spider webs allowed to grow to the size of hammocks in every corner; the French were lazy, which is why they chose white for all their furniture. They thought it didn't show the dust. But they didn't fool her, by Jesus. At least not anymore. It was just too bad she hadn't seen through them before furnishing Cathy's room with the darned stuff. But she wouldn't be fooled again, no siree.

Because of her injuries, progress was slow, which was frustrating because Cathy wanted to finish up quickly and go over to Janet's.

Guess what? I've got a job.

And she couldn't keep her mind on her work. Her thoughts turned repeatedly to Father Lauzon. Although he had been the pastor at her church, St. Mary, Star of the Sea, for six or seven years before this latest transfer to St. Alphonsis, she really only knew him to see him and say a shy hello. As far as she knew, he never bothered much with parish kids. He had a distinctly un-priestly air about him. To her, he seemed more like a businessman than a priest. Tall and deep-voiced, hands nearly always shoved deep into his pockets, playing with loose change, he was friendly and aloof at the same time. On Sundays, after mass, he always came out into the church parking lot. You could hear him talking to everybody in his big booming voice. Cathy'd heard him joking with men parishioners, asking when he could get a game in at their golf club. She'd even seen him pull a golf bag out of the trunk of his car, so she knew he wasn't just making conversation. And he whistled and sang all the time. Snippets of tunes from the radio. She couldn't imagine him looking over her shoulder and fussing over details of housecleaning, investigating her work and raising his voice if he found a spot of dust somewhere or a wrinkle in a bedspread. He certainly didn't look as if he'd care whether a rag was wrung out properly or not. In fact, Cathy was certain he wouldn't even realize that some people considered that there *was* a right way and a wrong way to do such a thing.

As she finished up in her room, the last thing she did was adjust the angle of the slats in her blind to let in as much light as possible. Her mother liked lots of light in a room, except when she was brooding behind one of her closed doors.

She was expected to scour the bathroom from ceiling to floor, ensuring that all its shiny surfaces — mirror, white tile, white porcelain fixtures, silver chrome taps, faucets, and cupboard handles — all sparkled. She even had to bring the step ladder in from the garage and take down the round glass ceiling light cover and wash it so that when her mother turned on the light and looked up, she saw only light and not the little dark specks of dead insect bodies. Finally, she had to replace all the towels and facecloths and the bath mat, making sure they all hung perfectly folded from their correct rack.

Then came the dining room, dusting and polishing all the dark wood furniture and washing all the little square windows in the French doors. Finally, she had to wash and rinse the floor in the front foyer, put two coats of paste wax on it, and then buff it to a gleaming shine, first with the brushes on the electric floor polisher and finally with the lambs' wool pads.

Her well-trained hands worked independently while her thoughts wandered, wondering about St. Alphonsis. She pictured herself answering a beautiful heavy dark door, placing a hat on a coat rack, and leading a visitor inside, settling him in a comfortable parlour before she went to knock softly on a study door and say, "Father, you have a visitor. Shall I make tea?"

★ ★ ★

Finally, at two o'clock that afternoon, having made sure that all the drapes and curtains in all the rooms of the house were wide open to the bright afternoon light, having checked that not a dish was out of place in the kitchen, and having changed her clothes and combed her hair, she was free. The last thing to do was to hunt through the lemon-, pine-, and vinegar-scented rooms for her mother. Cathy liked the sharp, tangy air. Along with the orderly appearance of the rooms, it was palpable evidence of all her hard work.

She knew to be diligent in her search. Sometimes you could miss Adele because she sat so silently, hidden in a corner of a room, sunk into a chair, staring at the carpet in front of her feet, with a cold cup of tea in her lap. This time, though, Cathy spied her through the dining room doors, sitting outside on the swing, with her head thrown back, her eyes closed, and the garden hose held tightly in her right hand. As the swing rocked gently back and forth, the water from the hose splashed across the trunk of the nearby hawthorn tree, tracked across the grass, spilled onto the soil beneath a lilac bush that her mother had recently transplanted, and then reversed its path. Cathy cautiously called out through the screen that she was going to Janet's. She knew enough to pause, looking towards her mother, just in case Adele was watching her through narrowed slits. There might be one more task that she wanted completed. But this time, her mother did not respond, and so Cathy quickly and quietly left the house by the laundry room door.

The Saturday-morning lawn mowers had fallen silent, and the smell of fresh-cut grass had drifted away. Now the hot afternoon air was scented with petunias. Oppressed by the sun, people had abandoned the street to their automatic sprinklers, which were busy *ffutt-ffutt-ffutting* arcs of water across the front lawns. Cathy stepped off the end of her driveway onto the gravel shoulder of the road, listening to the playful sounds made by the shooting water. *Ffutt … ffutt … ffutt … ffutt …* went Mrs. Munro's sprinkler onto her beds of pansies and then *chucka-chucka-chucka-chucka-*

chucka-chucka-chuck as it mechanically jerked away in another direction. *Quich … quich … quich …* said Mr. Grant's sprinkler.

"Kinda like one big conversation out here, isn' t it?"

Angela had fallen into step beside Cathy. She could have walked right out of a flowerbed in her hot pink silk top, bright green silk pedal pushers, and yellow sandals.

"Just goes to show you never know how many parallel worlds exist right beside yours, you know?"

Cathy was staring straight ahead to the end of the street. Angela followed her gaze.

"Ah! Tar bubble time."

Cathy smiled, her mind flooding with the memory of how, years ago, on a hot day like today, with the sun beating down so hard that her black hair felt almost on fire to the touch, and the heat waves rising from the scorching asphalt, the tar bubbles would always be up. Good big ones, ready for pushing down. And they belonged to her and Isabel Labelle.

She began to run towards the end of the street, pulled by memory back into the summers of her childhood. The crown of the road was scarred with cracks that had been filled in with tar. The tar was melting and bubbles were there now rising up slowly in the broiling heat, tiny reflections of the sun riding on their glossy thinning surfaces.

"This the place?" Angela asked, arriving at her side.

"Right here."

"How many on a team?"

"Doesn't matter. Just the same number on each side."

"Remind me of the rules?"

"You pair off your bubbles and just watch them grow. If yours gets to be the biggest, you get a point. Unless it bursts. Then you lose it and your team gets smaller. So that's why you have to decide whether you're going to push it down before it bursts so you can keep it. But if you push it down too soon, and the other team's bubble gets bigger and doesn't burst, they get the point."

"Hmph!"

"Isabel and I used to spend whole afternoons lying here," Cathy said, her hand drifting up to caress the side of her face, "with our cheeks on the road."

"Yikes. A hot asphalt facial."

"You can't see the height of the bubbles unless you're right down there beside them."

"Wanna have a game?"

"Naw. It has to be Isabel."

"Whatever happened to her?"

"Don't know. Moved away."

"You sure?"

"Yes. Years ago."

"No, I mean them. Look at them. They're just waiting for you."

"Well, they'll have to wait forever, now."

"You taking the shortcut to Janet's?"

"Uh-huh."

"That stinky dark little cave?"

"It's not a cave, it's just the underpass."

"I think there are rats under there."

"You sound like all the mothers on the street from years ago. They told us that just so we wouldn't play down there. I've never seen a rat."

"Just the same…"

"See you."

Standing alone in the middle of the deserted street, Cathy looked down at the tar bubbles. It felt like a lifetime ago that she and Isabel had played there.

There was a ditch at the end of the road with a little dirt path worn into the grass at the water's edge. Cathy left the pavement and headed through the little buffer of field and then down over the edge of the slope. Beneath her shoes, the coarse crunch of the gravel shoulder changed to the soft crackling of weeds and grass. Flowered walls rose up on either side of her. The slopes were covered in purple and white clover, brilliant yellow dandelions, pale pink and white bindweed blossoms, and tiny yellow hop flowers. In amongst the flower heads an army of insects bobbed and hovered, hunting for the things that sustained them. They brushed past her hair, intent upon their survival. On the opposite side of the water, a red-winged blackbird trilled from atop a stalk of last season's thistle.

When she reached the path the sound of trickling water blotted out the rasping, rustling vegetation. She paused to watch the stream for a moment, wondering how much water had flowed past, day and night, in the years since she had played here. This was one of life's mystery questions. There would be an exact number, but it would be unknowable.

The path threaded beneath the concrete underpass. As she stepped into the cool darkness of the cavern-like space, the sound of the moving water intensified. Her eyes adjusted to the dark and her skin rippled with goosebumps as she pressed close to the damp cement wall. It stank of mould and sulphur under there and was cool enough to chill meat. There probably could be rats.

Emerging into the sunlight again a moment later, the sound of running water dropped, replaced by more rustling and bird-song. She picked her way carefully across the water, stepping on protruding rocks and discarded half-broken cement blocks, refuse from past bridge-building exploits of excited little neigh-bourhood boys. Once on the other side, she followed another path for several more minutes until just before encountering another road crossing. Then she trudged up the angled slope, leaving the flowers and the sounds behind her, and set her foot upon the arbour-covered delight that was Whitehall Boulevard.

Janet St. Amand had been Cathy's best friend ever since the day, eight years ago, that Sister Gertrude brought her by the hand to the door of the Grade 2 classroom in the middle of the morning and asked Sister Joseph to make room for a new pupil. Sister Joseph took the delicate little blonde girl by the hand and sat her down in the empty desk right across the aisle from Cathy.

The newcomer obviously didn't own a school uniform yet. She was wearing a dress with bright coloured tulips all over it; Cathy remembered this because a tulip was one of the few flowers that she was able to identify at that age. When Sister Joseph turned her attention back to the examples of addition and subtraction on the blackboard, Cathy remained staring at the brilliant colours, unable to tear her eyes away.

Janet's house was midway down the boulevard, a lovely old English manor with a dramatic sloping roof above the front door and lead-paned diamond-shaped windows that twinkled in the sunlight like bits of treasure hidden among the dark leafy ivy that covered the brown brick exterior.

Just as her hand was in the air, about to knock on the screen door, Eva, with her shiny blonde hair caught up in a ponytail and tied with a bright blue scarf, came around the side of the house with Whisky, a blonde cocker spaniel, at her heels. She had been gardening and her hands were caked with mud.

"Well, hi there, sweetie. Long time no see. How come you've been such a stranger? Your timing is perfect, though. Now you can get the door for me. How many times do I have to tell you not to knock?"

She slipped past Cathy, followed by the dog, and paused to kick off her moccasins on the landing inside, calling up the stairwell to Janet that her best friend in the world was here.

The three of them converged in the kitchen a moment later, Eva going immediately to the sink to wash up, Cathy choosing to lean on a cupboard near the door, and Janet making a speedy arrival from upstairs right into the middle of the room, courtesy of a long skid in her stockinged feet. She narrowed her eyes at Cathy immediately.

"What happened to your face?"

"I know. I know. Nice mess, huh?"

"What's the problem, sweetie?"

Eva turned around to see what Janet was talking about.

"I'm so clumsy. My mother says I can't stand on my feet for more than ten minutes at a time."

Eva shook her wet hands in the sink and then took Cathy by the wrist and pulled her into the light in front of the window, sweeping Cathy's dangling hair out of the way.

"Ew, honey, that looks really sore. I didn't notice that at the door. How did you do that?"

"Oh, it's a really dumb story. My father was washing the car in the garage yesterday and there were soapsuds and water all over the floor and I was in a hurry to get to the bathroom. I shouldn't have been running, but I was desperate, and I slipped just when I got to the door. I hit the doorknob on the way down."

"Oh, you poor thing. Did you put ice on it?"

"Yeah, a bit."

"Well it sure looks like it could use some more. Here, sit down."

Eva dried her hands on a tea towel and took a tray of ice cubes out of the freezer. A moment later she swept Cathy's hair gently out of the way again and lightly pressed an ice bag to the swollen cheekbone.

"You should be more careful, sweetie. You could have put out an eye or something. It's hard to tell if you're gonna get a shiner or not. I don't see any blood under the skin near your eye. There's just a bit over the bump. It looks like there's been a very little bit of bleeding there. That's an awfully hard swelling though. You must have hit the bone. Did you hurt anything else?"

"No."

"Did your mother watch you for a concussion? You're not supposed to go to sleep right away after a bump on the head, you know. If it's a really bad bump and you get sleepy right after, then it usually means that you've got a concussion."

"Oh, it wasn't really that hard. It just looks worse than it is. I don't even know what a concussion is, really."

"A bruised brain."

"So why can't you go to sleep if you have one?"

"I'm not exactly sure, but any drowsiness after a bump on the head can indicate that you've actually bruised the brain, and I think if it's serious you can actually slip into a coma."

"Well, I guess I don't have one because I woke up same as usual this morning."

"What did you do to this?"

Janet was pointing to the adhesive tape on one of Cathy's fingers.

"Oh, that's not related. I'm just trying to save a broken nail, that's all."

She thrust her hand out in front of her, turning it this way and that, examining the white taped finger, surreptitiously widening her eyes to the evaporating air.

Janet poked her nose into a brown paper grocery bag standing on the table. She pulled out a chunky blue box of tampons.

"Yea. More corks. Huge box! They on sale or something?"

"Well at the rate you use them I'm beginning to wonder if you're smoking them or something."

"Ew. Yuck, Mom."

"Well. They sure don't last long with you around."

"Well, you're just lucky I'm not like Lucy De Finca then."

"Who?"

"Sandra De Finca's little sister. You don't know her. She's in Grade 8. She has to use two at a time."

"Two at a time? How can you do that?"

"Put the first one in really far and then hold onto the string so you don't lose it and put a second one in. Sandra told me it's the only way Lucy can use them without getting a leak."

"Hm. I never thought of doing that. It sounds like a good idea. Sure beats using those manhole covers. Poor kid, flowing so heavily at her age."

"Manhole covers?"

Cathy looked at Eva with even more wide-open eyes and started to giggle uncontrollably. Eva smiled.

"Well, what else would you call them? They make you waddle around with your legs two blocks apart, you can't wear anything tight, they bunch up in the hot weather, it's like sitting down on a stack of damp books, they're hot, they smell awful, you can't swim. Who the heck needs to live in the Dark Ages like that? You couldn't pay me to use pads ever again. You girls are really lucky that tampons were invented so you never have to go through that."

"And how."

Janet lifted a package of fig cookies out of the grocery bag and tore open the cellophane.

"Here," she said to Cathy, pushing the open end of the package towards her. "Have some. I'll get some milk."

"So, Cathy, besides beating up on yourself and nearly putting out an eye, what's new?"

Eva was bent over a vegetable crisper in the fridge, her voice coming out from behind the opened door.

"Yeah," said Janet. "I didn't see you at all last weekend. What's up?"

"Well, I've got a summer job."

"Really? How neat. Where?"

"Well, my mother got it for me. It's out at St. Alphonsis Church. You know, where Father Lauzon got transferred to?"

Eva had now closed the fridge and was rooting through the cutlery drawer looking for a knife to chop an onion.

"That's way out in the east end, isn't it?"

"Yeah."

"What's the job?"

"I'm going to be a housekeeper."

"What?"

"I know. Funny, eh? Me, a housekeeper. But the one that used to be out there died and they can't find anybody to replace her, so I'm *it* for the summer."

"You're kidding. What do you have to do?" Janet asked.

"My mother said it's nothing out of the ordinary. Just dishes and dusting and making beds and getting their meals."

"Just! It sounds like a lot of work to me."

Eva finished chopping, leaving a mound of onion bits on the breadboard, and turned her attention to breaking apart ground beef with a wooden spoon in a large bowl.

"How many priests?"

"Three."

"You have to cook meals and pick up after three men? Boy, I don't envy you that. How many days a week?"

"Monday to Friday. They have to fend for themselves on the weekends, I guess."

"Well," said Janet, pulling half a dozen cookies out of the package and putting them on a plate, "I hope they give you a vacation so you can come up to the cottage again this summer."

"Oh, I'm sure you won't be there that long, sweetie," Eva said, brushing onion off the board into the bowl with the meat. "That's a full-time job getting all those meals for three grown men and running a household. They're gonna have to find a permanent replacement fairly soon, I would think. I know you'd like the money and everything, but you're still just a young girl. You have the whole rest of your life to work. Besides which, keeping up with your own housework is boring enough without having to do someone else's. I don't know how Crystal comes here every week and puts up with us and this house. And she's been a cleaning lady for years. She sure does a terrific job, though. I couldn't survive without her. I'm sure you'll do a great job for them."

"As long as I don't burn everything to a crisp on the first day."

"Make sandwiches," said Janet. "What can go wrong?"

"Actually, before you go home, sweetie, I'll give you a copy of this recipe that I'm making. It's for Scandinavian meatballs. It's really easy. You just make these tiny meatballs here, like I'm doing, and then there's a nice rich gravy that goes with them that's also really easy to make. You serve everything over rice and you don't need another thing to go with it. The priests will love it."

"I've never made rice before."

"Oh, that's easy. You just boil water, add the rice, turn the heat down really low, and wait. That's all there is, really, to making rice. It sort of makes itself. Even Whisky could do that if she had to, couldn't you, sweetie."

Just at that moment, with her stubby tail stump vibrating rapidly, the dog shot out from under the table to retrieve a scrap of onion that had fallen off the breadboard onto the floor.

* * *

Later, when Cathy left, with the recipe for Scandinavian meatballs folded and stashed in her pocket, Eva called out to her from the door, "Get your mother to put some ice on that cheek for you. And cold cucumber slices, too. They'll help. Get her to slice them really thin."

Cathy paused on the path down beside the steadily trickling water and brought the piece of pale yellow writing paper out of her pocket. The golden late afternoon light sloped over her shoulder. Eva's handwriting was lovely, curved and tidy, pretty to look at. Cathy gazed at the cheerful scrolls and loops and then gently pressed them against her swollen cheek. The paper had picked up the scent of Eva's hand cream. She stood like that for a moment, eyes closed, with Eva's handwriting and the warm sun touching her face. *Get your mother to put some ice on that cheek for you. And cold cucumber slices, too. They'll help. Get her to slice them really thin.*

CHAPTER 5

A ngela Gordon was a blonde, green-eyed American actress whose pictures appeared in magazines all over the world. Her husband, Eduard Jorge Manrique, a Spanish film director, thirty years her senior, lived most of the year alone in Spain, in the province of Andalusia. Angela joined him there for extended periods whenever her schedule allowed. Together they had one daughter, who, in an impromptu burst of her mother's *joie de vivre*, had been named Andalusia. Andy, as she was called, was only seven months younger than Cathy.

One night, when Cathy was ten years old, Angela just came out of the television and got into Cathy's head. It was past midnight and Cathy had to be very careful and quiet. Her mother had just ended a four-day-long silence. Cathy sat close to the television screen with the blue light flickering over her pyjamas and the sound turned down very low. She wanted to see Angela's eyes. They seemed kind, and she wanted to see if they would look back at her if she looked directly into them. She leaned so far forward the tip of her nose touched the cool glass and the picture disintegrated into a sea of tiny black and grey and white dots. She followed the movement of dots in front of her, trying to anticipate which way Angela's eyes would move next so that she could go with them and make contact. And then the dots shifted, two little black pools formed right in front of her eyes, and Angela's lovely calm warm voice streamed out of the middle of all those little dots and the middle of Cathy's mind at the same time.

"Hi, sweetpea," she said, reaching out and stroking Cathy's long loose hair.

It was after that that Cathy began to steal.

The magazines at Gibson's Variety were kept at the back of the store. Mr. Gibson was partially lame, so he always sat on a stool behind the counter near the cash register. He had a little black and white television hooked up beside him and was always watching something. Cathy taught herself how to steal the movie magazines, picking up two at a time, sliding the bottom one under the cover of a school binder while pretending to open the top one and browse through it. After a few minutes, she replaced the remaining magazine on the rack and then went right up to the front counter and bought gum or a chocolate bar with her fifty-cent allowance. She couldn't look Mr. Gibson in the eyes. She felt bad about what she was doing to him. He was a nice man. He never seemed to mind the hordes of kids that descended upon the store after school. Sometimes, when he ran short of pennies, he'd push your nickel back across the counter to you when you still owed him two cents. Cathy had promised herself that if she ever got caught she would bring all the magazines back. They were in perfect condition. And then she would try to explain to him that this wasn't really stealing. It was just something she needed to do. She had to bring Angela home to be near her.

By day, she kept the magazines hidden between her mattress and the box spring. At night, she waited until the house was quiet and then she brought them out and spoke to the pictures in the dark. If it was too dangerous even for that, she just positioned her cheek against the mattress, right above the spot where she could imagine touching Angela's cheek on the cool paper below, and whispered through the thickness.

From the magazines, she had learned all sorts of things about Angela's private life. She lived in a beach house in Malibu, California, overlooking the Pacific Ocean, and also had an apartment in New York. Cathy had one picture of Angela and Andy sitting at a round kitchen table beside sliding glass doors that led out to the beach. There is a bowl of green grapes on the table, and the wall behind them is panelled in diagonal wood strips. Andy, who has inherited her mother's long legs and green eyes that disappear into little nests of eyelashes when she laughs, is barefoot and has pulled her knees up to her chest. Grinning, she looks straight out of the page at Cathy.

In another picture, Angela is sitting in a hotel room in Paris where she is on location for a movie. The location is a boon to her because, that particular year, Andy is attending a boarding school just outside of Paris. In the picture, Angela is dressed entirely in black and is drinking iced tea out of a tall slender glass. The interview is about motherhood. Cathy had read it so many times that large parts of it were committed to memory.

> What's being a good mother? Spending every waking hour at your kid's elbow? I gave Andy some space so she could learn to make her own decisions. Compared to other American children her age, she's a model of sophistication. She's been all over the world; since she's been five years old, she's been flying between her father and me by herself. She knows how to find her way back to Spain from Hollywood and I don't have to worry about her; I can just put her on the plane; she knows how to ask the stewardesses for directions to the washroom in three different languages and she knows her father will meet her at the other end.

What I gave her was the space and the opportunity to learn things. Most kids have the opportunity to think for themselves thwarted because their mother is always there to do everything for them. If I'd kept Andy at school strictly in America or in Spain, she would speak Spanish or English, but not both, and know her way from her house to the school and that's all. But life is what you make of opportunity and I wanted her to learn that early.

At this point the type ran onto the next page of the magazine. Before turning the page, Cathy always upended the picture to read the time on Angela's watch. It always said the same thing — 8:50. The detail was important to Cathy. If she met Angela someday, she could tell her that she knew exactly what time the picture had been taken. Angela might say that she was a bright, observant girl.

Why do I constantly have to explain my marriage to people? They are so bogged down they are incapable of accepting anything unusual. They see only the age difference between Eduard and me and the fact that we live apart much of the year, and based on that, they draw conclusions. What they don't see is that there is room for variation on a theme. A good marriage and quality parenting don't have to take place in suburban America behind a white picket fence with people crammed under one roof so closely that they trip over each other.

Who are strangers to decide that Andy is deprived and my marriage must be a failure?

Do you expect me to believe that there is a quality to life worth having that is found five nights a week on a Los Angeles freeway during rush hour or at the laundromat on weekends?

Do you know that a woman came up to me at a restaurant in New York once and told me that I should find a young lover so that my daughter could have a real father? She was sure Eduard would understand this. Can you imagine? She obviously thought that Andy was missing something. But with us, Andy has the best of both worlds. She sees things from my generation's perspective and she sees things through her father's eyes. Since she's been a baby, when she's living in Spain, the two of them go out walking in the evenings. They've enjoyed hundreds of hours of each other's companionship in this way. She's learned to speak perfect Spanish, and her father has read stories to her and told her about things that she never would have encountered had she grown up only in America.

I can't agree that Andy would be richer for having grown up in California sitting on the couch watching television with a younger father.

Besides talking to the magazine pictures, Cathy often found herself travelling to the kitchen in Malibu to visit. Andy pulled an extra chair out from beneath the table with her agile feet and motioned for Cathy to sit down; Angela nosed the bowl of grapes towards her.

"There you are. What took you so long? We were worried about you. Why don't you just live here with us, instead? Here, have some grapes."

"*Yeah! Come to school with me. It'll be way better. I can introduce you to some of my friends. You'll have a much better time. Do you want something to drink?*"

Sometimes they went for a stroll on the beach accompanied by Mickey, Andy's black cocker spaniel. Sometimes while they walked, with the ocean breeze lifting up the edges of their hair and caressing their faces, Angela reached up and gently took a shock of Cathy's hair in her hand and gave her head an affectionate shake.

It was on this beach in Malibu that Cathy spent the Sunday afternoon before beginning her new summer job. She stayed in her room all afternoon, sprawled across her bed, gazing quietly at her collection of magazine pictures. Angela danced around in the sand, making her laugh.

"*Just think of the creative possibilities of cooking for three priests. Our father, who art at the table, hallowed be thy grain. Hail Mary, full of grapes, the Lord is whiskey. Blessed be the beans that come unto you. No, no, even better ... blessed be the beans that return unto you. In the name of the fork, the spoon, and the holy roast. Almonds.*"

A barefoot Andy stood in ankle-deep water tossing a stick into the Pacific for Mickey. She looked back over her shoulder.

"*It's a good thing you act, Mom, instead of having a night-club routine. We'd starve.*"

"*Don't interrupt. I'm on a roll. You can serve spaghetti with saintly sauce. Holy hamburgers, although holy humbuggers would work too. What else? Mother of God's meatloaf.*"

Angela, laughing, turned into the wind to clear her hair out of her face.

"*Holy cow, this is too funny. Oops, there's another one. What's for dinner tonight, Cathy? Holy cow with massed potatoes and blessings, Father. Oh Christ, we are going to have a blast!*"

He'd been taught that in the end, there was no one left but God. But what if God had also turned away? Then what did a person have? Worse, what did a priest have? Nothing, of course. Absolutely nothing. Nothing to embrace, nothing to fall back on. No wife, no children, no job, not even a hobby. The very thought ground Jerome Martin to an absolute halt one winter morning, right in the middle of celebrating mass. As he bowed in prayer over the shiny gold chalice during the consecration, he suddenly saw the face of an impostor looking back at him. He wasn't changing bread and wine into the body and blood of Christ at all. He was droning sleepily over a stale wafer and sour cheap wine wondering where the draft was coming from because his feet were cold. He had no idea where God was. Or when the last time was that he had known.

He hadn't slept again. The wretched dream. Over and over, night after night, wandering in an austere dark landscape, listening to haunting whispers. He'd recognized the voices right away: himself as a child, as an adolescent, and as a man, whispering the words to every prayer that he had ever uttered. But, as the dream clearly indicated, the prayers had never come to rest in the sacred ear they were intended for. Instead, they had lost their way and were wandering in the bleak, dark, dead end of the universe, like undelivered mail.

He twirled away from the altar in his stiff white and gold vestments and headed down the three steps towards the altar rail. He knew he could get help if he asked for it. There would be counselling, a new posting perhaps. Things would be tried to rekindle his devotion. And he would be pressured to make a tremendous effort to rediscover God for himself. He would be reminded that prayer was his most powerful tool, that he had only to use it faithfully. He began setting sacred hosts on the quivering extended white tongues of the faithful of St. Alphonsis.

But Jerome Martin was dead certain that he was beyond help. He'd already tried to wring one last bit of devotion out of himself, begging God, every day for months, for guidance. But whenever he closed his eyes in prayer, kneeling alone in the church after it had emptied out, rather than sensing God's loving presence, all he could think about was how tired he was, how restful it was to close his eyes for a few moments. All he was certain of was that the stale words of his prayers dropped from his lips straight down onto the cold stone floor of the church.

Every night, the dream tormented him, pressing his nose right up against its whispering message. Every night he fled, flying through darkness, breaking through the surface, his eyes popping open to recognize, right there above his bed, splashed with street light, the familiar sloped ceiling of his dingy little room in the rectory of St. Alphonsis parish.

This was precisely how he awoke in the early hours of the first Monday in July, in the summer that he turned forty-six, rising once again into the familiar lonely solitude of the empty hours before dawn. He lay on his back, his long heavy limbs sunken into his sweat-dampened narrow mattress, his eyes tracking across the ceiling. Zigzagging right and zigzagging left, his eyes traced and retraced a jagged crack that resembled a staircase. Then they circled around and around and around over a patch of peeling paint that looked like the head of a bald man with a large round nose. Until recently, these small familiar things had usually helped to anchor him while the bad dream dissipated. But lately, the dream had begun to pursue him beyond the unconscious. He no longer felt safe now that he was awake. He lay in his bed with a racing heart. The voices that he used to leave behind when he awoke now whispered at him from inside the walls of his room.

And so, in the forty-seventh summer of his life, and the twentieth year of his ordination into the priesthood, Jerome Martin lay awake once again in his airless second-floor bedroom, staring at his ceiling, knowing that he had reached an impasse. God had never heard of Jerome Martin.

Through the window just beside his head, he could hear the sharp splash of rain on cement. It was the first respite from the summer heat in days. The heat and humidity had started early this year. Usually it was mid-August before the air grew so gauzy. Trying to sleep in a second-floor bedroom with only one window that faced east was nearly impossible without a fan. He had one, but it was still stored away on the floor in the back of his closet. Fetching it at this hour would only wake the others. After breakfast he could come back upstairs and see to it, since the heat looked like it was here to stay. The fan would be dusty and need a good wiping down and he had just the right worn old hanky ready to be retired from his drawer and reassigned.

The wispy window curtains suddenly lifted off the sill to let a thread of breeze pass beneath them. The delicate ribbon of cool air slid pleasantly down the outside of Jerome's naked left leg. A dozen more of these and he might be enticed to fall back to sleep. But the curtains sagged back down onto the sill and settled. Out of habit, his hand wandered to the bedside table where he kept an old black sock futilely draped over his

clock so that the faint glow from the illuminated face would-
n't keep him awake. He lifted the sock and confirmed what he
already knew. It was 3:05 a.m. Inhaling deeply, he let the sock
drop. His arm followed, crash-landing across his brow, forcing
his eyes shut. Three long, hot hours stretched out before him.
At six, he could get up and prepare for mass.

Thunder rumbled outside. He supposed he could sit up
and read. It wouldn't put him back to sleep again, but it would
ease his conscience slightly. Reading could always be considered a positive activity, even when undertaken to avoid something
else. When the thunder rumbled again, he half-heartedly
propped himself up on his elbows and turned toward the window. Blue reflections of lightning flickered across the walls of
his room, lighting up the closed dark door to the hall. If it
weren't for his insistence on keeping the door closed for privacy, there might have been a slight chance of generating a
cross-breeze.

On the other side of the door, the hall led to the rooms
of Ralph Lauzon and Gerry LeBlanc, two men who slept
soundly. Jerome could picture them both: Gerry thrown face
down on his bed in a heap, breathing deeply, a child of a man
who would scramble into action immediately upon waking;
Ralph on his back, spread-eagled over the wide mattress of his
pastor's double bed, his face undistorted, his businessman's
mind still at work down in the wells of sleep.

Still propped up on his elbows, Jerome looked down the
length of his long body and kicked the thin cotton sheet
loose from his right foot. His poor wilted penis jiggled slightly
like an infant limb. *Limb of God*, he thought, sadly, *have mercy
on me.*

He envied the others their sleep. Like their lives, it came so
easily to them. They could exhaust themselves each day with
their work; they spent themselves on meetings, telephone calls,

appointments, lunches, prayers, mass, errands. For him, though, there was something wrong; there was something desperately wrong with his ability to sleep. For months now, he had been continually paralyzed by exhaustion, day and night, so that even sleep had become a bizarre workload for which he did not have enough energy. He only fell into short periods of unconsciousness after hours of unsettled tossing upon his old lumpy mattress. Once asleep, he travelled all night, always ending up in that mysterious black infinity. And then he woke, exhausted, lonely, and worried about what was happening to him. He couldn't remember the last time he had slept, undisturbed, through an eight-hour night.

He lay back down and listened to the water trickling from the roof into the eaves that passed just below the window. His large hands rested one above the other in the black hair on his abdomen. The rain was stopping. Evidently the disturbance was only a small cloudburst.

He closed his eyes and saw Ralph's face pass before him, smooth and unmarred, with its cleanly shaved, darkly shadowed jaw. Then Ralph's car, glittering black with that fine red line of trim running along the doors and fenders. Ralph was like his car: clean and glossy, good-looking. Uncomfortable, he moved again, seeking a better position. In his memory, he could hear Ralph's deep masculine voice crooning snippets of tunes from old movies. It was one of several things about Ralph that he admired. He liked the way the man swung his long legs in and out of his car, the way he sported up any staircase two steps at a time, the way he rattled the ice cubes in his highball glass when they ate at the Bishop's and boomed out "Where the Sam-Hill've you been?" to someone he hadn't seen in a while. Jerome wished he could do those things and tired himself out with the longing to do so. But eventually his envy always reduced him to shame. What kind of a wasted prayer was it to beg, "Dear Father in heaven, make me like another man, make me different than I am?" Where was the vocation in that? Where was the love of God, the gratefulness for the life that had been given to him? In the dark, oppressive heat, Jerome shifted yet again and answered his own question.

His large spatulate fingers began to rove searchingly over his skin. They stopped to examine a small pimple beside his navel, but that was only to pretend that he wasn't going to do it again, that it wasn't already underway. It was a habit left over from childhood, when he'd believed that God could look down and see absolutely everything that anyone was doing at any given time. In a moment his fingers resumed their small circling motions and moved on. Softer than bird wings settling into place, St. Augustine's prayer passed over Jerome's lips: "Dear God, enter into my heart and whisper that you are here to save me."

He'd tried masturbating earlier. His hand had worked for nearly half an hour. He even gave up worrying about whether or not Ralph and Gerry could hear the creaking of his old bed or about whether he would give himself a blister. He did everything he could to make himself come, until, without warning, his mind suddenly emptied and his hands fell away. While his penis withered, he turned over on his side, facing the wall to wait for sleep. But, as abandoned as he felt, talking to God was a hard habit to break. And so, for the one-millionth time, he bargained with God for the return of regular, restful sleep in exchange for his chastity.

But now it occurred to him that the bit of cooling breeze that had touched his leg might be enough to help him out. His promise to God was already broken for that night; it didn't matter that he had been unsuccessful — he had tried, and that was enough to break the promise. You didn't give God half-promises.

If Jerome could have had a say in the matter, he would have preferred that the capacity of a penis for which a priest had no use would die. The ridiculous organ lay in wait all day in his underwear like a jack-in-the-box, ready to spring at the least provocation. At night, after it seduced him into touching it and rubbing himself to climax, it tormented him by stirring to life again within minutes, wanting more. Or, worse, it often humiliated him by wilting in his hands before ejaculating, leaving him lying naked in his sagging bed feeling like a failure. He had come to think of his penis as a wicked demon trickster attached to his body for the sole purpose of tormenting him, and he fervently wished to be rid of it.

And yet God, in His infinite wisdom, had made the organ the way it was. And He had made a priest what he was. A human. So Jerome reasoned that there must be a purpose in the brutal antagonism between his body and his soul. In fact, he wondered if abstaining from masturbating when he wanted to, when he thought he should try to, was a kind of underhanded insult to God. If St. Augustine was correct in believing that nothing about man could be corrupt because he is made in God's image and nothing about God can be corrupt, then this urge to touch himself must have some godliness about it. God made the urge as well as the organ. Perhaps the evil lay merely in the senseless enjoyment of stimulation, in the blatant favouritism towards one part of the body. Jerome didn't enjoy any other aspect of his physical self so much. In fact, he loathed his craterous complexion, his boils, his large clumsy limbs and uncoordinated gestures. But alone in a dark sweltering room, he overly loved a rubbery wand of temperamental fibrous tissue that resembled the neck of a skinned turkey. Perhaps God wanted him to succumb to this behaviour, not for the sake of pleasure, but for the sake of learning: to experience his baseness, his separation from God. If this was God's intent, how graceless to refuse the lesson.

Besides, Jerome was certain that in this soul-sapping heat, if he could just come once he would be able to sleep. All his sleeplessness would flow out of him. With sleep, he would be able to discipline himself. With discipline he would begin again to travel in the footsteps of Christ. He would work all summer to put himself back on track and be ready to serve with renewed vigour by the time school resumed in September.

While he continued to rationalize, his hand passed down through his pubic hair to his penis. His fingers began running little tests. They fluttered, stroked, moved in small, light circles. The earlier discomfort was gone. It would be worth trying again, just for the sleep that would follow.

He kept his eyes firmly closed to concentrate. Travelling slowly across the smooth old sheet that was worn to the softness of newborn skin, the open palm of his free hand found the edge of the mattress, no longer a firm sharp ninety-degree angle, but now compressed and rounded by age to the width of a woman's throat. His hand slid back and forth, back and forth along this column. His breathing, as well as his other hand, picked up the rhythm. After passing over imagined collarbones his hand searched for and found the partially firm mounds of budding, mattress-lump breasts, which he squeezed, first one then the other, one then the other. With each squeeze, he felt his testicles firming. This could have happened had he chosen another life; if people led parallel lives, this could be part of his life with a woman; this could be his marriage. There could be a soft warm breast filling his palm. Nipples could be rising on his tongue. There was no sin in merely enacting what could have been. This was normal; this was good. He hadn't noticed that he had pulled both his lips into his mouth and was sucking on them.

He was erect now, filling his working hand. He wanted to spit into his palm for more lubrication, but it was too danger-

ous to stop for even a second. If only God had made man flex-
ible. He tipped himself slowly, carefully onto his side so he
could lower his erection between the mattress breasts. His free
hand was frantically spreading the breasts, opening up a space
to receive him. If only the mattress could magically grow a little
receptacle, something wet for him to slip into. He rolled closer,
and as he did so, a trickle of perspiration ran down through
the hair on his abdomen, mimicking the rapid steps of an
insect. His torso jerked, his eyes flew open, his free hand let go
of the breasts, swatted at the distraction, jiggling the bed, and
his full hand suddenly emptied. Goddamn!

Defeated and ashamed, Jerome rolled onto his back. He
felt like a grown man who could not overcome a temptation
meant for a child. Exasperated, he closed his eyes, but it was
clear that he was not going to fall asleep again. If he got up,
he could at least occupy himself with making a cup of hot
chocolate. The thought of the hot chocolate reminded him
that a new housekeeper was coming in the morning. The
daughter of a former parishioner of Ralph's. They were low
on cocoa and he should leave her a note to get a new tin. The
trouble was his limbs were heavy as wet sandbags and the
kitchen seemed a very long way away.

Outside, tires approached on the wet pavement. Jerome
wondered where another human being could have been until
this hour. What did people find to do that detained them until
nearly dawn? Or was this someone just going out at this hour?
He opened his eyes to watch which way the blocks of light
from the headlights were going to travel around the walls.
Right to left or left to right? If left to right, which way was
the car travelling? Up or down the street? The squares
appeared above his desk and began their curious ritual, travelling slowly across the wall to the corner. Then, like live things,
they flashed into the mirror on the back of the door, raced

past his head and shot out the window. Absurdly, he imagined that they had fled from the gloomy solitude of his life.

Finally he swung his feet over the edge of the bed to the linoleum floor. He pushed himself up and stood facing the window. They had warned him in the seminary that a priest's life was one of constant temptation. But then they had ordained him; they must have seen something in him, must have believed in his vocation. It couldn't have just evaporated. Churches had always attracted him. Their cool, cavernous solitude drew him inside, even when he was a young boy. He liked the crisp echo of footsteps retorting from stone walls, the silent little eddies of scented air that surprised him. That was something, wasn't it? Some sort of sign?

Surely this insomnia was just something temporary. It had to be; he could not live out the rest of his life on so little sleep. He just needed to get back on track. A simple, small catalyst could knock him back into the right orbit. Maybe he should make a list of things that he could do to spark himself back to life. Things like painting this dull little room and getting rid of that annoying bald-headed man on his ceiling. He fished under the bed for his slippers and lifted his robe off of the back of the door. It would be cooler in the kitchen with the back door open.

★ ★ ★

The kitchen was located on the ground floor, at the back of the rectory. When Jerome pulled open the heavy wooden door leading to the backyard, the sharp smell of damp mouldy earth and the cool moist air that pressed against him like a wet cloth startled him. The sensation was so pleasant, so welcome after the stifling heat of his room that he remained standing at the door, looking out into the yard, mesmerized.

He had never really looked closely at the yard before now, although he had cut across it hundreds of times. His impression, by day, was of a grubby sad little patch of bare dirt and weeds, not worth a second glance. It had been years since anyone had cut the grass regularly and turned the soil in the gardens every spring. Now, the yard was ringed with trees of heaven and a few old maples that had long ago knitted a dense canopy overhead. The trees' hundreds of unchecked suckers had braided themselves into the chain link fence, causing it to twist and bow outward in some places and to sag inward in others. Neglect and overgrowth had nearly erased the outlines of the original flowerbeds. The only thing that remained fresh and groomed was the path that ran from the gap in the fence in the back corner where the garage stood to the back door.

But now, lit by the pale glow of the yellow street light slanting through the rusting fence, Jerome found the yard strangely enchanting. Every illuminated surface outside of the yard glistened with rain: the sidewalk, the visible corner of the garage eaves, the grey metal garbage pails standing beside the garage wall, plant foliage growing outside the ambit of the canopy, a bit of the top rail of the fence. But beneath the canopy, the yard remained a haven of dryness, a compelling high-ceilinged green grotto. Looking back and forth between the wet and the dry surfaces, indulging in the sharp contrast between the two, Jerome suddenly perceived this reverse oasis as a small miracle. Dryness in a surround of glistening wetness. Then his mind leapt. Contrast. That's all miracles were. Simple, startling contrasts. Dead Lazarus rising to life, the sick restored to health, one fish and one loaf, then fish and loaves in abundance.

Jerome pushed the screen door out into the fresh early morning air, descended the sagging back porch steps, and arrived, puffing with excitement, into the dead centre of this miraculous outdoor room beneath the magical green roof. His loosely tied robe had fallen open and cool air wandered deliciously into the folds of material and over his skin. He looked up. The treetops were alive with movement and sound. A party was underway. In the slumbering silence of the early morning. Another contrast. The trees were engaged in a joyous whispering conversation, every leaf and branch having something to say to its neighbour, while hundreds of gossiping water droplets slithered across smooth and rough surfaces, dropping down onto the next level to repeat what had just been said above. Now and again a little breeze wandered through the canopy, and hundreds of raindrops clattered softly to the ground. Jerome thought they sounded like hundreds of little feet, as if invisible elves or leprechauns were jumping out of the treetops and landing unseen bedside him.

He twirled around slowly, his head thrown full back so he could see the canopy that covered him. How freeing it was just to stand there in the cool temperature beneath the protective arch of foliage. He wondered why he hadn't ever even noticed the yard's chapel-like quality before. Had he known, he could have come out here every time it rained, stood here in the delightful chill and filled himself up on the thrill of this secret place. His mind leapt again. Of course. How could he not have seen it until now? This domed green chapel had been created just for him. Look how it contrasted to his room: large, cool, airy, filled with the present. Listen to the whispers. How joyous! The overhead trees must be filled with birds and insects. They must be tucked in up there, alongside one another, waiting for dawn. They would be beginning to groom themselves now, rooting beneath their wings, burbling softly to one another. Life. Bustling. What he so desperately desired. It was clear now what was going on. He was meant to discover this place. This humble little outdoor grotto was God speaking to him.

Jerome twirled around and around, searching the underside of the canopy for signs of the animal life that he was certain must be hidden there. He thought that each little bird would know his or her role in God's universe. And Jerome suddenly understood that each of them could teach him his place. They all knew that their purpose was to fly through their days with their wings extended to the heavens like Jerome's arms were extended now, unburdened by anything worldly, the way Jerome was now, his robe slipped to the ground, shuffling a slow circle beneath the green canopy of the miraculous outdoor grotto that God had made just for him.

"Knock, knock."
Who's there?
"Orange."
Orange who?
"Orange you getting out of bed this morning?"
"What?"

Cathy pushed herself up on one elbow, squinting across the room. Angela, grinning, was leaning against the dresser filing her nails. She wore dangling earrings and bangle bracelets, hot pink silk pedal-pushers, open-toed sandals with green, pink, and blue straps, and a green silk blouse tied in a fashionable knot beneath her bust so that her tanned midriff showed. She'd changed her hair from blonde to brilliant carrot orange.

"Rise 'n shine, my flea. Time's a-wasting."

Cathy glanced at her alarm clock. She had woken five minutes before it was due to ring. She reached over, shut it off, and sat up.

"That's it. Up and at 'em."

Angela stepped in front of the dresser mirror to inspect her hair.

"Today's the day."

Cathy got up, pulled open a drawer, and began to root

around for underwear. Then she found her tan skirt and madras blouse in the closet, nylons in another drawer, and shoes under the edge of the bed. As she dressed, she noticed that her hands were shaking slightly. What if she had just imagined that her mother told her about the priests needing a housekeeper? But no, that couldn't be true. Last night she'd phoned for the bus schedule right in front of Adele.

"And don't be calling here looking for a ride if you miss the bus at the other end, missy. I'm not traipsing all the way out to the other end of town to fetch you. Getting your butt on the bus on time is your responsibility."

"You've got a real job," Cathy whispered to her reflection.

"Of course you've got a real job. We're not all crazy, here. If you want to hang around and think about it some more, I can figure out where the place is."

Cathy smiled at the thought of Angela, the famous Hollywood actress, jiggling earrings, jangling bracelets, red hair, bare midriff, knocking at a rectory door, looking to cook breakfast. Then she zoomed back into herself. She had to brush her teeth and have something to eat before leaving the house.

"Big day, huh?"

Richard, who was on an early shift at Robinson's, was spreading peanut butter on a piece of toast in the kitchen.

"Guess so," Cathy said, pulling open the fridge.

"Here," said Richard. "I already poured you a glass."

He pushed a small glass of orange juice toward her.

"Thanks."

"Excited?"

"More nervous," Cathy said, putting a slice of bread in the toaster.

"Don't waste the energy. You could clean for the Queen."

Cathy smiled. She'd no idea Richard ever noticed anything about her.

"Gotta cook too, though."

"So? They're priests, for Christ's sake. They won't be used to anything fancy. And they're still just a bunch of guys. They're probably eating outa tins. My guess is they'll be grateful for anything warm that comes on a plate."

"Think so?"

"Know so."

He pointed to a small folded white cloth on the nearby table. "Think that's for you, by the way."

Cathy crossed the room and looked down at the note pinned to one of her mother's aprons. "Use it!" the note said in her mother's handwriting.

Richard swished his juice glass and small plate under the tap and set them in the drying rack.

"Gotta go. Bust a rosary," he called over his shoulder as he sauntered out the door.

★ ★ ★

Standing at the foot of the driveway five minutes later, Cathy looked up and down the dead-end street, first towards the ditch, and then towards the other end where Gibson's Variety and the bus stop stood, partially sheltered behind a hedge of overgrown spirea. She turned her back on the ditch and headed for the bus stop. Janet was leaving for the cottage this week and would be away until September. By the time she returned, the deep mustard goldenrod and the purple and white asters would be three feet high on the slopes. It would be impossible to walk without getting covered in pollen and thistle burrs. The redwings would be gone, the nights would be cool enough for sweaters, and ten-year-old boys who had stolen matches would be scenting the evening air with bonfires at the edge of the water. Her first and last visit for the summer down among the flowers and the insects

91

and the lovely sounds had come and gone two days ago. It would be a whole year now before she could go down those summer slopes again. Stung by the sharp slicing swiftness of change she hurried along, wondering what else she couldn't see coming.

The yellow and blue bus rolled into place beside her and the two great doors flapped open.

"Gateway to the future. All aboard."

Cathy watched her brown loafer swing forward and plant itself on the first step. Then she pushed herself up into the cavity of the bus.

"Well, you're a new one."

She stopped. The driver smiled. He had blue eyes and sandy hair. Cathy thought he looked kind.

"Come on up, hon. I don't bite."

"Do you go to the bus depot downtown?"

"Sure do."

"That's where I can transfer to the Number 16 East?"

"That's the place."

"Thank you."

"You're welcome."

She finished climbing the stairs, dropped her coins in the coin box, and turned away, heading down the aisle of the empty vehicle.

"You'll need one of these, hon, if you're gonna transfer."

The driver had torn a yellow piece of paper from a clip near the steering wheel and now held it out for her to take from his hand. She turned and looked down at it. They didn't have these on school buses.

He wagged his hand.

"Just give this to the driver when you board the Number 16. That way you won't have to pay again."

"Oh."

She took the paper.

"Thank you."

The bus roared ahead down the wide empty road.

She chose a seat beside a window, midway down the aisle, opposite the driver, and then turned to look back at her receding street. It really wasn't a dream. Her puffball-headed mother wasn't barrelling down the road after the bus in her pink fuzzy slippers and bathrobe, shaking a fist at the back window of the bus, hollering for it to "get back here."

"Bye-bye, neighbourhood," Cathy murmured.

She turned around and settled down in her seat. The inside of the bus smelled of the driver's aftershave and exhaust fumes. She was used to the stiff little yellow school buses. This was different. Her seat vibrated with every acceleration and the entire bus creaked like a giant mass of noisy cellophane and bounced like a giant loose spring over every bump. She could have been in the motorboat up at Janet's cottage pitching up and down in the wake of a passing yacht.

The platform at the downtown depot was terribly crowded with people. Cathy panicked slightly because she didn't know where to find the Number 16 bus. Just as she descended the steps, however, the driver pointed out the bus doors.

"Down to the end. All the way. It'll be sitting there waiting."

"Thank you."

She pushed her way through a thicket of slow bodies. The covered platform was dark and it smelled terribly of fuel and rubber and cigarette smoke. As she struggled forward, feeling like a hummingbird in amongst a throng of crows, buses released their brakes and let out great gasps of air and clouds of black smoke and then lumbered away from their platforms, brushing right past the arms of people, touching their clothes and parcels. She tried to read the numbers on the signs of the standing buses, but they didn't seem to be lined up in sequential order. Number 27 followed Number 9. At one point, she stepped into an empty bay to see if she could see how far the platform extended and only noticed at the last second that a bus was actually pulling into the empty space. When she looked up, her eyes locked into those of the driver. He raised his eyebrows and hesitated only an instant, long enough for her to jump out of the way, before sliding the huge bus into its berth. After that, her steps were more certain, as if her body had assumed command of physical activity, leaving her brain to drift behind through the crowd, searching for the Number 16 East.

Finally, at the end of the nearly block-long platform, she found what she was looking for. Clutching her damp, crumpled transfer she joined the line with men carrying silver lunch buckets and stout women gripping brown paper bags and big black purses. When her turn came to hand the transfer to the driver, he said, "Well, you're a new one, this morning." She'd had no idea drivers knew their passengers so well.

"Do you go to St. Alphonsis Church?"

"Sure do. It'll be a while, though. End of the line. I'll let you know."

This time she had to sit on an aisle seat beside a woman who looked down into her lap, turning her hands over and over. Cathy could see over top of the woman's bent head and now and again she caught glimpses down the side streets of the closely packed dark brick houses of the city.

Thirty minutes after leaving the depot, there were only four people left on the bus, not including her. Two of them got off at the very next stop and then one each at the next two stops. She was now the sole passenger and still there was no church in sight.

She glanced at her watch; it was twenty to seven. At that very moment, somewhere inside the rectory of St. Alphonsis Church, the three priests were dressing for morning mass, kissing stoles before ducking under them, murmuring ancient

Latin words over their rituals. She was to have breakfast ready
for all three men by seven-thirty. Could she do that in half an
hour? She squinted at the long stretch of road ahead and her
stomach fluttered.

The bus driver caught her anxious glance at her watch in
his mirror.

"You haven't missed it."

Cathy got up from her seat and staggered up the bouncing
aisle to sit in the lengthwise seat beside the door.

"You remember I want St. Alphonsis Church?"

"Yup. Guess you're a sinnin' type of young lady, huh?"

"What?"

He was not like the first bus driver. His shirt was open at
the neck and she could see coarse black hair tufts climbing up
his throat. His teeth were dark yellow and had big spaces
between them, and his eyes reminded her of big black olives
swimming in oil.

"You musta been up to somethin' bad to wanna be at
church at this hour."

Laughing, he clutched the steering wheel with both hands
and leaned his greased head towards her, running his thick,
maroon tongue over his glistening bottom lip.

"Find the nearest graveyard and check in, greaseball."

Cathy gripped the silver pole and stared straight ahead out
the windshield.

Two blocks later, the bus slowed.

"Here you go, darlin'. St. Alphonsis."

*"There isn't a detergent invented that can help you, ooze-monkey.
Come on, flea. We're outa here."*

Cathy got up and waited for the bus to stop. When the doors
opened, she scooted down the narrow stairs to the sidewalk,
stepping away from the curb to avoid the exhaust as the bus
lumbered away. She glanced up and down the street and saw no

one, not even a solitary parishioner heading to mass. She felt as if she'd just been dropped off in a desert.

The corner variety store across the street was padlocked shut. A diagonal bar ran across its front door bearing a giant Coca-Cola bottle cap. Twined around this and a nearby window bar was a heavy chain with the lock hanging from it. The insides of the store windows were plastered over with layers of posters and decals from soft drink companies and cigarette manufacturers. It had been years since the windows had been washed, and years since a piece of canvas had graced the naked iron awning frame that jutted out above the door. Next door there was a plumbing supply store with jumbles of metal pipes heaped in its windows. The storefront next to that was empty, its windows milky with grime. She found the whole street and these dismal old stores piercingly lonely and turned away.

Angela, shielding her eyes from the morning sun, stood in the middle of the street squinting at the drab yellow bricks of St. Alphonsis.

"Hmm. Not exactly the cheeriest of places, is it?"

The church and its adjoining gravel parking lot occupied the corner directly across from the variety store. The building, which was narrow across the front and long in the sides and had an extremely plain facade, stood back from the road, hemmed in between the parking lot and the dark brick wall of a shoe repair store. High up in the air, a small cross topped a grey wooden spire that rose out of a steeply pitched black roof. A flight of steep cement steps, divided down the centre by a rusting black iron handrail, led to six heavy wooden doors. On either side of the stairs, the grass had been worn away to bare dirt, and torn Popsicle wrappers nested in the dried mud of empty flowerbeds along the cement block foundation of the building. The sight of the cheerless church and the barren flowerbeds chilled Cathy.

She approached the staircase, noting that even the old cement sidewalk was washing away, its surface worn through to a layer of coarse pebbles. With her foot on the first step, she looked up the flight of stairs to the six windowless wooden doors that were closed against intrusion. Angela's bracelets tinkled.

"Hardly my idea of a welcoming place."

For a split second Cathy considered crossing the street to board the next bus back home.

"Naw. Where's the fun in that?"

Angela grabbed her elbow and towed her away from the stairs.

"Onward Christian soldiers, marching as to war…"

Word had been left that the back door leading to the rectory kitchen would be left open. They followed a sidewalk leading into a small scruffy backyard. Once inside the yard, Cathy saw that the rectory was indeed attached to the rear of the church. It was a two-storey building, made of the same dreary yellow brick as the church, with a similarly steeply pitched black roof. A large weathered cross with terribly blistered and peeling paint hung on the wall of the building, right beside a second-floor window. Stained, ragged drapes and their linings flopped listlessly over the edge of the open window, drooping against the bricks. Flakes of white paint collected below in the grey clay of another empty flowerbed and in the crabgrass of the small yard.

"Hmm. A few petunias would go a long way here."

"Oh, God," Cathy muttered.

The only entrance that was visible was the door to a rotting enclosed wooden porch, a mud room that sagged off the wall of the rectory. It sloped so badly that Cathy hesitated when she came to it and looked around to see if there wasn't some other, more appropriate, entrance. There was not.

"You know, I'll bet if we huffed and we puffed we could blow this place down. On my count, now. One…"

Cathy stepped past Angela and proceeded cautiously up the steps, pausing at the top. She was nervous now about getting inside and starting breakfast. She didn't want to get off to a bad start with the priests.

On the top step, a large, industrial-sized lard tin with a wire handle rested beside the back door. The sight of it made Cathy uneasy. She felt as if she were somewhere that would displease her mother, somewhere where standards were low. Moving closer, Cathy peered into the tin. It was filled with weathered wooden clothes pegs, the old-fashioned kind with the round button top and two prongs that you just pushed down over top of clothes to attach them to a clothesline.

"Why am I getting the feeling these folks don't own a clothes dryer?"

"Oh, God," Cathy whispered.

There were two doors, one with a badly torn screen and rusted hinges that squawked loudly when she gently pulled it open, and a weather-marked heavy wooden one. She steeled herself, turned the handle, leaned her shoulder against the second door, and pushed.

★ ★ ★

Three things struck her instantly: a penetrating stale odour, darkness, and prevailing silence. Angela pushed past and poked her head through the opening.

"Oh boy…"

Cathy stopped short of entering and stood in the doorway, letting her eyes adjust to the gloom. There was a kitchen in front of her, by the smell. Her nose picked up a mixture of old cooking grease, onion, fried meat, mildew, something sickly sweet, and just plain age. Despite standing in an open doorway, she longed to throw open a large window for some fresh air.

"Oh, I think this place needs more than a bit of air, honey."

The longer she stood, peering into the space, the more the room began to emerge from the dark. It was a large rectangular space with the door that she occupied standing midway along one of the long sides of the room. Immediately opposite, a door also broke the other long wall. On her right, countertops and cupboards ringed all three sides of the room. She could make out a narrow electric stove and a small fridge. On the short wall, the line of cupboards broke above a sink to make way for a window. There appeared to be some sort of wildly overgrown bush covering most of the glass on the outside, however, and consequently most of the light that might have entered the room through the window was turned back by the broad green leaves and dense collection of branches.

To the left, the room was empty, except for a tiny wooden table sitting snugly next to the far wall beside the door, both its wooden chairs pushed primly into place. The short wall on this side of the room did not meet with the opposite long wall of the rectangle. Instead, where the final quarter of this wall should have been, there was an opening leading to darkness.

Not finding a light switch beside the door, Cathy took a few tentative steps into the room, closed the door, and placed her purse on a nearby counter. As she walked, her shoes ground against grit on the floor. She headed for the door on the opposite wall, thinking to open it and find a source of light. Midway across the room, something soft came out of the air and touched her right cheek. She squealed and jumped back, but then recognized the feel of string. She reached up and pulled; something clicked and a pale yellow glow trickled from the ceiling. She stood beneath a bare light bulb.

The room was indeed a large kitchen. She saw now that the door she had been heading for was, in fact, a swinging door that looked like it led to the rest of the rectory. The break in the short wall on her left was actually an archway that led down a dark hallway. Closer to the sink, she found a second string. Even with two light bulbs burning, though, the dismal room resisted illumination.

"A bit like a morgue in here, wouldn't you say?"

Angela put a comforting hand on Cathy's shoulder.

"Actually, maybe dungeon is more accurate. Check out the cupboards."

Bracelets tinkling, Angela crossed the room and hoisted herself up to sit on the counter. She pulled open a cupboard door and examined the surface.

"How in the world did anyone ever think this was attractive?"

How indeed? The cupboards were plywood, coated with a dark, nearly molasses-toned varnish. Miserable compared to the bright white ones Cathy was used to at home. And the grey countertop was ancient, small, cramped, warped, and marred in several places with brown cigarette and pot-bottom burns. At home the countertop was smooth and perfect, white with lively flecks of peach in it. In front of the sink, Cathy noticed that the plaid patterned linoleum was worn through to its black subsurface in a shape the length and width of two small feet.

"Oh God. Don't look," said Angela, turning Cathy away. *"And these are pretty bad too. I don't know what you'd call this."*

Angela was squinting at a nearby wall, scratching at the surface with one long pink fingernail. The colour was indescribable. Cathy peered closely and discovered that the wall hadn't actually ever been painted; it was just a bare plaster surface gone dingy over the years, its history recorded in a Braille of grease splatters, food particles, and juice stains from slapped-dead bug bodies. She closed her eyes and drew in a deep breath.

"This can't be real," she whispered.

"Oh, it's real, all right."

Cathy frowned. Eva and Angela chimed together in her head.

Oh, I'm sure you won't be there that long, sweetie. That's a full-time job getting all those meals for three grown men and running a household. They're gonna have to find a permanent replacement fairly soon, I would think. I know you'd like the money and everything, but you're still just a young girl. You have the whole rest of your life to work.

"What a horrible place," Cathy whispered.

"But if you go home..."

Too much like work for you, is it, little miss I-want-to-freeload-through-life?

Angela slipped her arm around Cathy's waist.

"No, no, no. You don't want to do that. Running back home isn't a solution. What's wanted here is just a bit of light. We'll get some stronger light bulbs and some paint. Yellow ought to liven it up a bit in here."

Angela moved away to stand in the middle of the room, hands on her hips, eyes tracking across the bleak walls and ceiling.

"I'd say about four gallons. Bright yellow. New light bulb, a couple of fixtures... Maybe someone died or something before they could finish this place. That's what it looks like. And that bush has got to go. It's like working in a swamp. We should check it out, though. It might flower nicely if it was trimmed up. A radio would be good, too."

She clapped her hands and began dancing, eyes closed, head titled back, bracelets jangling. Her earrings flashed in the existing bit of light.

"Mairzy doats and do..."

Then from down the dark corridor a man's muffled voice and then little chimes. Angela stopped dead in her tracks.

"Well would you mairzy doats that! Correct me if I'm losing my mind, but did you just hear bells?"

Again, the same gentle tinkle of chimes.

"Bats in the belfry. Bats in the belfry. Quasimodo's swingin' on the bells."

A gasp of laughter burst from Cathy.

"You see. It's not so bad here. Sort of shaping up to be some kind of funhouse, I think."

101

Angela suddenly loped across the kitchen, half bent over, one arm swinging limply, her face twisted grotesquely, one eye squinted closed, her tongue tucked into her cheek. She grabbed the little string from the light bulb and hiked herself up onto the counter in her bright sandals and leaned over as if she would swing out into the room the next instant.

"Hunchback at ten o'clock high. Ha, ha, ha. Sanctuary. Sanctuary. Sanctuary. Ha, ha, ha."

A door closed firmly somewhere within the rectory. Cathy jumped. There had not been any indication of what the three priests expected for breakfast. The only things that she was confident enough to prepare were bacon and fried eggs and toast. But how many pieces of bacon for each priest, and how well done; how many eggs for each, and did they like the yolks soft or hard; how many pieces of toast for each of them?

"Two. I'll do two for everyone. Two of everything. Two eggs, two pieces of bacon, two pieces of toast."

Her eyes, having finally adjusted to the dimness of the room, suddenly picked out a tin with a note propped up against it standing in the middle of the little table. The words were scrawled in bad script: *Please buy more cocoa.*

While she stood, reading, the heavy swinging door beside her suddenly burst open.

"Aha! There's our new housekeeper."

Father Ralph Lauzon, former pastor of St. Mary, Star of the Sea, and now the newly appointed pastor of St. Alphonsis, strode into the room, redolent with aftershave. He was dressed in a black suit with its distinctive notched priest's collar. Cathy was used to seeing him at a distance. This close, his height was startling.

"Hello, Father."

"Good morning. What's your name? Karen, or something, isn't it?"

"No, Father, it's Cathy. I was just reading this note here about the cocoa."

"Cocoa?" he boomed, gazing around the room. "Not cocoa. Coffee! Where's the coffee this morning? I don't smell any. Haven't you got it going yet?"

He rubbed his big hands together expectantly and attempted a friendly smile, but his eyes were filled with criticism. Cathy began to stammer.

"No, Father. I'm sorry. I ... I don't know where anything is. I was just looking around for a moment. I just got here."

"Looking around? Looking around? You look like you're just standing around. That's not going to get breakfast ready, is it? You need to open cupboards if you're going to find any-thing. Just look around here for what you need. That's what we're paying you for. Here, look in here."

He crossed the room in two strides on his long black legs and pulled open several of the dark cupboard doors. Finding coffee on a shelf behind the first door that he opened, he removed the bag and plunked it on the counter. "See? Coffee. That should have been on ten minutes ago. Coffee should be the first thing you do every morning. And see, in here, sugar. In here, coffee pots, teapots. Everything you need. And in here, cups, saucers. Don't be shy."

He pulled things noisily out of the cupboards and plunked them roughly on the counter.

"There's bread in the breadbox over there. Just look around for whatever you need. And don't make anything for Father Martin. He left early to go baptize a sick baby at the hospital this morning. It's just two of us."

"Yes, Father."

"Now then, Christine, let's smell some coffee in here."

★ ★ ★

She retrieved the apron from her purse and tied it around her waist, tucked Eva's little yellow note with the recipe for Scandinavian meatballs in the pocket, and set to work. She found bacon and eggs in the fridge, bread, butter, and a frying pan. Cooking eggs and bacon was nothing. She'd seen her mother do it a million times. You just put everything in the pan together and the heat did the rest.

Midway through frying the bacon, she realized that she still didn't know how either of the priests wanted their bacon or their eggs cooked. She decided to try to make one set of each: two eggs with soft yolks, two eggs with hard yolks; two pieces of bacon with the fat still visible, two pieces cooked to a crisp. She turned the burner up a notch, put the lid on the pan, and left it to chortle and sizzle while she rooted through the cupboards.

She found plates and knives and forks, cups and saucers, and a sugar bowl and creamer and set the small bare wood table that hugged the wall just out of reach of the swinging door. The frying pan popped loudly behind her and she turned to find smoke rising into the air. Both sets of eggs were nearly hard by the time she managed to shave them loose from the bottom of the pan, and the bacon was turning an alarmingly deep brown.

She had just finished serving the meagre breakfast onto the plates when the door *whooshed* open and there stood Father Lauzon again. She froze with the frying pan in one hand and the spatula in the other. He looked at the table and frowned.

"Not there. What are you doing? We don't eat in here. That's for the housekeeper."

He went to the table, plucked up both plates, and backed through the swinging door.

"And the coffee?"

The door fell closed. He'd vanished again. Every time the heavy swinging door opened away from the kitchen, the back of the retreating priest blocked her view of the next room. The door then slipped past him to swing back into the kitchen, still blocking her view, and then swung away again, opening onto empty space. Now you see Father Lauzon, now you don't!

As if to add to her troubles, the coffee pot chose that moment to boil over onto the stove. Cathy set the frying pan down on the front burner, picked up the coffee pot, turned its burner off, and went over to the table to fill the cups. When she looked back, the frying pan was smoking badly again. She'd neglected to turn its burner off.

"Oh, God," she whispered.

"Jesus, Jesus, Jesus. What are you doing? You're going to burn the place down on your first day."

He was back. He snatched the two coffee cups.

"Bring ketchup for Father LeBlanc."

She found a gummy bottle of ketchup in the fridge and a moment later timidly pushed the door forward and discovered the small, nearly square dining room. A dark wood table surrounded by four plain dark wooden chairs occupied the centre of the room. A solitary buffet stood beneath a small curtainless, grimy window, beyond which she could see the badly neglected weedy little backyard. Every other wall in the room was completely empty. The plates and coffee cups stood on the table, one at the head, the other on the side. There were no placemats, no napkins, no tablecloth. Just the plates on the bare wood table. The room was empty. She tiptoed forward and placed the bottle of ketchup in the middle of the table.

She heard footsteps approaching and scurried back through the door.

"How about some toast, Karen?"

Her stomach went ice cold. She had forgotten about the toast. She'd made it earlier and had meant to sit it in the oven to keep warm while she prepared everything else. But she'd forgotten. It was on the counter, stone cold. There was nothing to do but take it out into the dining room. When she entered the room, she discovered Father Lauzon seated before the plate at the head of the table, eating noisily, obviously not waiting for anyone else.

"Aha!" he said with his mouth full, reaching to pull a piece of toast from the plate she held. He tore the bread in two and began mopping up his plate. As Cathy passed back into the kitchen, she heard a great gurgling burp behind her.

Eventually, she heard two male voices speaking on the other side of the door. She couldn't make out any of the conversation but heard the clack of coffee cups against saucers at odd intervals. Not knowing what to do next, she decided to explore the little hall that opened off the far end of the kitchen. She discovered a plain little bathroom and a narrow bedroom and more of the sickening sweet smell that she'd encountered when she first stepped into the kitchen. Little old lady perfume. Like crushed rotting flowers.

"No wonder she died," said Angela, poking her head into the room.

Mrs. Dupuis' room contained a narrow iron bed pushed against a wall, a black little steel cross on a nail above the bed, sooty faded pink walls, and a straight-back wooden chair sitting beneath a grimy little window that looked out onto the gravel parking lot. Cathy shivered and turned away.

"Let's see the other comforts of home."

Taking great care to be quiet, Cathy turned the knob on the door at the end of the corridor, thinking that she would discover a closet, but found herself, instead, staring straight onto the side of the main altar inside the church.

"I told you I heard bells, didn't I?" Angela again poked her head past the door jamb right into the church. She crinkled up her nose and sniffed.

"Kind of a clammy little place, isn't it?"

Chilly concrete. That's what it smelled like. Cathy closed the door. So she had heard the sounds of the morning mass seeping beneath the door. And if the sounds could come this way, did that mean the church filled up with the scents of coffee and frying bacon every morning?

"I'll bet it does, you know. And I'll bet once he smells breakfast, mass winds up pretty darn quick."

Nervous that she had stayed too long down the hallway, Cathy closed the door silently and hurried back along the hall to the kitchen, turning the light off as she passed the switch. The men were still talking behind the closed door. So she filled the sink with hot soapy water in preparation for the dishes. By the time she turned the taps off, the dining room had fallen silent. She crept to the door and listened for a moment. Nothing. Tentatively, she pushed the door open. The room was empty. Only the dirty dishes remained on the table, the plate at the head of the table pushed forward into the centre.

"Father Lauzon?" she asked timidly.

The rectory had fallen completely still. Where had they gone? She hadn't heard any doors. And the second priest. She hadn't even met him. After hesitating a moment, listening carefully for any sound that might give her information, she stepped forward, stacked the dishes, and cleared the table.

After washing the dishes and piling them into the rack to dry, she wondered what to do next. Make some beds, perhaps? That would entail finding the bedrooms.

"Well, nothing ventured, nothing gained, I always say. We might as well see what the rest of this haunted house looks like."

Angela strode through the door, leading the way. Now she wore turquoise slacks, white sandals, a white T-shirt with a matching white shell necklace and bracelets. Her hair was still carrot orange.

The layout of the ground floor was quite simple. The kitchen was the first of three adjoining rooms. The dining room lay on the other side of the swinging door and then flowed freely through an archway into the living room. Both the dining room and living room were carpeted with threadbare beige broadloom. The living room furnishings consisted of one sagging couch covered in faded autumn print upholstery with two brown limp cushions wilted in each corner; two arm chairs with sagging seats, one matching the couch, the other a dark chocolate brown, both facing the couch from the far side of a long narrow coffee table; one end table adorned with a black wrought iron lamp topped by a parchment lampshade that had gone nearly orange with age; one cardboard picture in a brown plastic frame of Jesus and his exposed crimson sacred heart hanging in the dead centre of the blank wall behind the two chairs; and a cloud of dusty grey sheer curtains covering the picture window, obstructing Jesus' view of the neighbourhood. Opening off the left side of the living room a bare wood staircase led upstairs and a dark wooden door opened to the front yard of the rectory.

"Well, at least they got around to painting the walls in here. Musta been before the flood, by the look of things, though. What would you call this? Pre-Christian bleak?"

Angela wandered away from the wall she had examined into the tiny vestibule between the door and the foot of the stairs. She rested her hand on the railing and a foot on the bottom step and squinted up into the darkness.

"Maybe these guys have a skin condition or something. They don't seem to like light."

Maybe they're vampires, Cathy thought back, *stealing souls.*

"Oh. Funny girl this morning! Well, there's a first time for everything. I can't say a priest's bedroom was ever anything I expected to go looking for in my life. But live until you're full, I always say."

Cathy tried a light switch beside the door but the bulb directly over Angela's head remained unlit.

"Too cheap for light bulbs, it looks like. We'll have to fix that."

The stairs were steep. As she cautiously climbed up, Cathy felt first her head, then the rest of her body, pass, as if through an invisible cloud, into a block of heat that smelled even more intensely than the kitchen. The further up she went, the more old dust, old cigarette smoke, and dry old wood scent she encountered.

The stairs led up to a dingy hall that turned 180 degrees, running back towards the front of the house, parallel to the staircase. A tiny bathroom stood at the head of the stairs, and then the hall passed by two bedrooms, two closets, a laundry chute, and finally ended at the door of a third bedroom, directly at the end of the hall opposite the bathroom.

Ignoring the bathroom, Cathy stepped into the first bedroom. It was small and square, with faint robin's egg blue walls that cried out for a fresh coat of paint. There was a strange musty smell in the room, strong enough to knock you over. It wasn't quite like basement mildew-must. But it was musty nevertheless. Maybe there was dampness behind the walls somewhere? Did the bathroom pipes run through here somehow? Cathy reached out to touch one of the walls as if she might feel dampness but stopped short of touching the plaster. The blue paint was dingy with a sooty film. Years and years of exhaust from the traffic drifting in through the window? She pushed her finger against the plaster and moved it sideways. Sure enough, it cleared a pale blue trail through grit.

Much like the housekeeper's room, there was a single iron bed pushed against the wall, a black steel crucifix above the bed, a small brown dresser, and a plain linoleum floor, but this one had no chair. The bed was rumpled. She moved towards it, automatically reaching for the sheets and the dirty beige cotton bedspread, pulling them up to the single flat pillow in one gesture. It was such a miserable little bed, it made her want to run out of the room instead of moving it away from the wall so she could tuck the sheets in and straighten the covers. It was all she could do to make herself go to the window and pull the over-long curtains back inside the room. This was the window she had seen from the sidewalk, curtains flopping outside against the bricks, beside the flaking cross.

The dented old tin wastepaper basket beneath the window was filled with crumpled Kleenex, and it was here that the smell of must intensified. She made a mental note to empty it on her next visit. Then, turning to leave, she saw the telltale elastic waistband of a pair of men's underwear peeking out from beneath the bed. There was no mistaking what she was looking at. She'd seen her father's and her brother's underwear in the laundry plenty of times.

"Oh, God," she whispered.

She would have to pick up strange men's dirty underwear. She hadn't thought about that. She'd only imagined towels and sheets and dishcloths — innocent things.

"You're on your own on this one, honey. I don't do underwear. Not even for little gods in training."

Cathy kicked the offending thing out of sight beneath the bed, hitting her leg against the steel frame in the process.

"Shit," she whispered and limped out into the hall.

Angela giggled and followed.

"Oh, God. Why did I do that?" Cathy muttered.

Now she'd contaminated her shoe with a priest's dirty underpants. She scraped the toe of her shoe back and forth against the old green hall carpet. She'd have to think of something. Gloves, maybe. Or a pair of tongs. Something. Something with long handles.

"Your father has that pair of barbecue tongs, you know. They'd be just the thing."

"You're right."

"I usually am."

Cathy looked longingly at the weak bit of light filtering up the stairs.

"Naw. We've gotta get this over with. Come on. Let's go. Door number two. Open sesame."

Angela was right. She had to find out what else was in store for her. She passed a closet door and came to the second bedroom.

It was so dark in this room that it was difficult to make out anything, but there was a bit of light leaking into the room from the edges of tall dark draperies. She could feel carpeting beneath her shoes, and so while she lingered at the threshold, waiting for her eyes to adjust, she gave her shoe another good wipe. Gradually, she could see the big dark shapes of at least a dresser, a bed, and two night tables with lamps.

"This must be the head guy's place. I mean, look at what the poor fellow next door had — a skinny single bed with an iron headboard. Those went out with asylums, didn't they? I mean why doesn't he just lie down and have tuberculosis?"

Cathy walked over to the drapes and pulled them apart. The room had blood red shag carpeting on the floor, heavy red, gold, and black flocked wallpaper, with matching brocade bedspread and drapery fabric.

"Humph. Marginally better than next door. But who the hell's taste is this? I mean, I know Spanish — the real thing — and this just isn't it. I don't even know what you'd call this. Pretend Madrid, maybe."

Standing in one corner, on shiny chrome legs, was a large modern office desk with a black vinyl swivel chair behind it and, facing it, two high-backed gold and black brocade chairs with miniature wooden spires extending from the corners of the headrests. How odd to have two chairs in your bedroom like this. Did the person who occupied this room conduct business up here? That's what it looked like.

"Humph. Wonder why he gets the double bed?"

This bed was unmade as well. Afraid of finding discarded underpants tangled in the sheets, Cathy reached only for the visible edge of the red bedspread and tugged it up and over the two plump pillows and smoothed out the largest wrinkles with her hands. No musty smell in here. Aftershave, though. Really strong. This *must* be Father Lauzon's room.

She went back out into the hall again. She was now at the end of the hall staring into the smallest room. She stepped just inside the door. Old dried perspiration. The air was scented with it. Someone lay up here at night and sweated in his sleep.

She looked from wall to wall. Not even twice her four-foot-ten body length, if she were to lay herself down, wall to wall. How could an adult live in this room? How could he even fit? It was the size of a nursery. And the angled ceilings made it worse. It was like a plaster tent.

This room, too, had a bare linoleum floor, a narrow iron bed pushed against the wall on the left, and a black metal crucifix nailed to the wall above the headboard. The walls were painted a dingy faded green, coated with the same sooty grit as the blue room. There was a bedside table with a small lamp, a black sock draped over a plastic alarm clock, and a black rosary coiled at the corner. Beside the table there was a tiny window. Near the foot of the bed, a wooden chair held a neatly folded white undershirt and a pair of black socks. A tiny wooden dresser, big enough for only a child's wardrobe, stood in the shadows against the right-hand wall. No desk, no little mat beside the bed. Nothing but the single crucifix on the wall. The bed, unlike the others, was neatly made, the bedspread tightly tucked under the single flat pillow. Into the bed and the tiny drawers, beneath the rigid little crucifix and the sloping ceilings, a whole adult life was tucked tightly into this suffocatingly small space. It was unbearably futile and lonely to look at, and so Cathy turned to leave, and that was when she saw a man standing in the dark hall, just three feet away.

He was backlit by the bit of light filtering up from downstairs. She could see that he was tall and darkly dressed with a large head and wide shoulders. In the dim light, she could just make out the flesh parts of him — his face and two large hands. One hand alone was large enough to cover her whole face.

"What are you doing? Do you need something?"

He stepped forward into a small patch of light falling into the hall from the room. She noticed a patch of white, a notched collar at his throat. Her lungs unlocked and filled.

"I'm Cathy, Father. The new housekeeper. I was just making beds. But this one is done already."

There was a funny smell. Sweet and gasoline-like at the same time. She'd smelled it before. Brandy. Or something like it. Her father poured it on his Christmas cakes.

"You don't have to make my bed. I always do it myself."

So this last room was his room. He was the one. He must have to stoop to clear the ceilings.

"I'm sorry, Father, I don't know your name."

He stepped into the room. The smell got stronger. There was also a spicy smell now, too. Aftershave, maybe? And fresh perspiration. The same as the stale air in the room.

"I'm Father Martin."

He extended his hand. Her heartbeat quickened. She had never shaken an adult's hand before. Her own hand shot out from beside her and deposited itself like a dead bird in his large damp hot hand and lay there, lifeless, while he pumped both their hands up and down in the air between them. Then he let go and her hand hung awkwardly in the empty space for a brief instant before dropping back to her side. She'd never felt the wet inside of a man's hand before. She felt like she'd been somewhere she oughtn't to have been.

She could see him clearly now. In the light, his head seemed even larger than it had in the shadows. He was balding, and what little hair remained he wore in long strands combed straight back from his prominent forehead and firmly pasted into place on his scalp. His brown eyes bulged, and the whites of them were shot with fine red threads. His cheeks were raw looking, as if they'd been recently scrubbed with a pumice stone, and his large red lips were split and chapped, encrusted with flakes of peeling skin, as if it were the dead of winter. From where she stood, she could see a few flakes of dandruff on the front of his black shirt. His complexion was badly inflamed with boil-like pustules along his jawline and on his neck. *This* was the one her mother had described.

He stared at her as if he could read her thoughts. He'd pulled his lips inward and was grinding them between his teeth. She suddenly remembered where he had been earlier that morning. That must be what happened. He came home and she didn't hear him come up the stairs.

"I hope the sick baby is going to get better, Father."

"Sick baby?"

"The one you went to baptize this morning. Father Lauzon told me not to cook breakfast for you because that's where you were."

"Oh."

Just then it occurred to her that he might have drunk consecrated wine at the hospital. Maybe baptisms on sick babies were combined with something else, like communion or extreme unction. She didn't know. But if he'd had wine, that would explain the smell.

"Is there any breakfast left?"

"Left? No, Father. I only made enough for the other two priests."

"Oh."

"Well, there's still a bit of coffee in the pot, I think."

He stared at her.

"Would you like me to make you something, Father? Bacon and eggs and toast?"

"Yes."

Now that she had a bit of experience, she knew what to do.

"How do you like your eggs cooked, Father?"

"Just once over."

"Do you want the yolks soft?"

"Yes, and I like the bacon crisp."

She stepped to the side and he moved away from the door.

"It'll be about fifteen minutes, Father. I'll call you when the table's set."

When she got to the top of the stairs, she remembered hearing the faintest click just before turning around to find him. At first, the sound had woven itself into the repertoire of all the other creaks that the rectory made. It was a very old building and it murmured to itself. But just now, as she headed down the stairs, the sound revisited her. There was something not right about it. Something unlike the other wooden sounds. As she headed downstairs, her mind replayed the sound, turning it over and over, *click*, *click*, examining it for a mystery.

★ ★ ★

Father Martin sat at the empty table and ate his breakfast in silence. Behind the closed door, Cathy put the now dry dishes on the little table. As soon as he was finished, she was going to get busy and empty the cupboards and rearrange a few things. While she waited for him to finish, she poked through the fridge looking to see what was available for supper. The fridge was a relic from another era, small, with round shoulders and a tiny, heavily ice encrusted freezer hanging down into the interior space. She found a frozen package of ground meat in this little ice cave, but nothing else. Meatloaf for supper? She could make that. Her mother made it at least once a week. Defrosted meat and what else? She remembered Eva chopping onions for her meatballs. Meat and chopped onions and what else? Eggs. She had seen her mother put eggs in her meatloaf. What else? Salt and pepper. Anything else? She couldn't remember. She'd think about it while she cleaned.

She closed the fridge and found Father Martin standing in the doorway staring at her. She had no idea how long he'd been there.

"Yes, Father? Is there something else I can get for you?"

"Is there any more toast?"

She wondered how long he would have remained there, staring at her, before he spoke up.

"I can get you some, right away. It'll just be about two minutes, Father."

When the toast popped up, she took it out to him on a clean plate. He was staring out the window, absently fingering the raw red bumps along his jawline. The thought of him picking up the toast after touching his pimples turned her stomach.

"Here you go, Father," she said, setting the plate down and whirling away on her heel to leave the room before she gagged.

A few minutes later, as she was rooting through a cupboard of canned goods, looking for a vegetable to serve with the meatloaf that evening, he came through the swinging door, one long index finger buried deeply in his cheek, picking something out of his back teeth.

"Thank you," he said, crossing the room and leaving by the back door.

★ ★ ★

"Humph. Mysterious bunch. No one talks. No one introduces themselves."

"Well he at least did that, remember?"

"*Just barely. How long did you say we have to stay here?*"

Angela was sitting on one of the counters, swinging her legs.

"Just until they find someone. That could be as early as next week."

"*Well, if they don't find anyone, we're stuck here for a while, so we might as well cheer ourselves up a bit. Let's get going on these cupboards. You empty and I'll organize.*"

Taking Father Lauzon's invitation to look around literally, Cathy stood on a chair and climbed onto the countertop and investigated all the out-of-reach back corners of shelves and then got down on her hands and knees and peered into spider-infested black holes underneath the sink. Nothing was arranged in any sort of order that she could decipher. The food seemed to be mixed in helter-skelter with the dishes; tins of soup stood beside a stack of dinner plates, and despite the breadbox a half-loaf of bread sat across the tops of soup bowls. Useful items like juice glasses were stored on a top shelf while a dozen china teacups and their saucers took up the more accessible lower shelves. She found a melted block of butter, gone rancid in the heat, sitting uncovered on a plain saucer in one cupboard, and a perfectly good covered glass butter dish pushed to the rear of a shelf at the top of another.

After completing her investigation, she emptied all the cupboards, depositing their contents onto the counters and the table, which she'd dragged into the centre of the room. Angela pulled a chair up to the table and sat with one ankle resting on her knee and one elbow hooked over the chair back. As each item was lifted out of the cupboard, she directed Cathy to sort things into one of two piles.

"*Love it. Love it not.*"

Cathy washed down the cupboards' bare plywood shelves, wiping up years of spilled sugar and salt grains, congealed syrups and liquids, crumbs and small black seeds that she intuitively guessed were mouse droppings. Gradually, the room began to smell of damp wood. It wasn't the most pleasant of smells, but it cut through the prevailing staleness.

She cleaned years' worth of burnt crumbs out of the interior of the toaster and polished its chrome surface and that of the kettle. She dismantled all of the stove's burners, cleaned them, and wrapped the catch basins in shining aluminium foil that she found in a drawer. As she worked, she made mental notes to get some 100-watt light bulbs for the ceiling lights. After changing the water in the sink, she cleaned the interior of the fridge and set a saucer of air-freshening baking soda on a shelf. One by one, small islands of cheer began to emerge around the room.

By the time she finished cleaning and rearranging, she was exhausted. The day had grown hot and humid and the kitchen was nearly unbearable.

"Let's get some air in here. Give me a hand with this thing."

Angela had pushed open the back door and was dragging the lard tin forward so she could prop it against the door. Cathy finished the job. The two of them stood on the back stoop surveying the yard. It was filled with cool green shady pockets despite the overhead afternoon sun. An old neglected flowerbed followed the rusty fencing all around the yard.

Lured by the cool green shade, she walked around the corner to investigate the bush that covered the kitchen window. She didn't recognize it. It had thin woody stalks, so thickly tangled at the base you would have had a difficult time slipping a piece of paper between them. The leaves were a plain dark green, more round than tapered.

"We'll just have to trim it up and wait and see."

When she went back into the kitchen, she noticed immediately that the air smelled better. The meat still hadn't defrosted, but she was able to scrape the first thawed layers into a bowl. Then, because it was nearing four o'clock and she planned to have dinner on the table for five, she decided to soak the rest of it in hot water. Meanwhile, she began assembling other things to mix into the loaf. She'd found onions and potatoes beneath the sink — long green tails sprouting through the little net bag, and little white stubs rooting inside the brown paper bag. Salt and pepper and eggs were handy. She thought ketchup might be a tasty addition so she shook the bottle twice into the mixing bowl.

When it came time to use the eggs, she realized she had a problem. There were only three left. If she used even one, some-one wouldn't be eating breakfast the next morning. She didn't know what would happen to the meatloaf if she left the eggs out but decided to risk it. She'd unearthed cans of peas earlier and decided to substitute this for the eggs. After all, what was the difference between eating peas that sat beside the meatloaf or were included in it? Not much that she could see.

When everything was ready she plunged in her bare hands and squeezed the raw meat together with the ketchup, chopped onion, salt and pepper, and a whole can of peas. Halfway through mixing everything together she wished she had drained the water off the peas first. So she held the bowl over the sink and drained off whatever was left. Some of the meat slipped into the sink, and she regretted not having used cleanser on the old porcelain first. But there was so little meat in the bowl that she didn't think she could afford to lose any. All she could do was remember for the next time.

She patted the green studded mixture into a loaf shape and set it in a roasting pan. It looked painfully plain. She pictured lifting something from the oven in an hour that was glistening with juices and an irresistible golden crust of some sort. She'd read an article about glazes in the back of one of the magazines with Angela's picture on it. Something about mustard and brown sugar. That would be easy enough. But she had found only white sugar so far in this kitchen.

"I don't want to be a spoilsport, but I think plain and simple for the first night is safest."

Maybe just a tiny bit of sugar sprinkled over the top. Just a very tiny bit to accent the flavour. That's what advertisements were always saying: accent the flavour.

So, at four-thirty, the meatloaf went into the oven, lightly sprinkled with sugar and covered in foil. On top of the stove, she set some potatoes to boil and a can of peas and carrots to heat. No sooner had she closed the oven door on the dinner than the back door opened and a man wearing grey work clothes and tan construction boots strode through the middle of the room.

"Hello." He nodded to Cathy, who stood at the stove with her eyebrows halfway up her forehead.

Then he plunged through the swinging door and vanished into the interior of the rectory.

"Like I said, talkative, well-mannered bunch we have here."

"Who was that?"

"Beats me. The missing link, I suppose."

"You mean the third priest? Dressed like that?"

Angela shrugged and ran her hands through the back of her hair, raking it up into untidy little spikes.

"Around here, I'm prepared for anything."

Cathy crept to the swinging door and listened. Silence. He must have gone upstairs. Oh God, into that nasty dry little blue bedroom. She pushed open the door and went into the dining room. Still nothing. She must be right. He must live here and he must have gone upstairs. They must have been *his* underpants. Right now he could be up there changing and dropping another pair under the bed for her to pick up. The vision made her shudder.

"Yuck. One detail too many. Well, at least we've got one for dinner."

Cathy pushed the thought of the strange man and his underpants aside. She stared at the bare table and then at the three drawers in the buffet beneath the window and then back at the table again. What would you have a buffet for, if not to keep things in? She stepped behind the table and began pulling open the drawers. She found a quilted table pad and a white linen tablecloth with matching napkins.

"Civilization."

Together Cathy and Angela spread the pad and the table-cloth over the dark table. Instantly the room brightened.

By 4:45 the kitchen smelled of roasting meat and boiled potatoes. Cathy had set three places, artfully wrapping the cutlery in the linen napkins and placing them on a diagonal across each plate. There was a fresh stick of butter in the butter dish, newly filled salt and pepper shakers, and teacups for each priest. Father Martin arrived at 4:55, stopping to stare at the stove and fold his lips inward. His bulging eyes turned toward Cathy.

"What are we having?"

"Meatloaf, Father. And potatoes and mixed vegetables."

"Oh," he said and continued through the door.

At five, she checked the meatloaf. It was grey all over on the outside and alarmingly moist and pink on the inside. She turned the oven up to four hundred degrees and removed the foil cover from the loaf.

"Holy mackerel, something smells good in here."

This was Father Lauzon's booming voice coming through the back door at five-thirty. Thank God he'd been late.

"You can serve up in five minutes," he said, passing from view behind the door.

So Cathy put the potatoes and the mixed vegetables in bowls and set them on the table and went back to attend to the meatloaf. When she opened the oven, what she found was a considerably shrunken loaf with a great deep crack down the centre. Any juice that had been at the bottom of the pan had evaporated. She tried lifting the loaf out of the pan to put it on a platter, but it began to break apart. Then she tried slicing it. Her mother's loaf always sliced easily. Her brother put cold slices between bread for lunch the day after and still the slices remained intact. But these crumbled before the knife was even finished cutting them. After three attempts, she had a mound of grey meat piled in the pan. She decided to leave what was left of the loaf untouched and to just tuck a serving spoon beneath the crumbling pile. She took the pan out to the table as it was and disappeared back into the kitchen just as feet sounded on the stairs.

She stood in front of the stove and looked into the empty potato pot, realizing for the first time that she hadn't eaten anything since breakfast. What was she supposed to do? Did they expect her to bring her own lunch? Could she have a bit of food from this place? She wished now that she had kept aside a potato for herself. She pressed her finger into some salt grains that lay on the counter and absently licked them. The back of her knees ached. She'd been on her feet for how long now? Ten hours. For the first time all day, she thought about going home. Home and her own room would be nice.

She began to fill the sink again for the dishes and tidied up the counter while waiting for the priests to finish. Again, she heard conversation and then the dining room just fell silent. No one came through the door to tell her they were finished. She waited until she was certain the room was empty before going in to clear the dishes. At seven o'clock she pulled the back door closed on a silent but tidy kitchen.

She walked into her own house an hour later, almost fourteen hours after leaving home. Her father's car wasn't in the garage and it was far too early in the evening for Richard to be home. On her way past the bathroom, she heard water slosh and knew her mother was in the tub. Cathy silently reversed her steps. She wanted to go down into the basement for a moment. Her mother could stay in the tub for hours, so this was a good opportunity. She'd think of an excuse on the spot if she got caught. On her way back through the kitchen, she noticed two pies cooling on the counter. She bent over for a sniff. Strawberry-apple. Tart on the tongue. Maybe she'd be allowed a piece before bed.

Mindful of making any noise, she carefully opened the door to the basement and descended into her father's oasis. Years ago, he had had a complete modern kitchen installed in the basement. It was a lovely basement anyway. Not damp and dank like some of them. It had hardwood flooring, carpeting, and windows that let in lots of light.

His kitchen was panelled in beautiful knotty pine and included every possible convenience for cooking. There were recessed ceiling lights illuminating all the counter space, cupboards with spinning lazy Susans, drawers with built-in divided sections for sorting odd-sized utensils, a full-sized stove and fridge, a dishwasher, and even a tiny chest freezer.

Her father liked to bake. His specialty was bread. He made wonderful loaves of white, whole wheat, rye, and pumpernickel. He also made bread sticks, rolled in fresh sesame seeds, and dinner rolls — soft white Parker House rolls with golden brown crusts. At Christmas, they were heavenly, dripping with melted butter and then dipped in rich brown turkey gravy. During Lent, there were hot cross buns with lots and lots of currants, and for Easter, tutti-frutti buns crusted with little cubes of brilliantly coloured dried fruit looking like miniature jewels beneath a snowy haze of powdered sugar. His cinnamon rolls were huge, unwinding for miles, dark sugary spice trails secreted between layers of fluffy dough. He made peanut butter cookies the size of small plates and the blackest gingerbread anyone could imagine. Best of all, though, were his Christmas cakes, both light and dark, so crammed with fruit and nuts the cake had to find tiny crevices between the fruit for itself. He made them every November and soaked them in brandy for six weeks before cutting them. When she was younger, one whiff of all the heady spices and the brandy was always enough to bring her history lessons to life — the tales of Marco Polo and the spice trade.

You could always tell when he was down there baking. The whole house filled with the wonderful aroma. Later, he'd quietly leave a plate of something delicious in the middle of the kitchen table and slip off to work. Pies were the one baked good Gerald never touched, however. They were strictly Adele's domain.

Cathy quietly pulled open several drawers before finding what she wanted. The barbecue tongs. She'd just tell her mother she needed them to barbecue at the rectory. Adele would be delighted that she was taking something of her father's without telling him.

She was able to make it all the way up to her bedroom without encountering her mother. She slipped the tongs down into the arm of a sweater and tried clutching the bundled-up garment under her elbow. It looked fine in the mirror. Tomorrow, nobody would be the wiser.

Suddenly, she could hardly stand up. How was it possible to have become so tired? She leaned on her dresser with her eyes closed for a moment, figuring out what to do next. She wanted a bath, something to eat, to sit down, to lie down.

Her mother found her standing in front of the open fridge eating a piece of cold chicken. Fresh from her bath, Adele smelled of talcum powder and soap. Her fuzzy red hair sparkled with a few water droplets beneath the overhead kitchen light. The sleeves of her pink bathrobe were rolled back beyond her elbows, and she was busy working hand cream into her forearms.

"So? Did a little work for a change kill you?"

Cathy kept chewing.

"What did the priests get for dinner? Burned beans? Cold porridge?"

"No. Meatloaf."

"*You* made a meatloaf?"

Adele began to laugh, raising her elbows higher so she could see where to put the cream.

"You've never made a meatloaf before in your life. What did it turn out like? A hockey puck?"

"No. I've seen you make them before. It wasn't too hard."

"What did you put in it?"

"Meat. Chopped onions. Salt and pepper. Eggs. It turned out."

"Eggs? How many did you use? You only put *one* egg in a meatloaf."

Cathy thought carefully for a moment.

"Two."

Adele laughed again, rolling the sleeves of her robe back down.

"Two eggs. It must have been glued together. What did the priests say?"

"Nothing."

"Poor things probably broke their jaws. Two eggs in a meatloaf. Who ever heard of such a thing? What did they get for dessert?"

"Nothing."

"No dessert?"

"There wasn't anything. They hardly have any groceries. The cupboards are nearly empty. The housekeeper died, remember?"

"Don't tell me they're going to set *you* loose to do the grocery shopping?"

Cathy shrugged. Angela held up a bowl of fresh grapes invitingly.

"I don't know who's going to do the shopping."

Adele pulled open a drawer and took out a small, coil-bound book entitled *A Guide to Good Cooking*.

"Here," she said, poking the book into Cathy's stomach. "You better stick your nose in this before you kill somebody. And you can take one of these pies tomorrow. I don't want a phone call from Father Lauzon telling me I haven't taught you anything."

★ ★ ★

Cathy sank into the folds of her bedcovers and closed her eyes. There was a robin high up in a tree somewhere in the neighbourhood, singing and singing and singing as the last of the light darkened into a summer night. How was it possible to be so tired? Were there even enough hours ahead in the night to get the sleep that she needed? Had this morning really been part of this same day? Her mind flashed with images from her day: the crack in the meatloaf; the revolting maroon tongue of the bus driver; the white paint flakes; the view of the altar from the door at the end of the hall; the cobwebs under the kitchen sink; Father Martin's hot damp hand. She had taken in a million new experiences. They were whirling around in her brain looking for a million places to settle. Her brain didn't have that much space. She began sinking, falling into darkness. *Click* went that curious sound behind her in the upstairs hall. *Click*. Not wood. Not a two-by-four ticking inside a wall. More outside than that. Close by. *Click ... click.* Metallic. What? *Click ... click.* How had he gotten there? All the way up the stairs without her hearing a thing? Just standing there, watching her. An empty dark hall ... *click* ... and then there he was. *Click* ... and the scent of her father's Christmas cakes, too.

Knock, knock.

Who's there?

I t wasn't until after she had placed three steaming bowls of hot oatmeal on the breakfast table that Cathy discovered the worms. It was her third morning at St. Alphonsis, and she had used the last three eggs the morning before, so she was at a loss as to what to serve next for breakfast. There wasn't enough bacon left for three servings, and only five slices of bread remained. She remembered the half-bag of oatmeal she'd found while cleaning the cupboards. It was folded closed and bound with an elastic. It had to do.

There wasn't any brown sugar to serve with the porridge, but she did find an old half-used can of corn syrup. She filled a small creamer with it, hoping to make it more appealing, and put it on the table. The coffee pot was the last thing to go out to the dining room, set on an old potholder.

She had no idea whether or not they would eat the porridge and was musing about what to do if they wouldn't when she spotted something moving in the little bit of dry oatmeal that had spilled on the counter. Thread-thin and the colour of rust, two tiny worms lifted themselves out of the pile of white oats, waving in the air, searching their new environment.

"Hmm. I see. Enhanced oatmeal. Oh well. It's only protein. What they don't know won't hurt them."

Angela sat on a nearby counter eating green grapes from a bowl in her lap. Andy sat cross-legged beside her on the counter, running her tongue over her front teeth, fishing pieces of grape skin out of her braces.

"Actually insects are a perfectly good source of nutrition that we completely ignore," she said. *"Eating insects is no more revolting than eating the flesh of bigger animals. We're just used to one thing and not the other."*

"Since when did you become so enlightened?" Angela asked, looking up over her shoulder at her daughter.

"Saw it on a documentary. Some tribes of people dig insects out of trees with sticks and consider them a delicacy. In fact, there's even a woman in California who cooks roaches along with rice for her husband and he says they taste just fine. I saw him take a bite. Some people even eat chocolate-coated grasshoppers."

Cathy knew this was true because she had seen that same documentary.

Andy had started to come along to the rectory too. Today, her long straight blonde hair was pulled tight into a ponytail at the crown of her head and hung down just past her shoulders. Cathy liked the way it swished back and forth. Her own hair was not as long and didn't hang as perfectly straight because of its slight natural wave. But whenever Andy was around, she pretended it did. The two of them swished through the rooms of the rectory together.

"Well, by the sounds of things, they seem to be eating behind that door. The boiling water will have killed the worms right off the bat and they're so tiny, mixed in with all the oats, nobody will be the wiser. But I don't think you can serve them this again tomorrow. The rest of the bag is probably crawling."

Revolted by what she imagined, Cathy swept the spilled oats, worms and all, back into the bag, crushed it closed and put it in the garbage beneath the sink.

So what was there to serve tomorrow? And the morning after that? The rest of the bread would be gone by this evening. The freezer was empty. The cupboards were bare. Was she supposed to just go out and get groceries somehow and then have the priests pay her back, or something?

"You know you're going to have to ask someone. Today. You can't leave it any longer."

"Yeah, ask someone what to do. It will be fun to shop for this place."

Andy was stretching her arms above her head, yawning. She had on lime green pedal-pushers, and her white cotton top rode up, showing her lovely flat tanned midriff. Like mother, like daughter. Adele never would have allowed a top that rode up like that, displaying bare skin. Never in a million years. It didn't matter, though. Cathy's midriff was luminous white and she wouldn't have wanted to show it to anyone.

She stood in front of the sink staring through the window into the underwater-green tangle of overgrown bush. She was thinking about the meals she had seen featured in magazines: summer barbecues, Sunday brunches, Christmas parties, spring lunches. She could bring some of her magazines with her to work and prepare some of those things for the priests. Broiled grapefruit would be easy. She could do that. Just sprinkle a bit of sugar on grapefruit halves and set them under the broiler until the sugar browned and formed a crust. Then put a red cherry in the centre and serve. That would be nice for breakfast one morning along with poached eggs and toast. She could make a cheese sauce for the eggs. That was in one of the magazine articles. Just a bit of butter in the pan, sprinkle in some flour and add milk and cheese. She could manage that. But she needed some groceries.

"Ahem!" Both Angela and Andy were looking at her with raised eyebrows, surreptitiously tilting their heads to indicate that she should turn around.

Father Martin had come into the kitchen without her hearing him and was standing just inside the swinging door staring at her.

Angela narrowed her eyes at him.

"Professional stare artist, this one."

"Oh, Father," Cathy said, a little uneasily, "you should have said something. I didn't hear you come in."

He reached up and ran his fingers along his bumpy jawline.

"Mr. Renaud will be here later this morning with an order of groceries," he said.

"Humph! Mind reader, too. Very handy."

"Oh. That's good, Father. I was just wondering what to do about that. We're running out of everything."

"Yes, I know. It's always like that just before he delivers the next order. He comes every two weeks and everything you need will be in the order."

Angela let out a big sigh.

"So if you run out of things before *the next order arrives, Bozo, you need to change the order, don't you?"*

She rolled her eyes and walked away, hands on her hips, shaking her head. Cathy heard her bracelets tinkle as she hoisted herself back up on the counter. Andy stood on the counter, edging herself along, opening cupboards and looking inside. She hadn't seen everything yet.

Father Martin stood perfectly erect beside one of the cupboards, staring at Cathy with his large pop-eyes. Did he have something else to say, or was he waiting for her to say something else? She found it awkward to look at him directly because of the staring and the way he kneaded his lips together. He looked as if he didn't know what to do with his long limbs and large hands and feet. So she picked up the dishcloth and began moving it around the already-wiped counters, waiting to see if he would speak again.

From her perch up on the counter, Andy mimicked him. Cathy could see her, even without turning around. Andy sucked in her lips, flared her nostrils, widened her eyes and then crossed them. Cathy had to bite the inside of her cheeks in order not to laugh out loud.

"What kinds of meals are you planning, this week? I've enjoyed everything so far."

So he did have something else to say. He wanted to talk more about food. About planning the food. The word "planning" threw her off slightly. Since arriving at the rectory, she hadn't really "planned" anything. Meals had just been scratched together with whatever was available. It would be lovely to plan ahead, to set beautiful tables for the priests and serve elegant meals that she'd had time to think about, meals that Angela might serve. But so far, she had just worked with whatever she found in the fridge. She thought the priests had eaten rather poorly since her arrival, at least compared to what she was used to at home.

He continued to look down from his great height and stare. Maybe she could talk him *into* a few things.

"Well, Father, I guess I'll have to see what kinds of things come in the grocery order. Then I can maybe plan ahead. Is there anything special you'd like me to cook for you?"

His eyes widened. How nice this young girl was. So eager to please. Mrs. Dupuis had been such a lifeless old woman. The same meals every day of the week, month in and month out. Leftovers Monday, meatloaf Tuesday, salmon patties every Friday. Everything over-salted, pork chops fried dry, coffee reheated all day so as not to waste a drop. They should have found someone young long ago. And it had been ages since anyone had asked him anything personal. Imagine. What did *he* like? Ah, God worked in wondrous ways. First the green miracle grotto, and now this.

Jerome drew in a big breath. What sorts of things did he like? He wasn't sure he knew the answer. What colours did he like, what foods did he enjoy? Those were normal questions answered by people everyday, and yet he couldn't remember if there was anything that he liked better than anything else. He couldn't remember when it had ever mattered what he liked. When had one thing in his life last risen above another to capture his attention? Everything in his life had blended to grey, ages ago. But maybe *that* was about to change. Maybe this girl was what he had been waiting for. Maybe this was the turning point. With a well-fed stomach, he'd be happy and able to sleep again. He'd have a remarkable life after all.

"What about shepherd's pie, Father?"

"Hmm?"

"Shepherd's pie. It's a casserole with ground beef and corn and potatoes…"

"Yes, I know what shepherd's pie is."

Mrs. Dupuis had served shepherd's pie. Her potato crusts were always grey and lumpy and the meat over-fried.

"I have a recipe for shepherd's pie with a potato-cheese topping, Father. Does that sound appealing? Do you know if any cheese comes in the grocery order?"

A potato-cheese crust. Now here was a tantalizing prospect. His tongue slid back and forth against the roof of his mouth trying to taste the suggestion.

"Yes. Yes. That would be fine. You just get whatever you need to make that. Mr. Renaud can tell you what kind of cheese he has."

He'd clenched both fists and was now gently knocking his knuckles against each other. Andy mimicked him, making long swinging chimpanzee arms. He continued to stare. His lips disappeared completely, folding entirely from sight into his mouth. Suddenly his ears, standing nearly at right angles to his head, looked huge. The boils along his jawline glistened with oil. Cathy looked at him and knew that he had looked like this, years ago, in a schoolyard. Awkward and oily and over-large, with big hands and feet and pimples, and that he had rubbed his lips between his teeth and taken too long to speak. "Big dumb lummox." Somebody would have called him that. What was a lummox? She didn't know. Something large and awkward? Something slow? "Pimple-headed moron." That's what he would get in a schoolyard today. "Moron" because his big-eyed staring and slowness to speak made him look dumb. "Loser" was another word he would get. "Big dumb loser." Cathy studied him, his large cow-eyes, his grinding lips, his boils and greasy skin, his nervous knocking knuckles, his hesitancy. He looked frightened, too anxious to settle any-where, as if expecting to be shooed away from every room he entered. How pitiful, she thought, to be so ill at ease at his age, in his own house, in the only world he had to inhabit. Despite the unease that had flickered through her whenever she discov-ered him staring at her, Cathy's heart softened towards him.

"Anything else, Father?"

Anything else? Anything else? She was so generous, this girl. His excited mind roamed wildly. What had he enjoyed before, years ago? What had he eaten at home? He reached up absently and tugged his earlobe.

"What about stew, Father?"

"Hmm?"

"Stew. Do you think the others would like that, one night a week? Beef or chicken stew? I can put any kind of vegetables in it you like."

Stew was easy. It had been her grandmother's staple. There'd been a pot perpetually simmering on the back burner of her stove throughout Cathy's childhood. Salted water, onions, carrots, celery, chicken, sometimes beef chunks, potatoes, broccoli, peas, whatever was handy. You just let it sit back there on a warm burner all day. It made itself. Just like Eva's rice. She could manage stew.

Jerome's eyebrows rode up his large forehead. Stew was an easy answer. He liked stew.

"Yes. I think so. What would you put in it?"

"Anything you like. Chicken or beef, first of all?"

So many questions.

"I like both."

He knew that Gerry didn't care much for chicken, but he didn't care about Gerry at all at the moment.

"Okay. What vegetables do you like?"

Verbal volleys. It must be that kids speak like this nowadays. What else? What did he like? Suddenly his mind opened up and he remembered that his mother used to make turnip for him when he was a boy.

"Can you put turnip in stew?"

"Sure, Father. What else?"

"Oh, I know what I like."

He was suddenly animated, rising up on his toes with one long index finger ascending slowly into the air. Childhood memories flooded into him.

Andy suddenly looked out from behind a cupboard door.

"Uh-oh! Look out. I think he's gonna sing."

"Peanut butter cookies."

"Peanut butter cookies, Father? In stew, Father?"

His eyes opened wider and his lips disappeared so deeply into his mouth his nose began to tilt downward. No. No. That wasn't what he meant. But the sudden memory of his mother's cookies, with the crisscross imprint of a fork on their surface, warm from the oven, burst into his mouth, making him salivate.

"Even more interesting. I think he's gonna swallow himself," Andy chirped.

"No. That's not what I meant. I mean, I don't like lima beans."

Lima beans. Where had *they* come from?

"Lima beans don't belong in stew anyway, Father." She'd only seen lima beans in canned soup. She wouldn't even have known where to get them if he'd wanted them.

"Can you make peanut butter cookies?"

"He actually has a fine idea there, you know."

Andy hopped down off the counter. Angela reached over and patted her daughter's bare flat midriff.

"Too many cookies, too many tummies, sweetie."

"Sure, Father. I can make peanut butter cookies. Do you know if peanut butter comes in the order? I didn't find any when I cleaned the cupboards."

"Just get whatever you need. Ask Mr. Renaud."

"All right then. You heard it here first. We can get whatever we need. All hands on deck. This rectory's not going to know what hit it."

Andy turned a perfect cartwheel right in the middle of the kitchen. She stopped in front of Father Martin, reached up, and patted a clear spot on one of his cheeks.

"Thanks, Padre. You won't regret it."

"Father?"

"Yes?"

"One more thing. Who's the other priest?"

He frowned for an instant, his lips popping out of his mouth to bunch together.

"Oh, you mean Father LeBlanc."

"He seems to wear street clothes, Father."

"Yes. He works in a factory. It's an experiment. Leave the bill for me right here."

He pointed to a nail protruding from the side of one of the cupboards. Then he pushed the door forward and left the kitchen.

★ ★ ★

135

Two hours later, as Cathy stood in front of the open fridge, wondering how to defrost the tiny ancient freezer, footsteps thumped up the back porch steps. A voice called out something that she didn't quite catch, and a short chubby man carrying a cardboard carton strode through the open door into the room. He carried the box right past her, setting it on the table. Then he extended his hand.

"Hello there, love. I'm Renaud. The grocer."

He didn't even wait. His pudgy, dry, room-temperature hand simply grabbed hers, gave it a quick squeeze and half-pump and then it was gone. No hot, damp flesh.

He had friendly dark brown eyes and, resting in grooves on his bottom lip, two of the longest front teeth Cathy had ever seen.

"Rabbit man," Andy blurted out. Angela elbowed her.

"Mind your manners."

He wore navy trousers and a short-sleeved white shirt with a bow tie. A bow tie!

"Would you look at this?" Andy chirped, tugging both wings of the tie. *"I think he's straight from vaudeville."*

His hair, still sandy coloured despite his fifty or so years, was combed neatly back in long strands from his forehead and slicked down to the nape of his neck with grease.

"So. You're the new housekeeper, eh? Just here temporarily, are you? Until they find someone permanent. From Father's old parish, I guess, eh? Out the west end? Well, it won't be long, I expect."

Before Cathy could respond, he disappeared out the door again. He made several trips in and out of the room, bringing boxes up the porch steps and placing them on the table and then on the counter, conscientiously pointing out that the meat was all together in a separate box. He huffed and puffed as he came and went, and his feet pounded noisily across the old rectory floor.

During one of his trips back to the truck, Cathy stepped forward for a quick snoop in the boxes. Her hands fingered unfamiliar, bargain brands of food: tins of fish and pudding, things with drab-coloured labels and unfamiliar names; things she somehow imagined having seen in old magazines, things associated with England and the war and rationing. Old-fashioned things. Maybe she'd seen some of them at her grandmother's when she was a kid. She wasn't sure.

Angela lounged at the table eating grapes.

"How bad is it?"

"Bad," Cathy said aloud into the empty room.

Thump. Thump. Thump.

"I'm gonna need a crane to do this soon," Renaud puffed. "Up and down steps all day. A person begins to get old."

"Would you like some help?"

"Help? Yes, but this isn't work the Lord intended *you* to do. You're the size of a little bitty bird you are, now that I look at you. I'll have to be bringing a separate order of liver out, just so's you can build up strength enough for your own job. No. No. Lifting isn't for the ladies. Here you are, then. Six boxes. Same as always."

"Psst," Angela tapped Cathy's shoulder. *"Remember how I told you that lemons make a room smell nice and clean? Ask him."*

Cathy timidly asked Mr. Renaud if he had any lemons.

"Lemons? Yes, I've got lemons."

"Could I have a couple every order?"

"Sure."

Mr. Renaud removed a notebook and a pen from his shirt pocket and readied them for use. Andy fished a half-eaten bunch of grapes from the bowl on the counter and wagged it at Cathy.

"And green grapes too."

"Grapes? Oh, Lordy, Lordy! That's different. You sure you're going to get these guys to eat grapes? That's dainty lady-stuff food,

137

grapes. But yes, I have nice seedless green grapes. California green grapes. Would you like to try a large bunch in the next order?"

Her heart stopped dead. California. She could get grapes all the way from California. They would be delivered right here to the rectory kitchen. Her heart fluttered to life again. Green California grapes, just like Angela and Andy had. Her grapes might even grow on the same farm, or in the same field, or maybe even on the very same vine together with their grapes. It was the closest that she had ever come, physically, to them.

"Well where did you think they grew? New York?" Angela crowed.

She glanced over the top of the unsuspecting grocer's head to where her friends stood and smiled.

"Yes. One big bunch should be fine to start."

"Okay. Grapes, lemons, anything else?"

The grocer was poised over his list, looking at her expectantly. She grew expansive with her happiness and the power of being completely in charge of something for the first time in her life. Angela popped a single ripe grape into her mouth.

"Get some tomato juice."

"Tomato juice, please."

Cathy pictured small juice glasses brimming with the chilled red liquid and wedges of lemon set against the brilliant white of the tablecloth.

"And an iceberg lettuce and some fresh tomatoes, a bag of rice, a box of raisins, and a bottle of salad dressing, please. French. A tin of cocoa, two packages of 100-watt light bulbs, a bag of oatmeal. A large jar of peanut butter. And some grape jelly, too."

That would be good for breakfast some mornings. Toast and peanut butter and jelly.

"And some cheese, please. Cheddar, extra old. One large block."

It was what her father used in his cheese bread.

"And I don't think I want some of the things that are in here. After I have a better look at them, can I send them back, next time?"

"Certainly."

Mr. Renaud nodded and dutifully wrote down her requests on his little pad and then whistled.

"Ah, the priests are in for some changes around here, I can see that."

Angela draped herself across Mr. Renuad's shoulder.

"Change, my weird little artifact, is what makes life interesting."

Cathy, grinning, was silly with happiness.

"I hope to cook some interesting things."

"Well, we'll see what they think about 'interesting' when you serve it to them on a plate."

Mr. Renaud tilted his head back, opening his mouth to laugh at his own little perceptions. Then his teeth re-settled themselves into their moorings on his bottom lip.

He left behind a handwritten, carbon-backed bill, which Cathy poked over a nail on the side of the cupboard for Father Martin, just as she had been instructed.

CHAPTER 9

The news came out of the blue. Adele heard it on the radio at midday. She was standing at the kitchen sink, swishing bits of potting soil down the drain after transplanting an African violet that she'd rooted from a cutting.

"There is going to be a new member of the White House family," the newscaster began.

Adele's wet hand shot forward to the radio and turned up the volume. The First Lady was expecting a baby in the second week of October, but because of a past history of miscarriages and stillbirths, the news had not been released until it was thought that the pregnancy would succeed. A special team would be assembled at Bethesda Naval Hospital to perform the Caesarean delivery in the fall.

That was it. No other details. Nothing about how the First Lady was feeling, no mention of what plans were in place for the name, the baptism, the first pictures. Nothing else.

Adele clicked her tongue and plugged the electric kettle in to make a pot of tea.

"Damn news people. They never tell you the whole story. Just keep all the details to themselves."

She went immediately to the china cabinet in the dining room and chose one of her best teacups: Royal Doulton, fine bone china, Arcadia. Pink wild roses on a white background. A hint of green on the handle. Delicate. Feminine. Refined. Proper for the occasion.

She set the teacup down gently on the glossy tabletop. The President watched her from his picture frame on the buffet. He was sorry he couldn't have told her sooner. He knew she would be delighted. He knew how much she loved children.

Her chubby hands fumbled beneath the heavy damask linen tablecloths in the buffet, pulling out all the hidden magazines. It had been a long time since she had them all out in the open. Today was perfect, though. They were all at work. Even Cathy. Way across town at St. Alphonsis.

It was quite a growing little collection she had. Eighteen magazines in all. She sorted through them, lining them up in chronological order while her mind worked away. If this is July and the baby is due in the second week of October … second week in October, September, August…. Adele rapidly counted backwards on her fingertips, little sibilant whispers escaping her lips. January! Her fingers stopped moving. She must have been pregnant by the second week in January. It was now July, so she must be exactly six months pregnant. Had there been a sign in any of the recent pictures? Something that had gotten past her? How far in advance of the printing did they take the pictures? Not too far, surely. What if she changed her hairstyle or something? The picture would be out of date. No. They must take the pictures just days before. So they were fresh. In *that* case, one of the pictures, the May issue, had been taken within the last six months. Adele tore open the magazine to the right page and bent over this most recent picture. Her eyes narrowed and her mouth twisted to one side as she absently chewed the skin on the inside of her cheeks. She must have been pregnant in this picture. Even if they'd taken it one, two, three, four months early, she must have been pregnant.

In the picture, the First Lady sat in a chair upholstered in cream brocade, her hands resting in her lap against a pastel yellow wool suit. Adele examined the suit front and the hands. You couldn't really tell. Nothing showed. So the picture must have been taken before she was showing. February, March, or April at the latest.

But you don't look at the stomach before you show. You look to the eyes. It's always there. That blissful, contented surrender to your womanly destiny. Along with joy, expectation, and, of course, fatigue. She saw it there now in the quiet deep brown eyes. She must have been distracted before, not to pick it up. But it was plain as the nose on her face, now. In fact, it practically screamed at her from the page. Her eyes locked with those of her friend. They exchanged little Mona Lisa smiles.

"You almost had me there," Adele said softly, "but your secret's out now."

Her friend looked pleased at having fooled her.

The kettle was boiling furiously in the kitchen. While she made tea, Adele's mind churned excitedly as she opened and closed cupboards, lifting down tea bags and the sugar bowl. Another Caesarean. Her third. Well, Adele certainly knew what difficult births were like. Both Richard and Cathy had been delivered by Caesarean section. The scar alone was enough to bear, running from the navel down to the hairline. Every time you showered or changed, there it was in the mirror looking back at you, discoloured and puckered, rippling down the front of your abdomen like a zipper.

And the pain when you woke up! It wasn't something you forgot, like the other, normal women's pain. The doctors masked it for you with morphine at first, but after that, you were expect-ed to deal with it on your own. When the nurses got you up to go to the bathroom the next day — *the next day!* — you could feel all your organs flopping into place against the incision. You had to put your hand gently over the bandaged area to be ready, just in case the stitches didn't hold.

She wandered back into the dining room with the teapot and the sugar bowl and settled into her chair. Six months along in July. She remembered exactly what it was like being that far along in the summer. Richard had been born at the beginning of November. The summer that she was pregnant with him, her legs swelled up so badly that her ankles disappeared. She sat out on the balcony of their first apartment with her feet elevated from July till September, reading gardening magazines. Then she went indoors to the living room couch for two more months. That was when they got their first television.

Now here it was, nineteen summers later, and she had the house to herself once again. And the President was going to have a new baby. She stared deeply into her friend's eyes. What could she do to help? What could she get for her?

The First Lady stared back with the faintest of smiles hovering about her mouth.

"I'll leave it all up to you, Adele. I know you have exquisite taste."

The picture was crowded with details. Patterns in the wallpaper, the carpet, the upholstery. Flowers. An enormous arrangement stood in a crystal vase on a pedestal just behind the First Lady's right shoulder. Cascading lilacs amid miniature yellow roses, baby's breath, and dark green fern. Beneath the vase the lattice-worked edge of a beautiful lace doily hung delicately over the edges of the pedestal. Adele stared at the lilacs and the yellow roses. At the white doily. Back and forth her eyes went. These things were there for a reason. She was meant to see them, to take something from them. She stared and waited. She was open. She knew something was coming to her. She could feel it advancing, advancing. Here it was, at last. Yes, yes, yes. They were perfect. Absolutely perfect. What a gift. She jumped up, went into the kitchen, and scrounged noisily in a drawer for a scrap of paper and a pencil. Back at the table, her tongue came out and worked the corner of her mouth as she began to sketch and make a list. She was on fire.

★ ★ ★

Everything that she bought she hid in the Christmas drawer, beneath the red and gold Christmas tablecloth and napkins, the box of unused Christmas cards, the tree, the bell, the sleigh-shaped cookie cutters, the little tin of silver polish, the candle-stick holders, and the bundles of candles wrapped in wax paper. It was the bottom drawer of the buffet. In a million years, no one would ever go in there for anything in the middle of summer.

In the mornings she bided her time, waiting for the house to clear out. Cathy was always gone before she got up. But some-times Richard or Gerald had late starts. Gerald would sometimes cut the back lawn and then come in for a cup of coffee before showering and leaving at eleven. When he asked her what she had planned for the day, she told him. Work. Just like him. There were all kinds of things to do around a house that men never even noticed.

By lunchtime every day it was safe enough for her to take the knitting out and work in the open. In less than a week, she had almost finished the sweet little white sweater and was hurrying carefully through the rest of it because she wanted to thread the lavender and yellow ribbons through the lattice-work to see the final effect. The bonnet and booties would take no time at all after that. Then she wanted to try making a cradle shawl to match the outfit. It didn't come with the pat-tern, but she was a good enough knitter to improvise one. Its latticework edge would carry the same yellow and lavender ribbons as the sweater, bonnet, and booties. She would draw the ribbons into a lovely bow at one corner.

She kept the work in her lap, below the level of the table so that the First Lady couldn't see what she was doing.

"It's a surprise," she said, smiling down at her hands, pleased at her clever reproduction of the lattice pattern from the doily.

"It's so sweet of you, Adele. I'm sure I'll love anything that you make."

She worried while her hands flew and the needles gently clacked together from time to time in the dead still house. She still hadn't found out how she was going to send the parcel over the Canada–U.S. border to the White House. She knew she could just send it to the White House and it would probably get there, but she wanted to be certain when she mailed it that it would get right to the President and his wife. She wanted to have the exact address of the White House. Those were technical problems, though, that could likely be solved in one phone call. She just couldn't figure out where to call for such information.

The other information that she needed concerned customs procedures at the border. She didn't want to put a return address on the parcel but thought that that would perhaps make it look suspicious. There *were* lunatics out in the world. The idea of big rough hands tearing open her parcel with its delicate contents, maybe slashing open an end of the box with a knife, worried her. She wasn't doing all this meticulous work to have it land on a post office floor somewhere, or worse, to be stolen en route.

But she also didn't want to take the chance of having the parcel returned to her. The risk that someone else would then learn about it loomed large in her imagination. She could just see her neighbour, Louise De Finca, that shapeless, woody, root vegetable of a woman, stepping back, blank-faced, wide-eyed, patting her throat, remarking that she didn't know why on earth anyone would even think to send a gift to the President of the United States for his new baby.

145

Well too bad if some people never took a chance in life. That was their business. She didn't see anything wrong with her idea. You never know in life unless you try. The sweater set might end up on the evening news or in the pages of *Life* magazine with the first portraits of the baby.

Adele already saw her friend, posing on a cream satin French provincial chair, wearing one of her bouclé wool suits with matching pillbox hat, the new infant on her lap. Almost certainly the child would be wearing a lace christening gown, but that somehow wouldn't interfere with the wearing of Adele's gift at the same time. The yellow and lavender ribbon pattern would become famous overnight because the White House baby would have worn the anonymous gift for his or her first magazine portrait. All of America would wonder where the sweater set had come from, which uptown Washington or New York or Boston department store had supplied the outfit. All of America's ensuing crop of newborns would be similarly attired.

Adele paused, smiled, rested the needles in her lap for a moment, took a sip of tea, and slid her hand down the side of her abdomen, checking for signs of life.

During the next several weeks Cathy plunged whole-heartedly into teaching herself how to be a house-keeper. After filling the kitchen too many times with black smoke, she learned to turn the temperature down on the burners. She learned to put enough butter in the pan so that the eggs no longer stuck to the bottom. She kept the first pieces of toast warm in the oven until the other pieces were ready and then carried them all out to the table with a pot lid over them. She found an old shot glass and filled it with Father LeBlanc's ketchup and set it beside his plate at every meal. After doing the breakfast dishes and vacuuming the living room and dining room, making beds and opening windows to air the rectory, she sat at the bare little house-keeper's table beside the swinging door and pored over the illustrated pages in the cookbook her mother had given her.

The book was old and almost everything in it too formal. The illustrations highlighted table settings and food that had gone out of style before she was born or that simply didn't suit an ordinary household or a humble rectory. Tables were dressed with linen tablecloths, linen napkins, good china, silverware, and serving dishes that stood in little silver wire stands. Suggested meals were too elaborate: beef Wellington; coq au vin. Fussy desserts stood nearby on a buffet, sitting on large fancy platters. Little iced cakes, pastel green, yellow, and pink, the flawless icing covered in tiny flowers or little silver candy beads. No hint in any of the pictures of paper napkins, plain, unmatched china, ketchup bottles, milk bottles. No illustrations of casseroles, meatloaves, or fruit cobblers, although the recipes were there, hidden at the back of the book under the title "Casual Fare." She took the spirit of grace and pride from the book, though, and did what she could, pressing odds and ends like the shot glass into use, mastering the recipes for scalloped potatoes and chicken pot pie. Anything was an improvement over plain plates on the battle-scarred old bare table, over the plain dry past of Mrs. Dupuis.

She could tell that Father Martin appreciated her efforts. She occasionally caught sight of him through the swinging door, standing behind his chair, surveying the table with its pitcher of ice water, the bouquet of Queen Anne's Lace that she picked along the back fence, the knives and forks rolled into the napkins. He looked pleased.

One evening, on a rare occasion when she brought something hot from the oven to the table after the priests had seated themselves, she heard Father Martin including her efforts in his grace. She'd pushed partway through the door, holding a steaming dish of potatoes before realizing what was taking place. Father LeBlanc lounged at the table, rumpling the tablecloth with his big elbows, supporting his head against one fist. As usual, his water glass had been banished to the centre of the table, and he remained oblivious to his napkin. While waiting for grace to conclude, he used his fork as a toothpick. *Ting, ting*, it went against his teeth. Cathy saw Father Lauzon, his head tilted toward the ceiling, pinch his nose and then begin to roll something absently between his fingers.

"Lord, we are grateful for the kind and caring manner that has blessed our table over the past weeks," Father Martin was saying, his huge oily head bowed low, "and we are grateful for the bounty that You have seen fit to provide for us and the refreshing manner in which Thy bounty has been celebrated. Amen."

Amen.

Cathy set the dish in the centre of the table and returned to the kitchen.

"Pleased" hardly did justice to Jerome's feelings. He was actually absolutely startled by the change that the simple white tablecloth alone brought to the entire dining room. In addition, this new girl used bread and butter plates, a butter dish, chilled water glasses, warmed plates, bouquets of flowers. She took care to fold the linen napkins in geometric shapes, or to wrap the knives and forks within them. Once he'd observed her from the living room, stepping back and examining each place setting, making small, fastidious adjustments until she was satisfied. What a delight! Such care directed toward him and his colleagues. She'd turned the dining room into an oasis. It was enough to spark a dead soul to life.

★ ★ ★

One evening, after she had cleared the table and stood at the sink, looking into the back of the green bush, the tips of her fingers wrinkling beneath the dishwater, the door opened behind Cathy. She turned to discover the third priest standing there. Father Underpants.

He was short, she noticed for the first time. Chunky. His face was scarred by long-healed acne. The lenses in his glasses made his eyes look like two oily brown prunes. She hoped she wouldn't have to shake his hand.

"Have you done any laundry yet?" he asked, scrunching up his nose to hoist his slipping glasses.

She imagined his dirty underpants, right where she had last seen them, kicked out of sight and out of mind beneath his bed by her own impatient, repulsed foot. Her father's barbecue tongs still waited patiently in a nearby drawer for their debut.

"No, Father. I'm sorry. I haven't done any laundry yet."

"Well, I'm outa things. Socks and things."

His hand waved awkwardly up and down in the air in front of his torso.

"I've been wearing the same things for two days now."

"Oh my God," Angela and Andy shrieked in unison. *"The same underpants for two days?"*

"Beach. Beach," Andy hollered, shaking her hands in the air, *"I'm gone to the beach. Don't call me until this is over."*

Oh, God, Cathy thought, staring at him in disbelief. And there was nothing clean for tomorrow. So that would be three days.

"Oh," she stammered, "well, I'll do the wash tomorrow for sure, Father. I just didn't know how often you needed things done. I don't know how much clothing each of you has."

"Yeah, I need some things."

He turned and vanished behind the door.

★ ★ ★

The next morning, after all three men had left the rectory, Cathy trudged reluctantly upstairs.

"Couldn't we bake instead?" Andy begged.

"Couldn't we do anything else instead?"

"Beach for me, then."

Cathy stripped the beds of their plain, white sheets.

"Boring, boring, boring," Angela had pronounced when the sheets were first discovered. *"You'd think colour was a sin."*

As she tugged at them now, Cathy turned her head away to avoid inhaling the perspiration.

"God, men smell," she whispered.

"Ah! But the right one smells like God, my dear," Angela quipped from the nearby windowsill.

"Don't let my mother hear that."

"She's not here."

Cathy picked up the barbecue tongs, got down on her hands and knees, and peered beneath each of the three beds. Just as she expected, Father LeBlanc's dirty underpants were still there, nestled up against the baseboard. Several other pairs and numerous black socks had joined them. She also found socks and under-wear beneath his dresser and behind the bedroom door. What did he do? Just strip and step out of things and walk away?

"Looks like."

Didn't he have any system of putting dirty clothes aside for the wash? Had old Mrs. Dupuis come up here every day and fished around beneath furniture with her bare hands, expecting that *that* was where she would find the things that needed washing?

Cathy looked only as far as it was necessary to grab the underwear with the tongs and then, as she dragged them out into the daylight, she closed her eyes against the horrific sight. She was particularly trying to avoid seeing hair. Her imagination had taunted her the night before, showing her thickets of dark, sweaty, curly priest-hair stuck in the folds of the laundry; black glistening things falling onto her bare skin. She could have retched. She had seen one or two of her brother's strays in the laundry at home. Little single brown, curly, coarse wires sticking up from bits of laundry. Sometimes with a little bit of skin attached. Sticking up and threatening to touch her. Sometimes dropping off and landing on the counter. Landing on her. Then she had to move them. Blow them away and hope that she didn't get mixed up and inhale. Her brother's had been awful enough. But black hair, from down there, from a priest? It was too horrible to contemplate.

"I'm baking," Andy called up the stairs.

"Tch. You went to the beach, remember?"

"I'm baking at the beach."

It was on Father Lauzon's exposed sheets that Cathy discovered a stain. First one, then, in a matter of seconds, several more. She stopped pulling the sheets off the bed and stared. They must have been there all along. She'd just missed them before. They reminded her of the water marks she'd seen on the ceiling in the lunch room at St. Joseph's. She looked up and studied the ceiling directly above the stains. But there was nothing there.

It was nine o'clock in the morning. There was no one around. Only the stain and Cathy. *Come closer,* it whispered. She sank down to her knees. *Now, sniff me,* it commanded. She put her nose down and sniffed. She had smelled her own body. Everything: breath, stale armpits, sour crotch, feet. Everything was bad, decaying, bacterial. This was different. Musty.

She stood up. Her mother was coming. All the way from across town. Pounding up the stairs, swollen with rage.

What do you think you are doing, missy?

Quickly, she drew the covers over the stains. She didn't want this. It was forbidden, dangerous. But what do you do with dangerous knowledge you don't want?

She flew up her string. The sky was dry as a desert, the sun broiling. If only she could just hand the knowledge over like a parcel and leave it up here where her mother would never find it. Maybe the sun would evaporate it.

"Come on back," Angela called up. *"She's not here. You can't sit up there all morning. You've got to get this stuff done. Otherwise Monsignor Underpants will be workin' on day four."*

Men have musty water come out from down there. Cathy pressed on, weighed down by her unwanted knowledge. She brought underwear and socks out of Father LeBlanc's room, and the same, plus crispy handkerchiefs, out of Father Lauzon's room, but nothing out of Father Martin's. She looked twice. Beneath the bed. Beneath the bedside table. Behind the door. Nothing. Not a scrap of anything. Bless his large oily head, he must be putting his dirty laundry down the chute. But when she stripped his bed, she noticed the same dried stains. She glanced up at the ceiling but saw only a long ragged crack and a round peeling patch of paint.

Angela occasionally poked her head into a room to comment, but Andy never came back from the beach.

"*She's sensitive,*" Angela said.

And lucky, thought Cathy.

Cathy stuffed the laundry, a tong-full at a time, down the chute.

Since no one told her anything about where to find things in the rectory, she had to search for the basement. Where else could the washer be? There wasn't a main-floor laundry room in *this* place. Instinctively she went back to the little hall off the kitchen. Sure enough, she found the door to the basement midway down this corridor. Now she had accounted for all the doors in this hall. One for the bedroom. One for the bathroom. One into the church. And one down into the basement.

The stairs leading down into the basement were new. The original wood should have been greyed with age by now, like everything else in the rectory. But this was new. As unexpected as the red Spanish decor in Father Lauzon's bedroom. What had happened here? Had the old stairs been so decrepit they had fallen apart? Had old Mrs. Dupuis put her foot through a rotten board and tumbled partway down the stairs? Had she paused to catch her breath partway up the stairs and leaned against a handrail that gave way? Cathy imagined a twisted, breathless old woman's body lying at the foot of the stairs, her face pushed into the floor, mouth open a crack, her tongue dry as sinew. What if she was still down there?

"*Maybe we can just send out, you know. Get a laundry service. I know a good Chinaman.*"

Angela stood at the top of the stairs.

"Don't be ridiculous," Cathy whispered.

"It's not ridiculous. He's very reasonable and he does good work."

"Not you. Me."

The entire basement consisted of a single small room with a dirt floor. One mud-splattered, west-facing window looked out over an unplanted flowerbed into the backyard, letting late afternoon light into the otherwise gloomy space. The only other source of light was a solitary naked bulb screwed into a ceiling socket in the centre of the room; she had found the switch at the top of the stairs. Like all the other bulbs she had discovered so far, this one too was of such low wattage that it barely had an effect on the small space it was supposed to illuminate.

"Think about that," Angela said, squinting up at the bulb. *"What was the cost to the pair of eyes over the years to work in such light, compared to the saving on electricity bills?"*

"And whose eyes paid the price?" Cathy whispered.

"Exactly!"

A pair of cement laundry tubs stood beneath the window. She recognized the faint blue of Father LeBlanc's room splattered against the tub surfaces.

Andy suddenly appeared sitting midway down on the stairs, chewing gum.

"Yuck. Do you realize how long those paint stains have been there, and that nothing has happened to that room since then?"

"God, it's like time has stopped in this place," Cathy muttered.

In front of the laundry tubs an ancient wringer washer stood on a large sheet of plywood that someone had once taken the trouble to paint grey. The washer was as ancient as the little fridge upstairs with its tiny clumsy icebox hanging down into its centre.

"Oh happy day! Good luck trying to figure this thing out."

Angela plucked the lid off the round machine. It was just like a lid from a giant soup pot. Cathy didn't have a clue how to operate the washer. She was used to a modern square machine with dials that you pulled and turned to the appropriate word. Hot. Cold. Rinse. Delicate. This washer had a dial that resembled an egg timer, a long handle on one side of its round body, and an electrical plug dangling over the edge into one of the laundry tubs. A short piece of black hose was screwed onto the sink faucet and hooked over the edge of the machine. She supposed that she had to fill the machine first, then plug it in and experiment with the switch and handle in order to get a load of laundry underway. She recalled seeing her grandmother's similar machine in operation, years ago, but couldn't remember ever seeing it started up. The interesting part had been watching the yards and yards of soapy wet laundry being fed into the rolling wringers and seeing them emerge all flattened on the other side before falling into the tub of rinse water.

Beneath the stairs, someone had stacked a few old bricks and planks together to make a small shelf. Cathy found several abandoned jars of homemade pickles there. Perhaps old Mrs. Dupuis couldn't manage the stairs during her last year and had been unable to retrieve them. But how would she have done the laundry then? Perhaps the housekeeper who preceded Mrs. Dupuis had filled the jars. How long ago would that have been? How many years had those pickles been sitting there, waiting?

She picked one of the jars up and held it up to the window. Huge open dill flowers, peeled white garlic cloves, and small round mustard seeds drifted slowly in the liquid when she moved the jar; the tightly packed pickles didn't budge. She knew what she was looking at. Her aunt used to make pickles. Cathy had seen the pickle jars all lined up, hot from the boiling canister. Her aunt pulled the big jars out of the water, the bath, she called it, with huge tongs.

"Don't touch, now. They're hot."

155

She'd asked for a pickle later, when she thought they were cool enough to eat. The adults in the room had looked at each other and burst into laughter.

"No, dear. They have to cure. Your uncle's going to put them under the porch for a couple of months."

So here they were. Someone's pickles, sitting under the steps, cured. She set one bottle on the stairs to take it up with her. It seemed a shame not to use them.

As it turned out, the laundry chute entered the basement ceiling right above the foot of the stairs. The laundry that she reluctantly sought was waiting on the bare dirt. A sordid pile of men's underwear and socks, sheets, and damp bath towels.

"Oh, God," she said quietly.

"Oh, I doubt He wants anything to do with this. Ew. Looks like this stuff belonged to John the Baptist." Angela carefully picked up a towel by its corner and held it up to the light. *"Great. Mouldy."*

Cathy clacked the barbecue tongs quietly. Angela let the towel drop back onto the heap.

"Just dump everything in together with a cup of soap and a cup of bleach. See what happens."

After a lucky fiddle with the side handle and a twist of the dial, the agitator jolted into motion. Cathy saw immediately why the machine stood on a piece of plywood; it wandered as it worked. Its four little wheels danced beneath the twisting motions of the agitator and the heavy load of wet laundry. Obviously the machine couldn't be left unattended, so she was now stuck in the basement.

"Oh happy, happy day. Last time I let you plan the itinerary."

The entire process of washing, wringing, rinsing and wringing, and rinsing and wringing again took more than two hours. She had to guess at everything. How many rinses before all the soapsuds go away? She remembered her mother saying something once about using cold water to get rid of

soap. So she rinsed in cold water. Again. And again. At the end
of that time, it still remained for the wet laundry to be carted
upstairs and hung up outside on the clothesline to dry. The
basement floor had turned to soapy mud where the machine
had overflowed or the water hose had slipped over the side of
the tub and poured overboard. Several articles of clothing and
bed linen had been accidentally dropped onto the dirt and
had had to be washed all over again. Cathy took a shortcut
and scrubbed two pillowcases by hand in the tubs and then
wrung them out herself rather than turn the machine on
again. By the time she returned upstairs to the kitchen for the
final time and filled the line outside with the last articles,
nearly emptying the old lard tin of its clothespins in the
process, she was exhausted. Her canvas running shoes were
soaking wet, as were the front of her clothes where she had
held wet sheets against herself to keep them from dragging on
the floor, and her arms trembled from the exertion of having
lifted the heavy, waterlogged loads.

At three-thirty, she made herself a sandwich and opened the
jar of dill pickles. Just as she had imagined, the aroma from the
open jar rose up like a genie and filled the entire kitchen. Had
someone once thumped across the old kitchen floor to the little
table carrying a bushel basket of muddy cucumbers still warm
from the sun? She cut one of the pickles into long thin strips to go
with her sandwich.

"*If only pickles could talk, huh,*" Angela said, biting down
with a loud crunch. The backs of Cathy's knees ached and the
sandwich plate shook in her hand. With yesterday's newspaper
tucked under her arm, she backed through the swinging dining room door and went to sit in the living room where she
could rest her feet up on the coffee table. She had just lowered
herself into the deep recesses of the ancient couch and had
folded the paper open to the entertainment page when she

heard someone come through the back door. Father Lauzon pushed aside the swinging door and crossed the dining room in four strides.

"What's this? What's this? Sitting down, reading the newspaper. What do you think you are? A lady of leisure? I'm paying you to work here, not to loaf and read newspapers."

Cathy shot up her balloon string, straight through the living room ceiling and the bedroom floors overhead, through the roof, up past the treetops and the church spire and the cross, high into the summer sky. There she looked out over the city. She could see the grid pattern made by the streets and the lake in the distance with the hazy white sky above it. Way below her, she heard her faint voice.

"I was just having my lunch, Father."

She saw herself staring at him, knowing.

"Lunch! You don't have to sit in the living room to have lunch. You can be doing something while you're having your sandwich. What about ironing, making the beds, vacuuming?"

Cathy rocked slightly in the breeze. The dull little churchyard was just a tiny green rectangle now, far, far below her, so small it was losing its colour. If she travelled much further away, it and the church and the rectory would all meld into a single dot and then vanish.

"It's all done, Father. I'm just waiting for the clothes on the line to dry."

"Well you should find something to do while you're waiting. That's what you're being paid for. You can read the newspaper on your own time. If I ask your mother if she puts up with this kind of work at home, I'll bet I know what the answer will be. And I'm sure you wouldn't like it if she found out about this, either, would you? Hop to it, young lady."

"Hop these, Lord Splattersheets," Angela said, holding both middle fingers aloft.

Back in the kitchen, standing before the wide open fridge door, distractedly feeding herself her sandwich with one hand, her cheeks flaming red, Cathy emptied the icebox of its contents, preparing to defrost it. She didn't much care that she didn't know how to do it. She'd just take everything out of the freezer and turn the whole fridge off. If food went bad, it went bad.

From up in the sky, she could see herself depositing everything with a loud smack on the countertop. If there were glass shards in the leftovers, it would serve the priests right.

CHAPTER 11

Gerald Mugan was having one of the best summers in years. The weather was fine, days were long and sunny, not too hot, evenings were cool, good for sleeping. His garden was doing well. He'd been spending some delightfully peaceful mornings working in it, weeding and watering the rows of green onions, tomatoes, cucumbers, peppers, carrots, and a few squash for the fall.

For nearly a month now a quiet and even-tempered Adele had been spending her evenings alone out on the swing. He'd find her there when he came home from work, even on his late nights. He'd bring her a plate of takeout potato salad, barbecued chicken, and a sourdough roll and they'd sit together on the swing having a light conversation about changing the wallpaper in one of the rooms, about moving a certain shrub to a better location. He ate quietly, listening and nodding. It had been a long time since there'd been such a good spell.

What it was, exactly, that facilitated a good spell was a mystery. He'd thought letting Cathy go to the St. Amand cottage last year had been a good idea. But he'd been kept up every night listening to Adele ranting about what a foolish tart Eva St. Amand was. So this summer he'd thought it best if Cathy stayed home. But then, out of the blue, this rectory situation cropped up, with Adele as the architect. It seemed like a safe, sensible place for Cathy. She was learning a few useful things. Just last week she'd asked him to teach her how to make peanut butter cookies. The job kept her occupied for ten and twelve hours a day. Her mother was quiet. And he was having a peaceful summer.

The trick would be to preserve the peace once school started. Getting Cathy on a school team of some sort and out of the house as much as possible would be the perfect solution. It annoyed him that she never showed any interest in joining things at school. All she seemed to want to do was come home and hole up in her room.

Not Richard, though. His room was for sleeping only. Gerald couldn't have said what kind of summer his son was having. Most mornings it was one o'clock before Richard came in, and by then Gerald was long since in bed. He knew Richard played late-night hockey in the winter months, but what he did in the summer wasn't too clear.

Richard's regrettable distance bothered Gerald. His son behaved like a boarder in his own home, privately coming and going, often offering only the barest of hellos and goodbyes. He never asked for the car, and nobody ever pulled into the drive and honked for him. He preferred walking. He held down his job and was impervious to offers of money. Gerald couldn't even give him twenty dollars once in a while. "No thanks, I'm fine," was the usual response. And the truth of the matter was, he was fine. As far as Gerald knew, he spent a bit of pocket money at the Rootbeer Palace with his friends and some on hockey expenses, but otherwise he added to his savings account every week. But in the competence of the son, Gerald felt a failing in the father. Still, rather than intrude, he thought it best just to wait and watch. Something would change eventually.

★ ★ ★

Save for the suspicions of a stranger, no one knew how much Richard Mugan thought about change. Ever since Grade 10 geography class and the introduction to maps, time zones, and the images of foreign cultures, change had fascinated him. He wanted to change his life by stepping out of it and leaving it behind. "Go west, young man," he'd joke with himself after work. And walking west he'd traverse the distance from the receiving bay at the back of Robinson's Grocery to the nearest curb at the Rootbeer Palace in exactly four and a half minutes. Striking out in the opposite direction, he would reach Routledge's Stationery in seven minutes.

At eighteen, he had grown to nearly six feet, but, like his father, he was underweight. His pale white skin seemed to lie directly over top of his long straight bones and slender muscles without allowing room for a single molecule of fatty tissue. With his straight rusty hair and fair Anglo colouring, he'd likely look like a boy all his life so long as his weight didn't change. From the back, people would never know he wasn't a lanky teen. It wouldn't be until he turned around to face them that they'd realize that he was a man of thirty, forty, or fifty.

His legs were strong from years of playing hockey, and his reflexes were quick for the same reason. At work, he was a minor celebrity for his quirky ability to stick out a hand or foot and retrieve, in mid-fall, an article that someone else had dropped. On his breaks, he would entertain his co-workers in the stockroom by wearing a purple cabbage leaf for a hat and juggling pieces of fruit that were on their way out to the display tables, without making even the slightest bruise on their surfaces. He could also take a green pepper and bounce it off several parts of his body, his bent elbows or his chin, before artfully trapping it behind his bent knee. Even Mr. Robinson was intrigued, stopping beside him one morning, picking up his own pepper, and asking, "How's that again?"

He never succumbed to the tedium of his job. Instead, he worked at his tasks every day as if it mattered to him to get everything right. And yet, he was a bright kid, and his co-workers and employer knew it wasn't the type of job he would have for the rest of his life. Eventually he would move on. Until then, though, by doing his job well, he gained his freedom and walked away at nine o'clock to get a cold root beer and maybe some onion rings and think about change.

Old Walter Routledge didn't know Richard by name. In fact, he'd never seen him before he started regularly stopping in at the stationery store a few months ago. Most of his other regular customers were his colleagues, local shopkeepers looking for cash register tapes and price stickers, or schoolteachers wanting pads of lined paper and boxes of pencils. This young fellow, though, liked to look at maps. He stood in front of the display, quietly pulling down maps that caught his attention, opening them and carefully folding them back upon themselves so he could study particular sections of them. He'd stand there for fifteen, twenty minutes sometimes, tracing little lines from one side of a page to the other with his finger.

Walter, pale as a root and stiffened by arthritis, stayed on his stool by the cash register looking out the large plate glass windows. He'd learned very quickly that this was not a boy that he had to worry about. He wasn't about to slip anything in his pocket and walk out. It was unusual enough to have a young man this age even enter the store, let alone frequent it. A young, serious lad with an interest in maps was a rarity. Walter took it as a positive sign.

Thus far the boy had bought maps of Canada, the eastern seaboard in the United States, Alaska, New Mexico, Mexico, Argentina, and New Zealand. Several of them had had to be ordered specially. The latest request was for Australia. Walter had taken a quick look at it when it arrived, poring over the strange names, the topographical markings, wondering what it was that interested the boy. Lots, obviously. Because even if there was a special order waiting for him at the counter, he still went over to the display to consider what was there.

"Big world out there," Richard finally said one day, smiling, taking the map of Australia from Walter's hand and tucking it into a little green canvas knapsack.

"Oh, for sure, son. For sure."

"See you again, then," he said.

Walter hoped so.

★ ★ ★

July slipped into August. Cathy couldn't believe that she had been at the rectory a month already. Displays of school supplies began appearing in store windows along her bus routes, nudging her thoughts towards September. Waiting for the bus outside of the church in the evenings she noticed a faint spicy tang in the air, a harbinger of the smoky, woodsy, vegetable-matter smell that she associated with autumn. The days, though, continued on, warm and humid, the afternoon breezes thick with pollen, making her drowsy and unconcerned with the passage of time.

The priests still had not found a permanent replacement for Mrs. Dupuis. Cathy imagined them fumbling around in the dreary kitchen in the winter, standing at the counters at seven o'clock at night, feeding ravenously on toast and peanut butter, gulping milk straight out of bottles. If it came to that, she imagined the impeccably mannered Father Martin would starve.

Once a week, letters from Janet, with their envelopes ruptured, waited in the centre of the breakfast table for Cathy.

"That mess there on the table is yours, missy. More nonsense from that lie-about friend of yours."

"I thought it was against the law to open other people's mail," Cathy complained in a barely audible voice one evening. Her mother was around the corner, wiping off the kitchen counter. Angela, sitting on the edge of the table swinging her legs, winced and covered her ears.

"God, you take chances."

"The law? That's for adults out in the real world. Around here, *I* am the law."

"Well law-dee-daw!" Angela sang, hopping down off the table, grabbing the letter, and heading upstairs.

Cathy pored over the letters in her room. Janet chattered from her beach-and-bonfire world about all of the activities on the lake; about how her water-skiing was really progressing this summer; about how her brother could swim clean across to the beach on the other side to visit his friends; about a storm last weekend that had loosened old Mr. and Mrs. McKenzie's canoe from next door, and how she had gone out the next morning to retrieve it for them after her father spotted it through his binoculars, resting in the reeds in the marsh at the south end of the lake. She urged Cathy to write back and let her know when she could take a week off and come up for a visit. Her father was still working in the city during the week and would be only too glad to pick her up on a Friday evening and take her up.

"What are you going to do," Adele exploded when Cathy finally asked permission to go, "just walk out on the priests and leave them stranded? You have a job to do. You're not a kid any more. All that girl is doing up there is lying around in a bikini all summer, not learning any responsibility. Besides, I don't trust that flighty mother of hers. She'll turn her head and the two of you will be off in a boat somewhere with boys. No siree. My father sent all of us out to work when we were your age and you're no different."

"But it would only be for one week. It would just be a little vacation."

Andy sat on the beach, digging in the sand, listening.

"Kids your age don't need vacations. I never had one when I was your age."

Angela, squinting against the sun, stepped closer to Cathy. *"Never mind. Come to us."*

Cathy grew bold and sent the rectory address to Janet, asking her to send mail directly there until the third week in August. After that she didn't want to receive any more mail in case it had to be forwarded to her house after she had finished working at the rectory. She explained that she couldn't leave the priests stranded and therefore couldn't accept the invitation this year, much as she would have liked to. Eva tucked a pale yellow single-page note into Janet's next letter, expressing regret at not being able to have Cathy as a guest and including a quick-bake recipe for a corn and tomato casserole. After gently sniffing the paper and once again admiring the lovely scoops and twirls of the handwriting, Cathy tucked this note next to the other in her apron pocket.

★ ★ ★

Despite the awfulness of doing grown men's sweaty laundry in the creepy basement, the repugnant task of fishing dirty underwear from beneath beds, the tedium of making beds, vacuuming a cheerless living room, and doing dishes three times a day, Cathy was having fun cooking. She could roast a chicken now. After spotting a mound of dark steaming things in the cavity of her first attempt, she'd learned to look inside beforehand and remove whatever it was that was in there.

"Giblets, maybe?" she whispered to Angela.

"Yup."

"I've heard of giblets. But that's with turkeys, isn't it?"

"What? You think chickens don't have innards?"

"Oh!"

Cathy hesitated. Angela jerked her thumb towards the garbage.

Cathy read about flour's usefulness. It thickened anything. If you mixed it with the drippings in the roasting pan that was how you got gravy. Although hers wasn't quite right. She had to mix it really hard and fast and then put it out on the table right away so it wouldn't separate and have grease floating on top. She'd been looking in the book but hadn't found out yet how to get the grease to stay inside the gravy.

She made peanut butter cookies once a week and served them with applesauce.

"Oh," her father had exclaimed when she asked him how to make them. "One of the Fathers has a sweet tooth, eh?"

The door to the basement had been open one evening and she found him down there emptying two brown paper grocery bags, putting things away into the cupboards.

"Well now, I can show you as long as everything else's taken care of," he said, tilting his head toward the stairs. "Is all your homework done and anything else that you're responsible for?"

"Uh-huh."

"You're sure? There isn't going to be some sort of incident with you down here?"

"No."

"Okay then..."

He'd been delighted to teach her. He cautioned her about creaming the butter with the sugar properly, making sure everything was evenly distributed. The cookies were all dropped onto the shiny silver cookie trays and she was just pressing a fork into the dough when the door at the top of the stairs suddenly slammed shut. Her father's blue eyes filled with panic.

"Better get upstairs," he whispered, taking the fork away from her. "I'll just stay down here while they're in the oven and then bring them up for everyone to enjoy. You've covered all the basics."

Her mother was out on the swing by the time she got upstairs. There wasn't going to be anything else this time. Just the slammed door. Later she even accepted a small plate of cookies to go with her tea. But once a week, every time her fork descended into the soft dough at the rectory, Cathy heard a door slam.

★ ★ ★

Early in August, Father LeBlanc announced that he would be going to his brother's cottage for a week. The announcement gave Cathy an idea. The August issue of a women's magazine ran a feature on *Celebrity Summer Entertaining* and included a menu plan of Angela Gordon's which featured cold cherry soup, fresh peach crepes, three-melon salad, and spiced iced tea. She'd plan a special going-away dinner for him.

Thus far, the priests seemed genuinely pleased with her cooking, although, ever since she had served them the strawberry-apple pie that her mother had made for them, they asked repeatedly if they were being served food that was sent from home. It happened the first time she brought a warm apple crisp to the table. Father Lauzon roared with approval.

"Fantastic. Your mother made something for us again."

"No, Father. I made it."

"You? My stars, you're going to make some man a good wife."

For the going-away meal, Cathy had to improvise slightly. She knew of only two kinds of melons, so she made a salad of cantaloupe and watermelon and added sliced apples and green grapes to it. The lack of a crepe pan actually proved to be a boon because she was not entirely sure how to make a crepe anyway. She opted for thin ordinary pancakes with the hot peach sauce drizzled over them rather than wrapped in the crepe itself. The same cupboard that had once yielded up the unused water glasses harboured an old gravy boat which, after another bit of artifice with a napkin and a bread and butter plate, was pressed into service as a hot sauce serving unit.

She made the spiced tea right after lunch on the Friday before Father LeBlanc's departure. It was only ordinary tea rather than one of the English ones recommended in the magazine, and the spices were from small tins rather than freshly ground, but she thought the pitcher of burnished liquid looked appealing once she added the ice cubes and lemon slices. She planned to take the pitcher to the table on a tray surrounded by the water glasses.

The only real challenge was the cold cherry soup. The magazine was spread out on the counter, weighed down by cans of cherries. Angela hovered nearby, waving off Cathy's misgivings with a cavalier swat of her hand. She'd made it a thousand times. Nothing could go wrong.

By the time Cathy put the finished soup in the fridge to chill, the kitchen was littered end to end with debris. She regretted the mess that she now had to clean up, but to her relief the soup tasted fine.

She went into the dining room and stood in front of the table, wondering what she could do tonight to make it look special. She considered borrowing a few votive candles from the church.

"Nice try, dear. As if they won't know where you got them!"

After a moment's further pondering, she knew what she would do and set out for the backyard to cut a bunch of Queen Anne's lace.

★ ★ ★

That afternoon, Gerry LeBlanc brought home a dozen cobs of
the first crop of early corn. He found a huge pot under the
kitchen sink to boil them in and set about shucking them on the
kitchen table. While he worked, stripping off the damp green
husks, his mouth watered in anticipation. The husks piled up
precariously on the tabletop before slipping off onto the chair
and then finally to the floor. The stringy corn silk clung to the
edges of the table and to his hands and clothes; much of it fell
to the floor and was ground beneath his work boots as he
walked back and forth between the table and the stove to
deposit the yellow cobs in the pot.

Cathy had not noticed him arrive, and he had not seen her
in the far corner of the yard. When she returned to the kitchen,
happy with her plan to cut the flower heads from their stems and
ring the salad bowl with them, she encountered him standing in
the middle of the room hugging a pile of corn to his chest. A
large pot of water boiled on top of the stove, sending billowing
clouds of steam into the air.

He grinned at her as she entered.

"I got this corn here given to me. Just picked this afternoon.
It has to be cooked up right away while it's still fresh. We can
just have it with the rest of the dinner."

Cathy's eyes wandered to the cluttered table surface that she
needed to prepare the pancake batter, to the corn silk all over
her nice clean floor, to his dirty shirt and the corn. Behind him
the water on the stove roared.

"What's the matter? Don't you know how to cook corn?"

"Yes, Father. I just wish I had known ahead of time, that's all."

"Corn goes with anything. What are you making?"

The answer felt like the most foolish thing she had ever said
in her life. She turned away from him.

"Peach pancakes."

He stepped up to the boiling pot and added more corn.

"Naw. We don't want pancakes. They're for breakfast. Haven't you got some pork chops or something that you can fry up to go with the corn?"

There were pork chops in the fridge, frozen solid in the freezer compartment, along with ground beef she was saving for next week's meals. "Nothing's defrosted, Father."

He looked annoyed.

"Well, make something to go with this for the others. I can just fill up on corn. There's plenty of it here for the three of us. Just make them anything. Not pancakes."

He brushed his hands clean of corn silk over the mess on the table.

"I cleaned them all. This stuff here is just garbage. They should boil in about twenty minutes." He waved his hand at the debris on the table and then plunged through the swinging door and was gone, his boots trailing corn silk.

★ ★ ★

She stood in the gloom of the empty late afternoon, stirring mayonnaise into chopped eggs for sandwiches, the only thing she could think of that would fill the priests up. She passed the aperitif cold cherry soup off as dessert, telling them it was a Norwegian pudding. By the time she brought the iced tea to the table, the ice cubes had melted and the apples in the fruit salad had turned brown.

True to his word, Father LeBlanc ate only corn. There were five stripped cobs piled on his plate when she went to clear the table. Neither he nor Father Lauzon had touched their cold cherry soup. Only Father Martin had eaten his. It took her an extra hour to finish up, and then she rode home on the bus in solitude. Angela and Andy were waiting for her outside of Gibson's, standing in the middle of a sunlit sand trail.

"Come on and spend the rest of your summer with us." Angela held out her arm.

"Yeah. California's great this time of the year." Andy, her blonde hair in braids, twirled around kicking up white sand with her tanned bare feet.

Cathy looked away. What if Father Lauzon called her mother?

"Flea, you tried to do something nice. Next time you'll know to add the ice cubes at the last minute. A little bit of fancy stuff now and again is good for the soul."

Good for the soul? she imagined her mother shrieking.

Andy stopped twirling and stepped closer to Angela. The evening sun stood behind them, rimming them in gold light against a pale turquoise sky.

What if the phone was ringing right at this moment? What if she walked right into a thunderstorm? Did she understand what her responsibilities were? Huh? Missy? Because if she didn't, the hairbrush could explain them to her.

The sand trail and her companions vanished. Cathy stared at herself in the pale turquoise windows of Gibson's.

Jerome Martin was beginning to think that God knew who he was after all. At ten-thirty on a Tuesday evening, he stood in his darkened room, leaning against his windowsill, enjoying the faint bit of breeze passing over his naked body. Lately, he'd been coming to bed willingly. He could fall asleep fairly soon after lying down, and some nights he slept right through till morning. He saw now that he hadn't lost his vocation. The horrible dream and the insomnia had just been a test. And he must have passed the test, because God had given him two miracles as rewards: a beautiful green outdoor grotto, right in his own yard, and a wonderful new young housekeeper.

On the few nights now when he did lie awake in the heat, he thought about her, the way she said, "Yes, Father," so sweetly, and "What would you like, Father?" It was obvious God was working through this fresh young girl with coal black hair and a cheerful eagerness to please. It had been so long since anything appetizing had been put before him. Now, though, every day she set down delights on a snowy white tablecloth before him. At three in the morning, rather than lying in despair on his fatigued old mattress, he thought about what his tongue might slide into later. Steaming dinner rolls split wide open, begging to be filled with yellow butter. Mounds of soft mashed potatoes. The thickened salted juices of a chicken stew. Sweet baked apples with darkened cinnamon interiors. Deep corridors that his tongue could slowly explore. He loved the exotic sweetness of brown sugar married to a spice, the pleasant waking shock of it. Life. Little pungent bits of it could be had in a teaspoon. *This* is what he'd been missing. God did work in mysterious ways, indeed.

* * *

The terrible phone call from Father Lauzon never came. Adele's angry footsteps didn't come pounding up the stairs. She never learned about the failed going-away dinner for Father LeBlanc. But Cathy spoke firmly to her reflection in her dresser mirror that night before turning out the light.

"You've got to stop this. Once and for all."

Back at the rectory on Monday, she served small pieces of watermelon with the morning's eggs and toast to try to get rid of the rest of it. Oddly, Father Martin sent his plate back into the kitchen with the watermelon slice intact. It was the only indication she'd ever had from him of a particular dislike. Apparently Father Lauzon liked watermelon, though. She found his empty rinds resting across his finished plate when she cleared the table.

She listened to her transistor radio all day now, singing along under her breath to each of the songs, making herself memorize all the words. She saw Angela sitting at her Malibu kitchen table, rooting through a bowl of grapes, watching her. Sometimes she knew she was standing in a corner behind her, waiting. But Cathy wouldn't turn around.

* * *

With the departure of Gerry for his brother's cottage, the entire responsibility for hospital visitations fell to Jerome. Because of his work schedule at the factory, Gerry usually took only evening and weekend visits. But for the week that he was away, Jerome happily assumed them all. He went to the hospital early and remained there most of the day. Anything was better than sitting in his dreary rectory office, bored to the bone, pretending to design a new catechism curriculum for the schools.

Ralph always wanted to know who was in the hospital.

"Anyone I know?" he'd ask.

The parish was large, but it was old and so were its parishioners. There were a few young families. But they were in the minority. They came from the new residential districts that were just developing nearby. It would take a generation before enough of these families developed into an established new core of parishioners. In the meantime, the mainstay of St. Alphonsis was dying out. In the middle of mass, when Ralph turned to face the congregation, a sea of bobbing white heads wearing flashing circles of glass stared back at him. A sprinkling of little old women, bundled in sweaters all summer. All of them blinking towards heaven, worried that their lifetime store of prayers might still fall short of ensuring salvation. Here and there he'd spot a solitary cap, a bowed bald head. World War I veterans. Those were the ones he liked to visit in the hospital.

Sick parishioners were always a boon to Jerome, though, because they put order into his day. When someone was hospitalized, he suddenly knew exactly where he should go, during which set hours, and what he should be doing. Visiting was more therapeutic for him than any other of his parish duties; it enlivened him, gave him a purpose, and filled the hours.

In the hospital environments, Jerome found it easy to slip out of himself. He noticed that his black suit and collar garnered as much respect for him in the corridors as the white lab coats and OR greens did for the doctors and nurses. He felt dignified. He strolled the halls, making eye contact, nodding.

During these outings he metamorphosed into a happy man. All he wanted, he told God in his private prayers, was to have something meaningful to do. While he prayed with sick parishioners, his mind guiltily mingled the patient's wish for recovery with his own selfish wish to continue to have a reason to come to the hospital, for there to be organization and purpose to his day.

"You must be patient," he found himself telling them. "God works at His own speed. Don't be in such a rush to outdo Him."

When his day ended, he was anxious to go home and see what waited on the dining room table for dinner.

★ ★ ★

While Father Martin was away visiting the hospitals one afternoon, Cathy took a load of freshly folded linen upstairs to put it in its usual place in the hall closet. Two days before, while she had been stripping the bed in Father Lauzon's room, she'd heard a muffled sound coming from the hall. It was difficult to tell whether the noise was stifled choking or low-pitched quiet coughing. The sound ceased when she stepped into the hall, starting up again only when she retreated into Father Lauzon's room. At the time, the door to Father Martin's room had been closed and she eventually assumed that he was behind it, praying, perhaps, saying his breviary, coughing and attempting to remain unnoticed.

Now, as she stood in the gloomy hallway with an armload of folded towels, she saw that his door was closed again, yet she was absolutely certain that he was not in the rectory. He had passed through the kitchen and spoken to her on his way out.

Something about the orientation of the sound from two days ago came back to her, something that had not been right but that she had ignored at the time. She stared hard at the closed bedroom door, listening to the memory of that sound. If he was not in his room now, it was possible that he hadn't been in his room two days ago. Just because his door was closed did not mean that he was behind it. So where else could he have been? Out, certainly. But what if he wasn't? What if he'd been right here in the rectory all the time?

"Mysterious, huh?"

Angela was back.

"Let's see here…"

There were six doors in the hallway: the bathroom door at the head of the stairs, one for each of three bedrooms, the door to the linen closet, and the one other door that had been locked when she had tried it. She assumed that it was a closet with church paraphernalia in it; she imagined cases of unconsecrated wine or cardboard boxes of hosts lying behind the door.

While she considered the locked door further, it occurred to her that it lay exactly the same distance from the door to Father Lauzon's bedroom as the door to Father Martin's room did. Sound travelling from behind either door had the same distance to travel to reach her ears in Father Lauzon's room. What if she had wrongly assumed the direction of the sound, encouraged by the sight of the closed bedroom door? What if the bedroom had been as empty then as it was now? She stared at the mysterious closet door. Then she stepped towards it and turned the knob; the door swung out towards her and a wall of suffocating heat hit her.

The baking hot air behind the door smelled like wood. Her hand found a light switch on the wall. Now she had accounted for all the doors. This wasn't a closet. She was looking up a steep, narrow wooden staircase leading into the inferno of an unfinished attic. And someone's private hell sat glaring from the fourth step: a plaster bust of the Virgin Mary staring out of dead blue eyes and a half-empty quart of whiskey. *Click* ... and the scent of her father's Christmas cakes, too.

That's what she'd smelled. The sweet strong smell that she'd noticed when she first met Father Martin. He hadn't had wine at the hospital that morning while baptizing a sick baby. He hadn't been at the hospital at all. He'd been right here, behind this door. Drinking. The smell had been whiskey. And Father Lauzon had lied to her.

She picked up the bust of the Virgin and passed her hand along the truncated edge of the breastless blue mantle. The paint was worn away along this edge. Is that what he did, then? Sat in here, in the dark so a crack of light didn't shine out from beneath the door, consoling himself with alcohol and a bloodless plaster companion? Drinking, sweating in the heat, stroking the smooth surface of this statue, his large roving fingers searching along plaster crevices, hoping to what? Miraculously slip up under the sculpted robes of the Mother of God?

Her mother was coming. Pounding.

What the hell do you think you're doing in here, young lady?

"You know," said Angela, stepping past her and sitting down on one of the stairs, "*I don't get self-denial. I mean, look at how bleak this place is.*" She elbowed Cathy aside so she could stretch forward and grab the doorknob. Then she patted the stair. "*Sit. And get the light, will you? Let's just see how miserable this is.*"

The door closed, Cathy sank onto the stair, snapped out the light, and entered Father Martin's world. Not a hairline of light penetrated the darkness. She could not see her lap, her shoes, her hands held out in front of her face, the back of the door that she had just closed. It was like being shut up in an oven.

"*Welcome to the stairway to heaven.*"

Cathy pictured clumsy, staring Father Martin folded into this narrow space, chewing his lips in the dark and fouling the air with his perspiration.

"I mean, have a drink with dinner once in a while, for Pete's sake. Jesus did. Ew! Probably not this stuff, though," Angela said, unscrewing the bottle cap, sniffing the contents, and screwing the cap back into place. *"Say, there's a thought. Think about the repercussions if Jesus had turned water into whiskey instead of wine, huh? The Bible would be full of drunks."*

Sweat bloomed on Cathy's forehead and upper lip. The air was hotter than anything she had ever experienced. She wondered if the entire attic could spontaneously combust.

"And if he wants a lady friend, then he should just get one and forget about being a priest. It's dead easy."

Cathy's head was beginning to swirl. She was going to faint. One of the priests would come home and find her spilled out into the hall, unconscious, with the door open behind her. She felt for and found the key resting in the lock on the inside of the door. He must have been distracted and forgotten to take it with him to lock the door from the hall side. She stood up. Angela kicked the door open.

"Sorry, flea, I got carried away. Go."

Cathy stumbled out into the coolness of the hall and stood, bent over, hands on her knees, panting. After a minute, she reached around behind herself and quietly pushed the door closed with one finger. *Click.*

"So then. Bit more of an adventure than we thought, this place, isn't it?"

Sitting in the silent rectory the next afternoon, absently examining the grease splotches on the unpainted kitchen walls, Cathy struggled with what she knew. Far away in her mind she could hear feet pounding.

And what are you doing opening doors that you have no business opening, anyway, missy? Huh?

Angela sat cross-legged on the counter behind her, filing her nails.

"The thing is to look at what we've got. There's the drinking and the statue thing — I don't know what to call that. Just plain loneliness, it seems to me. And then there's the fact that both these things are a secret. Except not anymore. Question is, who else knows? Father Lauzon because he lied to you about the sick baby at the hospital that morning, and my guess would be that Father Underpants at least suspects something. So now we have to ask, do we tell anyone, and if so, who and why?"

While her thoughts whirled, Cathy's hand roamed over the cool dull plaster, stopping now and again to pick at a minute bit of dried splatter. Then it moved on, circling aimlessly.

"Seems to me the best course of action is to pretend we don't know a thing. We're not the guy's keepers. And besides, we're leaving here in a few weeks anyway, right?"

"Trouble is, does it get any worse?"

"Yeah. Does he get up to any other weirdness, you mean? Good point."

"Right. And it's hard not to let on."

"Yeah … but…"

Suddenly Angela's bracelets jangled and her feet landed with a thump on the linoleum.

"Oh … you know what? You're brilliant."

She arrived at Cathy's side and began running her hand over the plaster too.

"I don't know why I didn't think of this before. A good diversion will do it."

With her eyes slightly narrowed, Cathy glanced around the room, sizing up all the walls.

"It'll divert you, him, the other two, me. It's perfect."

"Yellow."

"Yes."

That night at dinner, while the remaining two priests bent over their meal of meatloaf and scalloped potatoes, Cathy spoke to Father Lauzon.

"Father, the kitchen needs painting. The walls in there are bare plaster and they have at least thirty years' worth of grease and dirt worn into them. I can't scrub them any cleaner than they are and they still look dirty. Your new housekeeper is likely to be an older woman and she won't be able to clean them even as well as I have."

Ralph Lauzon put his fork down and rocked his chair back onto its hind legs, his businessman's mind engaged.

"The kitchen needs painting?"

"Yes, Father."

She knew that this appointment must have been a comedown for him. St. Mary, Star of the Sea, had a beautiful, modern rectory with a lovely patio that was screened for privacy with rose-covered trellises.

"And who would do this kitchen painting?"

"I would, Father."

"You would? You know how to paint?"

"Yes, Father. My mother does it all the time. I've watched her for years. She'll tell me how to do it."

Father Martin had completely ground to a halt and was watching his colleague's face intently. Ralph rocked back and forth, calculating, absently taking in another mouthful of meatloaf.

"By the way, this meatloaf's much better."

"Thank you, Father."

"The first one was mighty odd."

"Sorry, Father."

"How much paint will you need and how much will it cost? This is not a rich parish like yours back home, you know."

She was ready with information in a flyer that had come in the newspaper just that afternoon.

"There's a sale on, Father. Buy one, get the next one for half-price. It will take two gallons for two coats."

"Two coats? You think it needs two coats?"

"Yes, Father. The walls have never been painted before. The first coat will just barely cover the dirt. The colour won't show much until after the second coat."

He let himself down from his rocking position and shovelled his fork under half an inch of potatoes.

"You're sure you can manage to paint and still keep up with the rest of your work? I don't want to come home and find that there isn't a meal on the table because the cook's up a ladder somewhere."

He wore a mock serious face and winked across the table to Father Martin. Father Martin was waiting, his large clumsy hands folded in his lap.

"No, Father, I can do both things. I'll just take my time with the painting and get a little bit done every day until it's finished."

"Let me think about it."

She returned to the kitchen. Angela and Andy were waiting, sitting on the counters swinging their legs.

"Good work. When do we start?"

"He said he wanted to think about it."

"Yes, but we all know what that means. He'd have said no right away if it was out of the question."

"We'll see," she whispered, taking dessert bowls out of the cupboard.

"We should try for a contrasting trim, too. White would be nice. And then see if we can talk him into a couple of light fixtures to cover these bare bulbs."

"How about a spice rack?" Andy was lounging at the little table, playing with strings of red licorice. *"There's too much bare wall."*

"Well, first we need a couple of towel racks mounted on the wall or the side of the cupboard. Someplace out in the open so things will dry," said Angela, chewing the inside of her cheek thoughtfully.

"How about a rug, too?" Andy asked. *"There's too much bare floor."*

"Too much daydreaming."

Cathy put leftover apple crisp in the oven to warm. Angela began running hot water and noisily gathering dishes from the counters.

"If we get this mess cleared up quickly, we'll have time to stop off at the shopping plaza on the way home. Oh ... all those colours to choose from."

"He said he wanted to think about it. And I thought we said yellow already?"

"You know this is going to make you famous! By the time you're my age, people from all over North America will be clamouring for your services. Nobody else does this work. Think about how many dreary rectories there are in the world. And nobody else has noticed."

Andy was holding the last piece of licorice under her nose like a handlebar moustache.

"You know that bright lemon yellow in my room? It goes right through the walls. Ceilings too. It will light up this whole place. You watch."

Angela turned off the tap and swished her hand around in the mound of soap bubbles.

"Yeah, by the time we're through with this place, Father Confusion won't know where he is."

Andy's eyebrows shot up and she looked sideways at her mother.

"You think he knows now?"

Cathy set the warm apple crisp on a potholder in the centre of the table. She was regretting not having the foresight to keep vanilla ice cream on hand to serve with it, when Father Lauzon folded up the advertising flyer and spoke.

"Well, Miss Michelangelo, Michaela Angelina, Father Martin's going to pick up your paint for you on his way back from his errands tomorrow afternoon. He'll get you two gallons of this extra super special goof-proof stuff that you want here."

He tossed the advertising flyer over to Jerome and then turned to her wearing a big smile.

"Oh…," she said softly, raising an eyebrow and turning up the corners of her mouth. "Thank you, Father."

She finished the dishes alone, and then rode home with her head resting against the bus window.

August was slipping by uneventfully when a routine lunchtime news broadcast suddenly placed a cold hand on Adele's heart. Immediately she took to her bed. The sudden onset of premature labour was utterly unexpected; she hadn't even imagined such a thing, and yet, given the history, she should have known this might happen. But the First Lady had told Adele everything that she was doing, how she had been so careful, eating well, getting plenty of rest, not doing any excessive bending or lifting anything heavy. Her medical care was the best, the most sophisticated care in the world. How could this happen?

Adele lay in her bed, praying. She could take this burden, God. Let it pass from her friend to her. No need to bother that good family. She could cope with this. Let her have the discomfort, the pain. Give her whatever was needed, a tumour, a hemorrhage, she could bear it. She herself had never lost a child. This woman had lost several. Spread the sorrow around a little, God. She would be glad to do this for her friend.

Adele thought about what the reactions of her family would be if it were her lying there with a blue, veiny, undersized fetus struggling out of her body. Would Gerald call an ambulance, would he take her to the hospital himself? She caressed her stomach. How could they possibly relate to any of this? What did they know about your insides opening up like a mysterious mountain and yielding up a part of yourself that was as wet and moving as any other interior organ, and then having it lie against your skin, slick and slimy and demanding. What could they possibly understand about that? And what would the doctors do to save her? What if they couldn't?

She let her eyes open only the merest of slits so she could see a bit of light through her lashes. Languishing, viewing the disappearing light of the world through the weak drooping eyelids of a dying person, she slowed her breathing to see what it would be like barely having the strength to draw air. She made a doctor tell her family how he had never seen anything like it, how she was brave, how selflessly she had given of herself, all for the baby to survive. She made a baby cry in the next room, weak and helpless. Then she stopped her breathing, relaxed all her muscles so her head lolled to one side on the pillow and her eyes squeezed out the last bit of light. Dead in childbirth, she lay there for several minutes, savouring her performance. She liked it so much that she sat up and began all over again at the beginning. After several performances, she skipped off down the hall to gather supplies.

Cathy found her later that evening, propped up against pillows with a heating pad moulded around her abdomen. She entered the room warily, having been commanded to do so by an artificially weak voice. She noted the small touches of artifice, the hanky draped over the bedside lamp, the glass tumbler, the pitcher of ice water, bottles of pills on a tray — an actual silver tray unearthed from a box of old unused wedding presents in the front hall closet — resting officiously on the night table. She stood at a safe distance at the foot of the bed, trying not to notice too much. Adele's hand wandered up to her throat.

"I'm not feeling well. I have indigestion. Is your brother home?"

Cathy knew that Richard already thought her recent behaviour was odder than normal. Her hands constantly roamed over her abdomen; she asked people to pick up things she had dropped; she held cushions on her shoulder, patted them and rubbed her cheek against them affectionately.

"Didn't get back to the spaceship in time," he'd muttered one night.

Cathy could hear the television from where she stood. Although she had not seen him yet, she assumed that he was in the house, somewhere.

"I think he's in the living room."

"Have you eaten yet?"

"No. I just got in."

"Well then hurry and get yourself something because we're going to say the rosary."

The look on Cathy's face must have betrayed her. Adele placed her hand tenderly over her abdomen and raised her voice.

"None of your guff, missy. The President and his wife need our prayers tonight. Didn't you hear the news?"

Cathy looked at the carpet.

"The President's wife is in the hospital. Her pregnancy is not going well. She might be delivering by Caesarean section right at this very moment. The baby is two months premature. The least we can do is pray for them. That poor man doesn't deserve this. He's had enough tragedy in his young life."

Cathy swallowed carefully.

"Now, you go and get yourself something to eat and you be ready to say the rosary in five minutes, do you hear? Five minutes! And tell your brother that he can forget about hockey or whatever he has planned for tonight. I'm his mother and his friends don't run the show in this house every night."

★ ★ ★

Hail Mary full of grace,
The Lord is with thee.

They knelt, the three of them, on the dining room floor in the dark. Richard had refused at first, saying, "The hell I have to," when Cathy found him watching television and told him he had to say the rosary with them. He only relented when Cathy pulled at his shirt sleeve, begging him not to start a fight and leave because then she would be alone in the house with her mother.

"Please, Richard. You don't really have to pray. Just pretend. It won't take long and then you can do what you want. Please don't get her mad."

He'd pushed himself up out of his chair and whispered in her ear as he brushed past her.

"She's already mad."

Blessed art thou amongst women,
And blessed be the fruit of thy womb, Jesus.

Adele recited, over-enunciating, moist sounds like a cat eating canned food coming from her mouth. She knelt beneath the small chandelier, between the tea wagon on one wall and the buffet on the other, eyes closed, face bowed to the floor.

Holy Mary, Mother of God…

Her abdomen bulged in a fleshy mound beneath the waist of her housedress. Below it, she held her rosary in two hands, the yellow crystal beads mingling with her pink, hand-creamed fingers. Above it, her breasts and fleshy shoulders rode up and down with her dramatic breathing.

Pray for us sinners…

She wrung herself with a pious fervour, gathering together all of the sibilant sounds in the prayer words, all of the S's, all of the ST's and the soft C's, dragging them reverently across the edges of her teeth, praying for her *sssinzzz* and those of her children.

Now and at the hour of our death, amen.

Richard shifted his weight, trying to ease backwards across the carpet. The television was still on without the sound. From where he knelt he could see the bluish light flickering across the living room carpet. While he manoeuvred himself quietly, his mother advanced her chubby fingers to the next bead and began her prayer again.

Hail Mary full of graccce...

The tea wagon against the dining room wall was set with a silver tray upon which six china cups and saucers rested, waiting, the cups inverted so as not to gather dust. Behind Adele, in the middle of the dining room table, a large bowl of rose and gold dried flowers roosted on a frilly crocheted doily. Behind that, rose-coloured silk drapes were drawn shut over the French doors for the night.

Holy Mary, Mother of God...

Cathy's eyes wandered idly all over the shadowy room. It was a small measure of luck to have her mother so tightly closed up and engrossed in her prayers. She took the chance of letting her eyes rove freely over the top of the buffet, examining the doilies, the two glass lamps, the clock that chimed every half-hour, and the picture of the President. With the aid of the flickering blue light from the other room, she could just make out the wafer-thin profile of the framed picture nestled in a foam of tatting. The President was gazing, she knew, out over the top of her mother's bowed head.

"Such a good man," Adele said all the time, kissing the picture and then using her apron to buff the glass. "Such a gentle soul, a wonderful father and good husband, an example to the whole world, that man is. We don't know how lucky we are to have him."

Cathy wondered who else might be praying on their dining room floors for the President's wife. Were Sandra and Lucy De

Finca kneeling beside their mother with their eyes squeezed closed? Maybe the priests at the rectory had heard and were kneeling in a ring around the dining room table? Janet and Eva? No. Eva would hear the news and wrinkle up her nose and say, "Oh that's too bad. We'll have to keep them in our thoughts." Then she would finish arranging cut flowers in a bowl for the table near the front door.

While her mother droned on, Cathy stared at her blue flickering brother. He had sunk backwards and was now sitting on his feet, his arms folded across his chest, his hands stalled on his rosary, and his attention completely diverted to a baseball game.

Blessed art thou amongssst women...

She couldn't tell which way Richard was going in life — forwards or backwards. One minute he looked old, another minute he looked young. His features seemed to flow back and forth between childhood and adulthood, never quite resting long enough to solidify in either state. Now and again she saw vestiges of baby fat in his cheeks and around his mouth, despite his thinness. She could picture him in a crib, asleep on his side, pink mouth fallen open. Other times she saw what he would look like when he was older and fully formed. Now as she observed him, his baby fat appeared to have drained away, leaving contours of small tendons and miniature muscles and veins visible along his temples and jawbone and down his neck. A sharp, distinct skeleton with angles and hardness was rising to the surface from beneath his bluish-white Irish skin. Richard the adult was emerging. She wondered how much longer he would stay.

Glory be to the Father, the Son and the Holy Ghost, amen.

"Cathy, it's your turn to lead. Start the next decade."

Cathy hurried her fingers along to the correct spot and began to recite the "Our Father." Richard continued to watch television, having given a brazen thumbs-up gesture to his closed-eyed mother at the assignment of the next decade to his sister. As words to the prayer droned out of Cathy, her thoughts wandered away. The difference between her and Richard was courage. He wasn't afraid of being caught at anything, ever. But she was afraid of nearly everything, all the time. He somehow knew how to sidestep his mother's anger. At the least edge in her voice, he'd just walk away. And miraculously, she'd never follow him. It was as if she were afraid of him.

She finished the "Our Father" and began advancing her fingers over her small white pearl beads, at a loss to understand her brother's power, or how her mother stitched her contradictions together, embracing a religion that lauded humility and then finding humble things like rusted lard tins, poor priests, and quiet men repugnant.

CHAPTER 15

After carefully tucking the flyer for the paint beneath his alarm clock and then sitting on his bed to unlace his shoes, Jerome paused to marvel at God's imagination. In his darkest moments, he had not thought about paint. Yawning with pleasant fatigue, he nosed his shoes neatly under the edge of his bed, stretched his arms out above his head, and then lay down on top of his sheet. It never paid to try to figure out God. Faith meant simply accepting. Maybe the kitchen was chosen instead of his bedroom because it was closer to the green grotto. Maybe, on really sweltering nights, he could take his blanket and pillow downstairs and sleep in the kitchen where it would be cooler. Who knew what God had in mind?

★ ★ ★

Back at the rectory the next morning, Cathy dawdled through her chores, listening to the radio to see if the President's wife had given birth or died or if any other unexpected drama had unfolded. There was no mention of anything.

"Well, you know what they say. No news is good news."

Angela was poking through the little icebox, surveying the supplies. She was wearing lemon yellow summer pants with a brilliantly striped yellow, pink, and white top and huge hoop earrings.

"Sure would be nice if he'd get here with the paint, though. A change of pace will be nice."

"You know," said Andy from the middle of the room where she was bent over stretching, wrapping her hands around her ankles and touching her head to her knees, *"I don't think it matters so much that we didn't go shopping ourselves. He agreed to get yellow. But this way, he's stuck lugging the stuff and not us. Paint cans weigh a ton."*

Cathy, hands on her hips, stood beneath one of the bare light bulbs, turning a slow circle and looking carefully at the walls.

"I think I need to wipe these down," she said quietly.

"Okay, then. Let's each take a wall."

Cathy filled the sink with hot soapy water and began by wiping the baseboards all the way around the room. At one-thirty, Father Martin tramped up the rotting old back steps.

"Oh, good," he said, depositing the two heavy tins on the wooden table, along with two new rollers, a paint tray, and two small brushes. "I'm glad you've gone ahead and started preparing."

Cathy stared at the two rollers. Father Martin stood beside the table, looking over the top of her head, chewing his lips, pensively considering some private matter. She looked back down at the labels. He had purchased the right brand.

"Well, Father, thank you. I guess I better get going. It's going to be a big job."

He didn't seem to hear her.

"I have an old shirt you can put on. Do you want to have it?"

"Uh-oh," Angela gasped and hoisted herself up on the counter.

Andy turned a cartwheel across the room, stopping right under Father Martin's nose.

"No thanks, Your Oiliness. That will make her sick to her stomach."

"No thanks, Father. I'm all right with what I have."

"Did you bring any painting clothes?"

"No, Father. I forgot. But I can make do with these. I'll be very careful."

"Short sleeves would probably be better, don't you think?"

She looked down at her long sleeves and then, quick as lightening, flicked the buttons through cuffs and rolled the material back above her elbows.

"Yes, that's a good idea, Father. Now I'm all set."

"The door is open for air, is it?"

Cathy looked back over her shoulder.

"Ah … well, it will be in a moment, Father. There's a big tin out there that will hold it open."

He took hold of his lips again and ground them against his teeth as he looked towards the door through which he had just entered. Then his eyes moved to the window above the sink.

"It's sealed shut with varnish, Father. You'll never open that."

"You think just the one door will be enough, then?"

"Yes, Father."

"All right, then. Maybe I'll open the front door for a cross breeze."

Turning away, he finally passed through the door to the dining room and beyond.

Andy spun around on her tiptoes.

"Okay, that near-death experience is over."

Angela hopped down off the counter and shook herself like a dog.

"Ew! God! Near-death is right."

She walked over to the table where the paint cans waited.

"Let's see the colour."

The kitchen suddenly turned brilliant yellow and things began to move. Diagonal wood panelling from the wall in Angela's Malibu kitchen attached itself to one of the kitchen walls, and coloured glass knick-knacks, with sunlight shining through them, floated around looking for just the right nook to settle in. Copper-bottomed pots from cooking magazines hung themselves speculatively against the wood panelling. Cathy's spirit mushroomed. She twirled around on one foot, rubbing her hands together gleefully. In hours the kitchen would be transformed.

"In hours," Angela exclaimed. *"What are you thinking? This is a huge room."*

"Well, okay, okay," Cathy muttered softly. "Maybe not hours. But soon."

"None too soon," Andy chirped, poking her head through the door after Father Martin. Barely able to control her excitement, Cathy began prying the lid off a paint can using the stem of a fork as a lever. The kitchen grew more and more yellow. The fork handle worked frantically, slipping under the lip of the lid, pumping once or twice and then moving forward to repeat the same motions. Finally with a squawk of resistance, the lid yielded to her scrabbling, clawing fingers.

The light in the room dipped. The pots and the glass baubles and the rich wood panelling disappeared, and Angela and Andy vanished to a nearby cupboard. The colour of the liquid beneath the tin lid was a dull, flat gold. "Harvest Gold," as she now read on the label. As dull and thick and stupid a colour as Father Martin himself. She spun the second can around to read the label. "Harvest Gold," it said. She stared at the miserable colour.

"No wonder there's a half-empty bottle of whiskey on the attic stairs."

She sank down into a chair, glanced again at the loathsome colour, and then turned away to stare at her shoes.

"Goddamn you," she whispered. "God damn, damn, damn you. It was supposed to be yellow. Yellow! Brilliant. Buttercup. Yellow! You pimple-headed moron. You…"

Her next word died instantly as the dining room door pumped open and a foolish, pop-eyed Father Martin re-entered the room, having changed into old work pants and a worn-out sleeveless undershirt. Thick tufts of black hair peeked out from his armpits.

"Oh my God. The Bishop of Fluff," Andy shrieked, hanging partway out of a cupboard.

"Well, here I am," he announced, holding his arms out like a singer. "You'll have to help get me started. I don't have much experience with this."

Cathy, dumfounded, stared at his face, but the tufts were pulling her eyes like magnets. She dug her nails into her palms.

"Please, please, please don't let me look there," she prayed. Her frozen eyes were burning. She desperately needed to blink.

Father Martin looked at her.

"What's the matter?"

Still staring, she turned up the corners of her mouth.

"Nothing, Father. I just pinched myself by accident when I opened the tin. It's one of those pains that makes your eyes smart, you know?"

For three days Adele stayed in her bed, listening for radio bulletins on the condition of the First Lady. Outside of her bedroom, the house fell silent, the rose silk drapes in the dining room remained firmly closed against the daylight, Gerald, Richard, and Cathy came and went from their respective jobs, fixing their own meals and washing up after themselves. Outside in the backyard, the swing sat idle, the bird feeder stood empty, and the bird bath went dry. In the evenings, Gerald picked the accumulated mail up off the floor in the front hall and added it to the growing pile on the nearby desk.

"It's just this darn stomach flu that I've picked up," Adele said.

"It's her brain that flew," Richard quipped to Cathy.

On the second evening of her confinement, she called Cathy into the room and indicated, by moving her legs aside and patting the bed, that she wanted her to sit down. Cathy bit the insides of her cheeks and looked down into her lap. Her mother drew herself up out of her bedsheets and folded her hands upon the mound of her stomach. Then she inhaled, long and slow, sighed heavily, and cleared her throat.

"You know, Cathy, having a child is a very important time in a woman's life."

Zip! Cathy looked down at the black roof of the house. There were two sections to the roof: the one that covered the garage and the first floor, which was rectangular in shape with a ridge running down its centre so that it looked like an open book left to rest face down, and the smaller square part that covered the upstairs. It gathered to a point in its centre. When the maple trees moved slightly, she could see that the roof was glistening. It was raining, a fine cold drizzle that settled like a silver gloss on the surfaces of things. Down in the backyard, a block of yellow light from the kitchen window rested on a patch of silver grass. Cathy wondered if the light was strong enough to warm the patch of grass slightly, and if that was something that earthworms might like. Did they ever get chilly at night?

"A woman has a very special role in life, Cathy."

Come to think of it, what were worms, anyway? Reptiles, amphibians, insects? No. Insects had six legs. She had just learned that in science last year. Reptiles and amphibians didn't sound right. So what else was there?

"And it is the greatest role of all. It is the role of mother-hood. A woman was given the privilege by God to give birth with her own body."

Maybe earthworms had their own category. Just plain worms! There'd be a Latin term — *Wormus slimensus*, or something.

"It is a joy to carry that new little bud of life within yourself, to feel it grow and move inside you."

Maybe she was going to learn about worms this coming year. Sea worms and jungle worms. A whole new world that she hadn't even heard of. Worms that lived in trees and worms that could swim. The fascinating world of worms.

"It's not always easy to bear a child."

If it rained a lot tonight, hundreds of worms would come out of hiding and crawl all over the sidewalks. Was that because they were flooded out of their underground holes, or because it was easier to hunt for food when everything was wet? Regardless, she'd have to step over them in the morning. Richard usually found a little stick and flipped them back onto the grass. The stick wasn't because he was squeamish, he'd explained. It was just too hard to get a grip otherwise.

"It's often difficult to bring them into this world."

If a lot of them came out, there would be that horrid smell. The damp air filled with a clammy flesh smell, not quite like fish smell, but close. It made her almost retch. What would be the biological reason for smelling funny when you were wet?

"And some of us can't even do that naturally."

Naturally, smaturally, faturally, raturally.

Adele paused. She was ready, with her head tilted in supplication to one side, to celebrate the sisterhood of fallopian tubes and wombs. She smelled of talcum powder and floral oily creams, things she rubbed on her face and hands and shook down her cleavage in celebration of being female.

"You know that; I've showed you my scar."

Five cents. See the scar. Five cents.

Richard.

Cathy began to dig her nails into one of her palms. Her mother's gaze was like a heat lamp, pressing against her, willing her to turn her face up to it so that they could seal a bleeding pact of womanhood between them with their eyes.

"It runs from just below my navel to just above my, well, you know, my pubic hair."

Maybe she'd ask about the worms in the fall. Surprise her new science teacher with her interest. Ask if she could do a special project on them. Set up worm experiments. Worm mazes. See if they could learn.

Adele rubbed her abdomen.

"But you do it because you love them, and because it is your duty to do so."

199

Little worm gates. Worm hurdles. Put them through time trials. Salivation experiments. Who was that Russian guy with the dog?

"That's what a woman is put on earth by God to do. Your womb and your vagina are what you're all about."

If her nails broke through the flesh of her palm, could her fingers thread themselves through the fine bones and begin to emerge on the top of her hand?

"But oh, what a joy it is to be a mother."

The bed suddenly jiggled as Adele pulled her thick legs up to herself and wrapped her pudgy arms around her knees in a girlish pose.

"When you first see that little face looking up at you, your heart floods with love and you know that you have done the right thing, you know that you have fulfilled your destiny."

Cathy's legs, which were pressed together tightly, were beginning to shake. She shifted her position slightly.

Too much. Adele pounced, caught Cathy's chin in one hand and held it in an upward tilt, forcing the eye contact that she craved. Eyes glittering with forced tears, head dipped to one side, Adele smiled wanly and set her stubby thumb sweeping across Cathy's cheek.

"I wish no greater happiness for you, dear, than the blessing of motherhood."

Cathy jerked her head back. Her balloon string grew longer and longer, carrying her further and further into black night sky. There were stars on the right, and stars on the left, and stars straight ahead. And stars closed over the gap behind her. Blue and violet and twinkling. She'd go and see if they were the ancestral homes of worms. She'd get going on that special project right away. Tonight.

Flying through the void, she shed herself, like a chrysalis, escaping the hated touch of the creamy pink thumb. Far below her, a small receding figure, like herself, but not herself, sat on her mother's bed. She had no idea whom her mother was addressing. But she was just as certain that it was not her on this occasion as she had been at other times, when her mother, poisoned with rage, looked right past her and tried to drive a yardstick through the surface of reality.

★ ★ ★

Late in the afternoon of the third day, a news bulletin announced that the First Lady had been delivered of a son by Caesarean section. She remained resting comfortably at Bethesda, but the baby was flown to a hospital in Boston for observation. Adele lay in bed in her darkened room, listening to a radio program that played mushy string orchestra music. She sighed deeply at regular intervals and moved the heavy sheets and blankets away from her incision. A kindly nurse tended her. She encouraged her to sit up and then walk. She told the nurse she wasn't ready.

By the evening she was bored, so she called the other members of the family into the room. It was a rare night when everyone was actually home.

"Everyone get their rosaries. You too, Gerald. It's time to set an example for these children before they grow up to be pagans. Be back here in five minutes."

Cathy found Richard standing at the foot of his bed reading the lyrics on the back of a new album.

"Richard, come on. We can't be late."

"We?" he inquired, continuing to read.

"Tsk. Yes. You have to come too. She knows you're home. Richard, if we don't get down there right away she'll…"

"What? Do something?" he said, tossing the album on his bed as he turned to face her.

Cathy sighed. "Yes. I wish you'd be more careful around her."

"Ah ... that's where you make your mistake, my dear. Too much carefulness is the problem."

He stepped into the hall and together they headed towards the stairs.

"Sometimes, I just don't get you, Richard."

He smiled. "That's the whole point. And besides. You might. Someday."

They shuffled back into the room, Gerald looking as miserable as a trapped animal, Cathy fluttering in fear of the unknown, Richard detached and, to Cathy's horror, amused. He followed her into the room, whispering in her ear.

"Let's just see what kind of a freak show she's got lined up tonight."

Adele assigned various sections of the rosary to everyone. Then she ceremoniously draped her rosary over her stomach and solemnly closed her eyes. Angela, frowning, sat upstairs on Cathy's bed, watching everything.

"I'm up here if you can manage to get out."

Behind Adele's closed eyelids the First Lady returned to the White House with a small precious bundle swaddled in white. Adele knew that before Christmas there would be a photo session for the press in one of the upstairs rooms, two children at play on the carpet, one newborn sleeping sweetly on the First Lady's lap. The President told Adele how much he loved her, how lucky he was. She told him the pain didn't matter; she had had his baby and that was all that mattered. At the foot of her bed, her husband droned on in the dim light, begging forgiveness for his sins.

★ ★ ★

When the President's baby died, Adele abandoned her bed to sit by the television. She held a throw cushion in her lap and cried into it, rubbing her cheek against its soft damask upholstery, whispering, "Goodbye, goodbye little one." The lumpy, distended cushion attracted Richard's attention one evening when he found it on the floor in the empty living room. He unzipped it and found an entire set of knitted baby clothes, white with yellow and mauve ribbons, stuffed inside.

When it was finally announced that the funeral was to be entirely private, Adele snapped off the television and went into the dining room to her supply of pictures. Bits of the dining room, backyard, and St. Mary, Star of the Sea, figured in the funeral. She officiated at it, alone, several times, and then took herself out to the swing with a cup of tea. There she stared at the sky, counting the birds that flew south.

The next morning Cathy found the rectory kitchen door propped open with the old lard tin. From the porch steps she could smell fresh paint and Father Martin's perspiration.

"I think we've got com-pan-y," Angela sang.

"I thought I'd get an early start," he said as Cathy stepped into the room. "It seems to go kind of slow. How long do you think it will take to do the whole room?"

"Well," said Angela, resting her foot on the edge of the counter to tie the laces of a running shoe. *"Operation Diversion seems to be a total success with somebody."*

"The whole room, Father? The rest of the walls have to be cleaned first and then the paint has to dry completely before you put on another coat."

"Wait until you see this," he said, jabbing his roller toward the floor. There was a small paint tin sitting between his feet. He put his roller down and withdrew a brush from the tin and dragged it and its horrible green contents along the baseboard beneath where he was painting. The colour was truly appalling.

"Nice, isn't it?" he asked. "I remembered it was in the garage, last night."

He stepped back to admire his handiwork, the baseboard beneath the painted wall having been freshly coated in dull armoured-tank green.

"Oh…," Cathy stammered, "I … hadn't planned on painting the baseboards a separate colour, Father."

"I think it really adds something."

"Oh, it does that, all right."

"Huh … hum … different," Cathy swallowed.

"Thank you. I'm glad you think it goes well with the yellow," he said, his back turned to Cathy. "I wasn't sure. But I think you're right. It makes a nice contrast."

"You know? It's maybe not so hard to see why this idiot's been dumped and left to rot in this parish. He's a moron."

"A pimple-headed moron," Cathy thought.

Angela moved closer to the baseboard, bent over, examined the colour more closely, then straightened and looked directly at Cathy.

"Join you in the attic for a whiskey?"

"With the two of us working on it, it shouldn't take more than a couple of days," he continued. "Maybe you can finish washing the other walls and then I'll just follow you around the room with the first coat. Then we can divide up the second coat between us, one on the walls, the other on the trim."

Cathy went over to the fridge and pulled the door open. It was just as well that he was so enthusiastic. This room was never going to look like a sunny seaside California kitchen anyway.

"Actually, it's better if just one person does the painting, Father. Different people hold the rollers differently and you can tell where one painter left off and the other picked up. Since you've started, you might as well finish."

Angela, leaning against the counter, rolled her eyes.

"Nonsense artist."

"Hmm. I didn't know that. It's a good thing you told me.

You probably have enough to do with the housework and the meals, anyway. I'll finish this wall this morning and then I'll start that one over there next. I have to go out for a couple of hours later this morning, but I can start again after lunch. That will give you time to finish washing the other walls."

Cathy plunged her head into the refrigerator. Of course. How could she refuse to wash the walls? It was part of the housework; that was her job.

"Never mind, flea. It's only another few weeks."

So that he wouldn't talk to her while she worked, she snapped the radio on and turned the volume up. He bent over the baseboard again, attempting to add a second coat before the first one had dried. Half an hour later, she served him the darkest pieces of toast, the hardest egg yolks, and the fattest, most undercooked strips of bacon.

★ ★ ★

One morning, a week later, still bothered by the loss of her project and choking on the stench of perspiration, Cathy slipped outside for the first time since coming to the rectory. She didn't have a plan; she just needed a break. She walked around to the front of the church, half thinking she might go for a short walk. Uninspired to choose a direction after standing on the street corner for several minutes, she sat down on the worn cement steps of the church. She could get an orange Popsicle in the little variety store, but she couldn't spot any shady inviting harbour where she might sit on a bench beneath a tree to enjoy it.

Although it wasn't yet noon, the sun was overpowering. The light reflected off the sidewalk and stairs, pooling its intensity, it seemed, on the top of her head. She crossed the road and bought a Popsicle in the variety store anyway and returned to the cement steps, wedging herself into a small triangle of shade created by the building next to the church. From there she watched three grubby little boys emerge from the alley behind the variety store, carrying a worn cardboard box between them. They disappeared into the store, where they remained for several minutes, and then re-emerged, each with a bottle of pop, still struggling with the box.

They crossed the street towards her and plunked themselves down at the foot of the stairs, several feet away. Each wore makeshift shorts made from trimmed-off pants; two were bare-backed and the third wore a dirty blue T-shirt. Their hair had been inexpertly cut and grew in thick blunt mops from their crowns down across their sweaty foreheads and ears. Their bodies were long and excessively skinny. Where their joints bent, Cathy noticed sharp points and angles where she was accustomed to seeing the rounded shapes of the better fed. Mixed in with the boys' feet on the sidewalk was their cardboard box with its top flaps loosely woven together. One of the boys was scrabbling his fingers along the box wall and talking softly to the top of it. When he stopped, the box rocked slightly and the boys laughed. The boy in the blue shirt put his foot out to keep the box from straying.

"What's in there?"

Intrigued, Cathy had come forward out of her wedge of shade. The boys turned to face her, squinting and shading their eyes because the sun was behind her.

"Puppies. Wanna see?"

One of the boys peeled the flaps back and pushed the box towards Cathy. Immediately a fawn-coloured head and two paws rose up over the edge of the box. The pup sneezed in the bright light and then pushed himself further up over the box's edge and hung there, helplessly, suspended from his armpits. Cathy scooped him up into her arms and took a seat on the bottom step beside the boys. The pup squirmed to get to her face to investigate her. She felt hot little puffs of breath on her neck and ear and smelled the dusky odour of puppies. Her mother would have condemned it as a dirty smell, but she liked it. There was something of baking bread and hot laundry about it. Sharp little milk teeth and an unexpectedly cold nose explored her earlobe. Just as she was lifting the pup away to examine him more closely, he caught hold of her hair and began to chew it.

"There he goes, chewing again," the boy in the blue shirt said. "He's a chewer. He's chewed everything at my brother's. That's why my brother, he don't want them no more, cuz of this one chewing everything."

"Are they your brother's pups?" Cathy inquired.

"Yeah, but he don't want them. His dog just had them, eh, and he don't want no more puppies."

"What are you going to do with them?"

Cathy held the pup out in front of her so she could see his face. He looked back at her in a good-natured, quizzical way, and then glanced down to her lap beneath his dangling feet. Cathy set him down gently.

"Dunno what to do with them, cuz my brother, he don't want them. He said he don't want to see them no more. They bin chewin' up his place. He said for us to get rid of them. We gave two others away. Now there's just them two left. You want one?"

"No, I can't."

The pup was trying to straddle the distance between Cathy's lap and that of the boy next to her. His mouth was open, he was panting, and his one paw was stretched tentatively towards the boy's leg, testing the empty air for a footing. The white tip of his tail flicked back and forth across the end of Cathy's nose. She watched his sweet profile with its soft mouth and small wet nose, pink tongue that never rested, and one gleaming eye that watched everything around him with consummate curiosity.

While her own eyes roved over his baby features, another pair of eyes, dark and quiet but equally curious, stared up at her until finally Cathy noticed the other pup still sitting in the box at her feet.

One of the boys spoke.

"His brother's goin' to drown them if we bring them back."

Cathy looked at the boy in astonishment.

"What? These little dogs? When?"

"Tonight."

The pup in the box opened her mouth to pant. She was sitting directly in the intense sunlight but had made no move to escape from the box. Her eyes remained calmly focused up at Cathy.

"Can't you find homes for them? They're adorable."

"Nope. Don't nobody want 'em."

"We bin tryin'," said one of the other boys.

Cathy glanced down into the box again.

"Is there something wrong with this one? It's so quiet compared to the other one."

"That one in the box's a girl. This one's a boy. My mom says girl dogs make better pets 'cuz they're quieter."

"Why don't you take her, then?"

The boy bent over his own lap to pick at a hole in the toe of his running shoe.

"My dad doesn't want no dog. He says it costs enough to feed kids; he don't need no dog to feed extra."

The pup's gaze remained tethered to Cathy. She licked the end of her nose and then resumed panting. Cathy thought of her waiting like that, patiently, trustingly, later tonight, while a hand held her brother underwater.

The male pup had flopped on his side in her lap and was licking dried Popsicle juice from the palm of one of her hands. Now and again his baby teeth made a trial nibble along the edge of her thumb or at the tip of one of her fingers. For a moment, while she gazed at him, he stopped moving, his fresh little mouth open with its pink tongue flopping out of it, and looked up at her with one visible black eye. Then he snorted and scrabbled into another position so that his rear end came around to face Cathy and his white-tipped little tail flicked back and forth under her chin.

Her hands worked along his body, feeling out ribs and a warm potbelly. The puppy wriggled and jostled, chasing her fingers, finally tangling himself in the folds of her skirt. She untangled him gently, handed him to the boy next to her, and bent to retrieve the female pup, who looked up even more directly as she was being lifted.

Cathy took her to the crook of her neck and there stroked the soft fur and began to rock gently back and forth.

"How in the world," she whispered into the pup's fur, "could anyone hurt you?"

The pup lay still on her shoulder, panting. Cathy closed her eyes and let her cheek sink deeply into the warm, wonderfully soft fur.

"Be great in bed, huh?" Andy chirped. She was further up on the church stairs, perched sideways on the iron handrail. *"You could snuggle all night. That's what Mickey and I do."*

Angela reached over and stroked the pup's head.

"Such a shame she has no home."

"Mouse," Cathy whispered into the fur again, "you need someone to save you, don't you?"

She imagined two hands lowering the pup into a washtub of cold water, the hind feet going in first, the trusting quiet eyes looking up, unaware until the last instant. The image jerked her to her feet. Here was something much more comforting than either paint or whiskey.

"We just adore Mickey," Angela said, holding her face up to the hot sun. *"He's practically Andy's sibling. He comes absolutely everywhere with us."*

"Hey, I know," said Andy, swinging upside-down on the handrail. *"You can look after the pups in the rectory kitchen all day. At night they can keep Father Martin company. It'll be perfect."*

Angela, heading for the triangle of shade that Cathy had abandoned, shrugged her shoulders.

"It might work. We know damn well how lonely he is. Surely a pup is better than a statue. Won't hurt to try."

"You know," Andy continued from her inverted position, her loose blonde hair dragging on the cement steps, *"this might be a mission. God might want you to save them. He made you discover them. Why else did He let Father Renoir take over the painting? And why did you pick today to come out here, right now at this moment? Think about it."*

Cathy noticed one of the boys watching her.

"For someone who doesn't want a dog, you sure look like you want one."

"I said I can't. Not that I didn't like them. Why don't people like male dogs?"

"They do," one of the other boys replied. "It's just his mother said that about the girl dogs. Mrs. Traudechaud wants the boy, maybe."

"Yeah, maybe Mr. Traudechaud wants it too. His wife said he does, but he's not there. We're waitin' for him to come."

"Who's Mr. Traudechaud?"

One of the boys jerked his chin in the direction of the variety store.

"They own the store."

"Yeah, you know, the old lady with the thick glasses makes her eyes look big?"

"Oh, you mean *they* might want the boy dog?"

"She seen us playing with them over there in the school-yard and she told us to bring them over when her husband gits back."

"Probably they're gonna take him," said one of the bare-backed boys. "She really liked him. She called him Flapjack already."

"Yeah, he's gonna guard the store at night."

At the mention of the name, the male pup looked up and yipped, trying to entice a finger to play with him. The three boys laughed and swung their cramped legs out into various new positions on the sidewalk and the lower stairs.

"You see," Andy started up again, still hanging upside-down, *"that's even more of a sign. You'd only have to rescue her."*

"Tell you what," Cathy heard herself begin, "I'll take this one for now and you wait to see if that lady wants the boy, and if she doesn't, then bring him over to me and I'll take him too. I work in the rectory. Just come around to the back door."

"Great. Then his brother don't got to drown nothin'," one of the boys said.

Cathy pulled the little female pup away from her shoulder and held her out for inspection. The pup looked calmly into Cathy's eyes and licked the end of her own nose. Then she glanced down at the pavement far beneath her and back up to Cathy's eyes. Cathy brought her back to the safety of her shoulder, awash in a river of emotions.

"Thank you," she called over her shoulder, and then whispered into the soft beige fur, "What are we going to call you, huh?"

The moment that she stepped inside the kitchen with the pup and saw the hunched back of Father Martin, the certainty that she was doing the correct thing completely deserted her. She found herself hoping desperately that the pup would remain quiet.

She watched the priest in silence, noting how he made everything difficult for himself. Instead of squatting to reach the baseboard, he was folded over at the waist, his large upper body inverted and his pimply head cocked at a difficult angle to enable him to see what he was painting. His forearm and the top of his balding head glistened with sweat and he grunted intermittently with the strain of his position. The hair under his arms glistened.

While he remained unaware of her, she tried to think. What had seemed so clear out on the church steps just a few minutes ago was now muddled and incongruous. What had she planned to do? Just hand him the dog and that would be that? He would say, "Oh thank you, I was just looking for a dog"? The longer she stood there, the more certain she became of the error in her judgement.

Finally, Father Martin's paintbrush came to the end of the baseboard and he straightened up, nursing the small of his back with his free hand. When he turned to place the brush on the edge of the paint can, he noticed her.

She stood stock-still and met his gaze head-on. Her thoughts had never collected into a plan. She had only the exact truth to face him with. *"Father, I got you a dog because I think you are lonely and need something to love; I know all about you and the Virgin Mary; Father, God gave me a message that I was supposed to save this dog's life by giving it to you."*

He stared at the dog, and she stared at him. Nothing would come out of her mouth.

"What's that?" he asked, his voice guarded, his facial features turning slightly upward as if repulsed.

"It's a young puppy, Father. I found her out on the front steps of the church."

She turned the pup around and held her so that he could see her face.

"Well she must belong to somebody, then. You'd better take her back and leave her to find her way home."

"Well, I found her sort of in the process of being left on the steps, Father. She doesn't really have a home, and she's too little to be left near the road by herself."

"Well, that's none of our concern."

"Hmm. The all the compassion of a plough."

"Father, look at how small she is. If I leave her out there alone she might get run over by the bus that stops out front."

"Well that's unfortunate, but it *is* what happens to most dogs anyway."

"Oh boy! How did we miss this?"

Cathy's voice developed a quiver.

"Do you know anybody you could give her to, Father?"

"No. I'm not in the business of finding homes for unwanted animals."

He turned his back to examine the wall. Cathy put the pup back up on her shoulder, startled that she could ever have imagined this man sparing affection for an animal. The pup began to squirm, but Cathy held her firmly to her shoulder, determined to provide for her somehow. The priest dunked his paint roller in the tray of Harvest Gold, about to begin work on a new section of the wall. Noticing that she hadn't moved yet, he turned back to look at her, his roller suspended in the air.

"What are you waiting for? Take her back out and leave her where you found her."

Cathy was shaking. She swallowed and took a deep breath.

"I can't do that, Father, just leave her out there to be killed. I'll have to try and find her a home. There's half a meatloaf left over from last night's supper. You can make yourselves cold meatloaf sandwiches for supper. I'll be back in the morning."

Father Martin glanced first at the fridge and then at the puppy. His expression mixed disgust with fluster. In that last glimpse that Cathy had of him before grabbing her purse and exiting through the back door, he reminded her of a fussy, rash-covered, spoiled infant.

There was no sign of the little boys and their cardboard cargo in front of the church. Cathy considered trying to talk the old woman in the variety store into taking both pups but decided it would probably be a fruitless exercise. The searing heat and humidity sapped any ability that she might have had to think courageously or creatively. The pup panted heavily on her shoulder and began to lick her nose. There was not a single scrap of shade or a hint of breeze available to counter the temperature. Cathy found that the fur on the pup's head was red hot. She held her hand in place as a shade and was looking up and down the street, wondering what to do next, when the sudden sight of the bus lumbering towards her told her that she really had no other option now except to take the pup home. There, in the comfort of the air-conditioned rooms, she would be able to figure out a solution to her problem.

★ ★ ★

The bus driver recognized her.

"Well, well, well. Gotch yerself a little friend, eh?"

It was Mr. Hairy-chest-maroon-tongue. Cathy dropped her fare in the box without looking up and hurried down the aisle to the middle of the empty bus.

She chose the shaded side of the aisle and opened the window so a breeze blew on both of them. The pup's breathing slowed down and she fell sleep on Cathy's shoulder, the breeze having flapped back one of her ears. Cathy rode in transfigured silence, rethinking the conversation with Father Martin. The day she had found the attic stairs she had been able to feel such compassion for him, for the sad struggle he was waging against solitude. Now he repulsed her. His large roving eyes fevered with opportunism. It was a good thing the fall was approaching. The priests would have to find a permanent housekeeper soon and she could return to school. Her head drooped against the window and the heat closed her eyes. On and on beneath her, the bus's wheels spun, taking her home.

The pup, never taking her eyes off Cathy, squatted the instant she was set on the front lawn. Inside, a block of cool air met them at the door. The house was frozen in silence. Cathy got the pup a dish of cold water and left her on the plastic runners in the laundry room. The garage door was closed, so she didn't know if her mother's car was in the garage or not. The house had the aura of an old age home where everyone slept at midday.

In the dining room, she found a half-finished cup of cold tea on the table and a chair pulled out of place, as if someone had been sitting, observing the backyard through the French doors. The top of the buffet was slightly disturbed as well: the picture of the President was missing.

The sound that told her that she was not alone was so slight as to be practically indiscernible. She had to listen hard for it, as if it were a fleck of sound mixed into the air currents moving through the house. After an interval, it came again, as slight as the first time. Queer breathing.

The bathroom door was not fully closed. The sound escaping through the opening matched what she thought she had heard from the dining room, only now it came in brief, regular pulses.

Through the slice of view afforded by the opening, Cathy made out one-half of her mother's body lying on the blue carpet of the bathroom floor: the top part of her fuzzy red head, part of one arm, clasping something — the missing picture from the dining room — to her bosom, her floral print housedress pulled up above her waist, one leg with a bent knee, and abandoned underpants looped around one bare ankle. Her mother was rising rhythmically off the floor, sometimes shuddering at an apex before dropping down again. The hand of the arm that was not visible crossed into view at the spot where one thigh was visible and the other fell open to the side. The hand plunged down over her mother's pubic mound leaving the wrist in view, rising up and down in a regular stroking rhythm accompanied by accelerating breathing and a wet crackling. Her head began to move, rolling from side to side, coming into view, rolling out of sight. Cathy saw that her mother's eyes were closed.

The skin on the back of her neck tightened. She had to retreat but was so frozen with terror that she didn't have the ability to move. Her stomach squeezed hard, forcing burning liquid up the back of her throat. She dropped her mouth open to breathe so that she wouldn't vomit, but now her breathing grew crazy. All she could do was take in air, rapid little gulps, with no pause to let any air out. She was filling up with air and was going to explode. She felt her heart beating hard in her neck and heard it hammering against her eardrums. She needed to swallow but couldn't close her mouth; her bottom jaw hung loose, as if broken. White spots formed in the air in front of her and pulsed there like neon lights, and then a drool of saliva spilled out of the corner of her mouth down onto her foot and then the carpet. Her stomach heaved again and a small pool of vomit flooded into her open mouth. She needed to gasp. She had to go back. Putting her hand out blindly, she touched a wall. She could hardly get her legs to move. They felt as if they were wading through wet cement. Tilting her head towards the ceiling to keep the liquid in her mouth, she ran her hand along the wall. She tried to notice if her feet were moving silently over the carpet. Were they rasping, were floorboards creaking beneath them? The rooms receded behind her, one at a time. The dining room, then the kitchen, then the breakfast room, and finally she was back in the laundry room. She ran to the sink and vomited. Then she sank onto the carpet and with closed eyes stroked the pup, who had scampered over to play with her hands. Tears seeped from beneath her closed eyelids. How would she ever make her face neutral enough?

The pup wandered away and began calmly investigating the corners of the laundry room. Her water bowl was partially emptied onto the floor, and one wet front paw was leaving tiny dark imprints on the parts of the carpet that weren't protected by a plastic runner. Cathy, trembling, scooped her up and took her out to the grass again. When she re-entered, she slammed the door loudly, knowing that the air lock, as well as the sound, would travel through the rooms.

She didn't even have time to settle on the floor with the pup again before the laundry room door burst open and crashed against the wall. Her mother, eyes alight, filled the opening.

"What are you doing home?"

Cathy looked at the floor, not knowing whether to continue lowering herself towards it or to stand back up.

"I came home early."

"How long have you been here?"

"I just got here."

Adele stepped forward and hit Cathy hard on the left ear, knocking her down to the floor.

"How long have you been here?"

Cathy started to cry.

"I just came in this minute."

"It's the middle of the afternoon."

"I know. I'm ... I'm sick. I don't feel well."

Adele grabbed Cathy's clothing at the shoulder, hauled her to her feet, and pulled her close.

"What do you mean, you don't feel well?"

The pup began to whine, shrilling mournfully. Cathy's tears flowed more freely; her nose began to run. She could feel her stomach beginning to ripple. It was a matter of seconds before she would vomit again. Avoiding her mother's eyes, she struggled in the tight grip, speaking faintly.

"I think I have the flu. I threw up in the sink."

"The flu? It's the wrong time of year for the flu. People don't get the flu in the middle of summer. What's going on here?"

Adele shook Cathy violently. Cathy's voice died in a strangling cramp in her throat. Drool streamed from one side of her mouth. She spoke in a rasp.

"Nothing's going on. I'm just sick, that's all."

Adele's hand batted against Cathy's wet open mouth.

"This better not be another Linda Thomson situation, my dear, or I'll kill you, do you hear? The sex act is for married people."

Hearing retching, she stepped back and shoved Cathy roughly away. Cathy stumbled towards the sink, vomiting in waves. Behind her, her mother spoke again. "Oh! Whose dog is this? Aren't you cute? Come on, pup. Come here. Come and say hello."

CHAPTER 18

L ater that evening, Cathy slipped silently into her place at the table. Her head ached from swollen sinuses and her eyes still smarted. The centre of her chest felt heavy, as if weighted with sandbags, and beneath this burden, her stomach fluttered uneasily. She could feel the heat of her father's glare on the top of her bowed head. He spoke in a low voice, avoiding Adele, who was bent over the oven door retrieving a casserole.

"It goes back with you in the morning."

Struggling for control, Cathy spoke in a whisper, without raising her gaze from her lap.

"But she doesn't have a home. There's no place to take her."

"You can leave her where you found her."

"She'll be killed by a bus."

"That's not my problem. The dog goes back and I don't want any more discussion."

He straightened just as Adele arrived at the table.

"That smells good, dear. What have you made?"

"Just Salisbury steak. The President used to have a big dog, didn't he? One of those shaggy old sheepdogs. The ones with their hair all hanging in their eyes. I'm sure I've seen a picture of him with it on the lawn of his Cape Cod home."

Gerald's fingers drummed lightly on the tablecloth.

"Well, I'm sure he might have had a dog, dear, but that was a country house, a house full of servants and with an outdoor run for the dog and a barn or a kennel for it to stay in."

Adele asked for everyone's plate and served out portions of salad, potatoes, green beans in a cheese sauce, and meat. Cathy kept her eyes down, listening to the wet sound the serving spoon made every time it dipped into the cheesy green beans.

"They probably had him all bathed up for that picture," Gerald continued. "Magazines don't let you see the way they really are most of the time. They roll in things, other animals' droppings and garbage; they throw up worms, they smell, they chew things. A dog would chew up all of your baseboards and scratch up all of the wallpaper; she'll lift her legs to the furniture, shed her fur over everything. Animals were meant to live outside with other animals. Not indoors with us."

Richard and Cathy played with their food at their places, Cathy busying herself hiding hated radish slices beneath a lettuce leaf, while Richard guided pieces of his father's homemade bread around the rim of his plate sopping up gravy from his Salisbury steak. When his father said that dogs carried disease and vermin, a snort of laughter escaped him.

"Oh, come on. You make it sound as if we're living in the Middle Ages. There are such things as veterinarians, you know, not to mention hygiene and vaccines. And females squat. They don't lift their legs."

Gerald glared at his son.

"You just keep out of this now. I don't want any dog in this house."

"Fine. But that's the real issue. *You* don't want a dog. Not all these other excuses. They're just a lot of nonsense."

Adele puffed out her bosom importantly and moved food around her plate in the brisk, darting gestures common to poultry.

"Yes, for heaven's sake, Gerald. Do you think the President of the United States is going to live in a pigsty, with everybody sick with diseases? He has dignitaries to entertain. He's one of the wealthiest men in the world, even without being the President."

Gerald, arrested, stared out from beneath his bushy eyebrows.

"I'm just thinking of the work, Adele. Most of it will likely fall to you…"

"Like everything else around here."

"I just don't think we need an animal to look after."

"Well, now that's something entirely different," Richard began. "It's interesting that you feel you can speak for the *needs* of all of us without actually consulting any of us. I'm not exactly sure what *we* need in this house, but I'm certain I don't recall anyone assessing our needs, do you, Cathy?"

Cathy winced and took a small bite of meat. She kept her eyes down on her plate. Angela pointed to the meat and Cathy fiddled with her knife and fork pretending to ready another bite. In her peripheral vision she saw her mother's strong thick wrists fiddling with their own knife and fork.

"I actually might like a dog, come to think of it. It might be a nice change around here."

"Richard. No."

"See what I mean? Another fine unilateral decision arrived at in true democratic fashion."

"Never mind your smart talk."

Adele began to turn pink and to push her food around her plate more vehemently, afraid that she was being left out of something important.

"Yes, Richard. A kid your age, spouting off about democracy. What do you know?"

"I think I know more than most people in this house."

"Your statements don't even make sense half the time."

"What I said was perfectly intelligible. It means that four of us live here and only one of us is making this decision. That's the position taken by autocrats, and it displays a basic lack of respect for other people and for democratic principles."

Richard turned back from his mother to his father.

"Did you ever think to ask any of the others of us if *we* might like to have a dog?"

"Yes, Gerald," Adele jumped in, "you run this house as if you were the only one who had to live in it. Some of the rest of us have feelings, too, you know. I doubt very much if the President speaks to his wife that way. And as for you, Richard, giving yourself airs about being perfectly intelligible. When you've done something with your life, then you can expect respect, not before. If you can get to be President by the time you're forty years old, then you might have something intelligent and worthwhile to say. Until then, you're just an eighteen-year-old kid, and your high falutin' words don't hold much water with us, Mr. Bigshot."

"Nothing holds any water with you except your freaky damn President. And he was forty-three, not forty, and I can't run because I wasn't born in the States, and Canada, by the way, elects prime ministers."

Zip!

"I don't want a dog in this house."

Gerald's voice was artificially calm.

"Fine. You don't want a dog. I think that's been fairly well established. But tell the truth about it. Not all this other false crap about diseases and vermin."

At the sound of the word "crap," despite having two cheeks filled with green beans and cheese sauce, Adele began to sputter.

"Here! Richard. I won't have swearing at my table."

Richard arrested the progress of his gravy-drenched bread in midair.

223

"I didn't swear and this table doesn't belong to just you alone."

The balloon string kept growing. Cathy could see beyond the city limits now, out over the countryside.

Adele swallowed her mouthful and set down her fork deliberately, her face suddenly flared with heat. Her flat palm smacked down on the tablecloth, disturbing the bowl of red raspberries in the centre of the table.

"Are you telling me what I can and cannot have going on at this table, young man? I was not born yesterday, sonny. I know a swear word when I hear it. I've known them since before you were born."

Richard laughed and put down his bread and leaned towards Adele.

"So your point is what? That because you've known things longer you're infallible? What if your education was faulty? What if the meaning of a word changes? What if you just plain don't know what you're talking about?"

"You said 'crap.' I heard you."

"So? Look it up. It means feces, nonsense, or rubbish."

"Here," Gerald bellowed. "Such language at the table."

Cathy's string grew again. She was entering space now.

"Are you defying me, young man?" Adele hollered.

"Do you even know what defiance means? Maybe you ought to look that up, too. Just because someone has a difference of opinion with you, you think that's defiance. And while you're under 'D,' look up democracy too. It's the piece of vocabulary this whole family has the most trouble with."

"Here, Richard, don't you speak to your mother that way."

"And what way would that be?"

Gerald squirmed, attempting to lift his neck out of his shirt collar.

"Now, I said that's enough, Richard."

Adele suddenly hissed at Gerald.

"Oh, *you*, always entering the fray when it's too late. Look at the type of manners you've taught this kid. He doesn't get that cockiness from me."

She turned her attention back to Richard.

"Don't you sass me, son. You're not too big yet that I can't tan your hide."

Richard placed both his forearms on the table and again bent forward towards his mother.

"Sass you, my ass. Don't you accuse me erroneously when it's your own ignorance that's at fault. 'Crap' is not a swear word, I am old enough to speak with the vocabulary of my choice, and I am perfectly entitled to differ in opinion, with anyone, on any matter I choose. And furthermore, at my age, lady, you don't dare want to lay a finger on me, because you already know what will happen if you do."

"Now that's enough," Gerald raised his voice, hesitantly.

Richard tore a piece of his father's soft cracked wheat bread in two and deliberately returned to sopping up gravy from his plate.

"Enough what? Truth? Or gravy?"

Cathy began to fly faster.

Adele rose out of her chair and leaned over the table towards her son, hissing through clenched teeth.

"You insolent little bugger, when I say I don't want any swearing at my table I mean it. And only a pig eats that way."

She swatted his hand away from his plate, sending the soggy piece of bread into his chin, splattering gravy all over his chest and the wall behind him.

He rocketed out of his chair, bringing his plate with him, and with an athletic gesture flipped it forward and ground it into his mother's face, pushing her backwards into her seat.

Adele shrieked and twisted her face out from beneath the plate. Gerald hollered. The plate clattered to the table, landing loudly on top of another. Behind the laundry room door, the puppy started to whimper.

Richard stood, glaring at his mother from eyes that were bright as glass beads.

"You want to hear swearing? I'll give you some swearing. This place is a goddamned fucking loony bin and you are a goddamned fucking fruitcake. How's that?"

Angela grabbed Cathy's hand.

"Follow me."

They flew deeper into space. Cathy hadn't known her balloon string could be so long.

"You know," Angela whispered, *"all you'd have to do is say, 'This afternoon, when I came home, the bathroom door was open a crack and inside....' That'd shut them all up lickety-split."*

Cathy shuddered, closed her eyes, and muttered, "Oh my God."

Richard shoved his chair roughly aside and left the room. Cathy could tell by the retort of his footsteps that he had headed to the back door without bothering to change his soiled shirt, or, indeed, to wipe off his face. She pictured him using his shirt for that once he got outside. The door slammed so violently that the room shuddered. She glanced cautiously to the spot on the floor between her mother and herself.

Adele's hand went up to her hair to examine the clots of cheese sauce and gravy that had collected above one ear.

"So do you see now what you've raised? Never around when that kid was small. Always sitting in that basement of yours, never paying any attention to him. Are you satisfied now? Do you see how he talks to me? Maybe if you'd had the spine to be a firm father a long time ago, things would be different. It's too late now. The kid thinks he can do what he wants, when he wants."

"Adele, it's not worth losing your —"

"Don't lecture me about who's losing their head or not around here. Thank God one of us even has a head on their shoulders, and we know it's not you. I tell you, Gerald, almost anyone else would have made a better father than you to these two kids. One's heading for trouble with the police and this one here's sitting around dreaming about boys. At least I took her in hand this summer and got her into the rectory. If I'd waited for you to do something with her she'd be pregnant, just like across the street there."

"Trouble with the police? "

"You heard him. Did you listen to the language he's using? Where do you think that leads?"

She picked several paper napkins out of a holder on the table and began mopping the food off her face. Gerald dropped back down into his seat in front of his unfinished meal.

"God ... Adele..."

"That's it, go ahead, make fun in front of the remaining one. Teach her that she doesn't have to show any respect, either. Thank God small-time hicks like you are not running the world, Gerald, or we'd all be in hell of a mess. At least the President knows how to set an example. You. What do *you* know about anything? You're not even fit to polish that man's boots."

She pushed herself away from the table and went into the kitchen, deliberately crashing dishes together on the counter. Then she pounded off down the hall towards the bathroom.

The pup's voice rose in a high-pitched whine. Cathy's bladder burned, her stomach was churning, and great hot tears dropped down onto her hands. Her father spoke, his words fairly hissing like water droplets on a hot skillet.

"You see that that dog is out of here tomorrow morning and don't you *ever* — do you hear me? — *ever* stir up trouble in the house like this again, do you understand?"

★ ★ ★

227

Cathy waited until after midnight before tiptoeing down to the laundry room with a blanket and her pillow and her alarm clock. There she scooped up the little dozing dog and fell asleep with her curled against her chest in the faint glow of the pilot light of the hot water tank.

The bus driver cackled.

"Uh-oh! Your boyfriend's little bundle of joy didn't go over so well with the folks, did it?"

Cathy looked up from the pup, startled.

"What?" she asked.

The bus door closed behind her and the driver looked away into his side mirror, beginning to ease the bus into the flow of traffic.

"Ah well. Never mind. At least he didn't give you one of the other, non-returnable bundles of joy. Yet."

He erupted into lewd laughter, and his dark meaty tongue slid like a hunting reptile back and forth across his bottom lip. Clutching the pup closely, Cathy turned away and started walking towards the middle of the bus, her eyes filling with tears. She had hoped that by some miracle the corner store would be open early that morning, but she found the storefront as secured against the outside world as it always was at that hour. For the first time since arriving in that neighbourhood, she found herself wondering if the Traudechauds lived upstairs in the overhead apartment. If only she'd found out more information she could take the pup up there and ask the old woman if she would babysit for the day, until she could figure out what to do. It even crossed her mind to stand on the street and listen for telltale whimpers coming from the upper windows, indicating that the pup's brother was indeed in residence up there. But after a long minute of listening, her own pup made it known that she wanted to be put down. Cathy crossed the road and set her down on the scraggly church lawn.

When the pup finished her squat, she suddenly sprang up, yipped three times, and ran around Cathy's feet. She noticed the end of a shoelace, grabbed it with her baby teeth and began backing away from the shoe, undoing the lace and growling playfully. At the end of the tether, she wagged her head from side to side, growling as if the shoelace were prey. Cathy scurried her feet backward and the pup chased after them, grabbing at the trailing shoelace.

They played all the way down the sidewalk into the rectory backyard. There, Cathy scooped the pup and crept up the porch stairs quietly, hoping not to meet Father Martin just inside the door.

The kitchen smelled of paint but was otherwise dark, quiet, and cool, as usual. By her watch it was just seven. One, possibly two priests would be starting mass at that very moment, one at the main altar, the other in one of the small side alcoves. To buy herself a bit of time, she decided to make the priests boiled eggs instead of fried ones. That way she could leave the eggs to cook while she found a safe place for the pup. With the lively little animal hooked under one arm, she put on six eggs and a small pot of milk. Her intention was to quiet the pup with a breakfast of warm milk poured over pieces of soft white bread.

Her mind worked in high gear, planning every move of the morning, co-ordinating all her responsibilities with the priests and their breakfast and the requirements of the pup. She planned to feed her in the old housekeeper's room and let her stay in there to sleep on the mattress while she finished looking after breakfast. Then she would sneak across the street and beg the old woman in the store to keep her. If she was going to take one dog, what difference could a second one make? All the better to guard the store at night, especially if the Traudechauds didn't live upstairs. They could have one dog for the store and one for their house.

She worked with the dog in the crook of one arm, afraid to put her down because Father Martin's paint trays and brushes were lined up on the floor along one wall. Several times she darted in and out of the dining room to set the table, pup in tow.

The bacon finished cooking in record time, and she set it in a warm oven along with the six pieces of toast. When the priests began eating and the dog was safely stowed in the back room sleeping, she could arrive at the table with fresh toast. Since it was not unusual for the three men to gobble up nearly a whole loaf of bread in the mornings, there would be nothing suspect about this.

She broke the bits of soft white bread into a bowl and poured the warmed milk over them. While she turned to put the pot in the sink, the pup managed to put a small paw into the bowl and tip some of the milk out onto the counter. Cathy had been trying to ignore the obvious fact that the dog did not look the least bit sleepy, but now she knew with certainty that the pup wanted to play. Hearing the faint tinkle of consecration bells from down the corridor, Cathy whisked the bowl of milk and bread off the counter and headed down to the housekeeper's room, giving herself about ten minutes to feed the dog and coax her to sleep.

Once in the room, the pup showed little interest in the bowl of food, preferring instead to wander the old linoleum floor, investigating. Cathy busied herself pulling the bare wilted old mattress off the bedsprings onto the floor. Sitting down on the mattress, resting her back against the wall and closing her eyes for a moment, Cathy waited. She hoped that if she sat quietly, perhaps the pup would pick up on the atmosphere and settle down herself. Instead, the pup wasted several of their precious minutes wandering in the closet, clawing at a hanger she found on the floor. Bored of this, she eventually emerged and stood calmly in the centre of the room staring at Cathy. Hoping that her chance to influence the pup had now arrived, Cathy patted the mattress, meaning for the pup to come and settle down beside her where she could be stroked until she fell asleep. Enticed, the pup let out three sharp little barks and ran at Cathy's hand.

Cathy darted out to grab the dog, desperate to silence her immediately. She had no idea how well sound travelled into the church. When the dog continued to yip and growl at her, Cathy's composure evaporated, and she added to the noise by shushing loudly several times.

With the pup firmly trapped in her lap, she attempted to force-feed her the pieces of soggy bread, hoping that the warm milk would work its magic and put her to sleep. The pup settled slightly, waiting for the next piece to be presented. This encouraged Cathy. But as she fished another piece of bread out of the bowl, a noise outside the open window attracted the dog's attention. She responded with several short, sharp barks.

Cathy shook her roughly by the scruff of her neck, hissing, "No." The pup's huge brown eyes turned and looked at her, startled at the sudden shake. Cathy regretted her action instantly. Taking the pup up to her shoulder, she closed her eyes and rubbed her cheek on her fur.

"Mouse," she whispered, kissing the pup's head, "I don't know what to do with you. You can't make any noise."

The puppy squirmed to get down. Cathy set her back down on the mattress. The pup, growling, sprang after her hands in play.

Yip, yip, yip.

Cathy plucked her up roughly and buried her against her shoulder again.

"Shh. You can't do that." She bent her head into the dog's fur, tears sliding down her cheeks. "Angela, I need some help."

Angela's bracelets tinkled. Her head tipped to one side.

"Ah, flea. Think of someone."

"Eva."

"She's miles away. Think of someone else."

Cathy spoke into the pup's ear.

"Maybe Mrs. Traudechaud will help us, mouse. But you're going to have to be a good girl and stay in here until the priests finish breakfast. Then I can take you over there and see if she'll give you a home."

Down the hall, the swinging door opened into the kitchen. Frozen in fear, Cathy listened, stroking the pup anxiously.

"Hello?"

It was Father LeBlanc. The pup whimpered and Cathy moved her closer to her body. What did he want? He was the most remote of the three priests. He never came looking for her in the morning. What did he want with her *this* morning?

She held the pup against her chest, cooing softly, telling the dog to be quiet.

"Cathy?"

She would have to ignore him. He would see that she had arrived by the pot of eggs on the stove. If he thought she was in the washroom, that would buy her a bit of time. She set the pup down on the mattress where a small paw immediately landed in the bowl of food and upturned it, spilling milk and soggy bread chunks all over the mattress and part of Cathy's skirt. Frustrated, she stood up, towering over the small animal, which now made a game of diving at the wobbling bowl. She leaned on the windowsill, looking out into the church parking lot, trying to stem a flood of tears.

"God, I don't know what to do. I don't know what to do." she whispered.

A kitchen cupboard door opened and china tinkled. An instant later, the creaky oven door opened, paused, and creaked closed again. He was getting his own breakfast. He must want to leave early this morning and he came looking for her to ask if the food was ready yet. As if confirming her theory, the distinctive pump of the swinging door sounded and then the house fell silent.

She knew she had run out of time. The dog would not settle down and fall to sleep within the next two minutes. Her only option would be to leave her unattended in the room and hope that she would remain quiet. Resolved, she stepped past the mattress and headed for the door. When she glanced back into the room just before closing the door, she saw that the pup had followed her nearly to the door and stood staring at Cathy's feet, her small head tipped to one side. Cathy closed the door hurriedly but did not get two steps away before a high-pitched whimpering arose from the room. Her heart turned stone cold and she plunged back into the room. Behind her in the kitchen, the swinging door pumped again.

"Cathy?"

How long could she pretend to be in the washroom?

"Cathy?"

The voice was closer now. It was Father Lauzon this time, and he had advanced across the kitchen to where the corridor opened. Cathy answered from behind the closed door.

"I'm in the washroom, Father. I'll be there in a minute."

"Father LeBlanc needs a lunch this morning. Can you make him something? He's going to the worker's picnic. He needs a potato salad or something."

"Jackass!"

"Potato salad," Cathy hissed under her breath. "Why couldn't he have asked me yesterday?"

"Because we went home early yesterday."

Her shoelaces had been rediscovered. The pup was taking miniature dives at them, pulling and tearing at them, shaking her head from side to side. Panicked at her situation, and annoyed at the dog's complete lack of co-operation, Cathy picked her up roughly, took her to the mattress, shoved her down firmly and told her to stay. Before she was halfway across to the door the pup had followed her and was biting at her socks, yipping vigorously. Once again Cathy planted her on the mattress and tried to break away even faster. But the pup could keep up with her.

Desperate, she looked out the window again, wondering if she could lower the dog out into the parking lot.

"And then what?"

"Oh, God, Angela. I don't know. I don't know what to do with her. Help me."

With her small butt poised in the air, her tail wagging, and front paws extended along the floor, the pup challenged her running shoes to play. She sprang out of her pose, ran at them, and then retreated, resuming her hunting stance. Cathy couldn't believe her total lack of intuition regarding their situation. Weren't animals supposed to be able to sense danger? Wasn't that how they survived in the wilderness? Wasn't she herself giving off some sort of signal, some sort of warning scent that the dog should have recognized?

The kitchen door pumped again.

"Cathy?"

Feet were pounding.

What are you doing with a dog when you have responsibilities, missy, huh?

Cathy shot towards the door.

"Coming, Father."

The pup hung onto her shoelaces. Cathy bent to shake her loose, but her actions only escalated the game, inciting the pup to growl more intensely. She dislodged her and pushed her away across the slippery floor. By the time she reached the centre of the room the pup had rebounded and grabbed the back of one sock. Cathy shook her loose by raising her leg and kicking, again sending her sprawling across the linoleum.

"Cathy?"

"Yes, Father."

At the door the pup caught her sock again, this time more firmly, and Cathy, panicked because she recognized that she was shushing the dog quite audibly and had lost track of whether or not Father Lauzon was still standing at the entrance to the hallway, tore her away with both hands and pushed her away. The last thing that she saw was the pup, having been tipped up into a sitting position by the force of the launch, moving rapidly away, toppling over backwards, head first, her beautiful innocent eyes no longer alight with fun.

★ ★ ★

She boiled four eggs, peeled them under running water while they were still hot enough to scald her, chopped them, and mixed them with pickle relish, onion, and mayonnaise. Her tears fell into the mixture as well. She tossed lettuce with bits of crumbled cold meatloaf and cheese and tomatoes and combined everything in a bowl for Father LeBlanc. Her hands hardly knew what they were doing.

"*Come on,*" Andy said gently, waiting for her on the beach.

What the hell do you call this mess, huh, that you are making, missy? I've never seen such a sad excuse for a salad in all my life. Is that the best you can do, huh, little miss flighty, playing with a dog instead of doing your work?

"*Never mind. You can come with us.*"

By the gods, you're going to learn how to concentrate, young lady, do you hear me? Do you see what it says on this report card here, huh?

That you are inattentive and have difficulty concentrating. Concentrating on boys is what you're doing.

Fathers LeBlanc and Lauzon left directly after breakfast, Father LeBlanc snatching his contribution to the picnic off the counter as he passed by.

"You're welcome," Angela called after him.

Cathy fussed about the counters for a few minutes, listening anxiously for sounds from down the hall. Over and over she recalled the pup's worried eyes.

Father Martin soon arrived in the kitchen to resume painting. In her earlier anxiety to hide the pup, Cathy hadn't figured out how she could get her out of the rectory. With Father Martin's arrival, she recognized that she was now trapped until he left the kitchen area. Her mind worked like a butterfly, lighting only short seconds here and there. What should she do? What should she do?

"The dishes," Angela prompted. *"Fill the sink and do the dishes."*

Afterwards, she went upstairs, to the hall, to the linen closet, the furthest spot away from Father Martin that she could physically manage without actually entering the attic. There she sat down on the floor and mechanically emptied each closet shelf of its meagre stacks of worn, grey linen, unfolding and examining, with meticulous concern, each piece of material, running her hands over the fabric, noting the patches made thin and soft by wear, the edges left stiff and coarse through lack of wear. She worked with a bent head in the unbearably silent rectory, and after a few minutes, she felt Angela's kind hand stroking her hair. A painful lump in her throat strangled her and her tears dropped onto her hands.

Someone had once painstakingly repaired pieces of the linen, stitching, with delicate needlework, over small tears and holes. Several sheets had tiny holes plucked in them in one corner, as if a certain bedspring had a rough edge and clasped them when the bed was made or unmade.

When she finished with the contents of one shelf, she returned everything to its original position, just as if it had never been disturbed. Then, working mechanically, she proceeded to the next shelf to begin again. Her actions were like a ritual and she performed them with reverence. She pointed out to Angela how good the pup was being, how quiet and co-operative she was. Animals have a sense of danger, she explained. They naturally retreat and remain quiet for long periods until danger passes.

The linen smelled of old wood resins. The wooden shelves were unvarnished and lined only with sheets of old yellowed waxed paper, the surface of which had evaporated over the years, leaving behind the brittle parchment-like paper that crinkled with each disturbance. Cathy made a mental note to order proper shelf paper and a bottle of fabric softener from Mr. Renaud next week and to make a day's project out of laundering all the contents of the closet.

Buried at the back of one shelf, she found pillowcases that someone had embroidered with coloured threads; there were beautiful birds and flowers and small pastoral scenes lining the edges of several cases. These, she guessed, had belonged person- ally to the last housekeeper, Mrs. Dupuis. The present resident priests were likely not even aware of their existence. She set them aside. The priests might not appreciate their fussy ornate- ness, but they would provide something pretty for her to look at when she made the beds.

Various names and uses for sheets began to parade through her head, indeed, a whole miniature history of man's association to cloth assembled in her head like a sort of impromptu docu- mentary. The various lengths and widths of material presented themselves as sheets and then cloaks, mantels, capes, swaddling, winding cloths, shrouds.

Her thoughts wandered to her brother. How different they were. He'd never be in this situation. He'd have been more practical. He'd have stuck to reality. For her reality was like a narrow column of sunlight that she passed through only by chance. She couldn't find it when she needed it, and when it found her, she fled from it, it was so painful. For Richard, though, it was a familiar, infinite space through which he moved, as safe a place for him to occupy as was her sky at the end of a balloon string. She knew she could never tell Richard about this day in her life, about the need inside that made her take the puppy in the first place. He would never comprehend it.

The sun had moved around the outside of the house to pour in through the bathroom window, lighting up a large block of the tired old green carpet in the hall where she sat. Cathy watched dust motes begin to swirl up on the warming air currents and smelled the faint scent of late summer roses on the breeze that puffed through the open window beside the toilet. There were other things that she could be doing instead of what she was doing. The bathroom sink and tub needed cleaning, and the windowsill needed a good wipe to get rid of all of that dirty bus soot; the hall carpet could use a vacuum too. What else? Was there anything else that she had to do? Her hands moved restlessly over the embroidered pillowcases, smoothing away nothing. Her ritual had come to its end, and with it, for the first time in her life, an understanding of the purpose of ritual. It conveyed you gently between pain and acceptance.

She placed everything back on the closet shelves except for the embroidered pillowcases that remained resting in the sunlight in her lap.

Let what will be, be.

A familiar unpleasant odour wafted towards her. Father Martin suddenly stood behind her in the hall, dripping with perspiration. She had not heard him come up the stairs.

"What are you doing?"

"Just sorting out some old linen, Father. That's all. It needs freshening up. I'll do it all next wash day."

He looked like he had been working hard. He raised his forearm to sweep the perspiration away from his brow.

"Is there any lunch?"

You poor pimple-headed moron, she thought, looking up at him, her heart see-sawing back and forth between revulsion at his clumsiness and body odour and pity for the desperate eagerness with which he embraced the painting project. She could plainly see that his enthusiasm was born of a starvation not unlike her own.

How different things would be had she never suggested the project. If she hadn't she would never have been out on the church steps and she would never have seen the boys with the box of puppies. And Father Martin might have been, right at this very moment, sitting alone in the dark on the sweltering attic stairs, keeping company with a bottle of whiskey and a plaster statue.

"I've finished the two biggest walls. It's too humid to do any more today. The paint's just not drying at all. I'm going to give it a rest and have a shower. Can you make me a sandwich or something? I'll be down in half an hour."

"Yes, Father."

She knew when she bent over to pick them up why she had set aside the embroidered pillowcases.

The pup was lying on her side at the foot of the heavy iron radiator. Her mouth was opened slightly, but her eyes were closed. Cathy guessed that she might have lain there panting until slipping into unconsciousness. There was not much blood; what there was had drained out her right ear. The back of her head bore no mark.

Cathy scooped up the small body and cradled it, her tears dropping onto the still-soft and lovely fur.

"Dear God," she prayed, "couldn't you please make a miracle just this one time?"

But the little head flopped over easily in her lap, no longer supported by its neck.

She left the pup resting on the bed while she made Father Martin's lunch and set it on the table. The shower was still running, the path of the water through the pipes in the old house audible even as far away as the housekeeper's room. He would not miss her.

She took a tablespoon and several old newspapers from the kitchen, and, cradling the pup tenderly in her arm, descended to the basement. The early afternoon sun had come around to the window, and she was able to sit on the stairs in a narrow wedge of sunlight. Even in violent death, the pup's face remained innocent.

"It was an accident, flea. It's not your fault."

"She may have lain there in pain for most of the morning."

"No, I don't think so, sweetpea. Look at how peaceful she is."

The pup's worried little eyes returned to float in front of Cathy. She bent her head to the soft body.

"I'm so sorry, mouse. I didn't mean it."

Father Martin, freshly showered and changed into a clerical summer suit, ate his lunch in solitude and then left the rectory. Cathy heard his car pass by just beyond the window. The pup's body had conformed to the shape of her lap, appearing to be asleep, just as she had been twenty-four hours ago. Cathy left her in that position on the prettiest pillowcase while she dug into the gold-coloured clay beneath the stairs. She lined the small grave with newspapers, taking care to lap the corners so that no dirt could accidentally soil the pillowcases. Then she lay one pillowcase down as a ground cover and set the reposed dog down very gently on her own pillowcase. It had a pretty pastoral scene on it, a weeping willow tree beside a pasture fence with bright flowers twining around the posts and miniature butterflies hovering in the air above the flowers. She folded a third pillowcase in half and, after bending to kiss the tiny still head, covered the pup, leaving the brightly embroidered flowered edge of the pillowcase turned out. She spent several minutes arranging newspapers on top of the small sheet, until she was certain that dirt could not drop through and soil the dog or its covering. Then she covered over the grave with soil and patted the surface down. The crumbled clay mixture, dried with age, was so soft it felt like baby powder in her bare hand.

She lingered for a moment, unable to lift her hand away.

"You're safe now," she said softly, patting the soil. "It's not what you deserved, but it's the best that I can do for you now."

Some of the pillowcases were paired. She would take the mate to the one the pup lay on home for her own pillow.

After cleaning up the housekeeper's room and returning the mattress, inverted, to its original place, Cathy quietly left the rectory. There was a huge plate of cold sandwiches in the fridge for the priests with a note for them to leave the dishes for her to do in the morning. She made a mental note to get paper plates and napkins from Mr. Renaud.

She boarded the bus outside the variety store, giving thanks for one small mercy. The driver was a stranger.

Richard had not come home. Slipping in quietly through the laundry room door Cathy heard her parents arguing loudly in the living room about it.

"He's probably just at a friend's house," her father said.

"Probably? Probably? That's all you can say?"

Cathy took off her shoes on the plastic mat. She patted her eyes, trying to tell if they were still swollen. They felt normal beneath her fingers.

"You haven't a clue where that kid is and what's more you don't care."

"What do you mean I don't care?"

Cathy grabbed a banana and a glass of milk for a meal and sneaked past the living room archway. Her mother's right hand hung idly by her side, clutching one of the small throw cushions from the couch.

"Fine father *you* turned out to be. He could be lying dead in an alley somewhere with his head split open."

"Adele ... he's a grown young man. He can look after himself."

"Oh, big talker. Do you think the President wouldn't get on the phone in two seconds if it was his son that was missing?"

"Who said he's missing?"

"Don't change the subject. Any other father would have been on the phone by now and demanded that his kid come home."

"Adele, he's eighteen years old. You can't demand that he do anything anymore. Don't you realize that?"

"Don't tell me what to realize, you spineless coward."

Their voices travelled through the house, bouncing off the hard surfaces like jangling pieces of scrap iron.

Upstairs in her room, Cathy moved about like an automaton, putting clothes away, retrieving pyjamas from their hook, taking the braid out of her hair. The embroidered pillowcase sat on the bed, waiting to be slipped over her pillow. She pulled down the blinds, carefully lowered the light switch so it didn't make a sound, and changed the pillowcase in the darkened room before slipping under the covers. She lay there for several minutes in the still summer afternoon, resting her cheek against the pillow, listening to the foolish voices filter up through the floor. How could it be that less than twenty-four hours ago the pup lay safely curled up against her? How could the world alter so swiftly?

"Ah, flea, it wasn't your fault."

Cathy turned into the pillow and cried with a broken heart for the small life that had entrusted itself to her and that she had guarded so carelessly. She begged that she might undo the few seconds of that morning. What would that cost, over the course of all time? Just one small turning back? *Please, please, please, God, just this once.*

The house grew dark and still behind her as her friends slowly towed her away over a dark still sea and down, over the curve of the horizon. Beyond, on the other, lighted side of the world, Angela and Andy, dressed in colourfully embroidered ponchos, waited for her on a strip of golden beach with their dog, Mickey. When Cathy crested the horizon, their welcoming faces beamed at her and the pup rushed out from their shadows, heading directly for her, yipping with her sharp little voice, her beautiful brown eyes vibrant with life.

Gerald woke instantly when Richard arrived. He heard his son's stockinged feet rasp across the carpet in the hall and up the stairs to his room. When he thought he would not be noticed, he slipped out of his bed and checked that the doors had been locked. Only then was he able to return to bed and fall into a restful sleep, not hearing another sound until daylight.

The next morning, a Saturday, Gerald was up early before anyone had stirred. He fixed himself a cup of coffee and a piece of rye toast and parked himself at the dining room table to watch the birds along the back fence. Earlier in the spring, mourning doves had nested in the evergreens. He'd seen them coming and going bearing twigs and grass in their beaks. There was a family of cardinals nearby; they visited the feeder in the yard regularly, scavenging for seeds, the male hopping into the shadows of the hedge, bearing a treat for his secluded mate. Despite great effort, however, Gerald had not been able to locate their nest.

After he settled into his chair and scanned the fence perfunctorily, a bright blue object in the middle of the yard drew his attention. He considered it for several minutes, unable to decipher it. After more concerted study, he finally recognized it as the wastepaper basket from Richard's bedroom. He put his coffee cup down and padded off down the hall and up the stairs towards Richard's bedroom. His pulse rose steadily and he felt the first pricking of perspiration on his skin. His feet pressed along the carpet in a shuffling, building panic.

Stopping outside the room, he tilted his head, listening anxiously both for sounds on the other side of the door and elsewhere in the house. He heard nothing. He then knocked softly with one knuckle. Nothing. He knocked again, as firmly as he dared, and waited. When there was still no reply, he turned the doorknob quietly and opened the door a crack. The room was dark, so he pressed himself close to the opening. He was driven back by a harsh, acrid odour. Vomit.

He flung the door wide open. Richard lay flat on his back wearing only pyjama bottoms. Both his arms were flung out sideways, overhanging the edges of his mattress. The sheets and bedspread were pushed into a tangled lump at the end of the bed, partly trailing down onto the floor. Gerald stepped into the room a few feet but stopped as the smell became overpowering.

"Richard. Richard," he called in a hoarse whisper.

There was just enough light from a crack beside the window blind to see Richard's chest rise and fall rhythmically. Gerald smelled beer. Richard was dead drunk.

Now the wastepaper basket in the backyard was not so important. But he had to get it out of sight so Adele didn't see it and then come straight up here asking questions. He hurried out of the room and back down the stairs, still propelled by panic. At the back door, he slipped his bare feet into a pair of black galoshes and noiselessly let himself outside. He trudged across the yard to the abandoned basket. He saw flies lifting out of it. Peering over the edge, he saw vomit pooled at the bottom.

Now he had to have a plan. He swept up the basket with one hand, held it at a distance, and scurried back to the house.

Leaving his boots and the fouled basket inside the garage, he crept back inside the kitchen and paused to listen to the house. All was silent. He passed noiselessly through the main floor rooms, heading for the stairs.

He rapped impatiently on Cathy's bedroom door, and without waiting for a response pushed the door open, turned on the overhead light, and went to the side of her bed to shake her. She was huddled close to the wall, with her knees pulled up tight to her body and a clutch of sheets clasped to her chest. Her face was turned down into the pillow. She woke immediately at his touch and rolled over, squinting up at him through one partially opened eye.

"Get up and help me. Your brother's been sick. And be quiet."

Cathy's eyes burned. She propped herself up and groaned. She was confused about where she was. A moment ago it had been dark and then suddenly a guillotine blade of light had flashed, severing her from that moment. And now she was here. Awake in bright light. She wanted to go back to where she had just been. There had been something comforting there. What was it? It was right there, just frustratingly out of reach, draining away. If she didn't close her eyes and roll over again right away, she'd never catch up and it would be gone forever. She looked down and saw the embroidered pillowcase and the bunched sheets that she had clutched all night. That's where she'd been. Yesterday.

"Get a move on, now. I don't want your mother to find this."

"Find what?"

Her father had wandered off down the hall, motioning for her to follow. Cathy swung her legs out of the bed and moved about the room, finding slippers and a robe. She tiptoed quietly out into the hall towards Richard's room.

Gerald was holding the corner of Richard's window blind to one side. A wedge of light fell across the bed. When Cathy arrived, she caught her father muttering to himself that it was all over the carpet. She heard him say "shit" when his back was turned, a word he almost never used. She startled him by asking, in a loud voice, what was going on. Before he could reply, she was stopped dead in her tracks by a piercing sour odour.

"Go and get some clean sheets. He's thrown up all over everything. You'll have to change the bed and clean it up. Don't make any noise. I don't want your mother to know."

He continued to survey the disaster before him, wearing the helpless look of someone out of his depth. Cathy went down the hall to use the bathroom, opting not to flush and only to wash with a trickle from the tap. She found fresh sheets in the linen closet and obediently brought them back to the door of the room. Gerald was trying to sort out the tangle of sheets and blankets and bedspread at Richard's feet. In the dim light, he was not having much success. He was curled over at the shoulders, looking down, half-heartedly, at the mess at his feet, a sheet corner pinched gingerly by two fingers in each hand. Cathy saw that he resembled herself bent reluctantly over the priests' dirty laundry. Her father offered her the sheet corners.

"Here. You'll have to take the whole thing in a bundle."

He shook his hand impatiently meaning for her to relieve him of the sheets immediately. Cathy suddenly stopped moving.

"Tiresome, huh?"

She stared hard at her father.

"Heaven forbid he should wake Richard and make him clean it up. Heavens, no. That's what daughters are for."

He shook his hand again.

"Take this. I don't want to wake your mother. You'll have to get some cleaner in water and get it out of the carpet."

"Can we open the window?"

Cathy still had not reached for the sheets.

248

"Here," her father said, impatiently, extending his fistful of bed linen.

Cathy made no move to take the sheets. So her father bent down and scooped the bundle of soiled linen from the floor and pushed it against her.

"Get going before she wakes up."

The sheets fell to the floor. Her father looked at them and then looked up into her eyes. He narrowed his.

"Don't you get smart with me, young lady."

Cathy slid up her balloon string and looked out over the stirring city. She wondered if Bondy's bakery would be perfuming the neighbourhood air yet. Meanwhile, Young Lady took the acrid-smelling bundle downstairs to the laundry room, closed the door softly behind her and pulled the button on the washing machine. Partially digested pizza ingredients clung to the sheets. She should have taken the mess back upstairs and shaken the loose food into the toilet. But she didn't. She just shoved everything into the hot water and added a cup of soap. In thirty-five minutes there would be clean, unsoiled sheets ready to be put in the dryer.

Back in Richard's room, Gerald had unloosed the bottom sheet from two corners of the mattress and was attempting, clumsily, to strip it out from under an unconscious and oblivious Richard. When Young Lady reached the doorway, Gerald motioned for her to go to the other side of the bed to assist him. They managed to tug the sheet, by degrees, up along the back of Richard's legs and then under his torso and finally out from under his head.

Young Lady bent down to release the last corner of sheet from the mattress, and in doing so, set her slipper down into something slick on the carpet. She skidded forward, and at the same time, her hair dragged against the wall before falling against her cheek, bringing something wet and cold with it.

"Ew! God!" she wailed in a whisper, "he's got it all over here, too."

"Quiet. I don't want to wake your mother."

"It's in my hair, for God's sake."

Gerald stopped moving and glared at her.

"Since when do you use the Lord's name in vain?"

"It's on my face and I'm standing in it."

"Where did you learn to talk like that?"

"I meant 'gosh,' okay? It was just a mistake."

"You know better than that."

"It was just a slip, okay? I've got puke all over me."

"Here! That's another word I don't like."

Cathy watched from the sky. Young Lady stopped moving and stared at the shadows on Gerald's pale Irish face. She couldn't find the father of her childhood there. The one she had adored and worried about and tried to save. Instead, a fool stood before her, with no inkling of statues with worn edges and half-empty whiskey bottles on lonely attic stairs, or frightening narrow iron beds, or hands moving rhythmically between legs, or the musty stained sheets of grown men that she washed weekly.

"In three lifetimes it won't occur to you to ask about the dog, will it? Try it. I dare you. Just ask her what happened. What did she do with the dog?"

Richard's tongue came out and licked his lips. Gerald glanced down at him, hoping he was waking up so that he could be hurried off to the shower. Young Lady noticed that her father's face was scrunched up against the awful smell. He handed her his part of the sheet.

"It doesn't look as if he's ready to wake up yet, so just get rid of the rest of this and see if you can clean up in here a bit. I'll go back downstairs and wait for your mother to wake up. I'll tell her he had a touch of the flu."

"Well what did he have, anyway?"

"He's been sick on too much beer. After the way she went after him the other night, I can't say that I blame him, though."

Gerald eased himself into a sitting position on the footboard of the bed and spoke despondently to the carpet.

"I can't take any more nights like the one before last, either. The pressure's just getting to be too much. At your age, you should know better than to stir things up. Bringing that dog home was a foolish thing to do. I've had enough trouble for one lifetime without you dragging animals home to set her off. The sooner you can get into an out-of-town nursing course, the better. They'll give you a place to sleep and all your meals while they train you. Your brother's just now on the verge of manhood and I don't want anything to disturb him. A boy needs to be left alone. That's not something I expect you to understand, but I'm telling you that I don't want any more nonsense out of you. He'll likely be gone in a couple of years. I want what time he has left to live here to be peaceful for him."

Cathy watched Young Lady fumbling quietly through the sheets trying to find a clean edge to wipe her face. Nursing training as soon as possible was way too late. She'd needed to know about nursing yesterday, about how to fix a floppy little head and put blood back into a soft ear, how to get a heart going again that had stopped dead still, and how to relight an empty pair of brown eyes. She raised a clean corner of sheet to her cheek, wiped away the awful wetness, and then mopped the clot out of her hair as best she could. Then she turned her face away from her father and held the sheet against her eyes.

"Just clean up this mess. And be quiet when you go downstairs."

"What about him?" she asked, whispering, pointing to the bed.

"He'll just sleep the rest of it off. Cover him up with the clean sheets. I left his garbage pail in the garage. See if you can clean that out too."

"His garbage pail? What's it doing in the garage? What's in it?"

"He must have tried to help himself out a bit. It needs a good scrub. Thank goodness I saw it first. It was out in the middle of the yard. I brought it in before your mother saw it, though. See what you can do with it. And don't wake your mother."

During the last part of August, Cathy abandoned plans to cheer up the rectory, occupying herself solely with replicating meals that she found in magazines. Her feelings for Father Martin alternated between revulsion, when she was forced to endure his physical presence, watching his clumsy large hands and feet make the simplest task difficult, and pity, when he disappeared up the stairs after breakfast.

During the day she taught herself how to make lasagne, herbed rice, apple walnut stuffing for roast chicken. One quiet afternoon, she remembered Eva's recipes, tucked away in her apron pocket. She retrieved one of the pale yellow papers, sniffed its faint perfumey scent, and carefully placed it on the counter. For the next two hours, her eyes traced over the lovely comforting loops and curls, reading and rereading the directions as she created the Scandinavian meatballs for that night's dinner.

Father LeBlanc enjoyed a glass of milk with a serving of warm apple crisp one night and began to request milk with his meals regularly. She added more milk to the weekly grocery order. When peaches came into season and she served them as dessert, he suddenly asked if she could buy breakfast cereals instead of serving bacon and eggs every morning. The cereal and fruit then began to dwindle at an astonishing rate, and a bowl and spoon were routinely found in the sink in the mornings.

Mr. Renaud raised his long front teeth in laughter as the rectory's order evolved from week to week. She needed five loaves of bread a week, as well as three large boxes of cereal and five quarts of milk. Sometimes he clucked in disapproval, and other times he made suggestions based on his knowledge of special items that he had in stock. Father Martin was the only one who enjoyed tomato juice with his meal, but all three would accept apple juice. She bought both and served juice every evening. Ice cream was a favourite dessert, especially with fresh fruit or maple syrup. Fresh-made dinner rolls that came as ready-made dough in tubes were also a favourite.

By Labour Day weekend, the priests had still not found a permanent housekeeper. Father Martin had finished painting the kitchen, trimming all the baseboards and the window in the horrid green of which he was so proud. The ceiling seemed to have been overlooked. He knew nothing about preparing a surface for painting and so spread the harvest gold over the dark varnished cupboards without sanding them first. The end result was a dreadful streaky appearance that he managed to like, saying that it was a creative two-toned look that imitated expensive antiquing. Each little doorknob was painstakingly coated in green to match the trim in the rest of the room.

Inspired by his newfound vein of creativity, he moved into the front hallway and began to paint the balusters on the staircase with beige paint that he also found in the garage. As evidenced by his impatient daubing of test patches of colour here and there, he planned to paint the handrail glossy black, finishing with a brilliant red ball atop the newel post. Cathy learned to pass up and down the stairs marvelling more at the human capacity to differ from one person to another than at the striking ugliness of his conceptions.

She was content with her culinary progress in the kitchen. While she worked, she talked to Angela, asking her advice, listening to her suggestions about seasonings and menu combinations. She never went down the hall to the housekeeper's room and always fled up the basement stairs once she had put a load of laundry in the washer.

It occurred to her to speak to her father about learning to bake bread. She was certain Father Martin would make himself toast with jam before bed in the evenings if he had homemade loaves waiting for him in the breadbox.

In her mind she designed a corner of the kitchen to hold a small chest freezer. She toyed with the idea of suggesting to Father Lauzon that the rectory could save on its food bill by investing in the appliance, when, as if he had read her mind, he strode into the kitchen one afternoon. His face was dark.

"Where are the receipts from Mr. Renaud's?"

"On the nail, right there, Father, where they always are."

He snatched them off the nail and began to sort through them on the table, pausing to read certain ones and set them aside.

"I spoke to Mr. Renaud this week; I couldn't believe the size of the grocery bills I had to pay. He says that you have changed the standard grocery order quite a bit from what it used to be. You're ordering things you don't need. Look at this here, cocoa. We don't need cocoa. And all this apple and tomato juice with the meals. We don't need that. It's just money out the window. Salads, we don't need that. Those little bottles of dressing are expensive. Father LeBlanc can drink coffee and tea. Just get cream for coffee, no more milk. You're not running a restaurant here. Just stick to meat and potatoes. I'll tell Mr. Renaud what we need from now on. You won't have to bother with the order. Just cook with what you find in the fridge. We don't need fancy meals."

He swept up the carbon-backed bills and took them with him through the swinging door.

"Foolish spoiled kid," he muttered on his way.

Angela, bracelets jangling as she rammed her hands down onto her hips, stuck her tongue out at the swinging door.

"Look in the mirror, Your Pomposity. That's where you'll see 'spoiled'."

Cathy went to the sink and turned both faucets on full blast. She watched the water plunge into the black hole of the drain in the ancient sink, wishing she could stuff Mr. Renaud down there to die in the dark slimy pipes.

"You just couldn't keep your nose out of it, could you?"

"Ah, flea, he might not have said a word, you know. It could just be that the bills got too high."

"But they were the ones who asked for the dammed food. It's Father Martin's cocoa."

Cathy twisted the taps shut, and the kitchen fell silent.

"I didn't see Father Lauzon turn down any of the dinner rolls or the apple juice or the desserts. Did you?"

Angela shook her head vigorously.

"If all he wants is meat and potatoes, then that's what he'll get. Meatloaf and boiled potatoes five nights a week. No dessert, no dinner rolls, no bread, no ketchup, for that matter. And I can serve tap water as well as anything else."

Cathy angrily pushed the dishcloth around the counter.

"Why bother with tablecloth or the water glasses or floral centrepieces? Why not economize by not even heating the food? Leftovers can be served cold. Why change the sheets once a week? How 'bout I just turn them over? There'd be a terrific saving on soap and hot water and wear and tear on the clothes pegs."

"Flea, calm down."

"How 'bout everyone take a lesson from Father Underpants and just wear everything for three days running. Or more. How 'bout that?"

Angela put her hands gently on Cathy's shoulders and whispered in her ear.

"Why don't you just tell them you don't want to do this anymore? You start school in a week, anyway."

Cathy came to an abrupt stop. That's what Richard would do. When he was finished with Robinson's he would just say so and then walk out. No hesitation. Just perfect confidence in his right to move on.

"What's here for you now?"

Angela always made her think about the right things. With Father Lauzon controlling the food order now, even the distraction of experimenting and learning disappeared. There would be nothing to do except dust, vacuum, cook appallingly boring meals, and wash up dishes at the end of the day. The only thing that really held her back was the small grave beneath the basement stairs. She had covered it over with boxes of unused kitchenware transferred from the housekeeper's room and was confident that it would not be discovered. If only she could take the small grave with her under the crook of her arm and keep it safely with her in her room at home.

"Don't think about that. We've got her at our place, remember? Just come over."

She made scrambled eggs and green beans for the priests' supper. Father Lauzon, having a difficult time disguising his disappointment at the plain meagre meal, came through the door to ask for bread.

While she put two slices on a plate for him, he asked her if she could stay on after school started, just until they found someone permanent. She would only have to come in after school and make their dinner. They would make their own breakfasts.

Despising her lack of resolve, she dutifully replied that she would have to ask her mother.

Without waiting, Father Lauzon phoned Adele to ask if Cathy could continue to come in after school to make their meals. The request delighted Adele.

"It's about time you developed a sense of responsibility. At your age I had a job because I *had* to have one. You're too old to be running around playing games on teams. Don't think I don't know why you want to wear those short little uniforms. I wasn't born this morning."

Cathy stayed on the school bus until it dropped her at the bus stop in front of Gibson's. Then she travelled the usual route out to the city's east end. When she returned home in the early evenings, sometimes she saw a crack of light under the basement door and knew that her father was down there baking bread and sticky buns. Richard was not usually around. She ate alone and then, kneeling on the dining room carpet in the dark, droned through the rosary with her mother.

The President's dead infant had never left Adele's mind. She improvised prayers begging for mercy and the redemption of the baby's soul, mixing up snippets from the Sermon on the Mount with homemade proverbs about the souls of innocent angels.

She insisted on all five decades of the rosary, demanding that Cathy pray aloud, reprimanding her sharply every time her voice sank into a monotonous, flat tone. They alternated decades, Adele praying with closed eyes and whispering teeth. At the completion of the final "Glory Be to the Father," Adele insisted that they both bow their heads and beat their breassstsss while she intoned "Mea culpa, mea culpa, mea maxima culpa."

Cathy watched her mother's thick wrist and the attached clenched fist flopping back and forth in a regular rhythm.

★ ★ ★

September was unusually dry and warm, a boon to the nuns at St. Joseph's, who held their annual Mother and Daughter Welcome-Back Garden Party on the second Saturday of the month. Adele insisted on wearing a yellow pillbox hat and white gloves with her yellow summer suit. Cathy tried to tell her that the event was less formal, but Adele shushed her with a remark about fifteen-year-olds not knowing how to go out into the world yet.

By the time they arrived, Louise De Finca, crassly displaying her diamond-crusted fingers, had already assumed her usual position in the centre of the courtyard surrounded by her four immaculately starched daughters. Annoyed at her inability to compete, Adele admonished Cathy from between clenched teeth to stand up straight and look intelligent as they passed through the gate.

Janet St. Amand and her mother both arrived in bold floral prints with coloured shoes to match. Eva wore her hair loose to her shoulders, catching part of it up at the crown with a floral clasp that matched her dress. Anyone might have easily mistaken her for one of the senior students. She leaned against the trees, speaking to various people, tossing her head backwards, laughing with some of the nuns. She possessed an astonishing knack of looking right past their black linen habits, their little steel-rimmed glasses, their coarse, out-of-control eyebrows, to the girls that they all once were, and they, in turn, forgot their stations and became more animated around her.

The students noticed these changes and huddled in discrete clusters, observing the metamorphoses, speaking to each other from behind smiles, like ventriloquists, urging each other to watch what was happening. Even Sister Lumina, talking while waving a half-eaten cookie around, laughed when a breeze picked up her veil and blew it forward over her face. Peggy Jackson commented quietly to a circle of fellow students, "Christ Almighty, what Nolips lacks in lips she sure makes up for in neck. Would you look at the length of that thing!"

Even Adele had actually contrived to be part of a small crowd gathered around Eva St. Amand while she told a story about finding a rabbit on the boat at the cottage. Adele wasn't interested in the story. She was surreptitiously taking inventory of Eva's clothes and hair. It was irksome that this woman some-how approached the ideal of glamour and poise that had become synonymous with the President's wife. The suspicion that her loose youthful hairstyle and above average height created the glamour put stout, fuzzy-haired Adele into a sour mood. She pouted by officiously dragging Cathy by the sleeve to each of her teachers to inquire about her progress.

"Oh, but the term has barely begun," Sister Aline said. "We've hardly covered anything yet."

Sister Anne Rochelle, picking up her veil and holding it aloft to cool off, put her arm around Cathy's shoulders and gave her a friendly hug, remarking to Adele that she wished her daughter wasn't so shy and would come out for one of the school teams.

"Now that would be progress. We can't get her to stay one extra minute after school. She scurries out to the bus every day like a frightened little mouse. You'd think she hated it here. Surely we're not that bad are we, Cath?"

Adele bristled.

"She has other responsibilities after school, Sister. And quite a bit of homework each evening."

"Ah, well, you know the old saying about all work and no play…"

Here Sister Anne Rochelle paused for a moment and then suddenly giggled out loud.

"It makes you into an old ogre."

Her hand reached out and stroked the back of Cathy's neck.

"None of that in you, I hope."

Cathy swallowed dryly and looked down at the gravel between her black patent leather shoes.

Adele cleared her throat.

"Will you be teaching any poetry this year, Sister? Any Robert Frost?"

Cathy's ears jolted forward.

"Well, there is always something on the curriculum."

"I find it curious that at the age of fifteen Cathy hasn't yet learned 'Stopping By Some Woods on a Snowy Evening.' I certainly knew it at her age."

"Oh, yes," said Sister Anne Rochelle, clapping her hands together and rising up on her toes, "'Stopping By Woods.' That's such a lovely poem, isn't it? Well, you never know what's in store for you, Cathy."

She turned and winked at Adele.

"I don't want to spoil any surprises, do I?"

Adele puffed out her bosom and looked down, brushing imaginary crumbs from her bodice.

"The importance of that poem lies in its final lines, I believe, Sister."

"Yes," agreed Sister Anne Rochelle. "'And I have miles to go before I sleep.' Food for thought there. It's a *metaphor*, Cathy. You know the literary devices that we are starting to discuss in class? We haven't come to it yet, but it's in the chapter that we've just started."

Her enthusiasm bubbled out of her like water from a spring. Cathy wished it would dry up and disappear, because she could see plainly her mother's seething resentment at being overrun by its unchecked flow.

"Are you aware, Sister, that he wrote an inaugural poem for the President?"

"The President?"

"The President of the United States."

"Oh! Did he really? No. I wasn't aware."

"I'm amazed that you don't feel it is necessary to teach young people an important lesson from their own history like that. They should all know that inaugural poem by heart."

"Well, that would properly be American history, of course, and history is Sister Aline's domain. I'd love to read the poem, though. Can you recite any of it?"

Zip! Cathy was floating in the empty sky looking for a place to hide. Beneath her she saw the black convent roof, with its spectacularly steep pitch and green weathered copper railings and yellow air raid siren tucked into one corner. There'd be an amazing attic under that roof, she thought.

Adele's skin grew tight around her eyes and her round fuzzy head drew back, tortoise-style. She clasped her purse close to herself with both hands, a small white leather shield over her pubic area. Her cheeks flared pink. She cleared her throat.

"Well, no, Sister, I'm not prepared, at this very present moment."

"Well, why don't you send a copy of it with Cathy sometime. I'd be glad to look at it."

The nun, smiling broadly, rode up and down on her toes once more and shook a handful of Cathy's hair affectionately.

Cathy drifted slowly back and forth way up in the sky.

★ ★ ★

Adele finally released Cathy's sleeve when they passed through the garden gate. She stormed down the sidewalk towards the parking lot, her breath wheezing noisily. Beneath her, the too-high heels of her shoes clacked angrily against the pavement.

"Well, we'll see what kind of a year you have, miss, under that young nun. I don't think she's fit to be teaching students your age. She properly belongs in the grade school, teaching the little ones. If there is any nonsense, my dear, I will be speaking to Reverend Mother faster than you can shake a stick."

When they reached the car, she balanced her purse on her stomach and swished her hand down in the opening for her keys.

"And that phoney laugh of hers, trying to pretend she's a girl of fifteen. She's got a lot of growing up to do, that one, I can tell you. Giggle, giggle, giggle all the time."

Adele ground the gears of the Volkswagen ahead from second into third and announced to Cathy that from now on, after their recitation of the rosary in the evenings, they would begin going through the poetry of Robert Frost together.

"Oh Jesus, shoot me," Angela muttered from the roof of the car.

September slipped into October. The crimson-gold trees burned like bonfires against bright blue skies. The midday sun was still warm as summer, and the evening air was scented with ripe apples and wood smoke. It was Cathy's favourite time of year. She spent her lunch hours scrunching through the falling leaves on the school grounds. Angela kept her company.

"We never get this in California, you know. All the colours."

"I always feel like I'm waiting for something at this time of year," Cathy confided. "As if something is coming."

Angela kicked through a pile of leaves, nodding.

"Something always is."

In early November the temperature changed suddenly and the fall came to an abrupt end. Now the days were grey, short, and cold. Cathy left the house in darkness in the mornings and returned after dark in the evenings.

Holed up inside the house, Adele noticed nothing. The dining room floor was covered in paint cans and rolls of white brocade wallpaper. She was redecorating, singing softly while trekking up and down her stepladder.

"Don't let it be forgot, la-di-da-da-da-da, la-di-da-da-da-di-da, that was known as Ca … me … lot."

Her concept was rich in cream and gold details. Textured wallpaper with a gold metallic fleck, vanilla cream trim, cream silk drapes, a new crystal chandelier. She worked feverishly, her bottom lip pulled into her mouth and held tightly by her teeth.

"Oh my, Adele," the First Lady gasped.

★ ★ ★

On a Friday afternoon in late November, the final coat of paint applied, Adele bathed and left the house. She needed a new lamp for the buffet. Something to complement the new chandelier. Last month she had ordered a new hi-fi stereo set for a corner of the living room and would check again on the delivery date. Humming with energy, she parked the car behind Ableman Brothers Fine Furniture and struggled through slush to the front entrance where she found a group of people staring through the display window at several televisions.

"I don't know," she overheard, and "About twenty minutes ago."

Adele frowned. What was going on? Curious, she moved closer. Then Syd Ableman held open the store door.

"Come on in, folks. Get out of the cold. It's terrible news."

The crowd lurched forward, sweeping Adele inside.

"Terrible news? Is it a tornado or something?" she asked, swivelling her head to catch anyone's eye.

Once past the funnel of the door, the crowd broke apart, leaving her standing alone in the main aisle. Not three feet away, a man perched on the arm of a chair turned and looked right at her.

"No, ma'am. It's the President."

"Oh." Adele lit up. "What's going on? Is he going to speak?" She moved toward the chair. The man shook his head.

"No, ma'am. He's been shot."

265

"Shot?"

Adele's body began to tingle. Then her eyes narrowed and her bosom rose officiously.

"Oh, no. That can't be right."

She sped past the man to a seat in front of the largest television.

"How could he be shot?" she asked, backing into place on a chesterfield. "He's surrounded by secret service men all the time. They wear bulletproof vests."

She sank so deeply into the couch her feet left the ground.

"We're not back in the days of Abraham Lincoln," she said, propping her purse behind her.

Someone turned up the volume on all of the sets. The grey, serious-faced newscaster spoke against a steady background clatter of teletype machines. Words floated through the air like bubbles. "Shot." "Dallas." "The President." "Tour." "Shot." "Bulletin." "The President." "Shot."

She had not known that he was away from Washington. She was still getting over the baby. With Christmas coming, the dining room renovations, she had let go of him for a few days. What was he doing in Dallas?

The couch jiggled every few minutes as bodies shifted to make room for others. Adele's eyes strayed to the window. It had begun to sleet heavily but still a crowd stared, alarmed and disbelieving, at the flickering televisions. Adele studied several expressions and felt her own begin to change.

"Word now that the wound is serious…," the anchorman said.

A woman slid onto her knees, pulled a rosary from her purse, crossed herself, and began to pray. Adele immediately opened her purse, rummaged for a rosary that she knew was not there, sighed, extracted a Kleenex, snapped the purse shut, and crossed herself.

No prayers came to mind, though. Instead, she wondered if a bullet lodged in a shoulder muscle would be visible to the eye. She imagined them walking into a hospital emergency entrance, the President stoically grimacing against pain, the First Lady taking little skipping steps in her high heels to keep up with him.

The criminals would have tried to disable him, so the wound would be in his right shoulder. She saw it clearly: a single, neat, round hole through the summer-weight wool of a grey suit. The edge would be stained red. Beneath that, his white shirt would also be torn and bloody. His wife carefully slipped the clothing off his arm and then held cotton balls against the wound. They were in a small room in the emergency department, he sitting on a chair in his undershirt, secret service men clustering in the halls outside. The doctor came in and the First Lady removed the blood-soaked cotton ball. What did you see when you looked into a bullet hole? Could you see the butt-end of the bullet, a little grey steel disk sitting there like something in a nest? Or would the flesh have closed over it like a curtain?

If the bullet were not visible, then maybe the doctor would have to poke something into the wound, something with a tapered end, like a dental instrument. Maybe the bullet could be hooked or grasped with small tongs and pulled out. If only she could be there, in her nurse's uniform, rolling stainless steel trays of sterilized instruments up to the doctor's elbow, fetching ice, touching her friend on the elbow, consoling the President as the bullet was dragged from his body. She could swab his other arm and administer a shot of painkiller. She could go home with them to the White House to change the dressings.

★ ★ ★

At St. Joseph's, classroom loudspeakers crackled suddenly, startling the entire school. The teachers, forty minutes into the first lessons of the afternoon, halted in mid-sentence and turned to stare at the small brown boxes perched above the blackboards. The unusually sombre voice of "Our Lady of the Loudspeaker," as Reverend Mother was called, poured down on them.

"Students and teachers of St. Joseph's, would you please pause in your studies to pray for the President of the United States, who has suddenly taken gravely ill this afternoon."

The boxes crackled again and fell silent.

Sister Anne Rochelle's white hands came together instantly as she fell to one knee in front of the class, calling out the first words of the "Our Father." For the next moment the halls of St. Joseph's filled with the sounds of scraping chairs and shuffling feet. And then the sound of hundreds of chanted "Our Fathers" began to resonate up and down the corridors.

Cathy, kneeling in the centre of the class, mumbled along distractedly. Gravely ill with what? The President was a young man, too young for a heart attack. He lived in a safe country with clean drinking water. People like him did not just become gravely ill. You couldn't catch malaria or elephantiasis in North America. That was what the people in the missions caught. *Those* people got gravely ill. Something was not right.

Before the "Our Father" was completed, the loudspeakers crackled to life again. Reverend Mother waited for the stragglers to finish and then announced the first of the Sorrowful Mysteries. Sister Anne Rochelle slipped her rosary out of her deep pocket and held it aloft. Again the halls rustled while hundreds of rosaries were fished out of pockets or empty inkwells. Then the whole school resonated with chanted Hail Marys.

Cathy lifted her head cautiously and stared up at the loudspeaker. There was a lie here somewhere.

Holy Mary, Mother of God…

She remembered the yellow air raid siren on the roof. Maybe the mushroom bomb from the Russians had finally dropped. A huge poisonous cloud might be spreading over farm fields and highways from Washington, rolling north to Canada. There wasn't time to get home; the teachers decided it was best to have them all die in prayer rather than to succumb alone out on the roads. Her death was only hours, maybe minutes, away. She imagined her father, leaning on a dispensary, coughing, wheezing, one hand holding his chest. He would look out the window at the last moment, glancing in the direction of home before he fell to his knees and then collapsed. If she left right now, could she run fast enough and long enough to reach his side in time?

Sister Anne Rochelle caught her eye and raised an eyebrow. Cathy dropped her gaze to her hands but continued her speculating. Her mother would be pulling aside the drapes, crying at the windows of the house, terrified to be alone. Her last moments would be spent craning to see if someone was coming to get her.

Where would Richard be? Working at Robinson's? Would this be enough to make him lose his sarcastic smirk? Would he cave in and pray for himself? Or would he throw a leg over the back of a chair and lean forward on his knee, watching the sky, waiting?

And Angela? The real Angela. Where would she be? Was she just that moment crossing a room to answer a ringing phone? Would she know everything?

Two cassocks suddenly swished by in the hall. Cathy's eyes slid sideways just in time to see both Father McCoy and his assistant Father Roy pass by, headed briskly in the direction of the office. Cathy's heart fluttered; she might be right. The priests were here to read the last rites over the PA system. In a minute they would begin making the rounds of each classroom offering Holy Communion for the last time, hoping to be in time for everyone. But then, why hadn't the siren warned them?

Our Lady of the Loudspeaker finished the last prayer of the second decade, floundered and came to a clumsy halt.

Commotion filtered over the speakers: whispers, papers rattling, a hand over the microphone. Then the sad voice of Father McCoy flowed out of the boxes.

"Students and teachers, I ask that you pray for the repose of the soul of the President of the United States, who passed away moments ago in Dallas, Texas."

Sister Anne Rochelle twisted her head around as if to see the words coming from the speaker. Her face stricken, she rose, commanded Sandra De Finca to continue leading the class in the rosary, and left the room in a *whoosh* of black linen. From somewhere down the hall, a mournful wail rose above all the other commotion. Cathy's rosary began to tremble in her hands.

★ ★ ★

People continued to pour through the door at Ableman's. What was it, they asked. Voices rose up from all the furniture in front of the televisions. It was a Red plot. The Russians were still mad over Cuba. It was Mexican rebels close to the Texas border. It was a madman. Heads nodded. Adele listened, her head swivelling to locate each new speaker. It occurred to her to phone Gerald and tell him that the Communists had shot the President because of the Cuban incident. At dinner that evening she would explain it to the children in detail. They should begin to know how governments worked.

The bulletin banner flashed across the bottom of the television screen again for the umpteenth time. Adele wondered, with all of the racket coming out of the teletype machines in the newsroom behind the announcer, why there wasn't more information to pass on. Perhaps it was because they were going to cut to the hospital any minute and show the smiling President getting into a limo, leaving, waving with his good arm, his wounded arm held close in a white cotton sling.

The television camera dropped away from the face of a clock showing Dallas time — just passing two o'clock — to the waxy, slack-jawed face of the announcer. He folded his hands on his desk and, for a wordless moment, stared straight ahead into the camera. Then his mouth opened and his short chain of words sped like a locomotive out of the television, ploughing into the crowds gathered in front of him all over the world.

★ ★ ★

Gerald was just ambling in out of the sleet to begin his shift at Hooper's Pharmacy when an excited Gord McInnis motioned to him from behind the dispensary. Gord was bent to the radio, listening. The store was empty except for the two clerks and a woman customer trying out lipstick colours on her hand.

Gerald stomped the sleet off his shoes and hurried along the aisle to the dispensary to stoop beside Gord.

"President's just been gunned down."

"What?"

"Just heard. In Texas for something. Got him in an open car."

"Is he dead?"

"Yes. Just announced. He's gone."

The customer looked up at Gord, said, "Oh my God," and hurried out of the store. Gerald blanched, straightened, and ran his hand down the length of his tie.

★ ★ ★

After Father McCoy's announcement, the students at St. Joseph's followed Reverend Mother through the remaining three decades of the rosary and then were let out to the schoolyard for an unscheduled recess. Speculation bubbled up even among the younger students. One was overheard to say that this was where Khrushchev stepped in and threw his weight around.

Inside, phone calls were made, and within minutes altar boys arrived from St. Michael's across the street and a mass was arranged in the chapel. The bells rang and the uncertain students silently trooped back into the school, each grade sorted into meticulously ordered columns of two.

By four o'clock the sky had darkened enough to cause people to burn lights indoors. Cathy rode out to the rectory in silence, staring out the bus windows at the grey streets, watching hunch-shouldered dark figures disappear into cold, unlit houses. She had been wrong about the mushroom bomb and the Russians.

The damp and chilly rectory was completely deserted. She went through the empty rooms to the front hall, calling out to see if anyone was upstairs, but received no answer. She turned the thermostat up just enough to take the chill out of the rooms and lit a single lamp in the living room. She made a fresh pot of coffee, thinking that that was somehow appropriate, and then served out three plates with yesterday's leftover meatloaf and potatoes and green beans, and set the plates, covered in foil, on a rack in the oven to warm. She propped open the heavy swinging door into the dining room so that the priests would see through to the room immediately upon arriving home and know that at least the comfort of a meal awaited them. After setting the table, she left a note in the middle of the tablecloth, directing them to the oven for their plates, and then, having finished the previous evenings' dishes, she departed, pulling the old warped kitchen door closed behind her.

She found her mother in the living room, perched on the edge of a chair in front of the television, Kleenex wads littered the top of the coffee table. Lights blazed everywhere. Neither Richard nor her father was home. Adele turned her red swollen eyes to the sound of her daughter entering the room.

"Did you hear? They shot him. Killed him. That good man. Just gunned him down in cold blood. Hoodlums. No-good bums. Took those sweet little children's father from them."

The picture from the buffet sat on the coffee table amidst the Kleenex. Adele picked it up and polished the glass with a used Kleenex and began to cry harder as she stroked the side of the President's face. Her head shook sorrowfully.

"What a good man, what a terrible loss to the world."

Cathy stood still, noting how the palms of her hands were tingling slightly and beginning to sweat. Adele blew her nose and dabbed her eyes.

"Go upstairs and change. Put on your good brown dress. I'm going to call the church. There'll be some kind of service."

"They said a mass already this afternoon at school."

Eyes ablaze, Adele smacked her hand sharply on the table and flew to her feet.

"Do as you're told, you insolent little bugger. How dare you think of yourself at a time like this."

Cathy pivoted and sprinted up to her room, taking the stairs two at a time.

The phone rang five times in the rectory at St. Mary, Star of the Sea, before the housekeeper answered it. She wasn't aware of any service. None of the priests were in at the moment. She didn't know when to expect them. They had left messages that they wouldn't be home for dinner that evening.

Cathy heard the pounding footsteps on the stairs. She barely had time to glance around before the door flew wide open, banging loudly against the baseboard doorstop.

"Never mind. Get out of those good clothes and be downstairs in two minutes with your rosary. And no lip, either."

Adele advanced further into the room and cruelly snatched a handful of Cathy's hair and jerked her head forward.

"Let me tell you, my girl, the rest of your generation might be the ruin of this world, but you're not going to be part of it, if I have to belt you to within an inch of your life. Do you hear me?"

She shook the fistful of hair viciously. Cathy whisked upwards through the roof into the dark winter night.

All weekend the television remained on. Adele watched until there was nothing left to look at except the test pattern and then fell asleep in living room chairs. During a break for regular news, she rooted frantically through Richard's closet and found an old black and yellow atlas and a wall map mixed in with his abandoned school books and one or two oddly contemporary things — a map of Australia and a travel guide to New Zealand. She smoothed out the map on the carpet in front of the television and opened the atlas to the pages containing Washington, D.C. Then she got down on her hands and knees to run her hands over the distances and finger-trace spidery pink, red, or blue routes leading out of Ontario, down through the industrial heartland of America to its stunned core. Then she traced her chosen route to Washington with a ballpoint pen, connecting herself by delicate inky umbilical threads to her idol.

At three o'clock Sunday morning, unable to sleep, she lay on the couch, the living room ablaze with lights, contemplating various methods of transportation between her and Washington. Earlier, with a freshly sharpened pencil and a clean sheet of white paper, she had painstakingly totalled up all of the numbers in fine print beside the interstate highways on the maps and tallied the distance and the time it would take, at sixty miles per hour, to travel to Washington. At six-thirty in the morning she phoned the bus depot and the train station asking for information about the fares and the next departures for Washington.

There were no direct connections available. She had to pass through Buffalo or Detroit and wait to transfer or travel "express" to New York and then backtrack. She hung up and went back to her couch to fume and cry and finally drift off to sleep, lights still blazing.

Gerald, vigilant and hovering, monitoring the situation as if it were a critically ill infant, brought home bags of Chinese food and fish and chips for meals. He communicated with Cathy via lowered eyebrows, shifting glances, and barely perceptible punts of his chin hurrying her through wordless meals, steering her in and out of rooms and up to her bed. Richard, coming and going as he pleased, leaned in doorways, observing.

A slipper-footed Gerald trespassed as quietly as was humanly possible throughout the rooms of his own house, listening, reading the air currents for clues about what to do, what to adjust, what to anticipate so that the bomb in their midst did not explode.

★ ★ ★

Rum tum tum trrra
Rum tum tum trrra
Rum tum tum trrra
Rum-a-ter rum-a-ter tum

On the day of the funeral, Adele rose early, dressed in dark clothes, and hurried into the living room. She turned up the television volume and began fiddling impatiently with the rabbit ears.

"Come on, come on, come on," she scolded. "Of all the days."

When she was satisfied with the picture, she stepped back, looked around the room, and then suddenly darted over to a chair and pulled it away from the wall. Peering behind the chair she muttered "perfect" and then hurried out of the room.

Upstairs, Cathy could feel the newscaster's voice vibrating through her bedroom floor as she dressed for school. She also thought she heard the front hall closet door close. She frowned at herself in the mirror, wondering who would have been in there where everyone's good Sunday coats were kept.

Adele returned to the living room and bent over the displaced chair. Richard wandered through the dining room and leaned in the living room archway eating a piece of toast, silently watching his mother. The news finished and the coverage of the President's death resumed. Adele straightened and stared at the screen.

"The line of mourners outside the Capital Hill rotunda was three miles long at two o'clock this morning," the newscaster announced.

Richard shifted and drew his mother's attention.

"Did you hear that?" she spurted. "The lines of mourners outside the Capital Hill rotunda were over three miles long all last night."

"Line," said Richard. "Singular. And not 'over.' Just three. At two o'clock."

Adele narrowed her eyes, but just then Cathy arrived. Adele glared at her.

"Get that dangling hair out of your eyes. Have you no respect?"

"We're going back to the rotunda now," began the broadcaster.

"Quick. Richard. Turn on all the lights in the room. It has to be as bright as possible."

Adele began darting about the room slipping her hand up under lampshades grappling for switches. Barely moving, Richard slid his hand along the wall and turned on the dining room chandelier. Adele bent over the displaced chair once more. When she straightened and began advancing into the centre of the room, the Bell & Howell home movie camera was firmly pressed up against one of her eyes. The bank of powerful indoor floodlights bolted on top of it burnt away every other image in the room under its harsh, astral-white blaze.

"This is for posterity, kids. So you can tell your grandchildren you saw the greatest man in the history of the world. Live."

Rum tum tum trrra
Rum tum tum trrra
Rum tum tum trrra
Rum-a-ter rum-a-ter tum

She remained behind, alone in the house, while the others left for school and work, aiming the camera at the television for as long as the film lasted, capturing as much as she could of the pageantry, sealing it into the present so that not a moment was lost.

All through the heavy, dreamlike afternoon, the brittle hypnotic trilling of military drums rattled out of the television, filling the house. Long into that night she watched the endlessly looping news reels, bending to kiss the cold marble surface of her coffee table in farewell, raising her chin bravely to walk down the stately boulevards of her nation, setting an example to the world, falling asleep at last in blazing sunlight on the stone bench in the Rose Garden, the drums and the slow grinding wheels of the horse-drawn wagon echoing through the chambers of her wounded mind.

Ten days before Christmas, Ableman's had still not delivered the new hi-fi. Crackling with impatience, Adele demanded to speak to Syd Ableman personally. When he came to the phone, she gripped the receiver with her pudgy fist and spoke to him from behind clenched teeth, telling him that he had damn well better get that stereo out to her that afternoon or else. She had Christmas guests coming at the end of the week, and what was she supposed to do with the big gaping hole in the corner of her living room? Was he trying to embarrass her?

Gerald called an hour later, sounding artificially cheerful, explaining that he had had a call at work from Ableman's. They were willing to bring out a fruitwood stereo as a substitute until a mahogany one came in. Would that be all right?

"They can deliver it this afternoon," Gerald offered.

Tantalized, Adele agreed tersely and clicked the receiver in Gerald's ear.

Richard finished his shift at Robinson's that evening and met friends at the Rootbeer Palace. They dropped him off in front of Gibson's at eleven-thirty, and he walked the rest of the way home, his head thrown back in the cold air, looking at the pale blue stars.

"They don't sell maps for you yet," he said softly. "But when they do, I'll buy them."

Turning up the driveway, he noticed light spilling out from beneath the closed garage door. He found Adele in the garage, attired in painting clothes, her eyes lit by manic fires. She was poking about Gerald's workbench, her tongue working away at the corner of her mouth. Richard watched her use a kitchen fork to mash an entire tin of brown shoe polish to mush and then drop it into a brown liquid in an old mayonnaise jar. Next she added a few drops of pine tar and stirred the mixture vigorously with a discarded toothbrush. She didn't see him, so he pulled his head back in from the door and headed up to his room. He found the lights in the living room blazing, the middle of the floor covered with old newspapers, and a new stereo standing on top of them.

Gerald came out of the bathroom to find Richard standing in the living room doorway.

"Not a word, do you hear me? It's late. I don't want to get her going."

"Oh, she's already going."

"Please just go to your room."

"I'll go to my room when I'm ready."

"I don't want any trouble."

"Most people don't."

"Don't get smart."

"What would you prefer, stupidity or just obsequiousness?"

Gerald sighed; his shoulders drooped a little lower and his gaze dropped to the floor.

Richard turned towards the stairs.

"You might consider your room yourself. She's out in the garage, half-crazed, looking like she's getting ready to turn somebody into a pumpkin."

★ ★ ★

Adele, chewing the inside corner of her mouth, held her mayonnaise jar up to the light.

"Yes siree, boy, it doesn't take a genius to figure out how to darken a little wood."

She hurried in to the living room, stirring the toothbrush noisily against the jar.

"Just you wait," she hissed, tipping the jar and watching the dark liquid pour down onto the cabinet top.

She dredged her homemade paste all over the new hi-fi, meticulously working it into all the crevices. Then she went to the kitchen, made herself a cup of tea, and returned to pace before the cabinet, as if it could not be trusted to dry on its own. Finally, she buffed off the dried paste, stood back, and squinted critically.

"Oh … not bad, not bad."

The clocks ticked like metronomes marking the passing of midnight, then one o'clock, then two o'clock. Down the hall, Gerald, awash in horrible fumes, turned uncomfortably in bed every few minutes, listening to Adele's muttering. What he couldn't see, he could imagine: Adele puffing heavily, her cheeks pink with effort, her bosom rising and falling, her tongue held between her teeth.

The paste ran out after three applications. At four-thirty by the little pale green markings on Gerald's alarm clock she chuckled softly to herself.

"Fruitwood, my ass."

After several great grunts, crunching of newspaper, and a few thumps, she finally came to bed, trailing noxious vapours, muttering about a job well done. Gerald pretended to be asleep. But he remained awake long after she fell asleep, staring into the dark, wondering about the condition of the stereo cabinet, which was not yet paid for, and Adele's inability to accept the intrinsic nature of things, whether it was the colour of wood or

of tooth enamel, the texture of skin or hair, the degree of gum
that showed above a tooth line.

★ ★ ★

The Christmas guests were Gerald's three employers and their
wives. Gord and Anne McInnis owned Hooper's Pharmacy,
just down the block from Ableman's. Les and Joan Harwood
owned Southside Pharmacy down in Riverview, and Lou and
Winny Coulter owned the dispensary in the west-end Medical
Arts building.

Adele fussed for two days over baby-sized butter tarts, raspberry squares, made with her own raspberry jam, and butter-laden
shortbread. On Saturday morning she prepared creamy clam
chowder, which she then set in the fridge to ripen, as she called
it, cabbage rolls, and tuna-mushroom-salad, which would later be
topped with cheese and grilled on egg bread rolls.

In between kitchen preparations, she passed in and out of
the rooms where Cathy was scrubbing and polishing, her arms
laden with freshly starched and ironed drapes or sheer curtains.

"Look alive, there," she said tartly to Cathy's bent back.
"What kind of technique is that? An old woman could put more
elbow grease into it than that. Did you take a toothbrush to the
hinges of the bathroom mirror?"

By mid-afternoon, all the buckets of soapy water that had
been used in the cleaning had migrated, along with mops and
brooms and vacuum cleaner attachments and the electric floor
polisher, to the laundry room at the far end of the house. The
pile of fresh, clean cloths that had been pressed into service as
dusters, waxers, buffers, and scrubbing cloths, once a mound on
a chair at the top of the stairs, had dwindled to two unused
cloths resting on the top of the dryer. Behind them, they had
left a trail of rooms in which everything was so scrubbed and

buffed to perfection that, once again, the air in the house positively reeked of ammonia, pine-scented detergent, lemon-scented polish, and fresh paste wax. People could bend over and see their reflections in almost any surface they chose. Adele, her sense of herself enlarged by all of this cleanliness, wandered from room to room, pausing to stand in the middle of the carpets and rotate slowly, inspecting small details. Twice she tread across the thick, uniform pile of the vacuumed beige broadloom to the front hall closet, pulled open the door, and put her head inside to investigate something. Then she closed the door, patted it, and walked away.

"Get a move on," she barked as Cathy passed by on her way upstairs. "Company will be coming up the walk, for heaven's sake, and you still won't be finished."

At seven-thirty, after a brief bubble bath, Adele patted talcum powder all over her body with a huge blue powder puff, taking care that the residue landed only on the bath mat at her feet, coated her hair with hairspray, dressed as if she were going to church, and then, after checking the preparations in the kitchen and investigating the front hall closet one last time, she came to roost nervously in her newly renovated dining room. The cream silk drapes were partially swept back from the French doors and secured with new gold lamé tasselled cords. Cathy's clean windows sparkled like jewels in the light of the new teardrop chandelier. The "Regency White" wallpaper had surpassed Adele's expectations, looking exactly like an ornate brocade fabric. Her only disappointment remained the sharp contrast between the light woodwork and the deep rose broadloom. A cream and gold carpet set against a polished wood floor was still her first preference. She was playing with the dimmer switch, trying to decide upon the exact degree of lighting to enhance the rest of the room and detract from this nagging flaw, when the doorbell rang. Inspecting herself briefly in the mirror above the buffet, she glanced lovingly at the President's picture, then turned and sailed down the hall, swollen as a balloon, her chin in the air and her bosom in the lead. Pulling the front door open, she exclaimed loudly at her guests as if she'd unexpectedly found glittering gift boxes out on her front porch.

The cologne-scented coats were taken into Gerald and Adele's bedroom and laid carefully across the bed, the men's heavy wool topcoats separated so as not to crush the women's delicate minks. Everyone was invited to sit on the white brocade furniture in the living room, the plastic slipcovers having been whisked away. The men ordered highballs or martinis, the women gin and tonics or rye and gingers. Adele fluttered around the marble coffee table, doling out little party serviettes, refilling the three-tiered cake plate with hors d'oeuvres before it was really necessary. When she wasn't doing this, she settled in a chair, legs crossed at the ankles, hem tugged to persnickety decency over her kneecap.

"What do you think about the events of last month?" she asked when the room fell silent for a moment. "It's not likely we'll ever see the likes of him again, not in this century. They say you only see genius once in every several generations."

Startled by the abrupt shift in topic, the other women cleared their throats and cooed like nervous pigeons. They studied the carpet, their shoes, the legs of the furniture. The men's conversation faltered. Gerald gently shook a handful of salted redskin peanuts back and forth in his hand.

"He was such a good man. He was going to turn the world around. They say there would have been peace in our time had he lived. And those good little children, they would have been such examples to follow. Those lovely blonde curls. Did you see the little boy's salute?"

Here, Adele touched the corner of one eye with a manicured fingernail.

"So young to lose their father. They'll never remember him."

"Well, it's too bad, of course, a young man like that," said Gerald. "But life goes on. A powerful country like the States simply can't afford to flounder."

"Did you watch the ceremonies on television, Anne?" Adele demanded.

"Well," Anne said, flustered, raising her eyebrows as if she had suddenly learned she was to be tested. "We saw some of it, of course. What was on the news, mostly. It was pretty hard to miss. I guess that's all the networks were playing for several days."

"Yes," agreed Winny. "I turned it off after a while. It was too depressing. All those long faces and those lugubrious drums. It began to feel as if someone I knew personally had died."

"You turned it off?"

Gerald let the peanuts fall back into the bowl.

"Well, hon, not everyone is as interested in the family as you are. After all, I missed quite a bit of it, too, having to be at work. Winny's still nursing at the hospital, you remember. You were luckier than most, being able to watch the whole thing."

Adele turned to Anne.

"Did *you* see the little boy's salute?"

"Oh, not originally. I saw it somewhere, later. In the paper, I think. Sad, wasn't it?"

"It was in quite a few magazines, too, I think. One of them had it in that big memorial edition," Joan added. She too was beginning to feel as if they were being examined on something, although she couldn't exactly say what.

Now, suddenly, as if running to fetch a whistling kettle, Adele pushed herself out of her chair, puffing with excitement.

"Oh, well, you've got to see the little boy's salute. Magazine pictures don't do it justice. You have to see the way he steps forward, so cute, his mother standing beside him. Just wait a minute."

She flew from the room, leaving the guests speechless and Gerald rummaging through the bowl of peanuts. She only went around the corner, as far as the front hall closet, and returned in a moment pushing a small wheeled metal table before her with the movie projector perched on top of it, already threaded up with a reel of film. Gerald poked deeper into the bowl of peanuts.

"I have it all here, on film. History in the making. It's not the best quality picture, but you can see his little salute and the First Lady standing right beside him."

She parked the table in the centre of the floor, beside the coffee table, blocking any passage out of the room. Then she ran back to the closet and returned with the portable movie screen, which she set up in front of the doorway, completing the imprisonment. The entire time she worked, speech flowed out of her like a brook, telling them they were in for a real treat, that they were lucky enough to see these scenes for the second time. Nobody else was going to be able to do that in their lifetime.

Les looked at his watch and then shot a glance at his wife, who could only raise her eyebrows and surreptitiously shrug her shoulders. Gerald studied the melting ice at the bottom of his glass. Lou drained his glass and leaned forward to deposit it on a coaster on the table.

"Jesus, I hope you don't have the whole four days there, Adele. None of us brought a toothbrush."

Gerald swished his half-melted ice cubes around silently.

"Oh, don't be silly. Wait until you see this. It'll only take a few minutes, but it's well worth it, believe you me."

With her back to the crowd, she called for the others to put out the lights while she adjusted the focus and centred the cube of light on the pearly white screen. In the darkness, Gerald stared at the silhouette of his wife's round fuzzy head with flat, lifeless eyes.

★ ★ ★

Later that night, after their guests had departed, Adele finished packing the uneaten sweets back into plastic storage containers and then curtly turned out the lights behind her and headed down the hall to bed, leaving Gerald to grapple with the garbage in the dark.

Several minutes later, Gerald stepped out of his shoes and slipped off his slacks before sitting down in his shirttail on the foot of the bed. Adele's voice rose up out of bunched sheets behind him.

"That's the last time I have that uncouth bunch over here. Your friends are boors."

"They are my employers, Adele. I work with those people. They put the bread and butter on our table. Can't you understand that without them, I wouldn't have a job and you wouldn't have this house to live in? I don't know why you can't just pass a pleasant evening in conversation with people without dragging them into your fetishes."

He regretted using the word "fetish" as soon as he said it.

"Fetishes, my ass. The only thing those people are concerned with is putting on the dog. Not a one of them has the brains to recognize history in the making. Can't read any other page in the paper except the comics. And their snotty remarks!"

Adele's voice took on a bitter mocking tone.

"'My, what an odd thing to do. Filming a funeral.' And, 'Hmm. It looks like a very light mahogany to me.' Jealous. That's all. Just plain jealous. And *you* too stupid to even realize it."

"For God's sake, Adele, they just made a simple statement."

"Simple statement, my ass. It was the way they said it, in that whiny, superior tone of theirs. They didn't fool me for an instant."

Gerald slowly began to work open the buttons on the front of his shirt.

"My lord, you're hard on people, Adele. A person can't even make a simple remark without you finding some fault with it. We're lucky those people even agree to come over, once a year. What am I supposed to do, start fist fights in the living room because you don't like someone's tone of voice?"

"Well they've had their last invitation from me. You can get together by yourselves, next year. Bunch of boors."

Gerald reached around behind himself and peeled his shirt away from his body.

"They're decent people, Adele, with successful businesses and good homes and families, hardly what anyone would classify as boors. Maybe I won't ask them back."

"Go on. Whine. Big baby. Can't have your own way. 'I won't ask them back.' No wonder some men are president before they're forty and others end up as pharmacists."

"Off you go then, miss," Father Lauzon boomed unexpectedly through the swinging door on the Friday before Christmas.

Cathy, standing at the sink finishing up the dinner dishes, twisted around to face him.

"Pardon, Father?"

"Spend the holidays with your family and we'll see you in January."

The door swung shut and he was gone.

"They have families that will look after them," Adele pronounced the next morning. "I need you home anyway. Here," she said, pushing a scrap of paper across Cathy's dresser, "this is today's list. Look smart and get at it."

Silverware polished. Crystal washed. Table linen ironed.

"Yuck. Doesn't all this work sorta negate the idea of celebrating?"

"Shh. At least we can sit down while we do the silver."

★ ★ ★

Three days before Christmas, Jerome Martin left the rectory with a small black overnight bag and drove the 126 miles to Robert's Corners to visit his mother. They had spoken on the

phone the night before, and so when he pulled his maroon car
into the driveway, he was not surprised to find her watching for
him through the filmy curtains at the window, marking time
with her rosary.

Inside the tiny vestibule, she greeted him with upstretched
arms, patting his back with the one good arm that she could still
wrap around his big shoulders. Her dry old cheek, pressed up
against his own, was cool, and smooth as chamois. Struggling to
stoop low enough to reach her, Jerome realized that she was
slight as a bird and that if he straightened with her still clinging
to him, he would lift her right off the floor. He also knew, by the
way she clung to him, wordlessly clutching as much of him as
she could, that her loneliness was as profound as his.

"Oh, son. Son. It's good to see you, son."

"Merry Christmas, Mum."

The house hadn't changed. His father's umbrella still stood in
the stand in the corner, the tray for boots still rested against the
wall just inside the door. The odour of mothballs and steamed
vegetables still permeated the air, although it was partially masked
today by the aroma of roasting chicken.

Jerome removed his boots and followed his mother, who led
him inside like an honoured guest. After taking his bag down the
hall to his childhood bedroom, a room still decorated with pale
green walls, still occupied by his brown dresser and a bed as
narrow and frightening as the one he now had at the rectory, he
returned to the living room to sit in his father's armchair. His
head extended far above the white tatted antimacassar that
reposed on the headrest, and his long legs spilled across the small
patch of carpet in front of him and plunged under the coffee
table. Next to Ralph, he did not feel like a particularly tall man;
here he felt like a giant.

His mother made tea in a large brown pot and covered it
with a yellow and brown crocheted cozy. She insisted on serving,

holding her palsied left hand close to her body so as not to make a mistake. There were Christmas cookies on a plate, brought over for her this year by the next-door neighbour, Mrs. MacKenzie.

"The neighbours are very good to me, son. Mr. Stewart sends his boys over every spring to clean the leaves out of the eavestroughs, and all winter, my walk and driveway are always cleared of snow. This spring, they are going to see what they can do about the back porch."

"Something wrong with the porch?"

"The stairs are no good. The wood's rotting. All the water back there, you know. I had a plug in the eavestrough and it dripped for a long time before I noticed it. Those boys of Mr. Stewart's, they do a good job cleaning out the leaves, but a block got in there. The wind must have blown something up. All that water, it ruined the stairs. Mr. Stewart says he can maybe fix it up with a little bit of wood he has in his garage. All summer the boys mow the lawns for me. And I can't give them nothing for that. Their dad taught them to be good workers. Takes them only half an hour to do both lawns. They bring their own lawn mower over here to do it. It just goes like that through the grass."

Her good arm made a stiff little sweep in front of her.

"I make them lemonade, after. The garden is grown over now. I had to let that go."

She spoke in short little spurts, pausing after every sentence to suck in a shallow gulp of air. Jerome found it too painful to look her in the eye while she related these details, things that he knew nothing of until he came here, things that he could not help her with. Not knowing where else to look while she continued, he dropped his gaze to the plate of cookies.

"Mrs. MacKenzie, next door there, she takes me shopping every week. Sometimes she tells me to get extra bread when it's on sale and then she keeps the extra loaves for me in her big freezer."

Her old blue eyes turned to look out the front window, looking right through the white curtains as if viewing the world through a white haze was normal. Jerome told her about painting the rectory, realizing that this was the most interesting news he had had to bring her in years. He observed how she brightened at the disclosure, pouncing on it, taking it to her heart where she stored it away like a nut to be brought out for sustenance during the dark of winter.

"Well, you remember that you did the kitchen here for me, son, that summer you had off."

She was referring to the first summer he had spent at home after entering the seminary. He had painted her tiny kitchen for her then, realizing that his mother had waited twelve long years for his father to die, pretending every day during her long vigil that her husband would be home at any time to take up his place in the family. Instead, during those vigil years, the boxes that contained her husband's clothes remained packed in upstairs closets, and the car that she could not drive sat cold in the garage, year after year, while doctors stood by helplessly, not knowing what to do with his father's diseased spine. Jerome had grown up and gone away to the seminary before she could abandon the daily routines and the charade of hope and optimism that were part of the ritual of prolonged illness. Only during Jerome's visit home that summer, after the death of her husband, could she finally have the small present that had been promised to her the year they had purchased the house.

"That's nice, son. A clean kitchen. The rectory must look nice now. Paint cleans a kitchen up real nice."

They talked until the light disappeared outside of the windows, she rocking in her chair, her eyes never leaving Jerome's face, her trembling arm held tight to her body with her good hand.

"You look tired, son," she said finally.

"I am."

He smiled defencelessly. The clock on the mantle whirred and chimed the quarter hour. She rocked in silence.

"Must be the drive, I guess."

"Long?"

"Hmm."

When it was finally too dark to see one another, Jerome moved about the house turning on lamps. The old floorboards creaked under his weight, reminding him that his father had walked these same floors for barely a month before going into the hospital. Since then, they must have remained absolutely mute under the sparrow-like weight of his mother.

He turned on the porch light and stood for a minute looking out at the street through the three small windows at the top of the door. He knew his mother never turned on the light in expectation of anyone else's arrival but his, and he came home so rarely. All those years that other wives had turned on porch lights, expecting husbands home from work any minute, his mother had made a lonely supper for herself and her child, leaving the porch unlit, knowing that no one else would arrive that day to share their lives.

In the kitchen, he reached over top of her head, bringing down the dinner plates from the cupboard, sparing her the trouble of dragging the step stool across the floor and unfolding its two steps. The small wooden table was set festively, with a white linen tablecloth covering the usual daily oilcloth and with small cut glass serving dishes that she normally kept wrapped in tissue paper — the exact same piece of yellowed tissue saved to rewrap each dish year after year — in the back of the china cabinet. Into these dishes she had carefully spooned pickled beets and pearl onions and cranberry jelly.

"The beets and onions aren't my own anymore. But Lorraine, across there in the blue shutters, she does them every year, just like

I used to, and always gives me a few bottles. I get beautiful tomatoes and cucumbers from her garden all summer, too."

Jerome gently tucked the chair in close to the table beneath her and shook out the folded napkin for her.

"Lorraine's son and his wife bought the house behind them. They can talk over the back fence. He's got two kids, now. A nice little boy and a young girl."

Jerome opened his own napkin and smoothed it over his lap. Snow was falling outside the window, passing through the block of light that escaped to the outside.

They bowed their heads over grace.

"You say it, son."

He thanked the Lord for their bounty on this day, but the word "bounty" felt like a lie upon his tongue.

She ate like a bird, serving herself teaspoons of meat and dressing and potatoes on her plate. Jerome didn't know if this was because that was all she really wanted or if he was witnessing a lifetime habit of necessary parsimony. Afraid of forcing her to lie to him, he refrained from inquiring.

They stood at the sink to wash the dishes, he drying them and placing them back in their proper spot on the shelves above her head, she standing with her two small pink-slippered feet placed neatly side by side beneath her, her one good arm drawing the dishcloth over the surface of the plates. Her quivering bad arm was put to use as best as it could be, helping to hold a cleaned plate out of the soapy water by shakily clasping it against her body while she rinsed the suds off her other hand before carefully transferring the plate to the dish rack.

Jerome resisted the temptation to take the plate from her and rinse it himself, listening instead to her constant patter about the neighbourhood. She knew things about everyone on both sides of the street, where they worked, how many children they had, the names of all the children, all the cats and dogs, what people planted in their gardens, where they took their summer holidays. While she spoke, his eyes wandered over the kitchen, observing details that he had never seen before. Had the cupboards always been so inconveniently high? Did she have to drag a stool across the room several times a day just to get a plate or a teacup? And where had the stool come from? He didn't remember it; it was modern-looking, made of shining stainless steel. Had one of the neighbours bought it for her?

His hand returned the dried plates to the tops of stacks and the cups to the first row of hooks, behind which there was a second, untouched row of hooks and other hanging cups. Why were there so many of each type of dish? Had there always been eight of everything in these cupboards? Had some of these things been sitting there since the first time they had been unpacked and stored there, unused all these years because his father had never come home to eat with them, because the family had never grown? Were they the unused place settings for unborn brothers and sisters, for in-laws and grandchildren?

Before bed, he turned on the back light and slipped out to see the porch. Someone had taken an old clothesline and cordoned off the stairs. When he touched one of the support posts, it waggled.

Jerome lay down in his childhood bed, haunted by what he had witnessed all day. Rows of hanging cups and stacks of plates and saucers stared at him from behind closed eyes. The porch post rocked back and forth, threatening to break off at its rotted root; his mother's poor arm trembled beneath her sweater. He had never imagined this. The consequences of his priesthood upon his mother had never occurred to him. Back then, he had only been desperate to find a solution for himself. Impoverished parishes like St. Alphonsis had never occurred to him. Now, in his mother's hour of need, he barely had pocket money to his

name and no means with which to help her — the second man
in her life to abandon her.

But what could he have done differently? Stayed here, living
in this small bungalow with his mother, going to and from some
local job everyday, having neighbours watch him grow into
middle age without ever leaving home, having her make his
lunches and keep his dinners warm for him, viewed on the outside as some sort of stunted offspring that could not mature?
Becoming a priest was at least noble and courageous. Wasn't it?

The furnace came on, sending whispering warm air currents wandering through the old rooms. Jerome lay in his bed,
listening. Noble? With a faltering vocation in a menial role in a
down-and-out parish? Courageous? Overgrown into clumsiness, a homely clodhopper of a man with a large head, oversized
feet and hands, a face flared with eczema and acne, eyes bulging
and cow-like. Too awkward to ever try out for a team, too shy
to seek out friends, not clever enough to forge an academic
path, he'd ducked away, tricking his mother by choosing the
Church so that she would not maintain a vigil for a wife for
him. Maybe that's why he couldn't find God very often anymore. He hadn't accepted his lot. And so now his lot had
increased, at his mother's expense.

Jerome fingered the rosy eruptions along his jaw. He had
found two new ones this morning that he had had to shave
around, leaving ugly little rings of bristle standing like fences
around the swellings. By Christmas morning they would be fully
risen, flaming, oozing pustules that people would stare at as he
gave them Holy Communion. They would still be unhealed on
December 28, at the Bishop's annual Christmas reception for the
diocese. He'd have to sit in his usual chair close to the fireplace
watching: Ralph leaning on the mantle, Ralph standing astride
the centre of the carpet, Ralph lounging in a doorway, light
flickering over his clean dark jaw, ice shifting and crackling at

the bottom of his glass. And the long afternoon would drive home the secret he struggled to keep out of his eyes and away from his mother. That he was as awkward and clumsy a misfit there as he had been in the world he had fled.

He left his mother thirty-six hours later, just after lunch on Christmas Eve. She stood at the window holding the curtains aside with her bad hand and raised her rosary to him in farewell.

It was Jerome's turn this year to hold the fort at St. Alphonsis. The other two men went home to family for Christmas while he said three Christmas morning masses and then made himself scrambled eggs and toast for brunch. Jerry had invited him to help himself to his new portable television. He spent the afternoon staring at Hollywood confections. Later that night he emptied the last of the cocoa into a pot of warm milk.

Beginning in January, some of the boys from St. Michael's were to attend classes at St. Joseph's while construction of a new part of the boys' school was completed. Parents had been informed of the arrangements a year in advance and were given particulars in a letter that arrived in the mail the week before New Year's.

Gerald scanned the information contained in the letter and then returned to his newspaper. Adele studied the letter more slowly, scrutinizing every word as if there were a secret code embedded in the sentences.

"Well, there had better not be any trouble out of this, I tell you, because I won't stand for it. I already caught little miss hot pants getting secret letters from boys last spring and I nipped that in the bud right away."

Gerald spoke from behind his paper.

"The teachers will still be in charge of the classes. They just need a little bit of room for the other kids for a few months until the construction's over. She's never given us any trouble before."

"How would you know? You're never here. You wouldn't notice anything until it was too late. She'd be pregnant before you'd get your nose out of your paper."

Gerald allowed the top part of his paper to wilt forward.

"What do you want me to do right now? She hasn't done anything. It's just a letter telling you what the arrangements are going to be for the next few months. Why make it into something that it's not?"

"That's it. Stick your head in the sand."

"What do you mean, stick my head in the sand? What are we talking about?"

"Talking to you is like talking to a brick wall, Gerald. Go back to your damn paper."

Adele pushed herself out of the depths of the couch, clutching the letter so hard it rumpled to ruin in her hand. She headed off in the direction of Cathy's room, her feet pounding beneath her.

Hearing her mother approaching Cathy quickly buried her magazine between the mattresses of the bed. Just in the nick of time she was able to grab a geography book from her desk and arrange it and herself on her bed, as if she had been reading about the natural resources of Scandinavia for most of the morning. The door to her room flew open, banging against the doorstopper so hard that, despite the rubber tip on the end of the stopper, the wood was damaged.

Cathy froze.

"So, missy. There are going to be boys in your class starting next week. And I told you last spring what the rules are in this house. Absolutely no boys until you are out of high school. I will not tolerate any boy-crazy nonsense under my roof, is that understood?"

Cathy, her head lowered, began to stroke the page of her book, nodding.

"I told you I was having you watched, young lady, and I'm going to be kept well informed of all your activities. If I hear even one story about you acting up with boys and carrying on, you'll be shipped to boarding school out of town so fast you won't know what hit you. Do you hear me?"

Cathy nodded at the green and blue maps spread in her lap, wondering if Angela was filming a movie in one of these countries. Right this very moment were she and Andy getting off a plane, looking around at the unfamiliar surroundings of a foreign airport?

"Have you memorized 'Stopping By Some Woods' yet?"

Cathy nodded.

"Well then, instead of lazing around doing nothing, this afternoon would be a good time to get going on another poem. That man wrote hundreds of poems. If we waited for that English teacher of yours to get around to them, you'd be graduated and married. Where's your book?"

Cathy retrieved her poetry book from her bedside table drawer. It was a new volume of Frost's works given to her for Christmas by her mother. Adele flipped through the pages until she found "The Road Not Taken."

"Here it is. This is his other important work. I knew this by heart when I was your age."

She waved Cathy aside with a swat of her hand and lowered herself clumsily down onto the bed, beginning to read even before she was settled, announcing the title as if she were reading numbers out loud in a cavernous bingo hall:

"The Road Not Taken.
Two roads diverged in a yellow wood,
And sorry I could not travel both
And be one traveler, long I stood
And looked down one as far as I could
To where it bent in the undergrowth…

"Oh, this just takes me straight back," Adele said, wiggling her fat bottom deeper into the mattress. She continued:

"Then took the other, as just as fair,
And having perhaps the better claim,
Because it was grassy and wanted wear;
Though as for that, the passing there
Had worn them really about the same…"

She forced curious inflections onto syllables that wanted no inflections, fell into a rhythmic singsong for a few paces, clumsily stumbled over other text, and finally began the third stanza in a whisper.

"And both that morning equally lay
In leaves no step had trodden black."

Her voice rose: "Oh, I kept the firsssst for another day!"

Her spittle flew across the carpet onto the dresser mirror: "Yet knowing how way leads on to way…"

She roared like a five-star general: "I doubted if I should ever come back."

"Heil, Adele," Angela mocked, saluting and stomping to attention.

Cathy bit the inside of her cheeks.

"Ah, how true those words are, my dear," Adele said, smoothing the page with her chubby hand. "How true indeed. You, at your young age, no experience of the world yet, you have no idea when you leave here if you'll ever be back to your happy childhood home."

Cathy zipped up her balloon string and came to rest parallel to the top of the maple tree in the backyard. She looked back down through her floating feet and observed the back of her mother's fuzzy red head bowed over the book.

Stay still.

Adele was whispering again. Angela stood in front of her, parroting her.

> "I shall be telling this with a sigh
> Somewhere ages and ages hence:
> Two roads diverged in a wood, and I —
> I took the one less traveled by,
> And that ... has made ... all ... the difference."

Adele swallowed and closed her eyes.

Cathy stared at the maps in her geography book.

"Yes siree, boy," Adele said, rocking her bottom from side to side, "taking that road sure made the difference for me, I can tell you."

The maple tree had an old bird's nest tucked into one of its forks and a squirrel's nest in another. Cathy hadn't noticed either nest last summer. Both were dusted with snow now. Inhospitable. It was funny how you never saw baby squirrels. But they must be there, every summer. Coming down out of their trees for the first time, looking at their new world. But they seem to manage to go out into the world undetected. That's what she would like to do. Just crawl away from this inhospitable nest. Go out into the world undetected.

"Do you know what the two roads are?" Adele barked.

Cathy looked up.

"Life has more than one path, you know. When you get out in the world, you're going to have to make choices. See where he says, 'And sorry I could not travel both'? He's talking about being young and inexperienced there. When you are young, you want everything. You don't know how to make decisions that are responsible. So he's pointing that out here, saying that he wanted to travel both roads, he wanted every-thing in life right away, without having to work for it. If you read on, he says that the road bends in the undergrowth. Do you know what that means?"

From the sky Cathy watched herself tilt her head slightly to one side and raise an eyebrow.

"He's saying the undergrowth obscures his view," she said quietly.

"Well, that's what it says on the surface, but you have to read between the lines. That's what you get from not studying enough poetry from that young nun, who doesn't know what she's doing. He's talking about how young people are influenced the wrong way by undesirables. The 'undergrowth' that he refers to are the ones that you see hanging around at the Rootbeer Palace all the time, the riff-raff of society, the ones who aren't going to amount to much. They're the ones who are going to 'bend' you to their ways if you get mixed up with them.

"At the end of the second verse he says that just as many go down the wrong road in life as the right one. In the third verse he says, 'In leaves no step had trodden black.' By that, he means that you can't see the black influence. The wrong choice also looks appealing. Remember the old saying, my dear, 'All that glitters is not gold.' The two paths look equally the same to someone as naive as you. The wrong one is trodden with black footsteps, the footsteps of the sinful in this life. But you can't tell which path those steps are on, just by looking.

"The poet is a wise person, though. He knows that 'way leads onto way,' and that he will never be back. He's talking about choosing the wrong path. Once you've made the mistake, you get yourself in deeper and deeper. So he saves the wrong choice for another day. That's poetry for not wanting to take that choice, ever. Do you understand?"

Cathy drifted a little higher than the maple tree and turned toward the west, toward California. She could see Andy, Mickey, and the pup running along the beach, splashing in and out of the rough Malibu surf. She nodded appropriately at her mother's question as she slid down her balloon string to land on the beach beside her friends.

Ten days after the new school term began, the phone rang in the Mugan household. Cathy had just come in from the rectory and was settling herself at her desk to do her homework. She lifted her French scribbler and her French grammar textbook out of her schoolbag and was busy dumping the remainder of the bag onto her bed when her ears pricked to the sound of her mother's pounding footsteps. The door to her room burst open. Adele, in a puffing fury, her arm stretched across the expanse of the door, her pudgy hand firmly gripping the glass doorknob, spit out words.

"There's a phone call for you downstairs, young lady, and I want to know who it is."

Cathy frowned.

"But I didn't answer it."

"Don't get smart with me, miss. It's a boy. Somebody named Tim Okamoto. Now get moving and make it short and then you'll have some explaining to do."

Tim was one of the boys from St. Michael's who now shared her French classes. She had seen him standing out at the bus stop after school but knew little else about him. He got off the bus long before she did. Today, he'd missed class.

"Hello," Cathy said timidly. Adele leaned against her, her ear pressed to the receiver.

"Hi, Cathy. It's Tim calling. From French class. Do you remember me?"

"Yes."

"I had to get my braces tightened this afternoon, and I was wondering if you could tell me what Sister Aline gave out for French homework?"

"Oh ... yes."

She recited the pages and question numbers.

"Just those four questions?"

"Yes, and the reading assignment. The next story. You know."

"Great. More adventures of Toto and Fifi, I guess."

"Yeah, I guess so."

"Okay. I guess I can handle that. So how are you, anyway?"

Cathy swallowed.

"Oh ... I'm fine ... thank you."

"Would you like to go to the book sale with me tomorrow?"

Her mother stiffened. Cathy began to quiver.

"Book sale?"

Her mouth dropped open and she began panting.

"You know, the one in the cafeteria at lunch tomorrow."

"Oh. I forgot about it. No. I can't go. I have to go in for extra help with Sister Anne Rochelle."

Adele suddenly grabbed the receiver. Cathy spoke into the empty air.

"I have to go now, Tim. Bye."

As Adele spoke, her free hand gripped Cathy's hair.

"This is Cathy's mother speaking, son. I don't know who you are, young man, but you can get your homework assignments somewhere else from now on, do you hear? Cathy is much too young to date. She has her schoolwork to do. Now, off you go, son, and don't call here again or I'll speak to your mother about it, do you understand?"

Adele slammed the receiver down.

"So, miss. It's starting already, is it? What did I tell you about boys?"

Cathy's eyes filled with tears.

"He just wanted homework, Mom. You heard him."

"Just homework, and then a date for a book sale. I'm not deaf, young lady. I know what I heard."

"It's not a real date, it's a book sale in the cafeteria. We'll be in the cafeteria at the same time anyway, so it meant we would just be standing at a table looking at books together, that's all. All the teachers will be there. Anyway, I told him no. You heard me."

"You're damn right you told him no. Get going. Up to your room. Now, miss. March."

Adele released Cathy's hair and gave her a hard shove towards the stairs.

"Just standing at a table looking at books, my arse. And what's next, after that, eh, gullible little girl?"

She pursued Cathy down the hall, hitting her repeatedly on the head with the back of her hard hand.

"And I want to know why he's asking *you* to look at the books with him? What have *you* been doing to make that boy think that he can just phone here whenever he feels like it?"

"It was only one phone call."

"Don't get lippy with me, my girl."

"I don't know why he asked me. I didn't ask him to call me."

"Where did he get this phone number?"

"I don't know. Maybe he looked it up in the phone book."

"How does he know where you live?"

They had reached the top of the stairs. Cathy turned to face her mother.

"I don't know!"

Adele paused and narrowed her glassy eyes at Cathy.

"And another thing, miss. What kind of a name is Okamoto?"

"I don't know. I think he's Japanese."

"Japanese? What are the neighbours going to think, for God's sake? You running around with Japanese?"

"I don't know."

The back of Adele's hand, hard as a paddle, landed across Cathy's mouth.

"Well you're going to know something, young lady."

Adele's hand shot out and gripped Cathy's hair even more firmly than before. She bent her daughter's head backwards and leaned forward and spat words into Cathy's face.

"Do you think I'm going to have my daughter running around with a Japanese, making a laughingstock of this whole family?"

"He just wanted homework, Mom. You heard him. Damn you. You're hurting me. Let go."

Adele exploded. Her hand smacked loudly and rapidly back and forth across Cathy's mouth.

"Pardon me, miss? What did you say? Damn? Huh? Damn? Is that what I heard? I'll show you what happens to a kid who thinks she can talk to me like that. You're not so old that I can't still take a bar of soap to that mouth of yours. Get going. We'll just see if you think you can defy me, missy."

Cathy ran the rest of the way down the hall holding her numb mouth. In her room she stood shaking, desperately wishing she could fit through the small window above her bed. Realizing her underwear was damp, she tore open her drawer and pulled on two more pairs. Through the floor she felt the closet door slide across its metal tracks and slam into the wall. Hangers jangled like a choir of tin bells and then the footsteps resumed, harder and brisker than ever.

★ ★ ★

Richard entered the house to the sound of his sister's sharp cries and his mother's breathless and laboured shouting. He heard the *thwacking* of the belt and the heavy bumping of bodies and furniture upstairs. Standing in front of the open fridge, he listened to Cathy shriek after each lash hit its mark, his own back flinching involuntarily at the sound. Finally, he grabbed a quart of milk and took it to his room, violently slamming the door behind him.

★ ★ ★

Gerald arrived home at nearly ten o'clock. His day had been long. The phone had rung incessantly; it was flu season and doctors' offices from all over the city had called all day wanting to dictate scripts. He and Gord had been on their feet side by side from noon until seven, never walking any further than four or five feet at a time, tramping all afternoon between the dispensary and the shelves behind them, pouring and counting, pouring and counting. Both typewriters rattled away, hour after hour, with the two men tapping out the labels for antibiotics and cough syrups. Whenever the clerks on the floor could get their attention, one or the other of them went to act in his capacity as advisor to physician-phobic customers, recommending an effective throat lozenge, over-the-counter ear drops, or a routine that would lower a fever. By the time Gord had left, they were more or less caught up, having filled close to two hundred prescriptions between them. Gerald had finished the final dozen scripts alone, hiding behind the little dispensary wall to sip a coffee that had gone cold. The last he'd had to eat was rye toast before beginning his shift early that afternoon.

Adele snapped on the light in the laundry room.

"Well. Finally. Did it ever occur to you that you have a family that needs raising here? So you didn't think that there would be any problems with boys in the classes, eh? Well, that just shows how little *you* know."

"What's happened?"

"She's got Japanese phoning here, asking her out on dates, that's what's happened. Ten days with boys in her class. You can't turn your back for one minute on that kid. But *you*. *You* think she's an angel. Well let me tell you, I'm smart enough for both of you. She's not fooling me with that 'he only wanted to know the homework' line."

Adele returned to the kitchen and drove the dishcloth around the countertops, her large buttocks shaking back and forth.

"I tell you, Gerald, if it wasn't for me these kids wouldn't get any raising at all. I have to do everything around here by myself. If I waited for you to get involved, they'd be savages. A person would hardly guess you were the father of these two kids, you're home so seldom. The President was the busiest man in the world, and he still had time for his children."

Gerald deposited his newspaper on the kitchen table.

"Oh, for Christ's sake, the man's dead and buried, Adele. Learn to accept reality."

He stepped past her, working his tie loose as he did so.

"That's it. Bail out again. Leave everything to me. Jelly-spine. Won't even raise your own kids. He might be dead, but while he was alive, the President's kids at least knew who he was. You're a complete stranger to yours!"

Adele dropped her voice, talking as if conspiring with herself.

"I licked your problem but good tonight, missy. You won't be getting any more phone calls from boys."

★ ★ ★

Cathy slipped out of her clothes, turned out the light on her untouched French homework, crawled into bed, and closed her burning eyes. Only one nostril was clear for breathing; the other was swollen shut from crying. One elbow was painful to move and was beginning to stiffen.

Oh sweetie, that looks really bad. Did you put some ice on it?

"Ah, flea. Come and stay with us instead."

She sought the right spot on the sheet, and then she lay her head down above Angela's picture. Tears dropped silently onto her embroidered pillowcase. She sighed and fell headfirst into darkness.

★ ★ ★

Gerald waited until he heard Adele close the bathroom door. Then he slipped upstairs to his daughter's room. When his soft knock received no reply, he turned the handle and opened the door a crack. Cathy was lying in the middle of the bed, her knees pulled up to her chest and her back to the door. Twice, he called out her name. He couldn't tell if she was truly asleep or just ignoring him.

"I'm going to look into sending you away to school next year. After that you should think about what I told you about attending a nursing school out of town. I can't come home to a house in an uproar like this every night."

He closed the door quietly and turned to find Richard leaning in the frame of his own doorway. He straightened and spoke in an undertone.

"I don't know what went on here tonight, and I don't want to know. I've had all I can take of this stuff."

He turned, hurrying before Richard could speak, and headed back down the stairs.

C H A P T E R

C athy kept her head down during French class, absently
doodling in the margins of her notebook. At least Tim
sat two rows over and behind her.

Sssson. Don't call here again, sssson.

Sister Aline walked among the desks asking questions
about verb tenses. Cathy was thinking about the end of class.
There would be a bottleneck at the door. She might end up
beside him, shuffling forward slowly, the sleeves of their uniforms brushing.

Sssson. Don't call here again, sssson.

When the bell rang she was going to have to run.

"Cathy?"

She shot to attention beside her desk. What was the question?

"Yes, Sister?"

"Please stay behind for a moment."

Sssson. Don't call here again, sssson.

When had the bell rung?

She watched everyone's shoes shuffle past. Then she crept up
to the nun's desk and waited, with lowered eyes, to be addressed.
Her fingers fiddled with the belt on her tunic.

"You don't seem to be yourself, lately, Cathy. Is there anything
wrong? Anything I can help you with?"

Zip! She looked out over the dull winter landscape of the city. Everything was grey. Even the tiny voice below her.

"No, Sister. Nothing's wrong."

"You look very sad all the time."

"Oh? Maybe I go to bed too late."

"What time did you get to bed last night?"

"I don't know."

"You didn't answer any questions today. Is there something about this chapter that you don't understand?"

"No, Sister."

"You were doodling in your book. You know I don't like your notes to be messy like that."

"Sorry, Sister."

"You've never done that before. What made you start today?"

"I can erase it, Sister. I have a good eraser."

"I still think there's something you're not telling me. Is everything all right at home?"

Cathy froze.

"Yes, Sister. Everything's fine."

Please, God, don't let Sister Aline phone home and say I'm not paying attention.

"Nobody's sick or anything? Your father didn't lose his job?"

"No, Sister. Nobody's sick. My father still has his job."

"What about your homework? Why didn't you have it done?"

Cathy sucked on the lump on her bottom lip.

"Your book was open. I saw yesterday's date on the page, Cathy. You didn't have the correct assignment in front of you, did you?"

Cathy shook her head.

"No, Sister."

"Why didn't you do your homework?"

She couldn't move. Last night's tears had not receded very far. Holding them back took tremendous effort.

"Hmm? That's not like you. Please answer when I speak to you, Cathy, and make eye contact when you do. It's impolite to look at the floor when you're being spoken to."

Cathy took a deep, tired breath and looked up, but at a spot on the wall above Sister Aline's head.

"I just didn't do it, Sister. I didn't have time."

"You didn't have time?"

"I was late coming home, Sister. The buses were slow because of the weather, that's all. It won't happen again. I promise. Could I be excused, please? I have to go to the washroom."

By the time she got to her locker, tears were streaming down her face. She grabbed her lunch and took it up to the third-floor washroom. No one would use this washroom at this time of the day. She closeted herself in the end cubicle, sat up on the water tank with her feet resting on the toilet seat, spread her lunch of tuna sandwiches and an orange out on her lap, and then sank the heels of her hands into her eyes to dam the flood.

The variety store across from the rectory had a hot chocolate machine. For a quarter, a paper cup dropped down and foamy hot chocolate poured out right up to the rim. Cathy went in every night to get one as soon as she got off the bus. She had offered to get one for Father Martin once, but he made a disgusted face at her and shook his head.

Old Mrs. Traudechaud always had a French station on the radio. She warbled along to the maritime tunes, telling Cathy that that was music from "down 'ome." One of these days she was going to go back down 'ome to see her old brodder, dere, before he die.

"He's ninety, dis spring, my brodder. Dat's old, eh? Not like you, yong ting, got your whole life ahead of you, dere. You ain't even got star' yet. Dat's for sure."

She spoke on an uptake of breath, saying "for sure" in almost every sentence. "How old are you? Fifteen? *Mon Dieu*, dat's yong. For sure. I was marry at your age. Two years already. I got marry when I was turteen. Had my first baby at fourteen. It's a different world now, dat's for sure."

Flapjack was large enough now to rest his paws on Cathy's shoulders when he stood up. Whenever he did this, Mrs.

Traudechaud chastised him, without so much as glancing up from her knitting.

"Flapjack, dat's a bad boy. I'm gonna cut off your tail if you jump like dat on de customer."

He always came out from behind the counter to see Cathy, wagging his tail. Cathy loved to run her hands though his soft coat and to take hold of his big ears. He responded by leaning against her, his eyes glued to her face, his thick tail whacking against candy display shelves, knocking chocolate bars and packages of gum onto the floor.

One afternoon in mid-February, when the late afternoon light was beginning to last a little longer, Cathy walked into the store as usual. Flapjack trotted out from behind the counter to greet her.

"Did you know dey took one of de priest away in an ambulance early dis morning?"

Flapjack placed his paws on her shoulders.

"No," said Cathy, stroking a paw. "Which one? What happened?"

"I don' know. My husband, he saw. He was out wit de dog at five o'clock. I tought maybe you might know. I din't see noting myself."

"No. I just got off the bus."

"Well, was somebody."

"My, my, my, isn't this intriguing?" Angela said, hurrying across the road.

★ ★ ★

An older, grey-haired woman stood on a chair in front of the cupboards in her stockinged feet. At the sound of the door opening, she turned around, wiped her hands on Cathy's apron, and began to climb carefully down off the chair.

"Yikes. Something tells me our work here is done," said Angela.

315

At precisely the same instant, Father Lauzon pushed open the swinging door.

"Aha. At last. Here she is. We have news for you, my girl. This is Mrs. Guinney. She's our new housekeeper. She moved in last night and started this morning. After today, you won't have to come all the way out here anymore."

Cathy looked at the woman. She wore a shapeless navy blue housedress, silver glasses, and brown stockings rolled into tubes around her ankles.

"I just want you to show Mrs. Guinney around a bit, answer any questions that she has, and then, my dear, you can be on your way. We want to thank you for all your help. The meals and everything else were great. Your mother's doing a good job on you, I can tell."

He disappeared through the door.

Frail Mrs. Guinney, territorial as a bear, stood in the centre of the room, staring at Cathy. She had little steely eyes that bore down like gun muzzles. They had to. This job would put a roof over her head, a mattress beneath her tired old bones, and tea-spoons of food on her dinner plate.

Cathy glanced around the room. The kitchen table, the top of the stove, and the remaining counter space were all covered with the contents of the cupboards. A bucket of soapy water stood on the counter.

"You know, you probably don't have to go to all that trouble. I just washed everything down in here a few months ago."

"I don't like to work nowhere that I don't wash myself."

"Well, is there anything you'd like to know?"

"I don't see no big fry pan nowhere. Do you know where one is at?"

It was easy to see what was going to happen. She would make the priests fried pork chops and lumpy grey potatoes for their meals, resplattering the newly painted walls. She would send the cut glass water glasses packing to the back shelves of the top cupboards. Breakfast would be runny, undercooked eggs and flat little pieces of white toast spread with margarine, with miserly strips of bacon, jiggling with half-cooked fat.

"Yes, I think there is a frying pan in a box in the basement. Is there anything else you would like?"

"Too bad there's no curtain for that window there, eh, above the sink? I don't like it so exposed like that. I don't know who's looking in at me."

The mystery bush had never bloomed. After she and Angela had trimmed it, it had simply put on more green growth and climbed back up across the window glass.

"Well, maybe you can put some string up with thumb tacks and hang an old dish towel over it."

"Oh, that's a good idea. Do you know where there's some string at?"

"No. You'll have to ask Father. Anything else?"

Mrs. Guinney folded her hands across her stomach, wrinkled her nose up at the ceiling, and stood for a moment swivelling her little grey head back and forth, looking at the two light bulbs.

"Those light bulbs up there, I don't like them. They're too bright. It's not so good on my eyes."

"I'm sure Father will change them for you."

Mrs. Guinney shuffled over to the oven, shaking her head and making a dismissive, disgusted gesture with her bottom lip.

"Too bright."

She took a dishtowel in her hand and opened the oven door. A withered brown meatloaf sat, uncovered, in a pot with yellow grease bubbles popping beneath it. She stabbed the loaf two or three times with a paring knife, twisting it sideways, grunted, and then sprinkled salt and pepper on the loaf. She took peeled carrots and potatoes from a nearby bowl, dropped them into the grease, shook salt and pepper over everything again, closed the oven door, and straightened.

"Have you found everything else that you need, then?"

Mrs. Guinney blinked against the offensive ceiling lights.

"Oh, pretty much, I guess. Just that big fry pan, if you could get it."

"Did Father show you where everything else is? The front hall closet where the vacuum cleaner is, and the linen closet upstairs?"

"Yes, yes. I'll find it. He said he's going to show me."

"Not the gracious type, this one," Angela said, rattling her bracelets.

No chance of her opening attic doors out of curiosity.

"Or even dreaming of how the boys keep themselves company."

"I'll go get you the frying pan, then, and then I guess I'll be on my way. I'll need my apron back, though." She gestured towards the garment tied around Mrs. Guinney's waist.

"I found this on the back of the door. Father says it was okay to wear."

"Father doesn't realize that I brought it from home."

"Is there another one? I don't see no more around."

"No. That's why I brought it from home. You'll have to ask Father to get you a new one."

"You can't let me have this one for the night?"

"No. I live all the way across town. I'm sorry, but I'll have to take it with me when I leave. Tuck a tea towel in your waist."

"Well, aren't we getting assertive?"

She held out her hand. Mrs. Guinney reluctantly untied the apron and handed it across. Cathy felt the pocket and found it empty.

"There were two notes in here."

"Garbage. No good to me."

Cathy's eyes narrowed. Mrs. Guinney pointed to the door under the sink. Cathy crossed the room and tore open the door.

Eva's rumpled notes peeked out from the refuse, ruined by wet tea bags and bacon drippings. Cathy turned away, leaving the door ajar just as heavy boots tramped up the back porch and stomped. The kitchen door opened and Father LeBlanc entered in his stockinged feet, carrying his dripping jacket, looking a bit surprised to see two women standing there.

"*So ... it was the pimple-headed moron.*"

All that ear-pulling and lip-chewing, Cathy thought.

"*And trysts on the stairs with the Virgin of Plaster.*"

Father LeBlanc nodded to Cathy and then tromped across the floor, shedding snow from the cuffs of his pants in his wake.

★ ★ ★

She closed the door behind her at the top of the stairs and went straight down to the bottom where there was laundry piled on the dirt floor right beneath the chute. Father Martin's things were mixed in amongst the others' belongings. She could smell his distinctive perspiration.

The grave was so small that she needed to pull only one of the two cardboard boxes aside to reveal it completely. She looked at the soft brown soil that had swallowed up the secret. Andy and Angela had told her they had the pup with them. She'd seen her with them, bouncing across the sand, chasing Mickey, her pink tongue trailing out the side of her sweet little mouth.

She knelt beside the grave for a moment, resting her hand on the soft soil.

"Goodbye, my dear little friend," she whispered, kissing the soil right above the spot where she knew the pup's head was.

She looked around once more at the antiquated washer and the piece of warped grey plywood that it stood upon, at the ancient, paint-splattered cement sinks, the pickle jars on the crooked improvised shelf beneath the stairs, and the clots of spiderwebs in the old rafters overhead. Then she took the frying pan, trudged up the blonde wood stairs, turned off the light at the top, and closed the door behind her. How had she spent an entire summer down there, trying to wash the stains of loneliness out of the underclothes and sheets of three men?

CHAPTER 31

Jean McKenzie had a key to the side door of her neighbour's house. She never used it, though, without knocking at the same time as she turned the key in the lock so that old Mrs. Martin would know who it was.

On this particular Thursday in February, on her way over to share a cup of tea with her friend, a peculiar feeling overtook her out on the driveway. Looking up, she could see through the dry, steam-free window that the bluish fluorescent nightlight was still on above the kitchen sink. She put the key in the door, mentally listing the reasons for the light to be on. Perhaps Marg was just getting forgetful. Maybe she had turned it off but just hadn't flipped the switch all the way down, or maybe there was a short in the wiring. It was odd that Marg hadn't boiled her teakettle yet, though.

Pepper, Jean's poodle, ran circles in the snow, bouncing off the back of her legs, barking his delight to be outside. Once the door opened, he rushed past, frantic to get to the kitchen where a doting Margery always treated him to toast.

Jean let the dog go on ahead without bothering about his tiny snowy feet because she half knew in her heart that it wouldn't matter this morning about a bit of snow on the carpets. Something else was out of place, now. The rooms still retained their nighttime coolness, as if no one had yet woken up and set the thermostat to a daytime temperature.

Finding no one waiting for him in the kitchen, Pepper disappeared into the interior of the house, sniffing along pathways that he had never been allowed to investigate before. Jean stayed in the kitchen, hesitant to go any further.

"Marg," she called out into the still, cool silence.

The electric clock hanging above the stove answered her in soft regular clicks. She considered phoning her husband, Carl, at work to ask him to come back home and go into the bedroom with her. But, then, what if she was being silly? What if Margery needed help? What if she had had a stroke and was lying paralyzed in her bed, her eyes tracking across the ceiling?

She crossed the room and called out again. Then she called for Pepper. When the dog didn't come, she grew uneasy, thinking that she had perhaps walked into a trap. Maybe there was an escaped convict standing behind a door, clapping a big hand across Margery's mouth, just waiting for someone to walk into the room. But, then, Pepper would have barked at a stranger.

Pepper had skipped up the stairs and sniffed his way along Margery's invisible slipper tracks, all the way to the side of her bed. He paused over the pink slippers on the mat and then gently put his two front paws up onto the bedspread and leaned forward. Margery lay on her back, with both her arms concealed beneath the covers, her slightly opened mouth strangely dry and still. Pepper stretched forward tentatively, tilting his nose to the ceiling, cautiously investigating the air directly above Margery's mouth. When nothing bad happened, he leaned in a little closer and sniffed gently back and forth across her bottom lip, his own eyes rolled to the side, watching her eyes carefully to see if they would open. When she didn't move, he wagged his tail tentatively and gently sprang up onto the bed and settled himself quietly in a mound of covers beside her.

★ ★ ★

Jerome drove back to Robert's Corners and attended the requiem mass for his mother at St. Anne's. She was buried in the churchyard, next to his father. Jean MacKenzie held a small reception back at her house. Jerome asked her if she would continue to keep an eye on his mother's house until he came to a decision about what he should do with it.

Back at the rectory, he began to wake again at 3:05 a.m. Wooden posts, rotten at their roots, toppled over onto him.

Jerome knew there was wood stacked against the wall at the back of the garage. The light from his headlights bored into it every time he pulled in and out of his parking space. He'd also seen longer pieces threaded overhead in the garage rafters. All of it was old, remaindered from long-forgotten projects. When he arrived in the garage at three-thirty one morning after weeks of dreaming, the wood was right where he'd remembered it.

He didn't notice his slippers blotting up oil from the small greasy patch beneath them. He stood, gazing up into the rafters, tears running down his cheeks, searching for the piece of wood he had seen in his dream. It was suspended across two rafters above Ralph Lauzon's car.

He climbed up on the hood of Ralph's car, his slipper soles grinding little cinders into the glassy black paint. With his long legs, he was able to step up across the expanse of the windshield and onto the roof in a single step. He didn't notice the loud popping as his weight buckled the roof. He paused unsteadily for a moment, transfixed by the large, looming shadow he threw across the wall and part of the ceiling. He'd had too much whiskey on an empty stomach. The mixture of alcohol and digestive juices burned uncomfortably. He steadied himself, burped, and waited to see if he was going to vomit.

The chunky piece of wood that he wanted was very nearly his own height. He dragged it forward and began tipping it back over his shoulder, feeding it back down through the open space behind him. Then the mid-point slipped through his hands and the beam fell, first onto the roof, then the hood, and then finally down onto the oily cinders. Jerome looked at the large pock in the roof, bewildered. He decided to come back later with a soft cloth and polish it.

Forgetting the light on behind him, he dragged his beam around the outside of the garage, across the snowy backyard, through the centre of his miracle grotto, and bumped it noisily up the back steps and through the mudroom. He left tracks across the kitchen floor and down the narrow corridor.

At four o'clock, Mrs. Guinney went to the foot of the stairs in her robe and hairnet and turned on the hall light. Gerry LeBlanc awoke, stared at the crack of light beneath his door, and wondered why he knew something was wrong. He met Ralph in the hall, and together they looked down over the railing.

"Fathers, I think yous should come down. Something's not right in the church."

They found Jerome at the foot of the altar, sitting on the steps in the dark, the only light coming from the candles in the side alcoves and the red sacristy lamp above him. He was crying, slowly rocking the half-decayed beam in his arms, chanting over and over that he would fix her porch for her now.

T he maps with red, spidery veins creeping through Ohio began waking Adele. She spread them out on the living room coffee table at 5:00 a.m. and ran her index finger along the routes to Washington, building a column of mileage numbers on a piece of scratch paper. If they left at six in the morning, they could arrive at seven in the evening.

Two weeks before Easter she made a meal that had a favourite dish for everyone in the family. There were scalloped potatoes for Richard, salmon patties for Gerald, and a chocolate layer cake for Cathy. She set the table with the good china, the silver, and the linen napkins that were reserved for Christmas day. She set a crystal wineglass of ginger ale at each place.

"So what's the bad news," Richard asked, staring at the spectacle.

"I have a surprise for all of you. Come on, Dad, Cathy, take your place. Help yourselves to everything while it's still hot."

She stood by the oven door, waiting to snatch warm dinner rolls out at precisely the right moment.

Cathy eased herself warily into her seat.

"*Ah, me, another adventure,*" sighed Angela, leaning against the wall behind Cathy.

Richard shook out his napkin and proceeded to tie it around his neck.

"I think I'll tie one on tonight. Haven't done that in a while."

He winked at Cathy. She looked away.

Gerald glanced at the fancy table.

"Get going," Adele urged. "Eat up. Don't let it get cold."

"Yes, indeed," said Richard, "shrinkage sets in if you wait until it's cold. Eat hot, I always say. You get more."

Richard heaped his plate with scalloped potatoes, relishing the crispy browned cheese topping that clung to the corners of the serving dish. He gestured toward Cathy's plate. She pinched her thumb and index finger together and Richard dropped a minute bit of the cheese topping on her plate.

Adele retrieved the hot rolls, set them in a basket, and arrived at the table.

Richard addressed Gerald in a British accent.

"My God, Henry. Look at what Cook's done now. First scalloped potatoes, now hot dinner rolls. Why, she's a perfect genius. We'll have to reward her. Cook, two lumps extra of coal for your fire tonight. And as a special bonus, you may sup at our table. Have a seat."

Adele sat down, tickled at Richard's good humour.

"What's gotten into *you* tonight?"

Richard picked up his wineglass of ginger ale and waved it around the table.

"Oh, the usual. Fine spirits, good friends, peace in the kingdom. You've heard I'm to be crowned in the morning, of course. By the way, M'Lord, your cellar is superb."

He drank from his glass and continued.

"M'Ladies, how are you finding the boar meat, this evening? I killed it myself this afternoon, you know. Ran it to the very ground on horseback, I did. Had a bloody good time of it, too."

Adele, laughing, opened a steaming roll.

"Boar meat. They don't have boars in England, do they?"

"Well, boors, anyway, for sure," said Richard.

"No. It's foxes they chase, isn't it?" Cathy asked, quietly.

"Oh, no, no, no, my dear. You don't want fox. Fox is dreadful. It's a very hairy meat, fox. All that horrible red fur stuck between your teeth. No. Trust me. Stick to boar. Cook here's done an excellent job with the plucking. This must be the finest meal served in all of England tonight."

"And you have bats in your belfry tonight," said Gerald.

"Your Grace," replied Richard, nodding at his father and then upending his ginger ale.

The table lapsed into silence. Cathy idly pulled bits of green onion out of her salmon patty.

"So, what's the surprise," Richard asked.

"Well," Adele said, stabbing a piece of salmon patty, "we're going on a little trip. Cathy, you'll celebrate your birthday while we're away, so this will be an extra birthday treat for you as well. Over Easter weekend, everyone has four days off. Dad, you can ask for Holy Thursday off. They can get someone else for once. You work all the holidays. Richard, you can get Saturday off. We're going to leave early in the morning, so you'll have to get to bed early, kids. It's a thirteen-hour drive. We'll be there around suppertime."

"'There' being where, if I may be so bold?" Richard asked.

Adele squared her shoulders, set down her glass, and panned the table.

"We're going to Arlington National Cemetery."

Gerald stopped breathing.

"There's all sorts of history there for you to see, kids. Monuments and museums. Cathy, you can have a horse and buggy ride, if you want."

"That's not fair," Richard mocked. "She always gets the buggy rides through the museums."

"It's about time we showed them some of the world, Gerald. They're old enough to be learning. Eat up now, Cathy. I don't want you filling up on just cake."

Angela rolled her eyes.

ix hours south of Ontario, they encountered heat that was freakish for that time of the year. They pulled onto the shoulder of the road and opened the trunk to exchange their wool sweaters for short-sleeved shirts. Then they left the main road to go into a small town in search of cold drinks.

Adele told Cathy and Richard to go into the tiny grocery store and bring everyone something cold to drink. She stood on the sidewalk, studying the window display of a pharmacy, dangling her arm behind her with a five-dollar bill flapping in her hand.

"Here, kids. Get yourselves chips, too. There's still a long drive ahead."

An instant later she vanished inside the pharmacy door. When she returned, she sported a new pair of dark-framed sunglasses. Gerald was a few doors down the street, filling the car with gas and having the oil checked. Adele strolled up to the attendant, a young man in his early twenties.

"How long from here to Arlington, son?"

"Arlington, ma'am?"

"Yes. The National Cemetery. The one with the eternal grave. It's where the President's buried."

"Would that be in Washington, ma'am?"

"Yes. Your nation's capital. It was on television all over the world last fall."

"Well, I've never been more that thirty miles south of here, ma'am. I think Washington's still quite a drive yet, from here."

Adele made a face and climbed back into the car.

"Imagine not knowing where your own nation's capital is," she muttered as they pulled back onto the highway.

★ ★ ★

Thirty miles out of Washington, they began to see billboards for a restaurant chain. Their forte was family food at family prices. Pancakes were served around the clock, in addition to their thirty-five flavours of ice cream and the best coffee around. After passing several of these signs, Adele suddenly announced that it was time for dinner.

"Pull over, Gerald. The kids are hungry. Cathy, you can have a chocolate milkshake."

The decor was striking: an orange and turquoise colour scheme, booths rather than tables and chairs, and a paper sand-wich-board clown standing on the table with the dozens of flavours of ice cream listed in the coloured polka dots of his suit. They took a booth beside a window. Gerald stared out of it at the flowing traffic. A pretty teenaged girl, with straight blond hair pulled back into a tight ponytail, dropped off four water glasses and four menus printed on placemats. The room was packed with a supper crowd. Adele kicked off her shoes and began to talk to her feet as she simultaneously rubbed them and browsed the menu.

"Poor things, cooped up all day without a breath of fresh air. Sandals tomorrow. Have whatever you want, kids, Dad. This is a holiday. We're here to enjoy ourselves. They have pie, Dad.

330

Raisin pie. With ice cream. It's your favourite. Cathy, it says breaded shrimp. That's your favourite."

Cathy nodded.

"Richard? What are you having?"

"I think I'll come back tomorrow and have the sandals."

Gerald raised a cautionary eyebrow at Richard.

"Tch, be serious now," Adele said from behind her menu. "There's lots to choose from."

Ten minutes passed. Adele suddenly became impatient, slapped the table, and glanced around the room.

"Where is that girl? We haven't got all night."

"Relax. She'll get here."

Richard spoke from behind his menu. He could see the waitress across the room at a sideboard slicing triple-layer chocolate cake onto small plates. High-intensity lights poured down over her and the desserts. When she moved, her hair, which was tied back with a black ribbon, glittered in the lights. If she did nothing else for the rest of the night except bend over the cake platters with the light glittering on her hair, Richard wouldn't mind.

Adele squirmed.

"I tell you, if I was running this dining room, I'd really make these girls hustle. People have got things to do besides sitting around and waiting. I don't even see our girl."

"Maybe she's doing something."

"Doing something, my eye. I could have been back here five times by now."

Gerald's fingers drummed, once.

"Here she is," Cathy chirped.

The girl arrived, breathless, rolling over the first page of her order pad. Her face was flushed pink. She smiled brightly at Adele.

"Have you had enough time to decide?"

"More than enough, miss. Are you always this slow? People have things to do, you know."

The girl's face fell. Her hand rose nervously, curling a strand of hair behind her ear.

"Sorry, ma'am."

"I'll have two pieces of that chocolate cake," Richard declared.

The girl turned to him and began writing.

"Just cake?" Adele asked sharply. "After all day in the car, you're having just two pieces of cake?"

"Well, make that three, then, and a glass of milk to go with each one."

"Three cakes, three milks…"

"Richard, order a proper meal. Something that will fill you up."

The girl stopped writing and looked back and forth between mother and son.

"This will fill me up fine. You said to have whatever we wanted."

He looked directly at the girl.

"I'll have three pieces of chocolate cake, please."

"Anything else, sir?"

"What are tonight's specials, miss, if you don't mind," Adele interrupted.

"The fish and chips are nice tonight. Fresh cod in a batter with homemade fries."

"Fresh, miss? The fish is fresh, not frozen?"

"She said 'fresh.' Heard her with my own two ears."

Adele glared at Richard.

"Fish and chips will be fine for me. And coffee, please."

Gerald spoke quietly, then resumed watching the traffic.

"They have raisin pie, too, Gerald. He'll have raisin pie, miss."

Gerald turned back.

"No, I don't want pie."

"Oh, have it. You'll be glad once it's here. Bring him the pie, miss."

The girl wrote.

"And you say the fish is fresh tonight, is it? Well…"

The girl shifted her weight to her other hip.

"Yes, ma'am."

"Cathy, are you having the breaded shrimp?"

Cathy nodded.

"Does it come with shrimp sauce, miss?"

Adele spoke while reading the list of ice cream flavours.

"Yes, ma'am, there's sauce with the shrimp."

"Fine then, bring her the shrimp and I'll have the fresh cod and chips with my son and husband. Cathy, do you want a chocolate milkshake?"

"Just the cake," Richard said, holding up three fingers to the girl.

"Milkshake?" the girl clarified.

Cathy nodded.

★ ★ ★

They stayed within the city limits, in a three-storey motel called the Washington Inn. Gerald pulled under a carport outside the office, and for the last dozen feet of travel, Adele's right foot hung out of her door, dragging along the pavement, in anticipation of a landing.

"For God's sake," Gerald muttered, but she was gone before the words reached her.

The office was brightly lit with a combination of overhead fluorescent bulbs and conventional floor and table lamps. Some attempt had been made to create a living room ambience by placing a large rug over the linoleum floor and grouping chairs, end tables, and a small sofa around it. Travel magazines littered the tables, and a giant aquarium on a black wrought iron stand stood in the window. Two vending machines stood in an alcove near the door, one for drinks, the other for cigarettes.

A short, plump, dark-haired woman with two spit curls glued to her cheeks stepped out of a back room. She wore a sleeveless mint green mock-turtleneck jersey. Adele immediately engaged her in conversation.

Gerald, Richard, and Cathy watched. At first, the two women exchanged little else but nods. Then the woman looked out of the window above Adele's head and began pointing while she spoke. Adele's head turned to follow the directions. Gerald looked, too, and saw streams of red taillights and white headlights on a freeway. After a moment, the woman's arm came down out of the air, and Adele's index finger tapped the surface of the counter. The woman brought a map out from under the counter and unfolded it in front of Adele. She continued to speak while her finger traced routes on the map surface, and then she pointed out the window again. Moments later, she folded the map and replaced it under the counter. Then she began drawing on a piece of paper. Gerald let out a sigh and turned off the ignition. Richard snorted in the back seat.

"Maybe she's booking us a vault at the cemetery."

"That's enough. I don't want a scene tonight."

Gerald spoke into the rear-view mirror.

"I'm not the one who makes them, remember?"

"Just keep your comments to yourself. I don't want anything to set her off."

"What if she doesn't like the colour of the toilet paper in the room, if, in fact, we're ever getting a room here?"

"Just drop it and let's try to get through the rest of this trip without any incidents. Maybe, if we let her do this one thing, she'll drop this obsession when we get home."

Adele took the paper from the woman, folded it, and put it into her purse. Finally the woman began writing in a large book and Adele squinted out the window at the front of the car to read the licence number. Things from Adele's purse were handed across the counter and back again. The woman retrieved a key from a rack behind her.

"All right, Adele!" said Richard.

Gerald glared into the mirror while his hand reached for the keys. Adele, meanwhile, stopped in front of the vending machine and bought four cans of pop. Then she bustled into the car, crackling with energy.

"Here you go, kids. A before-bed treat. Happy birthday, Cathy. Dad, here's a ginger ale for your highball. Down the end there, Room 201. She says the cemetery's about a fifteen-minute drive from here. We can have breakfast in the little coffee shop in the morning and then be on our way first thing. The office was nice and clean, so the rooms should be the same. And it's air-conditioned, kids."

Gerald piloted the car slowly down the driveway, behind a row of parked cars. The motel was painted white and turquoise, with cement ramps, instead of staircases, leading up to the upper floors. Each door had a little flowerpot of pink geraniums fastened to it.

"Aren't those flowers cute," Adele remarked. "This place is just fine. We don't need anything that fancy. Look at that other place over there, just to put your head down for one night."

Across the street, there was a huge white stone edifice with floodlit pillars. A sign, lettered in black gothic script, welcomed travellers to "The Senator."

"No siree. The President didn't flaunt his money and we don't have to either. All I need is a clean set of sheets and soap and water to make me happy. Those people staying over there aren't going to get to the cemetery any faster than we are. No pool here tonight, kids, but it's late anyway. Tomorrow we'll find you one. For your birthday, Cathy. Two birds with one stone tomorrow. History and you turn sixteen. Keep going, all the way down to the end, Dad. Room 201."

Cathy took a cautious deep breath.

"Turn in here," Adele directed, her arm wagging out her window. "Okay, kids. Here we are. Everybody grab your own suitcase. Room 201, right up there, second floor. You can have your pop and watch a bit of television before bed. I have the key."

Richard got out and stood watching the traffic. In his peripheral vision he saw his father ease himself out of the driver's seat and take a few heavy, limping steps. He looked tired and beaten.

"Hurry up, Gerald, for God's sake. You'd think you're eighty. Get the trunk open."

Richard continued to stare at the streams of traffic. Behind him his father's keys jingled.

"We'll all have a nice sleep tonight and be up early tomorrow to go see history."

Cathy noticed that her father looked fatigued. His pale blue eyes looked through things. She reached out to spare him lifting a heavy suitcase. Richard intercepted, hoisting the remaining two bags out of the trunk. Adele, toting her own brown bag, led the way up the ramp.

"Tch. I just can't get past how cute these little geranium pots are."

C athy lay awake beside her snoring mother that night, staring at the ceiling. Richard and her father were asleep in the other double bed. Angela sat on the floor beside Cathy, her folded arms resting on the mattress, her chin resting on her arms.

"Don't be so glum, flea. Things will get better."

I can't believe I'm turning sixteen tomorrow. I feel like I'm four. Like time never passes in my life. Or like time passes and I don't go with it, somehow.

"I know, I know. But just wait a bit longer."

Waiting is all I ever do. Waiting for nightfall, waiting for daylight. I feel like I'm glued to the floor and I can't move on. Like nothing lies ahead for me except more waiting.

"Trust me, sweetie. Time really is passing, even though it doesn't feel like it, and you are slowly moving forward."

How come you're so sure?

"Picture yourself at twenty-six. Where are you?"

Cathy closed her eyes. Twenty-six. Where was that on the road ahead? How far forward? Where would she be? What would she be doing? It certainly wasn't visible from where she stood.

"Just keep looking ahead."

Twenty-six, thirty-six. How many more sixes lay ahead? Cathy sighed and drifted off into darkness.

The next morning they all awoke to the muffled sound of Adele brushing her teeth behind a closed bathroom door. Gerald resisted the new day, lying on his side facing the floor-length, horizontally striped drapes, which he knew, from having parted them the night before, closed over a view of a weedy grass alley and the cement block wall of an adjacent motel. Outside, doors opened and closed, footsteps passed along the walkways, children ran and shouted, voices admonished them to keep quiet, car trunks slammed. Coffee came to mind, and rye toast, a soft-boiled egg and bacon.

Laughter rippled behind the bathroom door, then speech, then laughter.

"Jesus Christ, she's talking to him." Richard, wearing only pyjama bottoms, jumped out of bed and stood in the middle of the floor, rumpling his hair. Gerald reluctantly opened his eyes and sat up, just as Adele, rattling the loose doorknob loudly, burst out of the bathroom.

"Come on, everybody. Up. Up. Time to get up. Rise and shine. Look at me. I'm way ahead of the rest of you. Big day for you today, kids. History in the making. Dad, you can have coffee in the little shop."

She wore a two-piece white knit suit with black piping, white stockings, white high heels, and a small white pillbox hat attached to the back of her head. Her red hair was so heavily shellacked with hairspray that it shone like plastic in the light. She scooted around the foot of the bed where Cathy now sat.

"Richard? The shower's free. Better get at it before Cathy, with her long hair. Here, use this shampoo, if you want."

She tossed a tube of shampoo in his direction. He let it bounce off his naked chest and fall to the floor. Cathy picked it up, setting it quietly on the end of the bed. Gerald sat perfectly still on the other bed.

"Here, Cathy. This new blouse is for you. Happy birthday. I've cut the tags off, so you can just put it on."

Richard crossed the room to the bathroom, ignoring the shampoo. He closed and locked the door. A moment later the spray of shower hit the floor of the tub.

Adele addressed Gerald's back. He sat, facing away, his hands hanging idly in the space between his knees.

"Did you bring in your suit bag, Gerald? The other men will be wearing suits. And have you got Cathy's fifty dollars? We always give her fifty on her birthday. No card this year, Cathy. I was too busy with this trip. But it's the thought that counts."

Cathy read the white, cold skin on her father's back, the collapsed slope of his rounded shoulders, the lifeless sag of his limbs. She had never seen him so still.

Angela, leaning in a corner, arms folded, watched him.

There was less than two feet of space between the edge of the bed and the drapes. Gerald thought about stepping across and slipping behind them. He could live there. He could install straps on the wall and bivouac. Men did it on the walls of mountains. He could fasten food pouches to the back of the drapes. During the day, he could use the room, relax on the beds, shower, watch television. He would learn to recognize the maid's footsteps, memorize the jingle of her keys. At night, he could sleep strapped in behind the heavy material. The drapes were long enough that they would cover his feet. No one would see his shoes. His family would never know what happened to him.

"Gerald. Where's your suit?"

He turned.

"I can't survive in this heat wearing a suit. Not driving in the car all day."

"Oh, all right then, wear what you want. You'd think I was asking you to wear a tuxedo, for heaven's sake."

It took them less than an hour to pack, have breakfast, and pull out into the stream of traffic. Adele spread a map of the city out on her lap and compared it to the one on the white piece of paper that the woman in the motel office had drawn for her. From time to time her hand floated up to the back of her head to pat the pillbox.

When they were within sight of a major artery that turned west, one that the motel woman had alerted her to, Adele abruptly rapped her knuckles on her window and ordered Gerald to pull into an adjacent plaza. After climbing out, she bent and poked her head back inside the car.

"Just wait here. I'll be right back."

She disappeared through the door of a florist's shop.

Richard slapped his knees.

"Well then, I'll be right back too."

He walked past the flower shop and entered the menswear store beside it.

What now? Cathy asked Angela.

"Not a clue, flea."

Adele emerged from the florist's carrying an elaborate bouquet streaming with green and white ribbons. But she didn't get beyond the window of the neighbouring restaurant before being distracted. She disappeared inside with her flowers. Two minutes later she arrived at the car carrying something wrapped in waxed paper.

Richard emerged from the men's shop. Gerald's eyes widened. Cathy inhaled sharply. Arriving at Adele's side, Richard asked, "Like this? I always wanted one of these. Very high class."

He tugged the wings of a black and white polka dot bow tie.

Adele regarded the tie curiously.

"Hmph. I didn't know you liked those."

She held up her flowers.

"You can't arrive at a big international monument like this without anything."

"I agree," said Richard, fingering his tie again.

Adele climbed into her seat, tossing the waxed paper parcel onto the dashboard.

"Here you go, Dad, your favourite. Raisin pie."

★ ★ ★

At Arlington National Cemetery the rows of headstones were as precisely ordered as if drawn across the green fields with a giant ruler. The detail fascinated Gerald. All the straight lines, the exact angles. You could look in any direction and see the same long lines of uniform white headstones. Obviously there was an art to all this and someone would be highly trained in it. *Other worlds*, he thought, following Adele along a gravel path. *Worlds that you never even guess at until you stumble over them.*

They eventually joined a queue that led them up an incline to the grassy hill. Several sombre-faced people were returning downhill. Adele put out her hand and stopped a woman.

"Is this the right lineup for the President's grave?"

The woman nodded. A few moments later Adele stopped another person.

"Did you see the eternal grave?"

The person, a man this time, smiled.

"I think all graves are eternal, madam? But if you mean the President's grave with the eternal flame, then, yes, you are in the correct line."

Behind her, Richard tightened his bow tie.

"Gosh Ollie, I didn't know that all graves were eternal. I was just planning a short visit myself. What am I going to do now?"

Gerald hissed under his breath.

"Oh, you know what I meant," Adele said, cheerfully. "Now be serious."

Cathy looked at her brother curiously. She'd been wondering all along why he even came on this trip. She'd expected him to refuse. In fact he had refused much lesser things. She couldn't shake the feeling that he was up to something.

After a few minutes progress up the incline halted. It was growing warm and the bouquet was heavy. Adele noticed people looking at it. The glances made her uneasy. She pushed her bosom forward and raised her chin defiantly, muttering under her breath.

"A big monument like this and I'm the only one with anything. Americans. No manners."

"Excuse me?"

Good thing you're invisible.

"It has its advantages."

The line began to inch forward again. People fell silent. When the grave came within sight, Adele opened her purse and pulled out two rosaries, her own and Cathy's white one. She kissed the crucifix on hers and nodded that Cathy should do the same.

"Show time," Angela whispered.

God, I'm afraid of that.

Cathy touched the rosary to her mouth, hung her head, and watched her slowly shuffling feet. They moved, they stopped, they moved again. Adele tapped Cathy's arm and proffered a Kleenex. Cathy shook her head. Adele shook the Kleenex and pushed it at her. Cathy frowned. Angela whispered in her ear.

"Cue the tears."

Adele pushed the pink tissue at Cathy again and nodded. Then she dabbed her eyes and nodded again. Cathy clenched her teeth.

Jesus Christ, now I have to pretend to cry, too?

"Not pretend, dear. She wants the real McCoy. Like this…"

Angela pulled up her skirt, dabbed her eyes on the hem, and then noisily blew her nose. Then she turned around, flipped up the back of her skirt, and showed her bright pink underpants to Adele. Cathy pulled her lips into her mouth, bit down hard, and bowed her head. Her shoulders began to shake. A moment later, tears ran down her cheeks.

"*That's it,*" Angela snorted.

Adele patted Cathy on the hand.

"That's all right, dear. Let it all out. He was a great, great man."

★ ★ ★

The line moved. They were getting close. Adele craned her neck to see. There was a small fence surrounding the grave. People just stood before it with bowed heads and then moved aside. Her heart contracted. She wanted more than just a two-minute pause; she wanted to kneel and pray; she wanted to visit her friend properly.

Gerald saw the four guards standing at the corners of the grave. The sight relieved him. She couldn't possibly make a scene.

Her turn came suddenly. The line moved forward, then the backs of the people in front of her stepped away. There at her feet was the President's grave with the eternal flame flickering in the warm spring breeze. Adele's hand twitched beneath the flowers. A guard noticed and held out a white-gloved hand.

"Sorry, no flowers, ma'am."

No flowers? All this way to see him and she couldn't even give him a simple bouquet of flowers? She grabbed Cathy's sleeve and pulled her down hard into the gravel.

"Say a prayer for the repose of his soul, dear."

Adele crossed herself and began to pray in a loud sibilant whisper. Cathy rolled her eyes. Gerald leaned forward and firmly squeezed Adele's elbow. He indicated the guards with his eyes and the people in line with a subtle jerk of his head. Adele yanked her arm free, turned away, and finished her prayer. Then she got up, took a long moment to brush gravel from her knees, looked pointedly at one guard, then another, and then huffed off.

Two of the guards watched the crowd in front of them. Another glanced down the length of the line. The fourth studied the buttons on his comrade's uniform. As he did so, a bouquet of flowers trailing white and green ribbons sailed past his head and landed on the grave. Several yards away, with her back to the grave and her heavy shoulders squared, Adele jutted her bosom out as far as it would go and marched resolutely down the gravel path.

Richard never dwelt on endings. Beginnings were what attracted him. Every one had the potential to flower into a remarkable journey. It was his father who feared the future, staring out the dining room windows every New Year's morning, saying, "Well, then, another year," always meaning the year that had just ended and never the new one that stretched out before him. But Richard believed the future could always be better. He also believed the future was where he belonged.

He announced this belief at dinner one evening barely a week after returning from Washington. Adele was bustling between the table and the stove prattling breathlessly.

"Honestly, you kids don't know how lucky you are, seeing such history. Here're the potatoes. The gravy's coming. And those little pots of geraniums? Weren't they just the sweetest things? We could do that to some of our doors. Peas, Cathy. That flame, too, is going down in history. Imagine, it never stops burning. You're living in the modern age, kids. Now, is that everything? Yes. Eat up, everyone. Apple crisp for dessert."

She finally sighed, scooting her chair into place beneath her.

"It was a such peaceful place, wasn't it? I'm sure he's happy there."

"Speaking of being happy in peaceful places," Richard began, without looking up from his mashed potatoes.

"Oh, boy! Torpedo at three o'clock."

Cathy's fingers tightened around her fork. Richard raised a forkful of chicken toward his mouth.

"I'm going to Australia."

Gerald's head swivelled. Adele raised an eyebrow and began to smile.

"Oh, Robinson's is sending you on business?"

"Yes. A little local grocery store is sending me halfway around the world on business. I'm to be the new head buyer of kangaroo meat."

"Kangaroo meat? Who eats that?"

"Jesus, Johnny, and Rebecca."

"I'm kidding…"

Adele puffed out her bosom.

"Tch. Clown."

"… about the meat, not about Australia."

Adele frowned.

"What do you mean, 'not about Australia'?"

"I'm going to Australia. Nothing to do with Robinson's. I've given my notice. Going by myself. Just to travel around and explore. Leaving a week from Sunday."

Adele shook her head as if she had water in her ears.

"What?"

Richard forked carrots into his mouth.

"Starting off in Sydney."

Adele straightened, puffed out, and began sawing through a chicken breast.

"Are you now?"

"Yup."

Adele clucked dismissively.

"And who's paying for this fairy tale?"

"Me."

"Well, we'll just see about that. Your father and I still have some say in your life, young man, as long as you're living under this roof."

Richard smiled.

"That's just the point, though. When I go to Australia, I won't be living under this roof anymore, will I?"

Cathy stiffened.

"Bombs away."

"Australia's halfway around the world. Who put this idea in your head, anyway? One of your hockey friends? Australia, my arse! No siree, no kid of mine is going to be a globetrotting beatnik bum, that's for sure. Wandering around all over the place, no job. Huh! Over my dead body are you going to Australia. What are the neighbours going to say, us letting a kid traipse halfway around the globe by himself, no money in his pocket?"

"I don't give a damn about the neighbours, I have plenty of money, it's my idea, and you can't stop me."

"Checkmate!"

Angela tapped Cathy's shoulder.

"Pay attention. He's very good."

Adele glared across the table at Gerald. He swallowed and shifted.

"Well ... he's right. It *is* his money and he *is* old enough to ... to ... to take a little trip. Bit sudden, though..."

"He's not old enough."

"I'm old enough to do anything I want."

"You're not of legal age, yet."

"I don't need to be of legal age to travel."

"You can't have a drink."

"I don't want to have a drink."

Adele glared at Gerald.

"This is your fault. Never laying down the law."

Gerald sighed.

"Adele, don't get started."

Adele slammed down her fork.

"That's it, teach them respect."

"Ah," Richard interjected, "there's that 'r' word again."

"Adele," Gerald begged, "look at how old he is. What do you want me to do? Sit on him?"

"Careful…"

★ ★ ★

Gerald bought a map of the world. He spread it out on a table in the stockroom of Hooper's and stared at all the blue water between North America and Australia. The fact that his son had chosen to flee to the opposite side of the world was not lost on him. He ached with guilty regret at the decision as well as pride at Richard's courage. The ache needled him to think of a way to wish Richard well.

Adele sat on the swing most evenings, bundled up against the spring cold. Gerald brought her cups of tea and enumerated things for her that comforted him. It was just a matter of hours away by plane; his money would run out eventually and he would have to come home; he might find it lonely. Some nights, finding that she had wandered off to bed, he disappeared downstairs, leaving behind a narrow line of yellow light beneath the stairwell door. And after midnight, the aroma of fresh-baked cinnamon rolls would visit the upstairs bedrooms.

During the day, Adele busied herself laundering Richard's clothes. She ignored his clearly stated insistence on taking only his backpack and bought him two new suitcases. She filled the side pockets with new underwear and socks, a new shaving kit, shoe polish kit, sewing kit, and a new rosary and pocket-sized bible. She hid these last items beneath newly laundered flannel pyjamas. Then she bought him a waterproof jacket and a New Zealand–wool sweater.

Hoping to assuage his aching heart, Gerald wandered about, visiting the bank to inquire about wiring money overseas, inquiring at the post office about *poste restant* addresses. Then, on the last Friday before Richard left, something in the window of Hicox's Jewellery store caught his eye.

★ ★ ★

Unable to fall asleep on Richard's final night at home, Cathy wandered down the hall towards the light in his room. His new suitcases were open, sitting in the middle of the floor. He was scooping out the side pockets, plunging what he found between the mattress and box spring. When he saw his sister in the doorway, he cleared clothes off a chair and motioned for her to come in and sit down.

"Great hiding place under the mattress. Room for plenty of secrets."

Cathy smiled.

He moved to the second suitcase and pulled the pyjamas out of the side pocket, uncovering the rosary and the bible. He held them up, shaking his head. "Never learns."

He rolled a pair of jeans into a tight bundle and fastened a belt around them. He scrutinized a pair of socks and then tossed them into his pack. Next, he stuffed the shoe polish kit under the mattress.

"She won't change sheets in here anymore, so there's not much chance of her finding this."

Cathy noticed that the vestiges of baby fat were all gone tonight. He looked like he was heading towards adulthood, polished and ready.

349

"You should get a plan going for yourself, you know," he said, continuing to pack. "School is going to be over sooner than you think."

Cathy watched his busy decisive movements, afraid to tell him how unprepared she was for her future. Richard suddenly sat back on his heels, seeming to read her mind.

"You look like you don't even know where to begin, Cathy." She bowed her head. "I don't."

"The first thing is to realize that you are going to have to get out any way that you can."

She looked down at him, tears filling her eyes.

"How? I'm not finished school. I don't have any money. Where would I go? What would I do?"

"Look, don't take all the big steps at once. Start small. First of all, carve out a little space for yourself for the rest of the time that you're here. Learn to say no once in a while. That will get you started."

"Richard, I'll get the belt. You've seen what happens."

Richard's voice softened. "Look, Cathy. You don't have to sit there and just take it. Don't follow Dad's example. What a moron to just sit there and let himself be hit in the face with a cushion all the time. Even a kid would put his hand up in defence."

Cathy hiccuped.

"But if he says anything, it only makes her worse."

"Then he should ramp it up. He's not an invalid."

"Then she'd only come after me."

"That's why you have to be ready to fight back."

"But nothing works."

"Well, what have you tried?"

"Well…"

"I've never seen you do anything except bow your head and run up to your room. Just grab the belt away from her and use it on her if you have to."

Cathy's eyes widened. The skin on the back of her neck moved.

"Oh God, Richard," she said in a terrified whisper, "I could never do that. She'd kill me."

Richard went back to his packing.

"If you want to be free, you'll have to."

"Richard, if I ever hit her back, it would make her crazy."

Richard snorted. "You think she's not already?"

Cathy raised her eyebrows. "What about Dad? He wouldn't let me…"

"And how's he going to stop you?"

His eyes, of course. His blue watery eyes. They had torn at her heart for as long as she could recall. Tonight, however, her brother's clear green eyes pinned her.

"Tell me something. If push comes to shove, who do you think he's going to look after?"

Cathy's eyes flashed with tears. Not her. Her father had never once looked after her.

"You're going to have to look out for yourself because they're never going to change."

"Isn't there any other way?" she whispered.

"Have you ever seen her stopped?"

Yes. She had seen Richard stop her dead in her tracks.

"She's nuts, Cathy. She lives in a fantasy world. That's why you shouldn't believe the stuff she says to you. She's arbitrary, inconsistent, and just plain arrogant."

Cathy flicked tears off her cheeks.

"It's easy for you to talk, Richard. She never touches you."

"Not anymore."

"Not anymore?"

"Not ever again."

"What are you talking about?"

"She knows she can't get away with it."

"How?"

"Because I fought back. I grabbed a yardstick out of her hand once."

Adrenaline shot through Cathy. She sat up straighter.

"You did? How?"

"Just twisted it out of her hand. Made sure it wasn't too comfortable either when I did it."

"Did you hit her with it?"

"No. I did something better. I backed her up to a wall and held her there with it pressed across her forehead."

The image of her mother pinned to the wall, a yardstick cutting its sharp-edged outline into her skin, shocked Cathy.

"What about her hands?"

"She didn't move."

"What did she do?"

"Nothing. She couldn't move. My knee was jammed up into her gut. I wasn't fooling around. I told her that if she ever touched me again she would get the same treatment."

"What did Dad say?"

"He doesn't know."

"She never told him?"

Richard shook his head.

"No point. There was nothing he could have done. If he had hit me, I would have fought back. She understood that."

Cathy breathed deeply.

"Told you he was good."

"It only works if you mean what you say, though. You can't bluff. If you don't back yourself up, you're right back in her control again. So, when the time comes, be sure you mean what you say."

"What about last week, though? She didn't accept your news about leaving very well."

"Yeah, well. Don't assume that you can alter her thinking. She needs reminding now and again. Remember dinner last summer?"

The sight of Richard's hand steadily grinding his dinner plate into their mother's face, of Adele falling backward into her chair, was not something that she would ever forget.

"How did you figure this all out?"

"Just got tired of being smacked."

"Well, I'm tired of it, too, but I don't think it would work if I tried something like that."

"Well then, that would be your fault. You have to make sure you win."

"You make it sound so ... so blunt."

"Sometimes life is blunt. You don't always have a bunch of cozy options to choose from. Either you dictate to her the way you want to be treated, or she'll dictate to you, the way she always has."

Richard stared at her, reading her thoughts again.

"Look, Cathy, it's really not as hard as you think. Just push the envelope a bit."

Cathy frowned.

"You already rebel a little bit. Like when you pretend you're sleeping when Dad comes up to your room, or like Arlington. You weren't crying. You were laughing. What was that all about?"

"*These,*" said Angela, bending over and showing her underpants.

Cathy grinned suddenly and shrugged.

"And something about working at that rectory, too. That whole dog episode, I think. Whatever happened to her, anyway? Did you find someone to take her?"

"*She sure did.*"

"Yes."

Richard began tightening laces on his backpack.

"Believe me, the whole rest of your life lies waiting on the other side of this. All you have to do is get out of this loony bin, as soon as you can, any way that you can. Watch for any opportunity."

He tugged on a buckle.

"And hang onto facts. How long until graduation? What can you do after that? How do you get there?"

Cathy watched his movements, looking for hesitation. She saw none.

"I wanted to ask you something about that trip to Washington."

"Ask away."

"You knew by then that you were leaving, didn't you?"

"I've known since last year."

"You've known for a whole year?"

He nodded and tossed a hairbrush aside.

"Then why did you even bother coming on the trip?"

"Oh, I don't know. I though it might be fun to watch her carry on. It was sort of like going to Disneyland for her, you know. Getting to see the real McCoy. For four days, I can put up with almost anything."

"I thought you were behaving oddly. Nothing seemed to bother you. It was like you were waiting to pull a trick on us, or something. I couldn't figure it out. But it was Australia."

"Yup. I was just going along for the ride. No point in letting anything get to me. She is what she is, and she wants to be what she is. I just don't want it touching me anymore."

The room fell silent, and for the first time since entering it, Cathy became conscious of the alarm clock ticking on the bedside table. It was 2:15 in the morning. Somewhere on the other side of the globe, people were almost through with the day that was just beginning for her. This time tomorrow, Richard would almost be over there, nearly a whole day ahead of her in his life.

"Think you'll ever come back?"

He shrugged his shoulders.

"Hard to say. Who knows what lies ahead?"

"Then this is the last night we'll be together…"

"For a while."

Lamplight bounced off of his shiny hair, a shock of which hung down over his eyes, just like their father's.

"I'll miss you."

He looked up.

"I'll worry about you."

She suddenly reached out and took a discarded shirt off the foot of the bed.

"Can I have this?"

"Sure. Same with the rest of this shit. And oh, by the way, I know where there's a great little bible and a rosary, if you're ever in need. I'll leave them in a secret hiding place just for you."

Cathy smiled.

"Thanks, but I've got my own secrets."

"Do you?"

"Yup."

"Wanna share them?"

"Nope."

"No matter," he said. "At least you've got some secrets. That's a start."

★ ★ ★

At the airport, Gerald waited until Adele and Cathy finished hugging Richard before extending his hand to his son. Resting in his palm was a tiny brass compass.

"To help you find your way," he said.

They stood in the parking lot beside the car, watching the plane climb out of sight into the midday sky, its silver body blending with the shiny blue of the atmosphere until it was no longer visible.

For days Adele slammed doors, cleaning out cupboards that had not been disturbed in years, sorting through old picture albums, setting aside photographs of Richard as an infant, as a toddler, as a first-time hockey player.

She met Louise De Finca at the plaza one afternoon and foolishly offered up the story of Richard's departure as some sort of trophy that Louise couldn't possibly duplicate. Louise remarked that she simply would not allow any of her children to wander that far from home, and they respected her word as law. After they were married, they could do what they wanted, but until then, she and Angelo decided what their children's activities were. They had responsibilities as parents, she said. Adele hollered at her that her kids probably didn't have the gumption or the wherewithal to find their way to the end of their own driveway, much less to look after themselves in a foreign country.

Returning home, she fed her anger on window washing, taking down drapes and curtains, stuffing them into the washing machine with cups of soap. While they swished back and forth in their sudsy bath, she climbed up on the wooden stepladder and ground imaginary dust and grime off the panes of glass. As she worked, spittle from her outbursts landed on the surfaces that she was cleaning, forcing her to respray and repolish.

She stormed up to Cathy's room ranting about Sandra De Finca, about how Cathy should look elsewhere for friends, about how that girl was just a carbon copy of her mother. After she retreated, Cathy heard the angry slaps of the iron from downstairs as her mother drove the wrinkles out of yards and yards of drapery fabric. Hours later she returned.

"Look at you, sitting around on your arse all the time, reading. Your brother went to work after school when he was your age. Two nights a week that kid hiked himself over to Robinson's, and he kept his schoolwork up at the same time, too. I never had to remind him to work at anything. You have a long way to go, missy, if you hope to be like him. You couldn't even hang onto the one job you did have, for Christ's sake. And I even had to get that one for you. I tell you, you don't hold a candle to your brother. And you don't take after my side of the family, either, that's for sure. You never caught me sitting around all day with my nose in a book, too lazy to work at anything. You're your father's daughter, all right."

When Adele finally left, Cathy closed her book, turned out her light, and slipped under the covers.

"God, I am so tired of this, Angela," she whispered.

One night, a month after Richard's departure, Gerald locked the door after the last departing staff member of Hooper's Pharmacy and remained behind in the darkened store. For a while he sat behind the dispensary, staring out over the darkened aisles, his gaze flitting here and there over the shelves of shampoo, cosmetics, and cough medicines. Since Richard's departure, he had begun spending less and less time at home. He left earlier than usual, pretending to have a sudden craving for the coffee of a particularly distant restaurant or to want to sample the rye bread of a bakery across town. In the evenings, he drove home slowly, creeping along residential streets, listening half-heartedly to the radio, hoping to find the house in darkness, with Adele and Cathy both asleep. But more often than not he walked straight into one of Adele's full-blown rages.

As he rocked back in the dispensary chair musing, his attention wandered to the patterns that the street lights and the occasional passing headlights made on the ceiling. It occurred to Gerald that shadows had grouped and dispersed up there, unseen, for more than forty years. They were like whole other lives that went on, parallel to his own, without ever being discovered. How he longed to float up there and become a shadow.

His eyes roamed the ceiling, peering into the darkest, emptiest corners of the shadows, skating across the central planes of light that the street lamp cast. Nowhere could he find salvation. Finally, he swivelled his chair around idly and his eyes slid down over the brown and blue glass bottles and odd little cardboard boxes on the dispensary shelves. And then an idea rose up before him, as clear and succinct as any image he had ever seen.

While the ceiling shadows continued their kaleidoscopic grey ballet over his head, he slipped some money into the cash drawer, rang off the till, and locked the day's cash in the safe. Then he diligently locked the store door behind him and walked down the block to where his car was parked, his hand occasionally drifting up to touch the breast pocket of his suit.

For a week he made tea and brought two cups upstairs along with fresh, warm coffee cake or tutti-frutti rolls.

"Here you are," he said, setting the tray down on the dining room table. "A little before-bed snack. Try the cake while it's still warm."

He watched her sip her tea until her cup was almost empty before reaching across the table and filling it a second time. When she finished her second cup he whisked it away. After she went to bed, he washed the cups out and put them back in the cupboard.

On the fifth evening, he turned to find Cathy standing halfway down the basement stairs. The open bottle of pills stood on the counter beside the tea tray. She came to the counter and picked up the bottle. It didn't have a label. What the pills were and what her father was doing with them was something she could only guess at. She returned the bottle to the counter. Her father remained motionless save for meticulously circling a spoon in the teacup.

Cathy's face grew perfectly neutral.

im Okamoto earned the award for the highest academic achievement in the Grade 11 class of St. Michael's, as well as a school letter for his sports achievements and a share in the trophy that the debating team won in a citywide competition. Father McCoy read aloud the names of all the prize-winners over the loudspeakers one morning in late June, three days before the end of term. Janet St. Amand got the prize for outstanding Grade 11 geography student at St. Joseph's, and Sandra De Finca received a St. Joseph's school letter for being an all-around athlete. Sandra's older sister, Christina, received three Grade 12 awards, one for English, one for French, and one for debating.

Cathy sat quietly at her desk, listening to the announcements. The mention of the awards to the De Finca girls made her uneasy. Cathy wondered if there was a way to keep Adele away from the plaza all summer. Perhaps she could keep an eye on the De Finca driveway, observing when Mrs. De Finca's car was there and when it was not. She could volunteer to go on all the errands to the plaza for her mother.

During French period Sister Aline hosted a class party, supplying colas and a strawberry-vanilla cake baked in the convent kitchen. The students arranged all of the desks in a large circle around the room and milled around in groups, carrying cake on paper napkins and pop in paper cups, talking, reliving the year's memorable moments and disclosing their plans for the upcoming summer vacation.

Cathy had studiously avoided Tim since the night of his disastrous phone call to her house. Throughout the entire remainder of the year, she had avoided making eye contact with him, mostly by looking at the floor whenever he was around or ensuring that she always left a room before he did. When entering a room, she focused on her desk, never looking away from it until she was safely installed behind it. Then she busied herself copying the date from the blackboard, underlining the title of the day's subject with red pencil, sharpening her pencil and collecting the shavings in a Kleenex.

When Janet casually remarked once that she thought Tim liked Cathy, Cathy snapped at her to shut up.

"What's the matter with you? What did I say wrong?"

"Just shut up. I don't want any boy liking me."

Cathy stood in a triangle with Sandra and Janet during the class party, listening to Janet tell of her plan to swim in a cross-lake fundraising event at her cottage in July. Then something tapped her on the shoulder and she turned around to face Tim.

Zip. The sky was very hot and empty today. So empty, it was lonely.

"It was really nice having you in some of my classes this term, Cathy. I'm sorry we didn't get to know each other better."

The quiet self-assurance in Tim's dark eyes unnerved her. Her breathing quickened and her fingers worked themselves in and out of fists. She had no idea what to say to him. What had been nice? They hadn't even talked except for the time on the telephone. And that had ended so horribly. Hadn't he been able to pick up that she couldn't see boys? Why didn't he like Janet, instead? She was much prettier and she had a mother who wouldn't have minded a bit if Janet had a boy for a friend, or even a boyfriend.

"Oh," she heard herself stammer.

Something was different about her string today. It had shrunk. Instead of hovering over the roof, her feet were skimming the tops of the maple tress in the convent garden and she could see into the classroom window.

"Oh," she heard herself stammer a second time. "Well, it was nice having you in the classes too. You're so smart."

"Oh," Tim laughed. "Well so are you."

"Me? No, I'm not smart. I didn't win anything. You did. You got top student and two other things."

"Well, that still doesn't mean you're not smart."

"Oh."

"You seem smart to me. You're just quiet about it."

"Oh."

He smiled. She shifted painfully from foot to foot.

"I guess they're going to finish the addition across the street in time for September, so you girls can get your school back to yourselves again."

"That will be nice."

Tim laughed again.

"Were we *that* awful to have around?"

"No, I didn't mean that like it sounded. I just meant that it will be less crowded for everyone and you guys will have that nice new addition to use. That's all."

"Well, I'll still see you at the bus stop in the afternoons, sometimes. Maybe we can talk a bit then."

"Hmm."

Cathy was horrified. Her eyes were beginning to water. She dug her nails into her palms.

"So, what are you doing for the summer? Will you be around much?"

Her blood turned to ice water. She shot straight back up into the sky.

"No. No. I won't be around at all. I'm going up north for the whole summer to the cottage. I'm leaving the day after school gets out."

Janet's ears perked up.

"What? You have a cottage? You didn't tell me that. Where is it?"

"Well, my father just bought it last week. I don't know where it is. I haven't been there yet."

"Oh, this is such neat news. You'll have to find out which lake it's on. Maybe it's close to ours. We can visit."

"A cottage! Wow! That's great. You're lucky," said Tim. "I, on the other hand, will be cutting grass for my father all summer. Not too glamorous."

"Do you have a really big lawn or something?" Janet asked.

"No, my father owns a landscape company. I work for him all summer because it's his busy season."

Tim turned back to Cathy.

"I thought maybe we could go to a movie or something this summer if you were going to be around, but I guess you'll be soaking up the sun at your new cottage. I'd sure do that if I could, boy. It's a lot better than mowing grass eight hours a day. See? I knew you were smart."

Cathy looked at her feet and pushed her nails deeper into her palms.

★ ★ ★

That night she lay in bed staring at the ceiling wondering how to get to Janet as soon as possible and tell her that the cottage was a lie and not to tell anyone.

Don't tell anyone, don't tell anyone, don't tell anyone, she thought until she fell asleep, a small doll lying on a huge bed in a room with gargantuan furniture.

Tim's warm calm voice washed over her like sun-warmed shallow water. *I knew you were smart.*

★ ★ ★

"I lied because I didn't know what else to say, Janet. I didn't know he was going to ask me out. It just slipped out. I didn't even know I was going to say what I did."

"Why didn't you just agree to go out with him? He's pretty nice, I think."

"I can't, Janet."

"Why not?"

"My mother will kill me. He already called the house once last winter asking for homework and I got in big trouble."

"How come?"

"My mother just doesn't want me going out with boys. Somebody sent this thing in the mail to me last year signed 'Your Secret Admirer' and she went nuts. She thought it was from a boyfriend."

"Well, who sent it?"

"I don't know."

"So why didn't you just tell her that?"

"I did, but she didn't believe me."

"Oh," Janet said, softly, puzzled. "Why not?"

Cathy sighed.

"She's just like that, Janet. There's nothing I can do about it. I can't go out with him."

"How 'bout next year? You'll be seventeen, going on eighteen."

"No. I can't date until I'm out of high school."

"Really? Wow! That's strict."

"I can't ever go out with Tim, either, because he's Japanese." Janet frowned.

"What's wrong with being Japanese?"

"Nothing that I can see, but my mother hit the roof when she found out."

"Who told her?"

"I did. She made him identify himself on the phone and then asked me what kind of a name Okamoto was. I didn't realize what her reaction was going to be."

"Hmm. That's weird."

The two girls walked along in silence for a few minutes.

"Janet, please promise you won't say anything to anyone about the cottage."

"I already told my mom. She said she'd drive over to pick you up if your lake was close to ours. Too bad."

"Oh, God. Now what am I going to do?"

"Don't worry about it. I'll just tell her it's not true after all. She won't have told anyone."

"She's going to think I'm a liar."

"Naw. My mom's okay. I'll just tell her the truth about your mom being strict and stuff. She'll understand."

Janet bent over a water fountain in the school hall. When she came back up, she spoke again.

"How are you going to avoid him all summer?"

"I don't know. I guess I'll just stay inside and read a lot."

★ ★ ★

On the last day of school, Sister Aline left the room for a moment to collect the report cards from the Reverend Mother's office. Cathy sat drumming her fingers on her desktop. Behind her, she could hear Tim talking to Peggy Jackson. He was turned sideways in his seat with his elbow resting on Peggy's desk. Peggy was saying that she would be spending the summer in Pembroke at her grandparents' again. She had cousins there and together they helped her grandfather and uncle take animals to be judged at the county fair.

"That sounds like fun," Tim said. "The closest I've ever gotten to a big animal is the buffaloes on the back of the Indian-head nickels in my coin collection."

A dele stood in the middle of Cathy's room, her eyes wild with rage. The white chenille bedspread trailed off the end of the bed resting in a heap on the floor. The mattress had been upended and rested against the wall, partially obscuring the window and exposing the surface of the box spring. Several empty tampon boxes sat in the centre of the blue quilted surface. Adele clutched another, partially full box of tampons in one hand and grasped two individual tampons in the other. The carpet was littered with torn magazines. Whole issues lay at her feet, ripped apart clean through the centre of their pages; others had been dismembered a page at a time, with entire sheets of paper reduced to confetti-sized scraps of colour on the floor.

Adele became aware of Cathy only when she heard a gasp in the doorway behind her. She whirled around. As she did so, one of her feet ground into a picture of a young girl's face. It was what was left of the picture of Angela and Andy sitting in their Malibu kitchen. The rest of the page was missing. Scraps of torn pictures were scattered across the vanity. Cathy recognized a piece of Angela's arm wearing the watch that said 8:50.

"So, little hussy! Thought you could fool me, did you? I've found your little secret hideaway with your cheap movie trash and these things."

Adele shook the two tampons in Cathy's face.

"What were you doing with these, you cheap little tramp? Practising up? Huh? Just can't wait to get your pants off with some boy at school? Huh? I'll teach you to go behind my back and defy me, missy."

She threw the tampon box directly at Cathy's face, hitting her on the forehead. Then she snatched a hairbrush off the vanity and whacked the side of Cathy's face, hitting part of her jawbone.

"How long have you been using these things, you little bugger? There's more than one box here, so you must have been at it for quite some time. I'm a married woman and I can't use these things, so I want to know how a little sixteen-year-old can use them. Where have you been getting these, huh? Who showed you how to use these things? I come in here to clean this pigsty of a room of yours and what do I find out? That I've got a six-teen-year-old little slut living under my roof. Do you think Mrs. De Finca's girls have gone and ruined themselves? Huh? Their mother would half kill them if she found them using tampons. Who do you think you are, using these things at your age?"

She grasped at Cathy's sleeve and shook her. The brush caught Cathy on the shoulder and upper arm. Adele grabbed Cathy's hair and pulled her further into the room.

Cathy's foot slipped on a piece of the glossy magazine paper and she began to fall. Her mother yanked her back up to her full height. Cathy's neck cracked.

"And what were you doing with all of this crap, huh? Is this what you do with your spare time up here, then? Sit around dreaming bird-brained ideas about being a movie star? Huh? Can't concentrate on your schoolwork but you can daydream about Hollywood, eh? Your problem isn't concentration, it's just plain laziness. I know how much effort you've been putting into your schoolwork, spending hours up here with the door closed. I wasn't born half an hour ago."

She swept the box spring clean of the remaining magazines and threw Cathy down on top of it. The force of Cathy's landing dislodged the mattress, and it folded over top of her like a giant clamshell. Her legs hung out from beneath the mattress, and Adele used the hairbrush to repeatedly hit the thigh that was most exposed. The pain was so sharp that it caused Cathy to jolt into an upright position, trying, as she did so, to heave the mattress off and fling it back against the wall. In all the wild commotion, the hairbrush landed, with a loud crack, squarely on one of her kneecaps. Cathy shrieked and folded herself over the injury, cupping both hands over it, whimpering for her mother to stop.

Adele landed a couple of blows with the brush on the back of Cathy's bent head before becoming distracted by another picture. She plucked Angela's face off the vanity, swept the surface clear of all remaining articles with a single swoop of her arm, and shook the picture an inch from Cathy's face.

"So this is what you call good taste, eh? Reading about the life this painted blonde tart leads, huh?"

Her fingers curled around the picture, crumpling it into a ball.

"I knew it wasn't a good idea to let you attend classes with boys. I knew you couldn't be trusted, but your father felt sorry for you and said to give you a chance. Well you had your chance, missy, and now I see just what you did with that chance. Your father might think you're perfect, but I know what goes on in that idle little mind of yours. From now on I am going to count every single sanitary pad that leaves this house, do you hear me? You will not use another tampon again before you are married."

Adele grabbed Cathy by the hair again and turned her red, tear-streaked face roughly upwards.

"From now on, missy, there are new rules around here. I wasn't wrong about that letter you got last summer. Secret admirer, my ass. That was the start of all this. I warned you then what I would do if you continued, and now, my girl, you're going to learn the meaning of obedience. Tomorrow I am phoning the Reverend Mother and finding out from her which boys were in your classes and who that so-called secret admirer of yours is. Then I am going to call Father at the church and have him pay a visit to the boy's parents. And you, my lady, are heading straight for boarding school with the nuns in September. I'm not having any daughter of mine hanging around waiting to get pregnant by some good-time Charlie. You're so gullible, you wouldn't even recognize when a boy just wants a cheap thrill from you. You'd give it to him first and ask questions later. Over my dead body are you having boys in your class again next year."

Cathy floated upward and watched everything from a corner of the ceiling. She saw her mother's face zoom up close to hers and then retreat. Her eyes squinted and then widened. Her teeth flashed. Her words became indiscernible. Her mother looked like a yapping dog. Adele suddenly grabbed one of Cathy's ears and pulled her to her feet.

"Are you listening to me, you little bugger, or are you daydreaming?"

Cathy caught sight of both of them in the vanity mirror. Her mother was breathing heavily, her flushed face glistening with perspiration; she herself was totally dishevelled. Her hair hung in hanks across her face, the elastic from her ponytail dangling uselessly beneath one ear.

Adele's mouth dropped open and she began to puff with the effort of her movements.

"What did you think you were going to do? Flunk out of high school and go off to Hollywood to make movies? Huh? Be famous? Parade around in skimpy clothing at pool parties? 'I want to be popular with the boys.' Do you even know what goes on in those places? Do you know what a casting couch is, you stupid little fool? You're so naive, all anyone would have to do is tell you that you had a little bit of talent and you'd believe them. Then you'd come running to me once you'd gotten yourself into trouble."

Cathy's ears and eyebrows moved at the same instant. She raised her head and looked straight at the crazed images in her vanity mirror, a small smile turning up one side of her mouth.

"Be good."

With her legs and arms quaking she gripped the edge of her dresser and addressed her mother.

"Running to you?" she said, forcing her voice past the cramped muscles in her throat. "Oh, believe me, you are the last person on earth that I would ever come running to, for anything."

Adele froze and squinted at her daughter. Then she took a brisk little step forward, so that her tuna-sandwich-lunch breath puffed across Cathy's chin.

Cathy's fingers gripped the dresser, turning white. The blood vessels in her throat beat roughly beneath her skin and her limbs trembled visibly, as if they would explode and splatter the walls red with the rage that they could no longer contain.

"What did you say to me, miss?"

Cathy turned away from the mirror and looked directly into the wild eyes that confronted her.

"No bluffing."

"I said ... you are the last person that I would ever come running to for anything. Ever. And what's more, if you lay one more hand on me I'll break your goddamn arms."

Adele's eyes widened. Her hand shot up.

One of Cathy's swept the small lamp off the edge of the dresser, raising it high in the air. Adele paused.

"Don't you get smart with me, missy."

"You're the one who needs to get smart," Cathy said.

Adele charged. Cathy brought her weapon down, hard, intercepting her mother's attacking arm. The lamp broke in half with a sickening shatter of glass and metal, deeply gashing Adele's forearm. Aghast, Adele screamed. Then, jolted by a fresh supply of anger, she recovered and took another step forward.

"How dare you..."

The force of Cathy's knee plunging into her stomach silenced her.

She remembered calling the ambulance herself, calmly
dialling the phone and giving out succinct bits of information about the address and the type of injury. She led
them through the rose and cream dining room and up the stairs
to her room. When one of the ambulance attendants asked what
had happened, she answered very matter-of-factly.

"I kicked her."

"Who is she?"

"My mother."

"You kicked your mother?"

Cathy nodded.

"Wearing shoes?"

"No. Just with my knee. We leave our shoes at the back door."

"Were you guys fighting or something?"

"I guess."

The attendant looked at her with his head slightly cocked as
if he didn't understand something. Adele grasped his sleeve.

"Good Shepherd. Good Shepherd. Please take me to Good
Shepherd. Please call a priest."

Another attendant grabbed Cathy's wrist and held it up to
the light.

"It looks like you'll need this looked at."

He pushed her hair off her forehead, fingered a goose egg, and then shone a small flashlight, first in one eye, then in the other.

"Look me in the eye for a minute and follow my finger. Did you hit your head at any time?"

Cathy snorted softly.

"At any time? At any time when? In the past sixteen years?"

★ ★ ★

Gerald signed the papers to have Cathy admitted to the psychiatric ward. She saw him do it through the window in the emergency room office. After he had finished, he came over to where she sat and placed his hand on her knee.

"I think it best if you stay here for a couple of days. The situation at home has gotten out of hand. I can't function in an environment like that and I can't be responsible for submitting your mother to further danger. You'll have to cooperate with the doctors here to see what can be done for you."

She could have sworn the sound of him cutting her loose was audible.

★ ★ ★

The room, located on the top floor, looking north, was comfortless: a hard mattress, steel bed frame, stiff white sheets, a sterile white bathroom in the corner, a heavy door with a window that let in a sleep-disturbing block of hall light. She wondered if the treatment for madness was punishment.

She stood at the window fantasizing about lowering herself down the outside wall on yards and yards of bed sheets. There were people standing on corners, waiting for traffic to pass. She wished she could join them. But she was trapped, and the realization filled her with profound loneliness. Despite everything, she wanted to go home, to be in her own room, with everything in order on her dresser and all of her magazines lined up beneath her mattress. Tears rolled down her cheeks and dropped onto the cold terrazzo window ledge. Perhaps it hadn't been the right opportunity.

Her feet grew cold on the linoleum floor, so she climbed into the bed and stretched out under the hard uncomfortable covers, wondering how she would get out of this place. By the time sleep overtook her, she had at least decided how to protect herself.

★ ★ ★

She was taken to Dr. Marvin Elliott's office and invited, in a carefully regulated voice, to talk about herself. The room made her tired. She sank into the red leather chair, her limbs heavy as wet sand. Dr. Elliott's questions floated past. She let them go by, unable to respond, even if she were interested. She struggled to keep her head from sinking onto her chest and her eyes from closing. She tried staring out the window, counting the number of seagulls that soared past or sorting the clouds into different groups based on their shapes and sizes.

Angela, legs hugged to her chest, sat on the windowsill, listening. Dr. Elliott stared patiently at Cathy, waiting for responses that never materialized. Eventually he jotted notes in a pad balanced on his knee and asked his next question. After forty-five minutes, he announced that that was enough for the day and escorted Cathy to the door. Before she got halfway to her room, the fatigue and heaviness vanished.

★ ★ ★

Because she posed no danger to herself or anyone else, she was allowed free rein in the halls. Her feet took her up and down the halls on a restless circuit, her hospital slippers rasping beneath her on the slick tiled floor. Some patients propped open their doors during the day, affording glimpses here and there. That was how, one week after her admission, she caught sight of an arm moving tentatively up through the air. Long fingers stretched forward to explore something hidden from view. A jawbone. She froze. She had witnessed that gesture every day for months and would not mistake it anywhere.

How? How? How? The question pursued her all the way back to her room. How had she ended up in the same place as the stupid, loathsome, pimple-headed moron? Quaking, she went to the window and scanned the horizon for the direction of Australia.

"How come it worked for you?" she hissed at her brother.

D r. Phillips welcomed Gerald into his office with a brisk handshake. Gerald took a seat in front of the doctor's desk, letting his hands dangle off the ends of the armrests. Dr. Phillips, a tall blonde Englishman with tightly waved hair, slipped in behind his desk, placed a file folder down on the blotter in front of him, and turned bright green eyes towards Gerald.

"Now then, your wife's prognosis is excellent. She'll make a full recovery from her injuries. However, there is another matter."

"Oh?"

"Mr. Mugan, is your wife under psychiatric care with anyone?"

Gerald's eyebrows rode up his freckled forehead in surprise.

"No. She's never seen a psychiatrist. I'm sure she wouldn't go to one. Why do you ask?"

"Is it possible she might be seeing someone, without your knowledge, perhaps?"

"I'm virtually certain she would never agree to go to a psychiatrist. She doesn't believe in psychiatry, and frankly, I don't put much stock in it myself."

Dr. Phillips stared at Gerald for a moment, then flipped open the file in front of him, pausing to read for a moment.

"Your daughter's with us now on our psychiatric ward, isn't she?"

"Well, yes, temporarily. Troubled teen…"

"I see. The reason I'm asking is because on the day of your wife's admission, your daughter was the only one who could give us a medical history of your wife before we took her into surgery. When we asked about any medication that your wife might be taking, Cathy said something quite peculiar.

"Oh?"

"Yes. She said your wife was taking 'funny-farm busters.' But then she wouldn't elaborate."

"Hmph."

Gerald pursed his mouth.

"Pre-op blood tests found significant levels of antidepressant medication."

Gerald frowned.

"Hmph."

"After surgery, when we tried to get a history from your wife, she denied being on any medication or under any physician's care."

Gerald frowned, shaking his head.

"Hmph."

"I didn't want to pursue it with her until I had spoken to you. She might be embarrassed to admit that she is seeing someone. I am not concerned with that. Something else troubled me, though. According to what your wife told us the day after the surgery, your daughter had been behaving very out of character lately. She had become rebellious and secretive."

Gerald shifted.

"Yes. There have been a few minor problems at home, lately."

"I take it there was some friction between your wife and your daughter?"

"Yes."

"That happens."

"Yes."

Dr. Phillips ploughed on, his green-eyed gaze holding Gerald.

"You're a pharmacist, are you not, Mr. Mugan?"

Gerald felt fluttering in his chest.

"Yes."

"Do you keep any literature on medications at home?"

He pretended to think. His mind had turned into a giant wad of cotton. He could not weigh the pros and cons of various answers. He couldn't see where the conversation was headed. He swam around inside himself, aimlessly. What would be the best answer? What would be the safest thing to say?

"Yes. There is a pharmacopoeia at home."

"Do you suppose your daughter could have come across the description of antidepressants in your pharmacopoeia and then, perhaps, somehow gotten her hands on the drug at your pharmacy?"

Gerald's breathing quickened. He scratched his jaw.

"Well…"

"Understand, your wife was not in any danger. She was not overdosed. That's why I wondered if there was any possibility of her seeing someone. But you say that's not likely. Under the unfortunate circumstances, I had wondered about the possibility of your daughter's involvement, having a father who is a pharmacist and all."

Gerald's mind and blood raced together. He had never even remotely considered that a blood sample would ever stray into the hands of doctors.

"These results were, and still are, just a medical mystery at the moment. Despite your thoughts, she may be under legitimate medical supervision that we simply don't know about. Now, I suppose, if your daughter or anyone else is responsible for medicating your wife without her knowledge…"

Gerald tried to swallow but he didn't have any saliva. What did he mean, "or anyone else"?

"…that might be another story. But as I say, there is nothing overtly criminal about finding legitimate doses of this type of medication in someone's blood. We are just trying to gather as thorough a medical history on your wife as possible, and this cropped up as a little inconsistency, that's all."

"Hmph," Gerald frowned and bobbed.

"Does Cathy ever have access to your dispensary?"

Gerald looked at the neatly groomed, calm, rational professional sitting in front of him. What would he know about the dead ruling the living?

"I suppose it's possible," he heard himself say.

"We can't get Cathy to speak to anyone here, so I doubt she'll cooperate if we ask her about this. If you think it might possible that she was involved, then perhaps you would be the best one to handle the situation. I'm sure you would like this to remain in the family."

"Oh, yes. Absolutely."

"As I said, there was no risk posed, so there is nothing criminal to deal with under these circumstances, unless it comes to our knowledge absolutely that your wife was not being prescribed by another physician."

"Does my wife know what you've found?"

"No. We thought we would ask you first. If she was seeing someone, she obviously didn't volunteer the information to us for a reason."

"I'd prefer it if she wasn't told. I think I can get this matter under control myself."

Dr. Phillips nodded.

"By the way, we think that Cathy needs to see someone who specializes in working with young people. She's fallen mute since she was admitted. I believe Dr. Elliott is going to explain things to you after our meeting. He recommends transferring her to the psychiatric facility at the Great Lakes Regional Hospital. I thought you should be aware of what we found, however."

"Thank you, Doctor."

Gerald floated up out of the chair and extended his hand to Dr. Phillips.

"Cathy will be going away then?"

"Dr. Elliott thinks it's a good course of treatment right now."

"Well, if that's what's best. She can come back and make a clean start of things. Meantime, I can look into getting her a new bike, perhaps. A ten-speed. All the kids seem to be getting them. Something to give her a bit of independence. I guess she's at that age."

Two nurses finally emerged through the sliding glass doors of the emergency department, one with a beige raincoat slung over her arm, both carrying small zippered portfolios. Cathy saw them laughing and waving goodbye over their shoulders to the hospital windows. They boarded the van through its side door, and while one of them closed and locked the door, the other glanced towards Cathy.

"Are you all right, Cathy? It's a bit chilly in here. It'll warm up as soon as we get going, though."

She waited for a moment to see if Cathy would respond. When she didn't, she headed towards the front of the van and took her seat beside the other nurse.

The driver eased out into the traffic and began threading through the city. Cathy noticed instantly how foreign his driving was: the sudden stomp of his foot upon the accelerator or the brake; the tight, aggressive turns around corners that made her put her hand down on the empty seat beside her to steady herself; even the way the truck bounced on its mushy suspension from the direct hits on potholes and manhole covers — things that her father had always taken such meticulous care to avoid. Her father would have said that this man drove like a maniac.

Cathy leaned her head against the cold glass window and looked out at the rain. A rainy day had always been her favourite. It emptied the world of people and filled the outdoors with the most comforting hush and patter. From her bedroom window she had been able to see into the green depths of the hawthorn trees in the side yard and watch the robins or sparrows preening in the drizzle, carrying on as if the rain was as convenient as sunshine. Growing up, she'd spent hours at that window, listening to the rush and drumming of the rain, enjoying the fresh cool air puffing in through the screen, the sharp odour of damp soil. Lying in the dark, late at night, she'd loved the way the pounding rain embraced the house, locking her inside its powerful downward rush. And she liked what came afterwards, too. Rain always left behind change. Things were washed clean; light bounced off all the shiny surfaces. The world always looked full of promise after it rained.

The van turned a corner and proceeded down a tree-lined street. Cathy recalled the sound of the lower revolutions of her father's car engine, the distance he kept from the curb as he drove. His eyes. He had such eyes, her father: blue-grey and watery, as if perpetually on the brink of tears. Last night in her sleep, they had floated up through the depths of her dreams, begging her not to leave.

But she'd realized something this morning while sitting on the edge of the hospital bed, threading a sock over one foot. More of her had left already than either her father or she had ever guessed. The leaving that she did today was merely a formality. Time really was, after all, carrying her along in its current.

The van accelerated onto a ramp and merged into the right-hand lane of the highway. A strip of motels with names like the Sea Horse Inn and Rainbow Gardens flashed past the windows. Then the waterfront park with the brightly painted swings, the dinosaur-shaped climbing bars, and the World War II Lancaster —

the last vestiges of the city — flowed by. Cathy slumped down in her seat, breathing in the faintly fishy smell of the lake, thinking.

Change, my weird little artifact, is what makes life interesting.

You weren't crying. You were laughing.

Richard. So sure of everything he knew. Of his facts, of his decisions, of the way life worked. Born sure, she'd thought. But no. Made sure, he'd said. Start small, and hang onto facts.

Cathy looked at the jiggling water droplets collected on the window, at the ragged-edged trails they left as they slid down the glass. And as her depth of field lengthened, passing through the scrim of slanting rain to where lampposts and park benches stood to the line of dark trees stretching away along the curve of the beach to the horizon, the things that she sought took shape. It was Thursday, the ninth of July. Janet was at the cottage. Richard was in Australia. The van was heading east in the rain.

ACKNOWLEDGEMENTS

I wish to express my thanks to a special group of friends who have cheered me on. In particular to Judith Drost Storey and Barbara McDonald, both of whom read this manuscript during summers when they had newborn children to care for. To Magda Augustyniak, Kerri Launder, and Dana Hansen for their suggestions. To Leslie Galloway for her rampant excitement. Thanks to Jane Irwin for a well-placed "good word" and Richard Bachman for his enthusiastic support. Kudos to everyone at Dundurn for guidance and joyous cheerleading. Thanks also to authors Sarah Ellis and Roo Borson, who read portions of the manuscript and provided insight during their terms as Writers-in-Residence at the University of Toronto. My gratitude extends to Isabel Huggan for her encouragement, and my most humble thanks to her colleague at the Humber School for Writers, M.G. Vassanji, for his careful and intelligent mentoring of part of this manuscript, and for his generous endorsement. Finally, my deepest appreciation goes to David Oliver for selflessly assuming all the burdens connected to supporting a writer. This is our success.